MONTANA ANGEL

"I know why you schemed to keep me here," Nell told him.

Ross pushed away from the porch railing to tower above her. "You're right, Nell," he said in a thick, raspy voice. "I'll admit it. I want you. I'm burnin' up with it."

"Well, you can burn in hell for all I care," she whispered. "If you think I'm going to let a practiced womanizer seduce me, you're in for a big surprise."

"I'm not a womanizer." His words were clipped and short. He took a menacing step closer. The wariness in her gaze told him she wasn't ready to listen to anything more he had to say that night. "I'll see you in the mornin'."

Then Ross leaned his shoulder against a porch column and stared absently out at the gathering dusk. Now that he'd found her, now that he'd kissed her, now that he'd breathed in the intoxicating scent of gardenias in her hair and tasted the honey-eyed warmth of her sweet mouth he had no intention of ever letting Nell Ryan go.

Other **AVON ROMANCES**

EMBRACE THE WILD DAWN *by Selina MacPherson*
HIGHLAND JEWEL *by Lois Greiman*
KENTUCKY BRIDE *by Hannah Howell*
THE LADY AND THE OUTLAW *by Katherine Compton*
PROMISE ME HEAVEN *by Connie Brockway*
TENDER IS THE TOUCH *by Ana Leigh*
VIKING'S PRIZE *by Tanya Anne Crosby*

Coming Soon

MIDNIGHT RAIN *by Elizabeth Turner*
SWEET SPANISH BRIDE *by Donna Whitfield*

And Don't Miss These
ROMANTIC TREASURES
from Avon Books

CHEYENNE'S SHADOW *by Deborah Camp*
FORTUNE'S BRIDE *by Judith E. French*
GABRIEL'S BRIDE *by Samantha James*

MONTANA ANGEL

KATHLEEN HARRINGTON

AVON BOOKS ◆ NEW YORK

MONTANA ANGEL is an original publication of Avon Books. This work has never before appeared in book form. This work is a novel. Any similarity to actual persons or events is purely coincidental.

AVON BOOKS
A division of
The Hearst Corporation
1350 Avenue of the Americas
New York, New York 10019

Copyright © 1994 by Kathleen Harrington
Published by arrangement with the author
Library of Congress Catalog Card Number: 93-90817
ISBN: 0-380-77059-8

First Avon Books Printing: May 1994

AVON TRADEMARK REG. U.S. PAT. OFF. AND IN OTHER COUNTRIES. MARCA REGISTRADA, HECHO EN U.S.A.

Printed in the U.S.A.

RA 10 9 8 7 6 5 4 3 2 1

With love to five fine young men,
my stepsons:

Craig Patrick
Timothy Daniel
Scott Michael
Daniel Robert
and
Kevin Matthew
Harrington

In memory of
your great grandfather
Edward Farren
who, as foreman of the Anaconda Mine,
disregarded personal risk to remove explosive powder
from a burning magazine on the
fourteen-hundred-foot level
and assisted in extinguishing the fire,
for which he received a commendation for bravery
from the
Anaconda Mining Company
Butte, Montana,
December 1, 1924

Acknowledgments

There are several people to whom I must express my sincere thanks:

to our Butte cousins, the Downeys, the Harringtons, the Farrens, and the Christiaens, whose warm Western hospitality first welcomed me to Montana;

to Mary Lou Farren, who spent several days taking me to the historical sites of Butte, including the Clark "Copper King" Mansion, the Arts Chateau Mansion, and the old parlor house on Mercury;

to Leena Hannonen, who guided me in the depiction of the Finnish immigrants, their speech and culture;

and to Burl Estes, Deputy District Attorney, County of Orange, California, who took the time to explain criminal procedures in the 1890s.

Special thanks must go to two gentlemen, without whose generous help this book could not have been written:

Daniel Farren, O.D., who gladly shared his experiences working in the hard-rock mines of Butte as a young man and who edited my manuscript for accuracy in the depiction of mining;

and James Persinger, Deputy County Counsel, County of Orange, who edited my manuscript for accuracy in the details of law and whose advice was invaluable.

Her skin is like silk, and her speech
  is softer than the zephyr passing
  over the flowers of the garden;
The moisture of her lips is sweeter than syrup;
Her figure puts to shame the branches
  of the Oriental willow.
The locks on her brow are dark as night,
  while her forehead shines like the gleam of morning.
Her eyes, God said to them, Be,—and they were,
  affecting men's hearts with the potency of wine.
May my love for her grow more warm each night,
  and cease not until the day of judgment!

—THE THOUSAND AND ONE ARABIAN NIGHTS

MONTANA ANGEL

Chapter 1

July 4, 1894
Butte, Montana

"Miss Ryan's here, boss."

Rossiter Morgan looked up from the chart spread across his battered desktop and scowled at his redheaded mine superintendent. Eben Pearce grinned back with fiendish delight, apparently taking some perverse pleasure in his employer's forthcoming interview, unpleasant as it undoubtedly would be.

"The old bat can wait awhile," Ross growled as he returned to his perusal of the wrinkled parchment in front of him. He glanced over his wire-rimmed spectacles at Eben. "Tell her to park her carcass on the bench out there, and I'll be with her shortly."

Eben's blue eyes fairly sparkled. He held the door only partly open as he leaned around its edge and spoke in a low voice that betrayed his hilarity. "I'll fix her a cup of coffee and try to keep her occupied."

Ross absently grunted his approval, and the door was shut with a soft click. But his mind was no longer on the map.

Damnation. That was just what he needed to ruin his holiday completely. Sean Ryan's sister had come all the way from Massachusetts to find out personally how her brother had died in the Glamorgan Mine. She hadn't wasted any time about it either. Ross had received the letter from Miss Elinor Ryan of the esteemed firm of Ryan, Sheehy, and O'Connell

1

only five days before, telling him she was traveling to Butte to investigate her young brother's death. *Investigate.* What colossal nerve—even for an old maid who actually claimed to be a Boston attorney. Hell, he'd never even heard of a female lawyer. He doubted there really was such a creature.

But the old bag's letter was real, all right. He could tell from the precise, businesslike format, flawlessly typed with perfect punctuation and grammar, that she was a real prig. No trace of a heartbroken sister's tears from Miss Ryan. No bewailing the cruel fate that had taken her only sibling. Just a brief, formal acknowledgment of Ross's handwritten note of sympathy—one that had twisted his guts in the writing—and the bald statement that she was leaving Boston immediately to pursue an investigation of Sean's untimely demise.

Untimely demise.

God, what an ice-hearted biddy.

Standing in front of the desk, Ross bent over the mining map and traced the veins of copper ore with his forefinger. But a corner of his mouth curved up in a wicked half grin.

She was probably sitting out there stewing in her own juice. Served her right. When he did get around to seeing her, he was going to explain in the simplest terms possible—simple enough even for an uppity, swell-headed, Eastern female—that she was wide of the mark when she wrote of her suspicions about the safety of the Glamorgan Mine. His mine, for God's sake, his mine! After he threw her incredible audacity back in her face, he was personally going to march Miss High-and-Mighty Ryan back down to the station and see her on the next Northern Pacific train leaving Butte.

Forty minutes later, Eben tapped on the door and poked his head inside. "Miss Ryan asked me to remind you that she'd been waiting for over a half hour now. She came right here from the depot and hasn't even checked into the hotel yet."

Ross straightened, sank down in his beat-up desk chair, and rubbed the tense muscles of his neck. If she really *was* employed by Ryan, Sheehy, and O'Connell, he'd better not keep her waiting any longer. Ross had hired the Boston firm to represent him in court at Sean Ryan's urging. Two weeks ago, they'd sent out a green, citified lawyer who hadn't managed to offer anything since he'd arrived except pessimistic conjectures about the eventual outcome of the pending lawsuit against the Glamorgan Mine. If Gavin O'Connell was the best they had to offer, it was no surprise the legal firm numbered a female among its attorneys.

"Okay, send her in," he growled. When Eben just stood there grinning like an idiot, Ross glared back in mounting irritation.

"Holy Jesus," Pearce silently mouthed. He rolled his eyes in warning, then flung the door open and gestured with a dramatic flourish for the woman to enter the room.

Ross sprang to his feet the moment Nell Ryan stepped over the threshold. He shoved back his chair and started toward her, accidentally kicking over the wastebasket beside his desk in his haste. It fell with a bang and rolled across the room, its contents spilling out across the rough hardwood planks at her feet.

"Miss . . . Miss Ryan," he stammered. "Please . . . please accept my condolences on the loss of your brother."

Nell looked up from the litter of paper spread across the room's bare floor and met the large man's startled green eyes. He was obviously waiting for her to extend her hand in greeting. She nodded a curt salute instead, and watched silently as he pulled up a rickety cane-back chair to a position in front of his desk.

"Thank you, Mr. Morgan," she said and sat down. She placed her handbag on her lap, folded her gloved hands on top of it, and waited for him to be seated.

"That'll be all, Eben," he told his superintendent without even bothering to look at him. Dismissed so summarily, the kind Mr. Pearce didn't say a word as he closed the door behind him.

Morgan ignored the mess on the floor. Rather than take a seat, he propped his lean flanks against the edge of his desk just like the uncouth Westerner he was. Back in Boston, not even a common street vendor would stare at her so blatantly. But heavens to Betsy, it was no more than she expected from an avaricious mine owner.

They looked at each other for a long moment while neither spoke.

He started to say something, stopped to clear his throat, and started again. His deep bass was low and subdued, and he spoke with a slow, Western drawl. "What can I do for you, Miss Ryan?"

Instinctively, she realized that he'd purposely gentled his voice to a level just an octave away from being seductive. The hushed timbre gave his words a second depth of meaning, as though he were implying that he'd do *anything* she asked, if it pleased her.

"You can explain all the circumstances surrounding Sean's accident, Mr. Morgan," she answered crisply. "Tell me exactly what happened."

He folded his arms across his chest. The muscles beneath the rolled-up sleeves of his work shirt bulged, straining the material alarmingly. Morgan was a big, powerful man. Dressed in khaki shirt and pants and scuffed miner's tie boots, he appeared extraordinarily robust and athletic, clearly able to do any of the mine work he assigned to his crews. She had to tip her head back to look up at him and suddenly wished she hadn't taken the seat he'd so hurriedly provided. She was tempted to climb up on the chair and stare down at him. Let him get a taste of what it was like to be scrutinized so thoroughly. But she had a feeling he just might enjoy it.

"Sean was at the twelve-hundred-foot level," Morgan explained, "when he was struck on the head by fallin' timber. The heat and humidity in the drifts rot the beams pretty quickly down there."

"Was anyone with him?"

"No, he was alone at the time."

"Did he suffer long?"

"The doctor who examined him said he probably died instantly."

Nell let out a ragged sigh, lowered her lids, and studied her interlocked fingers. Exhausted from the arduous train journey across the country, she had to fight the urge to cover her face with her hands and bawl like a baby. When she did manage to speak, her voice cracked, betraying just how close she was to breaking down.

"Thank God, at least for that. I had visions of Sean lying alone for hours, waiting in agony for help." A tear plopped on her ebony glove, and she searched in her bag for a handkerchief.

Guiltily, Ross stared down at the top of her black straw hat with its wide velvet ribbon and jaunty black feather. He shouldn't have let his temper get the best of him. He'd been a stupid ass to keep her waiting needlessly. And a worse idiot to react to her presence like a randy eighteen-year-old buck. At thirty-three, he ought to be able to control his baser needs, for Christ's sake.

Here she was, grieving over the death of her young brother, and he could already feel the surge of carnal desire spreading through his veins. When she'd walked through his office door, he'd been nearly bowled over. Sean had spoken of his older sister with such offhanded, brotherly affection that he'd given no clue to her appearance. The young Irishman's nonchalant words had portrayed a determined, narrow-minded spinster, who'd practically raised him single-handedly since their mother died. Mentally, Ross had prepared a scathing reception for the woman he'd pictured as plump, overbearing, and prudish. Nothing Sean had said could have possibly prepared Ross for the vision sitting before him now. He'd been expecting a woman at the wrong end of her forties. She looked as if she were still in her twenties. But that wasn't the half of it.

Miss Elinor Ryan was what men called a "knockout." Crowned by a mass of thick reddish-brown hair the color of deep, rich mahogany, she had a figure that would make a monk vault over the monastery wall. Her enormous, dark brown eyes were velvety soft, framed by arched brows and long, curved lashes. Glittering with tears, they were the eyes of a houri, a nymph straight from the Muslim paradise. The smoothness of her ivory complexion was enhanced by a tiny mole above her full lips, accentuating the aura of opulent sensuality she created.

To Ross, she seemed to have stepped down from a painting of a Moorish harem, despite the fact that she was dressed in a no-nonsense Newport ladies' suit, dusty now from the long train ride. It wasn't the conservative attire with its fitted jacket, gored skirt, and white shirtwaist that staggered him, but the voluptuous curves beneath the somber black gabardine. Full, high breasts, tiny waist, slim hips: It was a figure that was certain to haunt a man's dreams. And without a doubt, Ross knew he wanted to do a whole lot more than just dream about Nell Ryan.

Usually he had a gift for smooth repartee when it came to the ladies, but the thoughts running through his mind couldn't possibly be shared with the beautiful woman sitting so rigid with disapproval before him.

Suddenly remembering the eyeglasses perched on the bridge of his nose, he pulled them off and tossed them atop the opened map on his desk. He offered his most engaging smile in a belated attempt at an apology for his insufferable behavior. "If I can be of any help while you're in Butte, Miss Ryan, please don't hesitate to let me know."

Nell looked up and met Morgan's hypocritical gaze. She didn't want his unctuous sympathy, just his full cooperation. Ignoring the ache of grief that threatened to engulf her, she blinked back her tears. "You said in your note that Sean was given a Catholic burial. I'd like to stop by the mortuary tomorrow, before I visit the grave, and pay the bill."

"The funeral expenses have already been taken care of." He waved his hand in dismissal before she could even offer to reimburse him. "And I'd be glad to escort you to the cemetery whenever you wish."

Nell rose. "That won't be necessary. I'm quite used to fending for myself."

He pushed away from the desk and towered over her. His head was bent, as though to catch her every word. The smile on his lips was clearly ingratiating, meant to flatter a love-starved spinster.

If Mr. Rossiter Morgan had any intention of starting a flirtation, she'd quickly disabuse him on that score. She'd disliked the man immediately. Aside from the fact that her brother had perished in his mine—quite possibly because of poor safety precautions—Morgan was one of those broad-shouldered, good-looking devils who thought he could work his way around any female, married or single. With his golden-brown hair and bronze tan, he was far too handsome for his own good. He might look like some conquering Norseman, and sound like one too, with that deep, intimidating voice of his, but if he thought he was going to lay siege to Elinor Margaret Ryan, he was greatly mistaken.

"There is one more thing, Mr. Morgan," she added. "I'd like to see the exact place where my brother died. If it's too much of a bother for you, I'm sure Mr. Pearce would be happy to take me down to the twelve-hundred-foot level. He was kind enough to spend the forty minutes I waited to see you telling me about Sean's life in Butte and his work as a shift foreman in your mine. Since Mr. Pearce is a native

New Yorker, I'm sure he and I have much more in common, including the little niceties of genteel civilization."

Morgan's granite chin jerked up on that one. His thick-lashed eyes sparked with glints of green and gold.

She smiled up at him sweetly in return.

"No," he said. He didn't bother to flash his crooked grin in an attempt to soften his refusal. "You can't go down there."

"Why not?" she shot back. "Isn't it safe?"

"It's perfectly safe. All the timberin' has been inspected. What happened to Sean was a freak accident."

"Then you can't possibly object to my examining the area."

"I can object. And I do. And since I own the Glamorgan, I decide who rides down in the cage and who doesn't. Women don't go down into hardrock mines. It's not decent."

Nell lifted her brows in scorn. "Why? Are you afraid someone will get a glimpse of my ankles?"

Despite his annoyance, Ross grinned at the thought. Wouldn't he just love to get a peek at those long, black-stockinged legs hidden beneath the full skirt.

"I refuse to be held responsible for what might happen if they did," he told her. "Gettin' caught in a narrow drift with a bunch of stampedin' miners would be mighty dangerous."

"I'll take my chances."

"No, Miss Ryan. You're not descendin' to the twelve-hundred-foot level or to any other level of the Glamorgan. And that's my final word."

Nell glared up at him. If you won't willingly take me to the place where my brother was killed so I can assess its safety for myself, I'll have to apply to the courts."

"You just do that, ma'am. And when you have the court order in your hot little hand—if you ever

get the court order—I'll have Mr. Pearce, that genteel New Yorker with whom you have so much in
common, escort you down there."

She ignored the sarcastic remark and moved
toward the exit. "I'd like to go through my brother's personal effects this afternoon. Do you know
where they're stored?"

"Sean's gear is still at the boardin'house where he
was livin'. I'm sure the landlady has taken good care
of it."

Unperturbed by her ridiculous threat to sue, Ross
moved past her, and the faint, elusive scent of gardenias swirled around him. He swung the door open
with unnecessary force. "Eben," he called, "accompany Miss Ryan over to Kuusinen's and introduce
her to Hertta. Then take the rest of the day off and
enjoy the celebration." He turned and nodded a brief
dismissal to the gorgeous and aggravating spinster.
"Good day, ma'am."

From the window of the trolley car, Nell surveyed
the sprawling mining camp with disgust. Butte was
as ugly and shabby as a toothless old harlot. Frame
and brick cottages were huddled against the barren
mine dumps and scattered up and down the hills
and gulches. Tall steel and wooden gallows frames
could be seen throughout the busy frontier town,
while smoke belched from the rows of tall stacks
atop the smelters. Crooked dirt roads led up the big
hill to the mines past dilapidated, unpainted shacks,
leaning crazily askew. There wasn't a single tree or
a blade of grass alive in the whole place.

On the slatted wooden seat beside her, Eben
cheerfully pointed out the sights. He seemed
totally unaware of the camp's abysmal dreari-
ness.

"Up on the top of the Hill are the Alice and
Moulton," he said with a jab of his finger toward the
crest. "Over there's the St. Lawrence and the Anaconda. Butte's got more than three hundred mines

working 'round the clock, plus nine quartz mills and four smelters."

Nell covered her mouth and nose with her scented handkerchief to combat the acrid fumes billowing from a nearby smelter and nodded politely.

"Some of the miners are from the mother lode diggings of California," he continued breezily. "Others—like Ross—are from the hard-rock mines of Nevada and Colorado. But most are greenhorns just off the boat from the old country. There's the Irish in Dublin Gulch and the Cornish in Centerville. Most of the Finns are on the east side, and the Italians live in Meaderville, north of the camp. But you'll find Swedes, Turks, Jews, Greeks, and heaven knows what else."

From her spot on the trolley, Nell could see the truth of Eben's words. The populace was made up of widely diverse nationalities. Many of the immigrants still wore the colorful garments peculiar to their native lands, making them easily recognizable.

"That's Maguire's," Eben told her with obvious pride as they drove down Broadway past a large rococo building. "It's the finest opera house in the West outside of San Francisco. Last month, Rose Osborne played in *A Celebrated Case*. There wasn't an empty seat in the house."

Nell looked out at the thoroughfare's string of saloons with dubious curiosity. One thing was certain. No one in Butte was going to die of thirst. What the city lacked in aesthetic refinement, however, it made up for in unabashed zest. The downtown streets were crowded with people, some gazing in store windows, others chattering boisterously with one another, while more than a few milled about aimlessly in a holiday spirit. What looked suspiciously like a Muslim, complete with caftan, turban, and red leather boots, was peddling hot tamales. Two Chinamen, wearing long, braided queues and loose silk blouses and trousers, stood in front of a restaurant decorated with indecipherable celestial writing and topped by an ornate pagoda roof. It seemed as though everyone was out in the warm summer sunshine, bent on enjoying the Fourth of July.

When the trolley stopped at a corner, Eben hopped nimbly down and turned to assist Nell.

"The Kuusinens are Finns," he explained as he led her up the wooden steps to the huge three-story frame home. "Finnish women are known for their marvelous cooking, and Hertta sets the best table in Butte."

A comely, fair-haired woman in her mid-thirties met them on the wide front porch. Her deep blue eyes twinkled with friendliness. Large-boned and glowing with health, Hertta Kuusinen shook Nell's hand with exuberance as Eben introduced them.

"Come in, come in." Her welcoming smile carved twin dimples deep in her rosy cheeks. "I vill make us a pot of tea."

"None for me," Eben answered with a shake of his head. His thick, unruly hair glinted like a copper kettle in the sunlight. "I'm going to have to leave Miss Ryan in your very capable hands, Hertta. I promised to meet some friends before the parade starts and give them a little help with the decorations." He turned to Nell. "But I hope to see you again soon, ma'am. Please let me know if there's anything I can do for you."

Nell offered her hand, and he took it with a smile that lit up his freckled face.

"When I get permission to inspect the Glamorgan," she told him, "I'll have you take me to the exact spot where Sean was struck by the piece of rotted lumber."

Eben's brows met together in a worried line. Beneath his great, red handlebar mustache, his lips pursed unhappily. "That's Ross's decision." He tipped his head to one side and grinned in good-natured supplication. "You wouldn't want me to get in trouble with the boss man, now would you?"

"Mr. Morgan promised me that once I obtained a court order, he'd have you accompany me to the twelve-hundred-foot level."

Eben scowled. "There's no need for that, Miss Ryan. If you're doubting the security of the mine, you can set that worry aside right now. The Glamorgan is the safest mine in Butte. Ross wouldn't have it any other way." He nodded farewell to Hertta and descended the porch steps.

The landlady opened the screen door and motioned Nell into the house. The tantalizing smells of ginger, cinnamon, and warm cookie dough floated in the air. To the right of the entry hall stood a front parlor filled with ponderous black walnut and red horsehair furniture. On the left was the dining room. Through its open doorway, Nell could see a huge, cloth-covered table stretching the room's entire length. A massive carved oak sideboard nearly covered one wall.

"First, I vill show you your brother's room," Hertta said. "Afterverd, ve'll sit down at ta kitchen table and have a nice visit. I've just made some *pepparkakor*." She nodded her head with complete self-assurance. "You vill like my gingersnaps."

She led the way up the narrow stairs to the third floor and into a small bedroom. It was austerely furnished, but scrupulously neat.

"Sean vas such a fine young man," she told Nell. "Everyone here vas so fond of him." As she spoke, she smoothed the colorful hand-stitched quilt on the narrow brass bed and plumped up the pillow. "Vhen Ross told me you vere coming, I left everyt'ing just as it vas for you to see."

Hertta was filled with an irrepressible energy. She flitted about, wiping imaginary dust from a marble-topped nightstand with her apron, checking the water level in a pitcher decorated with hand-painted flowers, then repositioning it in its matching washbasin. It was apparent that she took great pride

MONTANA ANGEL   13

in her boardinghouse and worked hard to make sure her clients were well taken care of.

Nell took in the bedchamber's homey atmosphere. On the papered walls, printed vines of deep green ivy twined up tall white trellises that stretched from baseboard to ceiling. The striped curtains at the window were a matching green and white.

"I think Sean must have been very happy here," she said softly. Her lips trembled at the comforting thought that her brother had slept his last night on earth in this spotless, cheerful room.

She walked over to the birch bureau across from the bed and picked up a small oval frame. It held a photograph of Maude Ryan with her arms around her two children. Brother and sister stood on either side of their mother, smiling for the camera as though they hadn't a care in the world. The picture had been taken a year before their mother died, but even then the family's carefree smiles had been nothing more than a charade. Tears misted Nell's eyes, and she set the frame back down on the chest of drawers.

"I vill leave you alone," Hertta said with quiet compassion. She moved to the door and then turned to face Nell again. "Your brother had paid two months' rent in advance. Please consider staying here vhile you're in Butte rather t'an at a hotel. I vould so love to have another female to talk vith."

The Finnish woman had a cheerful glow about her that would have warmed the coldest heart. After the long, solitary, grief-filled journey to Montana, Nell felt as though she were standing in front of a toasty oven on a frigid winter day.

"Thank you, Mrs. Kuusinen. I'd like that very much."

The landlady beamed fondly. "You must call me Hertta, just like all ta other boarders. We do not go in for fancy airs around here."

"Then please call me Nell."

"Come down to ta kitchen vhen you're ready, Nell. I vill have a teapot hot, and ve'll have a cozy chat."

After Hertta left, Nell wandered around the room. She lifted Sean's brush and comb from their place beside the photograph and stared down at the strands of dark brown hair entwined in the bristles. Then she opened the dresser drawers, lifted out his shirts, pants, and underwear, and laid them on the bed in neat stacks. She found the sweater she'd knitted for him that past Christmas and carried it over to the brass bed. Sinking down on its soft mattress, she stared at the bright green cable-stitched wool.

"Oh, Sean, Sean," she whispered with a broken sob, "why did you have to come to this horrible place?"

She tried without success to push back the weight of guilt that lay like a yoke across her shoulders. She'd been responsible for her younger brother since their mother had died fourteen years ago. God knew, she'd tried to talk him out of going West. But like his father before him, Sean had dreams of striking it rich in the mining fields of the Rocky Mountains. The memory of her father's departure, so long ago, brought a fresh ache of misery. She buried her face in the sweater as the tears began to flow.

Jack Ryan had headed for Colorado in 1873, leaving behind his wife, his nine-year-old daughter, and his infant son. The family never saw him again. When they'd learned he'd died in Leadville in a saloon brawl four years later, Nell had been devastated. In his long absence, she'd idolized her charming, ne'er-do-well father. She'd prayed nightly that he'd come back to them. Only as she matured and gained the wisdom of adulthood did Nell come to despise her father for abandoning his loved ones in his greed.

And that was what it was all about. Greed. For gold. For silver. For copper. It made no difference which mineral they sought. Men left their families distraught and penniless to follow their lust for the precious metals hidden deep in the earth. That dislikable mine owner, Rossiter Morgan, was of the same ilk. She knew his kind. She had firsthand knowledge of their selfish, driven natures.

Nell laid the sweater on the bed beside the pile of folded shirts. Wiping the tears from her cheeks, she rose and walked over to the open window. From the third-floor room, she could see across the shingled rooftops of the nearby homes. They were built on the side of a great hill that sloped steadily downward to the wide flatland that lay just south of the camp. High above in the limitless azure sky, white cumulus clouds skirted the range of mountaintops to the east. It was all so wide, so open, so endless.

She missed the familiar, narrow confines of Boston's crooked streets with their rosy brick colonial houses. In her mind, she could envision her own elegant bedroom in her aunt and uncle's home, filled with graceful Hepplewhite furniture. She hoped Uncle Cormac and Aunt Lydia weren't needlessly worrying about her.

It had been her father's older brother, Cormac Ryan, who'd come to the rescue of the impoverished family. A successful Boston lawyer, her uncle had helped his sister-in-law time and again while his foolish brother wandered the goldfields. Aunt Lydia was barren, and Cormac loved his nephew and niece as though they were his own children. After Maude Ryan's death and Nell's disastrous affair at seventeen, he'd moved them from their tiny home in Bar Harbor to his Boston mansion. Uncle Cormac was the only person who'd ever suspected the full tragedy of Nell's involvement with the thirty-one-year-old Charleton Blevins. Once Cormac had become convinced that she planned never to marry, he'd steadfastly supported her goal of becoming a lawyer despite all the opposition they encountered.

With a resolute shake of her head, Nell turned to face the boardinghouse's tiny bedroom and the awful reality of her brother's death. Dredging up old memories served no purpose. She'd come to Butte to investigate the circumstances surrounding Sean's accident. Once she was satisfied that no violations of basic safety precautions had contributed to the mishap, she would gladly return to Boston and leave this sprawling, ugly, wide-open mining camp to the likes of the detestable Mr. Morgan.

Chapter 2

Nell stepped off the trolley car and joined the throng of people elbowing one another for a better spot along the curb. She purposefully shook off the lingering melancholy that haunted her, determined to enjoy the holiday as much as possible. After her visit with Hertta Kuusinen, she'd decided to take her new landlady's advice and go uptown to watch the frontier city celebrate the grand old Fourth. When she'd asked her new friend if it was safe for a female to walk the streets of Butte alone, Hertta had burst out laughing.

"No one vill hurt a lovely lady like you," the Finnish woman promised. "If anyone should try to bother you, just give an itsy-bitsy scream. T'ere vill be a dozen burly miners rushing to your defense, and t'ey vill gladly beat ta fellow to a bloody pulp for you."

On that holiday morning, the city's business district, comprising seven or eight blocks of brick and stone Victorian buildings, was a marvel of patriotic decorations. Everywhere, red, white, and blue bunting proclaimed the nation's one hundred and eighteenth birthday. Dozens of flags snapped in the breeze. Bronze eagles adorned every street lamp.

An atmosphere of high excitement reigned. All around Nell, onlookers milled about on the crowded sidewalks. Butte was clearly a man's town. There seemed to be ten males for every member of the weaker sex. And it quickly became apparent that

17

Hertta had failed to mention another very important fact.

The place was an armed camp.

Nearly every male inhabitant carried some type of weapon. Even businessmen had pistols tucked into their belts, the handles protruding boldly from the fronts of their black frock coats in silent warning. Others wore holstered guns openly strapped to their sides, with no attempt made to conceal them. Certainly, there were an uncounted number of wicked hunting knives tucked into boots and equally sinister derringers concealed under coat sleeves. She felt a shiver of apprehension go through her. Boston had never seemed so far away.

Most of the men, dressed in sturdy work trousers and shirts, looked as if they were probably miners. But not all of them. Some were attired in expensively tailored business suits with silk top hats and canes. Several wore the flashy clothes of a professional gambler. One man sported a diamond stickpin the size of a jawbreaker on his striped cravat. He had a woman on his arm who wore the flashiest promenade gown on the street that day. Nell studied the garish couple out of the corner of her eye, certain that both were employed in nefarious activities. But no one else seemed to give them a second glance. In fact, nobody appeared to be the least disturbed by the strange commingling of apparently upright, law-abiding citizens with brazen representatives of a wilder element. She suspected that the residents continued to refer to the place as a mining camp—which it had been called from its earliest days—because a frenzied air of impermanence, fatalism, and rakish dissipation still pervaded the city.

Hertta had told her there was to be a grand parade, complete with a marching band. Nell could hear the sound of its stirring music coming closer as the procession approached the intersection of Main and Broadway. Suddenly, the crowd surged forward. She was caught up in the swelling tide and carried to the edge of the sidewalk, where she had a front-row view of the parade's participants. Numerous Butte social societies, including Swiss, Scandinavian, Irish, and Cornish, had decorated phaetons, surreys, buckboards, livery wagons, high-sprung traps, and tallyhos—as well as the horses that pulled them—with flowers and tricolored bunting. Buckskinned Indians in full native regalia marched along the route, as well as the Elks, the Knights of Pythias, the Montana state militia, and various trade associations, including the printing office clerks and members of the Butte Butchers Union, who were decked out in white jackets, flat hats, and ankle-length aprons. The city's new fire wagon, its alarm bell jangling merrily, was nearly buried in red, white, and blue streamers. Even an ambulance wagon drove by, covered with garlands of red and yellow roses, reportedly brought in from Helena that morning.

Everyone cheered when the thrilling sound of "Semper Fidelis" filled the air. The sunlight glinted off the polished brass of the trombones, French horns, and tubas as, twenty-one strong, the Boston and Montana Band marched past, attired in splendid red and gold uniforms.

Amazed, Nell spotted Mr. Rossiter Morgan in the second row, blasting away on a trumpet. When he caught sight of her watching him in openmouthed wonder, he stopped playing just long enough to flourish the shiny brass instrument in a mocking salute. Several people turned to stare at Nell in amused curiosity. She scowled at the irksome mine owner and then pointedly looked away. The man had no manners whatsoever.

When the pageant was over, the crowd gradually began to disperse. Nell wandered down Broadway, looking in the wide front windows of the stores, which had all been closed for the celebration. She was surprised to see the vast array of high-priced merchandise displayed, including fashionable dresses and hats that rivaled anything she'd seen in the fanciest shops on Beacon Hill. To the west, a great butte rose like an ancient pyramid above the city, and she slowly rambled in its direction.

Hertta had been right. No one bothered Nell. Most men politely lifted their hats as they passed by, though some of the rougher-looking miners stared openly at her, no doubt thinking she was a lonely young widow. Her mourning garb brought the usual sympathetic nods from other women.

She passed noisy gambling halls that were quickly filling with customers now that the patriotic festivities were over. Through their large front windows, she saw numerous faro tables with their stacks of twenty-dollar gold pieces.

Nell was passing in front of the Sazerac Saloon, when, without warning, the terrifying roar of an explosion rocked a similar establishment directly across the street. The Columbia Bar's big bay windows were blasted into fragments, raining shards of glass and splinters of wood out onto the cobblestones. She instinctively shielded her face with her hands as she backed up against the brick wall of the building behind her. Across the crowded thoroughfare, high on the shattered barroom's false front, a bright orange shield adorned with the letters APA had somehow survived the blast. Nell recognized the initials of the American Protective Association with astonishment. Evidently that secret organization, with its philosophy of intolerance toward the Irish and other new immigrants, had found its way to Butte.

"Dynamite it again!" someone yelled.

The gathering crowd surged toward the gaping, jagged cavity that had once been the front of the Columbia tavern.

"Let's teach those bigots a lesson!" another strident voice cried.

Only then did Nell realize that she'd strayed into the middle of a group of angry men, who were looking up at the orange bunting with undiluted hatred in their eyes.

"Come out of there, you snivelin' cowards!" hollered a burly man. He held what looked like a shillelagh gripped in one massive fist. Standing scarcely a yard away from Nell, he shook the gnarled black stick at the shattered barroom in open contempt.

No sooner had he issued his challenge than a dozen men dashed from the Columbia swearing epithets at the fuming mob, which had swollen to frightening proportions in the short time since the blast.

"Come on, ya dumb Mickel" one of the saloon's defenders mocked. He gripped a pick handle in both hands and swung it in a menacing arc. "Let's see which one of you has any guts when it comes to a real fight."

"It's a real fight I'm looking for," the strapping miner with the shillelagh taunted, "but all I'm seeing is a bunch of lily-livered Cousin Jacks. We'll be making you bastard Cornishmen crawl back to where you came from on yer hands and knees."

Despite the lethal pick handle circling over his opponent's head the Irishman launched himself at the APA sympathizer. The sickening crunch of bones being broken could be heard as the heavy wooden club smashed downward and found its target.

In less than two minutes, there were at least fifty fistfights raging in the middle of West Broadway. Men were snatching up paving bricks, sticks, stones, anything that came to hand, and hurling them at one another. A crowbar flew through the window beside Nell. The explosive sound of the shattering glass petrified her, and she was certain her heart had stopped beating. She cowered against the nearby wall of the Sazerac, keeping her face covered with her gloved hands. Unable to make her way through the howling throng, she was forced to stand there in the open, her black garments in stark relief against the red bricks.

From the taproom behind her, more men raced into the street, armed with clubs fashioned from the legs of chairs and tables. People were swearing and screaming in pain, as skulls were cracked open right and left. The wounded lay where they fell, blood streaming from their gory head lacerations.

Shaking with fright, Nell peeked between her fingers just long enough to see the silvery flash of a knife blade, and immediately closed her eyes tight once more. Groans, shrieks, and ethnic curses filled the air. She realized with dismay that she was whimpering in terror. Scarce wonder. She was caught in a crazed horde and totally unable to protect herself, pinned to the rough brick wall with no chance to escape. She was certain, by now, that nobody had even noticed her. It was only a matter of minutes before she'd be struck down by some wayward missile.

Where, in God's name, were the police?

Ross had been looking for Nell Ryan since the band dispersed at the library auditorium. After the parade, he'd quickly changed his clothes, wrapped his trumpet in his uniform, and entrusted the bundle to a fellow bandsman. Hoping the beautiful lady lawyer would roam down Broadway sightseeing, he headed in that direction. He'd caught sight of the little black hat with its perky black plume just as the dynamite exploded, rocking the storefront windows up and down the entire length of the street. When the fighting broke out, he started to race toward her through the surging, roiling crowd of angry combatants.

He hadn't gone half a block when he was stopped short by a vicious right hook that spun him backward, nearly knocking him on his can. He was suddenly grateful he'd taken the time to change into faded Levi's and a cotton shirt. He'd just paid five silver dollars for that fancy, gold-braided band uniform. Shaking his head to clear it, he saw the pug-nosed face of a beefy Irishman leering up at him. The sandy-haired fellow was a good head shorter than Ross, but he was built like a frigging bullwhacker.

"I'm in a hurry, you Irish sonofabitch," Ross said with a determined grin. As the beet-faced man charged, Ross sidestepped, then struck out with the chopping edge of his hand. His attacker hit the cobblestones like a felled tree, his head striking the causeway with a dull thud.

Ross sprinted away, grinning in happy satisfaction. There was nothing he liked better than a knockdown, drag-out free-for-all. It really got the blood pumping. There were no holds barred in Butte fights. Biting, gouging, kicking, kneeing, and kidney punches in the clinches were all part of the fun. The only thing that beat that kind of all-out exhilaration was sex with a beautiful woman.

With no warning, a powerfully built man jumped Ross from behind. They crashed to the ground together. Rolling across the paving stones, each sought for a vital hold. The big miner clutched a fistful of Ross's hair and jerked his head back viciously against the curbing. Stunned, Ross saw stars. He fought the blackness that swirled around him as he diverted his weight and feverishly searched for leverage. Twisting to his knees, he dragged the pale-haired fellow up in front of him. With lightning speed, Ross shifted his grip and tightened one arm around the man's throat. He placed his knee against his foe's spine and pulled his jaw upward relentlessly, till the miner's body was curved back like a drawn bow.

"I'd rather not kill you," Ross said in his opponent's ear, "but I'll break your blasted neck, if I have to." He slowly squeezed against the exposed windpipe. "All I want to do," he continued, "is to go to the aid of a lovely lady trapped against that saloon over there."

The quiet determination in his voice must have communicated itself to his adversary. The man went suddenly still. Ross leaped up and pulled his attacker to his feet.

"Go on. Get back in there," Ross said with a jerk of his bruised head. "And give 'em a couple of licks for me."

He jabbed the miner on the shoulder encouragingly. The stalwart fellow mopped his face with one shovel-sized hand, grinned, and lurched back into the fray.

When Ross reached her, Nell Ryan was crouched against the Sazerac's brick front, her gorgeous brown eyes squeezed tight. Her lips were moving, but she wasn't making a sound. The minute he touched her shoulder, she screamed loud enough to wake up the night shift in Walkerville. He should have known she'd have a great pair of lungs.

"It's me, Miss Ryan," he said in calm reassurance as he gently lifted her to her feet. When she still didn't open her eyes, he added a little louder, "It's Ross Morgan."

Nell raised her lids to gaze into the now-familiar eyes of the vexatious, uncouth owner of the Glamorgan Mine. She suddenly realized how much she admired sea-green eyes framed with thick brown lashes.

"How . . . how do you do, Mr. Morgan?" she stuttered in confusion, her Boston-Irish accent sharper and more pronounced than usual. Utterly disoriented by the mayhem that swirled around them, she tried to regain control of her jangled emotions by reverting to the precise, socially correct manners that had been drummed into her since childhood. She knew she sounded like a persnickety old maid, but Lord have mercy, it was a far sight better than howling like a banshee in total hysteria.

Morgan leaned both palms against the bricks behind her, casually shielding her with his large body, and bestowed his lazy half grin. He spoke in his irritatingly unhurried Western drawl. "Why, I'm fine, thank you, ma'am. Just havin' a nice, quiet Butte stroll."

At that moment, a brickbat smashed against the tavern wall. Nell gasped in horror. She clutched the front of Morgan's striped shirt and tried her best to bury her face in his chest as she huddled up against him. Tears of fright blurred her vision, and she started to shiver uncontrollably.

Not one to fight fate when it showered him with such extraordinary largess, Ross promptly slid his arms around her shaking form. He pulled her shapely curves tighter against his much larger frame, not hesitating for one minute to take advantage of her unreasoning panic.

"Let's find a better place to talk," he said in her ear. She tipped her head to stare up at him in dazed confusion, and wisps of silken chestnut hair brushed against his lips.

His body reacted instantaneously. Heat flooded his veins. His heartbeat accelerated as his breath caught deep in his chest. He could feel raw, sexual hunger tighten into a knot of primal need that only her dainty fingers could unravel. His mind might tell him that he should beware of any involvement with a snooty Eastern female, but his flesh and bones had no reservations about seducing the curvaceous lady attorney.

Hell, he admitted it. He wanted Miss Elinor Ryan. And he was going to move heaven and earth to have her.

He practically lifted her off her feet as he guided her to the dry-goods store next to the saloon. With one arm still around her waist, he kicked open the locked door of Barnaby's Mercantile. Then he ushered her inside and pushed the door shut with the heel of his boot.

She wouldn't let go of his shirt. Ross had to pry her gloved fingers away so he could check to see if she'd been injured. He tried to slip her suit jacket off in the attempt, and she became nearly hysterical.

"What are you doing?" she sobbed. She slapped at his hands ineffectually. "Stop that!"

Her stylish hat, which had been knocked askew earlier, tumbled to the floor, its broken feather fluttering slowly down to lie beside it. She stared for a moment at the ruined headpiece in horrified silence and then looked up at him as though he were attempting to rip her clothes off.

"Now calm down," he ordered in his deepest, most authoritative voice. "I just want to be sure you're not hurt."

Suddenly aware of that frightening possibility, she meekly allowed him to remove the form-fitting black jacket with its wide, puffy sleeves. He searched her white shirtwaist for any sign of blood and, to his great relief, found none. There were smudges of dirt on the previously spotless lace at her neck, as well as on her nose and cheek. Strands of her lustrous brown hair, which had once been piled on the top of her head in a smooth, perfect chignon, fell loosely about her shoulders. All the damage appeared to have been self-inflicted, probably when she'd crouched against the dusty tavern wall. Otherwise, she was unharmed.

"You're fine," he reassured her with a rallying smile.

"I could have been killed!" she cried. "What kind of a place is this, anyway? What kind of people are you?" She balled her hands into little fists and batted at him. The blows glanced harmlessly off his chest and shoulders.

Like an illogical female, now that she felt safe, she was furious. And even though he'd just rescued her from a mob of rioting miners, he was the closest male, and therefore the natural target for her temper.

Her anger didn't last long. With an ear-splitting crash, a brick came sailing through Barnaby's big plate-glass window, and the din of the carnage taking place outside filled the store.

Ross immediately crouched and pulled her down with him. Half crawling, he hustled her behind a display counter piled high with bolts of cloth. They sank down to the hardwood planking together. With their backs to the polished oak counter, they sat on the floor and listened to the roar of the multitude as the turmoil in the street steadily increased.

Nell huddled against him, fighting the urge to crawl into his lap. Morgan sat with one knee drawn up, his elbow propped nonchalantly atop it. His other arm was wrapped protectively around her shoulders. She could feel the bulge of his biceps flex against her back as he gave her a comforting squeeze. A wavy lock of his disheveled hair fell across his wide brow, softening a profile that was as sharp and clean as the blade of an ax.

He didn't seem the least bit worried. In fact, a smile of some secret, inner amusement flitted across his lips when he turned his head to find her staring up at him in befuddlement. He leaned toward her, and Nell quickly looked away.

All around them, shelves of expensive fabrics were littered with pieces of broken glass. Silks and velvets from France, the finest wools from Scotland, Irish tweeds, English printed broadcloths, and camel's hair serges were gracefully draped into stunning displays on the mercantile's glass showcases. On the counter directly across from them, imported trimmings of delicate, handmade Swiss lace lay in elegant profusion. The expensive, high-quality goods displayed in Barnaby's Mercantile were in blatant contrast to the savage melee taking place only yards away.

For Nell, the scene lacked only a war party of hostile red men ambushing them from behind, or a frontal attack on the store's cash register by gun-wielding desperadoes, to fulfill all her worst expectations of the untamed West. She looked down to discover she had a death grip on the front of Morgan's shirt again. Biting her lower lip to keep from moaning out loud, she forced her fingers to let go.

Dear Lord, she silently prayed as she clasped her hands together, *all I want is to go home to Boston.* Her head drooped in contemplation of what might happen to her if the rioting worsened and things really got out of hand.

Morgan pulled her closer. She could feel his steadying strength surround her. Even sprawled negligently on the floor, he possessed the controlled tension of a successful prosecutor about to hammer home a final summation before an enraptured jury. She'd never known a man who radiated such inner power, such resolute self-assurance.

At last they heard the shrill sound of police whistles above the tumult.

"Heavens to Betsy, it's about time they arrived," Nell said with relief. She attempted to rise, but Morgan held her effortlessly in place beside him.

"Not yet," he warned. "Let's give them a chance to bring some law and order to bear before we stick our noses outside." He touched the tip of hers with his forefinger. "That's such a pretty little nose. I wouldn't want anything to happen to it."

Nell felt the warmth of a blush spread across her cheeks. "Nor would I, Mr. Morgan," she answered in her best courtroom manner. She was determined not to show how unsettling she found his attentions. It wasn't as though she'd never been the target of a man's artful flattery before. She tried to lean away from him, but he retained a firm hold on her shoulders. Tilting her chin up, she pursed her lips and glared at him.

Despite the arrival of the Butte police force, the bedlam outside grew ever louder and more frenetic. Together, the two refugees from the war zone rose to their knees and peeked between the bolts of herringbone flannel piled high on the display case that protected them. Through the large, smashed window, they had a panoramic view of the chaos.

The police had, indeed, arrived. But they sure weren't winning the battle. Brandishing nightsticks, the lawmen charged into the rabble only to be attacked by APA sympathizers and Irish miners, alike. It wasn't long before the cops were retreating with bruised heads and swollen eyes.

"Here come the reinforcements," Morgan said with a chuckle.

"Where?" Nell looked in vain for more gendarmes.

Instead, her companion pointed to a fresh influx of rioters, armed with anything they could lay their hands on. "I'll bet some of those boys came all the way from Centerville," he told her with unnerving complacency.

She realized with a sinking heart that even more miners, carrying pick handles, clubs, and heavy sticks, were pouring into the fray.

The street looked like a grisly battlefield. Ambulance wagons, private coaches, and hired hacks came and went as the wounded were removed and carried off to the hospitals. An elderly man in a business suit clambered up on a packing crate and called out to the combatants to cease their fighting. But he was soon dodging paving stones hurled at his gray head. One neatly knocked off his top hat. Before long, he was forced to scramble ignominiously to safety.

"What a fight!" Morgan exclaimed in admiration. He lounged forward eagerly on the bolts of cloth, as though longing to join in the fracas.

Nell clutched his elbow. "Don't leave me here alone!"

With a crooked grin, he slid his arm about her waist and hauled her to him. He bent his head, and when he spoke, his words were husky and filled with an unexpected tenderness.

"Believe me, angel eyes, leavin' you alone is the last thing I intend to do."

Outdoors, the policemen had been reinforced with deputies from the sheriff's office. They'd decided on the strategic use of flying wedges and were fighting as one body now. But for every miner they dragged away, it seemed that three more took his place. Another brick came flying through the shattered storefront window, and the two unwilling onlookers were forced to hide behind the counter once again.

Morgan leaned his head back against the display case's polished oak side and immediately sat forward with a jerk. Reaching up, he gingerly touched the back of his scalp.

"Are you hurt?" she asked.

He shrugged off her concern. "I'm too thick-skulled to be seriously injured. I just met the pavement a bit too suddenly, is all."

Nell tugged off her gloves and scrambled to her knees. "Let me see," she insisted.

He tipped his head forward and patiently allowed her to inspect the goose egg that had risen on his crown.

"Ouch!" she said sympathetically when she felt the large bump hidden beneath his tawny hair. She touched the swollen knob lightly with her fingertip and spoke with stern reproach. "You should have a cold cloth on this."

"Yes, ma'am," he meekly agreed.

Since his head was bent, she couldn't see his eyes, but she suspected they were sparkling with merriment. What was it about her that amused him so? Usually, a strong dose of her most disparaging manner was all it took to keep any gentleman with dubious intentions at arm's length. She suspected the problem centered around the fact that Rossiter Morgan was no gentleman. Still, he'd come to her rescue like a gallant knight of old, and, for that, he deserved to have his injury tended.

She looked around in frustration. The store was filled with bolts of material, ribbons, laces, dress forms, netting, and hand-painted fans. There was a

display counter stacked with Irish linen tablecloths,
another with Reynier kid gloves. On the far wall
were shelves of toilet preparations, fine soaps, and
perfumes. But not a thing to help reduce the swelling on his battered head.

"Well, drat it," she muttered in disgust. He looked
up to meet her gaze, and she noticed, once again, the
golden flecks in his deep green eyes. There ought to
be a law against a man being so good-looking.

"We hid out in the wrong place," he admitted
with an irrepressible grin. "If we'd have ducked
into the barroom next door, we could have found
some ice for my head and had something cold to
drink at the same time."

Nell smiled reluctantly at his carefree insouci-
ance. "Next time you're caught in the middle of a
riot, sir, you'll have to plan your retreat more carefully." She slipped back down on the floor beside
him. "Meanwhile, I'm afraid there's not a thing I
can do for you."

"You could hold my hand till the pain goes away,"
he suggested.

"And how long might that take?"

"Oh, not more than a week or so."

His words conveyed a lighthearted teasing, but
his gaze was suddenly dark and predatory. Not
waiting for permission, he took her bare fingers
in his callused ones and ran the pad of his thumb
across her knuckles with casual familiarity.

Tugging unsuccessfully, Nell tried to free her
hand from his strong grasp. She looked up with
irritation to meet his smiling eyes. "Did anyone ever
tell you that you're an outrageously bold man, Mr.
Morgan?"

"Me? Never!" he protested, as though genuinely
shocked. But she could hear the smothered hilarity
in his deep voice.

The sudden sound of rain pounding on the
roof forestalled Nell's reply. Thunder crashed and
boomed above them. Through the broken front

window, bolts of lightning lit up the darkened sky.

"Now that ought to put an end to the fighting," she said. Together, they rose to peer over the stacks of flannel once more.

But the thunderstorm didn't stop the battle. Irishmen, Italians, Finns, Cornishmen, and Swedes all kept at it, hammer and tongs. It seemed that no one was about to forgo willingly the pleasure of making mincemeat out of his enemy just to avoid getting a little wet.

Then a gunshot rang out.

From their vista, they saw a police officer, caught in the middle of the fighting, fall to the pavement. More shots sounded, and another man pitched to the ground.

Without a moment's hesitation, Ross pulled Nell to the floor and completely covered her with his body.

"Get off me," she said in a muffled voice.

"Lie still," he commanded. He braced his elbows on either side of her head and cradled her face against the hollow of his neck. If a bullet did strike her, it would have to pass through him first.

"Don't move, little darlin'," he soothed when she tried to buck him off. "I don't think my heart can take any more excitement at the moment."

He waited, listening tensely. Scores of bullets were flying in every direction. Several whistled over their heads to bury themselves in the back wall of the store. As the broken toiletry articles crashed to the display cases below, the sound of splintering glass filled Barnaby's Mercantile. Beneath Ross, Nell froze in terror.

Outside, the gunplay must have sobered the rioters as well, for the crowd grew suddenly still. The clanging alarm bells of the city's new fire wagon could be clearly heard and then the sound of torrents of water being sprayed into the Columbia Bar across the street.

Ross smiled to himself. Why hadn't they thought of that before? No doubt the Irish fire crews were having a field day hosing down the offensive APA shields from the false fronts of both taverns. After that, the firemen turned their powerful streams on the inside of the bar next door. Through the adjoining wall, he could hear them smashing every mirror, shot glass, and beer mug in the place. Next, they'd be aiming their hoses at the rioters themselves.

With relief, Ross looked down at the attractive woman trapped beneath him. He'd supported the bulk of his weight on his forearms so he wouldn't crush the life out of her. One of his heavy thighs was pressed between her slim legs in an added attempt to keep from smothering her. Her full skirt was bunched up around her knees in a scandalous display of intimacy.

She lay perfectly still, staring up at him with wide brown eyes filled with utter bewilderment. Just above her full lips, which were opened slightly, revealing a glimpse of even white teeth, was a small, dark brown mole. She looked as if she'd been mixing a cake and had greedily licked the spoon, only to leave a tiny, telltale drop of batter as permanent evidence of her naughty behavior. The effect was incredibly erotic and unbelievably tantalizing.

The air between them was charged with excitement. He was amazed at the intense physical attraction he felt toward this peppery female who'd seemed to take an unreasoning dislike to him from their first introduction.

She stirred ever so slightly, and her firm breasts brushed against his chest, sending sparks of molten energy to every nerve ending in his body. His palms ached to cup her soft curves. Intoxicated by her sensual beauty, he fought the temptation to lower his head and test the hidden sweetness that beckoned to him like some honeyed and magical aphrodisiac.

The delightful scent of Hertta Kuusinen's ginger cookies lingered about Nell's clothing. With his hands still cradling her head, he traced the line of her jaw with his thumb and told himself he was a blasted fool. But he had to discover something he'd been wondering about since the first moment they'd met. Unable to resist any longer, he bent even closer and touched the tiny dot above her lip with the tip of his tongue.

Shocked, she drew in a deep draft of air. "Why did you do that?" she demanded in a scandalized whisper.

"I had to find out if it tasted like nutmeg or chocolate."

"And what did you learn, Mr. Morgan?"

Despite his desperate attempt to calm his erratic breathing, his voice was hoarse with desire.

"That I want to taste you all over."

Chapter 3

Nell's heart paused for a split second before kicking into a wild, uncontrolled gallop. He couldn't have meant what it sounded like. A man just didn't say that kind of thing to a woman.

Speechless with disbelief, she stared up into his hooded green eyes. Those gold-flecked orbs had that predatory look again. Morgan had said *taste*, but in the depths of his smoldering gaze, she read the word *devour*.

She tried to hide her confusion. For a lawyer to be struck dumb was nothing short of disgraceful. After all, words were her business. She'd spent years studying legal statutes of the most complex nature, filled with complicated arguments, pro and con, on countless points of law. But the startlingly erotic image he'd painted with such ease in one simple sentence had left her as tongue-tied as a bashful junior law assistant who'd just been given her very first case by the firm's benevolent senior partner.

Morgan didn't seem to expect a reply. At least he didn't wait for one. With her face still cradled between his large hands, he lowered his tawny head and slowly covered her lips with his open mouth. His movements were unhurried, eminently proficient, and filled with self-confidence. There was nothing hesitant about the man. Or his kissing. When he traced the outline of her mouth with his warm, moist tongue, Nell clamped her lips tight in adamant refusal of the unspoken request. He wasn't the least bit daunted by her cold response, but slanted his mouth across hers in a sizzling kiss that would have set an icehouse on fire.

She inhaled the spicy aroma of shaving soap, and her heart lit up inside her with a warm glow. The fleeting picture of Morgan stropping a razor, with his chest bare and his rugged chin covered in soft white lather, revived a barely conscious, unidentifiable yearning that was somehow bound up with half-forgotten dreams of marriage and children.

With amazement, she realized she wasn't afraid, despite the fact that she was alone with him and stretched out on the floor of a dry-goods store in a scandalous and compromising position. She sensed that he was prepared to stop the moment she attempted to repulse him. That intuitive knowledge kept her from feeling threatened by his far superior strength. Curiosity and a budding excitement surged through her. Outside of a friendly buss, she hadn't kissed a man in nearly fourteen years. So long ago, in fact, she couldn't remember what it had felt like, only the painful months of heartache and searing mortification that had followed. She certainly couldn't recall these breathless, nerve-jangling, toe-curling sensations she was experiencing now.

Within a few days, she'd be leaving to return to the familiar routine of her well-ordered life. What could it possibly hurt to discover if kissing this golden-haired skirt chaser was as pleasant as it promised to be? Slowly, tentatively, she wrapped her arms around his muscular torso and returned the pressure of his inviting lips.

The feel of her sweet, timid response sent shock waves of pleasure through Ross's taut frame. He slipped his arm beneath her shoulders and rolled to one side, gently taking her with him. He was racked with desire. His body responded to her feminine allure like that of a sex-starved prospector just returning to civilization. She was beauty, enticement, and female mystery incarnate. He splayed his fingers across her rib cage, barely able to refrain from cupping her breast. Beneath her white cotton blouse, he could feel the stiff whalebones of her corset protecting her charms like a flimsy wooden barrier thrown up against some rapacious, plundering Hun. And he was that Hun.

Breaking the kiss, Ross drew back slightly and met her bemused gaze. He waited in patient resignation for her to have a sudden change of heart and slap his face soundly, all the while knowing the kiss had been well worth any punishment she might decide to mete out. But she didn't try to bite or scratch in belated outrage. Like some ethereal being, she stared up at him in solemn fascination, as though completely mystified by this strange, exotic, human ritual of lip touching.

The only sound was the pounding of rain on the roof. They were so close, he could feel her breath fan out like a warm caress on his face. A lock of her dark chestnut hair fell in long satin strands across her smooth cheek, and he tenderly brushed it aside, his fingers lingering on her fine-grained ivory skin. Carnal excitement thrummed in the air. Yet she lay so quiescent in his arms, he wasn't sure she even recognized the lustful attraction between them for what it was. There was an aura of shy uncertainty, of equivocal wonder about her that seemed strangely incongruous for a woman who had the physical attributes of a pagan love goddess.

"Sugarplum, you're makin' me crazy," Ross murmured. He bent his head to kiss her again.

This time she returned his kiss without hesitation. She gave the faintest of sighs as she slid her graceful hands up and locked them behind his neck. The twin mounds of her bosom pressed against his chest, and Ross groaned in hedonistic pleasure. He moved his hand upward to bracket the outer swell of her breast, certain that he was going far too fast and ready to pull to a screeching halt at the slightest indication of unwillingness on her part. Yet the longing to take her there on the hard floor of Barnaby's Mercantile drove him onward, willing, eager to test the limits she would set in their first romantic encounter. That this might be their last, Ross refused even to consider.

The minute Nell felt the pressure of Morgan's thumb on the side of her breast, she stiffened in alarm. This foolishness had to stop now, before he misread her intentions completely. An exploratory kiss was one thing. Shameless fondling was quite another.

She pulled back and braced her palms on his broad shoulders. The sight of her own small hands pressed against his solid, muscular frame unleashed a whirlwind of conflicting emotions. Fear that he might not heed her wishes and cease his unwanted attentions, after all. Desire to bury her fingertips in the tousled hair that curled around his collar and resume the kiss that had awakened such a deep hunger inside her. Anger at her foolish, female compliance.

She fought to keep the betraying unsteadiness from her voice. "I think we'd better see if it's safe to go outside, Mr. Morgan. It sounds as if the rioting is over."

"Let's wait awhile longer," he suggested huskily, "just to make sure it's okay." He bent his head to kiss her again, and Nell quickly turned her face aside.

"Let's check right now," she countered. When he smoothed the palm of his hand across her midriff in a persuasive caress, she tilted her chin up in dogged perseverance. "I'm afraid I must insist."

Morgan expelled a long, slow, ragged breath that brushed across her ear like warm velvet. "All right, little darlin'." He released her and moved to his feet with the sleek, easy grace of a hunting cat. Reaching down, he offered his hand and assisted her up.

As Nell rose to stand in front of him, her glance couldn't help but sweep over his magnificent physique. The snug, copper-riveted Levi's he wore revealed massive thighs corded with muscles. The faded indigo-blue denim was stretched taut across the crotch, clearly revealing the bulge of his hardened manhood. She tore her gaze away and stared in mortification at the display counter piled high with bolts of flannel behind him. But not before he'd caught her shocked reaction.

"Some things a man just can't help, angel eyes," he said in soft apology.

"Don't call me angel eyes," she snapped. She ignored the betraying flush that burned her cheeks. Meeting his look of tender amusement, she continued with peevish irritation. "And I'm not your little darling or sugarplum, either. My name is Elinor. It's a perfectly good Irish name. Use it."

"But Sean spoke of you so often, and he always called you Nell," Morgan hedged. "I don't know if I'd feel comfortable switchin' to Elinor at this late date."

Her voice oozed with condescension. "Then you can call me Miss Ryan."

"Doesn't that sound kind of formal, considerin' how we just—"

"All right, call me Nell if you must, Mr. Morgan. But from now on, please remember I have a strong aversion to trite, meaningless endearments."

His lips quirked in a wicked half grin. "Well, now, I don't have that problem. You can call me by any trite endearment you want. Darlin', honey, or dearest won't bother me in the least. I'll answer to any and all of them."

"Not on the longest day you live, Mr. Morgan."

"Ross would be just fine for starters."

She flounced past him, skirting the counter of herringbone. At the front of the store, the floor was littered with shards of broken glass. It crunched noisily under the soles of her laced kid oxfords with their patent-leather tips as she strode majestically toward the door. She paused only to pick up her jacket, handbag, and featherless hat from the display table where Morgan had laid them.

He was right behind her. He put out his hand to take the wrinkled suit jacket, and she grudgingly allowed him to help her on with it. There was something about the man that told her he'd brook no argument when it came to seeing to her needs exactly as he deemed fit. Heavens to Betsy, she wasn't some helpless schoolgirl. She'd been making her own decisions for far too long to be dependent on any egotistical, proprietary male now.

"I'll walk you to your hotel, Miss Ryan," he said. "The Thornton is just up the street." He tossed a silver dollar on the counter and pulled a brand-new umbrella from its display stand nearby.

"I'm not staying at the Thornton," she answered, only slightly mollified that he'd finally acceded in using the proper form of address. "I've decided to stay at Kuusinen's Boardinghouse, since Sean paid in advance for his room there. The landlady promised to send someone to collect my bags. I had them taken directly to the hotel from the railroad station before I went up to your mine this morning."

Morgan nodded his approval. "Hertta will take good care of you." He swung the door open, popped up the umbrella, and waited for her to step beneath. "I'll escort you to the boardin'house."

"That won't be necessary," she said as she sailed through the smashed portal and out into the downpour. Shielding her face with one hand, she blinked away the raindrops that threatened to blur her vision. "I wouldn't want to take you out of your way."

With irritating composure, he slipped one hand beneath her elbow and pulled her under the black umbrella's sheltering circle. "You won't, Miss Ryan. As it happens, I reside there myself. In fact, I was the one who helped Sean find a place to stay when he first came lookin' for a job at the Glamorgan. I can recommend Hertta's cookin' from personal experience, along with her clean sheets."

The street in front of Barnaby's Mercantile was a shambles. Up and down West Broadway, nearly every window was shattered. Over half the paving bricks had been pried up and launched like stones from a dozen catapults. The fronts of both the Columbia and Sazerac saloons were nearly demolished. It was nothing short of a miracle that the maddened crowd hadn't razed the two buildings entirely. In the pouring rain, the fire crews were busily unhooking their hoses, rolling them up, and storing them on the fire wagons. A fire captain hurried over the moment he saw the two civilians come out of the store.

"You a'right, ma'am?" he asked. "We'd no idea anyone was trapped in that building." Through the pelting rain, his dark brown eyes squinted at her in concern.

"I'm fine," said Nell. "I was caught in the middle of the riot, and Mr. Morgan came to my assistance."

The captain's wide-spaced teeth flashed beneath his thick mustache as he grinned at her companion. "Now, that don't surprise me none. If there's a pretty lady around, it's a sure bet the Colorado Cougar won't be far away." Nell stiffened and tipped her chin upward in frigid disapproval. The firefighter touched his hat in an apologetic salute. "No offense intended, ma'am."

Before she could answer, her tall rescuer put two fingers between his lips and whistled shrilly. A hack, which had just driven onto the scene, pulled to a halt in front of them. Morgan called instructions to the driver, opened the door of the cab, and hustled her inside. She'd barely had time to settle back on the seat when the team took off at a smart trot.

All along the thoroughfare, groups of uniformed state militia watched with fixed bayonets as the first of the wounded were carried away and the area was roped off and cleared of combatants and spectators alike.

Nell brushed the raindrops from her skirt and the puffed shoulders of her new walking suit. She looked down at the hat and bag she'd placed on the seat beside her and realized she'd left her gloves on the floor of the mercantile.

"Heaven save us," she said indignantly, "I've never seen the likes of such barbarism."

On the seat across from her, Ross leaned his bruised head back on the leather upholstery and enjoyed the enchanting sight before him. Even completely disheveled, with her lovely forehead creased in a frown, she was a delight to the senses.

"That was one grand Donnybrook Fair," he cheerfully agreed in an attempt to soothe her. Inwardly, he was relieved to know that his son had been nowhere near the riot area. Early that morning, Luke and his two Finnish friends had taken their fishing poles and a pail of worms and headed toward Bell Creek to spend a lazy summer day.

"Grand?" Her soot-covered nose twitched contemptuously. "There was nothing grand about it. It was the worst possible kind of behavior." She favored him with a scathing look. "Lawless violence can never be condoned, Mr. Morgan. I hope every man who was arrested today pays the full price for his misdeeds."

"You can't blame those Micks for dynamitin' the saloons. Anyone foolish enough to put up APA signs on the Fourth of July, or on any other day for that matter, was askin' for trouble. And a good head-thumpin' free-for-all is nothin' new for Butte, especially on a holiday. But things did get a little out of hand toward the end there," he conceded. "With all those bullets flyin', someone may have been killed."

Her eyes widened in horror, then filled with sudden tears. "I sincerely hope not." She put a finger to her trembling upper lip and turned to look out the window.

"Accidental deaths can happen anywhere, Nell," he said softly. "Even back in Boston."

She jerked her head to meet his gaze, and her chin quivered with wrath. If she knew he was referring to Sean and was trying to offer her comfort, she gave no indication.

"Something like this would never happen back home!" she disclaimed. "Differences are settled in court. That's why we have laws, judges, and juries. Civilized men don't go around carrying guns in their belts or blowing up the fronts of buildings. Or getting themselves killed in drunken saloon brawls."

Ross leaned forward and braced his elbows on his knees. He tried to take her hands, but she snatched them away. "I'm sorry you were so frightened, little girl. But I promise, the worst is over. This doesn't happen every day, not even in a minin' camp."

"I'm not a little girl!" she cried. "I'm thirty-one years old, Mr. Morgan. And I've been responsible for myself since I was seventeen. I don't need you or any other man to look out for me. Or to . . . to rescue me. And until I get out of this horrible place, I can take care of myself, thank you very much."

"My apologies, ma'am. When I saw you crouched up against the front of the Sazerac Saloon, I didn't know you'd just bent down to retrieve a lost hairpin or two. I mistakenly thought you needed some help."

Her words crackled with resentment. "I wasn't speaking of being protected from a crazed mob. I was referring to the antiquated belief that every unmarried woman is waiting for some knight in shining armor to deliver her from a life of spinsterhood."

"I hadn't realized I'd already proposed marriage," he said with a chuckle. "I'd planned to save that for later this evenin', after I'd taken you out to supper and dazzled you with my debonair charm and rapier wit."

She nearly ground her teeth in vexation. "I suggest you keep your well-polished line of flattery for the next woman you rescue. With any luck, she'll be

44 KATHLEEN HARRINGTON

For a love goddess, she had a tongue like a rattler. For a fast-talking Eastern lawyer, she wasn't doing too bad either. They were interrupted by the coach's halt in front of the boardinghouse before he could get out a single word in his own defense.

When they entered the front drawing room, Gavin O'Connell sprang up from the ugly horsehair settee and hurried over to them. The worried look on the attorney's handsome face made it plain that the two lawyers from Ryan, Sheehy, and O'Connell were well acquainted. O'Connell definitely had a proprietary air about him as he rushed toward her. "Nell!" he exclaimed. "Are you all right? For Christ's sake, I've been half crazy with worry!"

Ross had been disappointed in the Boston greenhorn when he'd arrived two weeks before to represent the Glamorgan Mine in court. That vague feeling of dissatisfaction took a sharp dive into outright male jealously at Nell's look of relief when she saw her friend.

"I'm perfectly fine, Gavin," she answered. She took her colleague's outstretched hand with a wan smile and then glanced up at Ross. "We were both trapped in a store right in the middle of the fighting. Mr. Morgan risked his life to protect me."

Gavin turned to Ross, clasped his hand, and shook it. "God, if anything had happened to Nell . . ." He swung back to her and placed both hands on her shoulders. "Are you sure you're okay? You look like the very devil."

Nell glanced into the large, brass-framed mirror on the wall over the sofa and drew in a startled breath. She was a complete disaster! Splotches of dirt covered her nose, her cheek, the crumpled lace at her throat. Her damp hair was half up in a stylish chignon and half down in long, snarled strands that hung limply around her shoulders and down her back. The expensive traveling suit she'd purchased for the trip was rumpled and covered with streaks of mud. She whipped around to stare at Morgan, who'd affected an air of complete ignorance. If he'd looked up at the ceiling and broken into an unperturbed whistle, it wouldn't have surprised her.

"That's because I've spent the afternoon with Lucifer," she grated through clenched teeth.

"If he hurt you . . ." Gavin began. He looked back and forth at them, his eyes filled with rising doubt.

Morgan's granite chin jutted out ominously. He folded his arms across his chest and braced his legs apart in a stance just short of insolent. "Miss Ryan came to no harm in my care. Nor will she."

"I've not been hurt by anyone," she said. She placed her hand on Gavin's arm. "And I've seen enough violence today to last me the rest of my life."

Gavin was only a few inches taller than Nell, and he met her eyes in a searching gaze. They'd been friends since the day she'd first met him in her uncle's law office when they were both still in their teen years.

"I'd planned to meet you at the station," he said, his brow knitted with worry, "but I was unexpectedly delayed. When your trunks were delivered to the hotel, I assumed you'd reached Butte safely. But when you didn't show up after several hours, I started to get anxious. Just about that time, a boy arrived at the Thornton, saying he was from Kuusinen's, and that he was to bring your baggage to the boardinghouse. I suspected some kind of thievery. So, naturally, I accompanied him back here instead of sending the trunks."

"I wanted to see where Sean had been living," she explained. "After I decided to stay here rather than at the hotel, I took Mrs. Kuusinen's suggestion and went uptown to see the parade."

"You can't remain here!" protested Gavin.

She released his arm and stepped back. "Whyever not?"

"This is a Finnish boardinghouse, for Christ's sake. Nothing but rough, vulgar miners live here."

"Sean lived here," she reminded him quietly, "and he was neither." She turned to stare blindly out the parlor's front window. "I saw his room this morning. I think he must have been happy living here."

Gavin put his arm around her shoulders in a gesture of understanding and reassurance. He pulled her toward the large red and black sofa and urged her to sit down. "Nell, Nell," he said soothingly as he sank onto the cushion beside her and took her hand. "I think you're in shock." He looked up at Morgan, who happened to be a very wealthy client of Ryan, Sheehy, and O'Connell. "Tell her, Morgan. Tell her she can't board at Kuusinen's. It's out of the question for any decent woman to stay here."

Nell looked up at Morgan, who'd followed them to the sofa and now towered above them. His eyes twinkled as they met her questioning gaze. A smile flickered across his angular features, and he cocked his head to one side in mirthful consideration.

Before he could answer, Hertta whisked into the room. "Nonsense, Mr. O'Connell. It is perfectly decent for Miss Ryan to board at t'is establishment. I live here." With one hand on her hip, she leaned toward Gavin and shook her finger under his nose. Her bright blue eyes crackled with ire. "So, you do not t'ink I am a respectable woman? You had better not say such a t'ing in front of my Kalle, I can tell you t'at!"

Gavin sprang to his feet, his face red with embarrassment. "Mrs. Kuusinen, I meant no disrespect, I assure you. But don't you see, that's just the point. Your husband lives here with you." He looked at the three of them, his lips pursed in exasperation beneath his light brown mustache. When they continued to stare at him in puzzlement, he ran his slender hand across his creased forehead and finally blurted out, "Nell's an unmarried woman."

"Oh, for heaven's sake," said Nell. "I'm staying here and that's the end of it." She rose and swiped vigorously at her dust-streaked skirt. "Right now, I'm going to my room and tidy up. After that, I'll go over to the Thornton Hotel and collect my luggage."

Ross stepped closer and spoke quietly to Nell. "I'll wait till you're ready and then escort you there. That offer to take you to supper this evenin' was genuine. We've some wonderful noodle parlors in Butte. I hope you like Chinese cookin'."

"There's no need for that," Gavin said. He waved his hand in dismissal of the entire proposal, as though Ross had included him in the invitation. "I'm returning to the Thornton from here. I'll take Nell uptown. We can have supper at the hotel, and I can catch up on all the news from our firm. I'm sure she has some detailed instructions for me from my father and Cormac Ryan. Afterward, I'll bring Nell and her trunks back here." He turned to her and added dubiously, "If that's what you still want to do by then."

Ross tried to conceal his irritation. He'd already gotten off on the wrong foot with the beautiful attorney from Boston. There was no sense in aggravating her any further by insulting her law partner. "I believe I made my offer first, O'Connell," he said as amicably as possible. "But you're welcome to join us, if you'd like . . ."

To butt in.

Gavin met his gaze and took the hint. "We'll leave the decision up to the lady," he replied. His white teeth flashed beneath his closely trimmed mustache in certain triumph.

Nell, however, wasn't amused. "I've already taken up far too much of your time, Mr. Morgan. I'm certain you have many demands on your busy schedule. I'll contact you when I have the court order allowing me to go into the Glamorgan." She paused, then continued sweetly. "Unless you've changed your mind and decided to allow me to descend to the twelve-hundred-foot level?"

So they were back to that again. Lord, she was a stubborn little thing.

"I'm afraid not, Nell," he said in a tone of quiet authority. "My refusal still stands. And so does my offer for supper any evenin' you find yourself without other plans."

Her dark brows arched in cool disdain. "And I'm afraid we'd have so little in common, we'd find absolutely nothing to talk about after the first awkward five minutes." With a barely polite inclination of her head, she glided out of the room.

Clearly disappointed, Hertta made a wry grimace and followed suit.

"Sorry, old chap," Gavin said with what appeared to be honest sympathy. "I could have warned you ahead of time. Nell never accepts a gentleman's invitation to a restaurant or anywhere else unless it's directly related to legal matters. She's just not interested."

"Why?"

The Easterner's hazel eyes clouded with misgiving. It was apparent the man cared very deeply about her. "I'm not sure," he admitted. "I've known Nell since she was seventeen. Believe me, in all those years she's never once shown the slightest romantic interest in any man." He shoved his hands into his trouser pockets and shrugged fatalistically. "Some females are just born with ice in their veins. Frigid when it comes to sexual congress. I guess Nell is one of them."

Remembering the breathless, heart-stopping kiss he'd shared with her on the floor of Barnaby's Mercantile, Ross stared at Gavin in disbelief.

Frigid? Like hell.

Chapter 4

Except for the tiny yellow blossoms of the ubiquitous tansy weed, there were no flowers in the cemetery. Not on Sean Ryan's grave or on any other. Nell stood before the fresh mound of earth with its crude wooden cross and willed herself not to make a sound. While the steady prairie wind ruffled the veil that spilled over the brim of her black felt hat and pried loose wisps of her tightly bound hair, she remained completely still, her head high, her shoulders back, her hands clasped on the funeral wreath she held in front of her. Sorrow, sharp and keen as a knife edge, ripped through her at the horrible sight. Clenching her teeth, she swallowed back the ache in her throat. She'd never beheld, or even imagined, such a lonely and forsaken place.

Graves couldn't be dug on the rocky hills of Butte, so the cemetery had been located in a desolate section of the valley south of the mining camp. There the coarse, sandy soil could be easily removed for a burial and as quickly tossed back on the waiting coffin. Somewhere close by, ore was being roasted out in the open, and the fumes swirled about the deserted graveyard like an invisible, noxious mist, killing every living thing but the tenacious dune tansy that covered the otherwise barren knolls. The dark green herb permeated the air with its strong aroma of camphor. Concoctions of its dried flowers were credited for curing skin irritations, bruises, sprains, and even rheumatism. To a heartbroken

Nell, the medicinal smell was fittingly reminiscent of sickness and death.

Directly behind her, she heard the sound of muffled footsteps and knew that Gavin had finished speaking with the waiting hack driver and had joined her at the graveside. Earlier that morning, Gavin had taken her to St. Patrick's, where she lit a candle before the Sorrowful Mother and spoke briefly with the priest who'd buried Sean. Then the two friends had ridden out to the flat together in near silence. On their arrival, Gavin had purposely lingered by the coach to give her some time to be alone with Sean.

"It's a terrible tragedy," Gavin said softly as he stopped just behind her. "That anyone so young . . ."

She bit her lower lip and blinked away the tears. She couldn't speak. She knew that if she attempted to express her grief, she'd scream over and over again in mindless, keening agony. She'd turn her face up to the blue Montana sky and howl like a wild thing at the obscene sight of her beautiful young brother's last resting place.

Unable to answer Gavin's words of comfort, she bowed her head and looked down at the circular ring of deep red roses she held in her gloved hands. The scent of their perfume rose up from the blooms, bringing the memory of a very young Sean in their mother's flower garden in Bar Harbor.

At ten years old, Nell had been responsible for the care of her baby brother while Maude Ryan worked during the summer months as a housekeeper at the Frenchman's Bay Inn. The inn, built to resemble a Swiss chalet, sat on the side of a high hill above the town and its picturesque harbor, which was filled in the summertime with yachts and naval vessels. On balmy evenings, sister and brother would walk up the steep path that overlooked the bay to meet their weary mother as she made her way homeward. The little boy, his big brown eyes glowing, often held a rose he'd picked from the garden clutched in his chubby fist. With a smile of welcome, Momma would reach out and swing him up into her loving arms. Two-year-old Sean would snuggle his head against her shoulder and hold the treasure beneath her nose. Their mother would breathe deeply and sigh with exaggerated pleasure. Then she'd give Nell an affectionate hug, and the three of them would return to the little summer cottage that belonged to Uncle Cormac, where they'd lived since the day Jack Ryan had left them to search for gold.

"Nell," Gavin said at last, clearly distressed by her long, disheartened silence, "this wasn't your fault. None of it. Why, I heard you try to dissuade Sean from coming out here many times."

"I should have stopped him, somehow," she said, her gaze still fastened on the knoll in front of her. "He was only nine when Momma died. She asked me to look out for him, to take care of him. I promised her I would." Her voice quavered and broke on a sob, but she forced herself to continue. "You can see how well I kept that promise."

Gavin moved a step closer. His words were gruff with compassion. "Stop torturing yourself for what couldn't have been changed. Sean was twenty-three years old. Short of tying him to the bedpost, there was no way you could have stopped him from going."

Nell stared blindly ahead, refusing to accept the consolation offered by her kindhearted companion. Gavin had no inkling of how badly she'd failed her younger brother. Through the chicanery of a very persuasive, smooth-spoken scoundrel, she'd lost the entire nest egg Maude Ryan had worked so hard to accumulate. Only two months after their mother's death, Nell and Sean had left the tiny home in Maine as virtual paupers. If it hadn't been for Uncle Cormac's generosity and love, they'd have been homeless as well. And all because Nell had become infatuated with a handsome chiseler named Charleton Blevins, who'd lied to her from the moment they'd met. That had been fourteen years ago. Now, at thirty-one, she still felt the unrelenting shame of her childish gullibility. She'd vowed at the time that no man would ever deceive her again. And in those long, lonely years since, no man had even come close.

Gavin touched her elbow, bringing her back to the present and its almost unbearable pain. "Would you like me to put the flowers on the grave?" he asked.

"No, I will." She looked over her shoulder to meet his worried gaze and managed a weak smile. "Sean especially loved roses."

She bent and draped the wreath on the wooden cross. Before she left for Boston, she'd have a proper stone set in place with her brother's name engraved in marble, so that a hundred years from now someone would read it and know how much he was truly loved. Tragically, that thought brought Nell no serenity. Dear God above, how could she leave her baby brother in this horrible place?

"Let's go back to the carriage now," Gavin urged. "I want to get you out of the sun."

She could hear the concern in his voice, as though he were afraid she'd suddenly collapse in a heap of black mourning weeds. He needn't worry. She was made of sturdier stuff than that. She never swooned. Like her mother before her, she'd never been able to afford that luxury. Foolish women, who became involved with ne'er-do-wells, rarely did.

With a brief nod, she allowed Gavin to guide her away from the gravesite. But before they'd gone five yards, Nell stopped and looked back at the wreath of red blossoms that adorned the roughly hewed marker. White satin streamers from its huge bow blew in the morning breeze, the gold lettering on the ribbon clearly visible.

Beloved Brother
Sleep in Peace

She stared for one long minute more, then turned and quickly walked with Gavin to the waiting hack.

Placing his bowler hat on his thick brown hair, he opened the carriage door, ready to assist her inside. "Where would you like to go now?"

"Back to the boardinghouse, I guess." She shrugged with indifference. "I've made no plans for the rest of the day."

"I'm going up to the Glamorgan," he told her. "I have a meeting scheduled with the owner and his superintendent to discuss some points regarding his court case. Why don't you come with me? You can listen in and offer any suggestions you might have. Then, afterward, I'll take you to lunch."

"I'm not too sure I'd be welcomed at the mine," she said with a wry smile. "The last time I spoke with Mr. Morgan, I threatened to sue him." She had no intention of telling her colleague what else, of a more personal nature, lay between her and the handsome mine owner.

Gavin chuckled. "Considering the fact that he's a rich client of Ryan, Sheehy, and O'Connell, I think that might be a rather inappropriate course of action."

She laughed softly. "At the time, of course, I was only bluffing. I don't really want to take my uncle's client to court. Not that I'm going to tell *him* that. But I intend to talk Morgan into allowing me to see the place where Sean died." Sobering, she frowned in sudden perplexity. "I can't tell you why, precisely, but it's something I need to do for my own peace of mind. I just have to see it, that's all."

"You don't think there was something suspicious about Sean's death, do you?" Gavin's expression revealed his surprise.

"I don't know. Mr. Morgan wrote me a brief letter, conveying his sympathy. From his words, I could tell that he was sincerely grieved about what had happened. Yet when I read between the lines, I felt as though he were holding back information, as though he'd purposely left something unsaid. That feeling of uneasiness has only increased since I've been here."

Gavin didn't pooh-pooh her reliance on feminine intuition. In the years that Nell had worked as her uncle's legal assistant, she'd garnered a reputation at their firm for an extraordinary ability to judge a stranger's character. She seemed to have a knack for assessing people's flaws and weaknesses, no matter how upright and honest they pretended to be. From cheating businessmen to grasping socialites, Nell could see through their alibis, evasions, and half truths with unerring judgment.

"Then let's go up to the Glamorgan together," Gavin said. "I'll insist on Morgan taking you to the exact spot where your brother died." He helped her into the coach, called out the directions to the driver, and climbed inside.

Nell picked up the handbag she'd left in the cab and scooted over on the leather seat to give him room to sit next to her. "Are the preparations for the trial going well?" she asked.

"Darned if I know." He grimaced in disgust. "I tried to talk my father out of sending me here to represent the Glamorgan's interests. I told him I was the wrong man for the job. What the heck do I know about mining?"

"You may not know much about mining, but you certainly know the law. Uncle Cormac and your father have complete confidence in you." She wrinkled her nose at him mischievously. "Besides, anyone with a degree from Harvard Law School shouldn't have a thing to worry about in a rustic district court way out here in the middle of nowhere. I doubt there's another attorney with your eminent scholarly background in the entire county of Silver Bow. Or in the whole state of Montana, for that matter."

Gavin grinned at her. His Harvard law degree
was a long-standing source of playful bickering
between them. Nell, being a female, would never
have been allowed to set foot in that prestigious
university's hallowed halls as a law student, even if
she'd had the unmitigated temerity to apply. There
were law schools that did admit women, but she'd
not attended one. After graduating from Wellesley,
she'd studied under her brilliant uncle's tutelage,
reading the law in his extensive personal library.
Yet since the two friends had first begun to practice
before the bar, Gavin had come to Nell for advice
far more often than she'd gone to him.

"You're right," he admitted smugly. He straightened his narrow bow tie with a gesture of droll
self-importance. "I'll dazzle the opposition's illus-
trious New York lawyers with my silver-tongued
oratory. All half dozen of them."

"A half dozen?" she exclaimed.

"That's the rumor going around. And Felix Hegel
has the bankroll to afford them."

"Bless us and save us," she said, "your adversary
intends to win or go broke trying." She smiled her
encouragement, hoping to tease him into a more
optimistic frame of mind. "You'd better hope the
jury understands your cultivated Harvard accent.
They'll probably be a bunch of slow-talking Montana
cowboys who drawl and say 'Howdy, pardner!'
when they meet you."

Gavin's grin faded. "I'd like nothing better than a
dozen honest cowmen. At least that way we'd have
a chance at a fair trial. But the jury's far more likely
to be twelve miners taking bribes that come straight
from Mr. Hegel's pocket."

"Surely not!" Nell protested. "You should be able
to weed out suspicious candidates at the time of
their selection. Have you investigated all the names
on the list of potential jurors?"

"Every man on that list is involved in mining in
some way. Between working either for the mines

directly or in a business that supplies equipment to them, hardly anyone who lives in this hellhole of a place isn't touched, somehow, by the search for precious metals below ground. This isn't going to be a cakewalk," he added with a grim look. "Any time you have a civil action with millions of dollars at stake, the most despicable shenanigans can happen—and usually do."

She patted his arm encouragingly. "Don't worry, my friend. You'll do fine."

His hazel eyes were filled with doubt as he slowly shook his head. "I told my father not to send me. He should have paid more attention to my wishes."

Nell sat on a high, three-legged stool in the Glamorgan's office and listened to the two mining engineers try to instruct Gavin on the basic points of their defense in the coming court battle. She'd learned from their conversation that Rossiter Morgan and Eben Pearce were graduates of the Columbia School of Mines. Both were experts in geology as well as mining technology. From her position by the door, she had an excellent view of the three men clustered around the scarred oak desk. While Morgan persisted in explaining to his apparently indifferent attorney about stopes, drifts, cross-cuts, and extralateral rights, she used the opportunity to study the mine owner himself.

Totally involved in the one-sided discussion, Morgan was bent over a large map spread out across his desktop. Well over six feet tall, he was slim-hipped, deep-chested, and corded with muscles. His angular profile, with its square jaw and straight nose, made Gavin's sculpted features appear almost girlish, while Morgan's unruly golden waves made her friend's light brown hair appear nondescript by comparison.

Earlier, Morgan had slipped on a pair of wire-rimmed glasses to study his charts, and whenever he glanced up over the spectacles at the two other

men to make a point, his green eyes sparkled with
excitement. It was obvious he loved the challenge
of wresting a fortune from the depths of the earth.
That didn't surprise her. Greed for precious metals
had always been one of mankind's more abiding
passions.

Unaware that he was the focus of Miss Ryan's
complete attention, Ross was trying hard not to lose
his temper with the dapper Irish lawyer sent out
from Massachusetts to be his legal counselor. Gavin
O'Connell made no attempt to hide the fact that he
was barely listening to the discussion at hand. From
what little he did add, it was clear that, although the
pretty-boy Harvard graduate might know the law,
he knew next to nothing about mining.

"Look here," Ross said, as he pointed to the map
showing the geological formations underlying the
Butte hill. He traced a vein of copper with the tip
of his finger, certain in his heart that it foretold nearly inexhaustible riches. "This is what we've been
followin' all the way down to the twelve-hundred-
foot level."

"I'd thought we'd lost it for good in May," Eben
interjected, "but Ross refused to give up. He insisted
on continuing the exploration for at least two more
weeks."

"Last month," Ross went on, "we opened up a
drift that promises to produce millions of dollars in
high-grade ore. But we have to be able to mine it.
We can't sit around on our backsides and wait for
Hegel to steal it out from under us."

O'Connell gave the map a halfhearted glance.
"Where's the Forrester Mine again?"

Ross jabbed emphatically at the wrinkled parchment with his forefinger. "Right next door. Hegel
studied old surveys of the surface lines on all the
mines in Butte and secured title on about forty
square yards that had never been recorded or
patented. Now he claims that all the remaining
ore in the Glamorgan actually apexes on his tiny

fraction of the Hill." Ross shook his head in disgust. "It's a triangular piece of dirt no bigger than Hertta Kuusinen's drawing room."

"What about a compromise?" O'Connell suggested. He fidgeted listlessly with the gold watch chain looped across the front of his gray tweed vest. "We could seek a settlement out of court and avoid a very costly litigation that you might lose anyway."

Ross straightened, folded his arms across his chest, and stared with mounting dissatisfaction at the Easterner in his fancy, twenty-five-dollar suit. In the stark environment of the mining office, Gavin O'Connell was a real fish out of water. Standing on the other side of the desk next to Eben, who, like his boss, was dressed in dusty khaki work trousers and rolled-up shirtsleeves, the Boston attorney looked exactly like the useless playboy Morgan suspected him of being. More than once since O'Connell had arrived two weeks ago, Ross had regretted taking Sean Ryan's advice to hire his uncle's firm to represent him. Until this morning, O'Connell had avoided a prolonged meeting with his client, making one excuse after another for not preparing the reply to Hegel's complaint or the counterclaim against him. Ross knew he'd need topnotch legal representation if he was going to have a chance against Felix Hegel and his cadre of wily lawyers.

"That vein of copper apexes on my property, O'Connell," Ross said, making no attempt to conceal his annoyance. "And furthermore, I don't intend to lose my court fight."

"What exactly do you mean by 'apexes,' Mr. Morgan?" a feminine voice asked from behind him.

Ross swung around to face the delectable creature perched on the tall stool by the office door. Temporarily derailed from his train of thought, he gazed into a pair of gorgeous brown eyes, bright with curiosity. Their long, thick lashes curved upward in effortless allurement. He'd taken three steps toward

Nell before he was even aware that he'd moved. His voice softened automatically when he spoke.

"The federal minin' laws protect the prospector who first discovers and registers a claim on a mineral vein. The surface outcroppin' of the ore is known as its apex. The owner is guaranteed the right to follow the vein that apexes on his property downward, even when it leads under the surface holdin's of the mine located beside it."

"I see," said Nell thoughtfully.

He doubted she did, but he wasn't about to tell her that. He smiled tenderly instead, delighted that she'd accompanied O'Connell that morning. She wore a fashionable black walking suit that subtly displayed her enticing figure. The front of the short jacket, with its enormous puffed sleeves, was striped diagonally with rows of narrow gold braid and trimmed down the front with shiny brass buttons. Beneath her chin, a white silk jabot was tied in a pristine bow. The light from the nearby window bathed her in a soft glow that revealed the smooth curve of her cheek and the delicate lines of her forehead and nose. Even in the ebony mourning costume, she was a feast for the soul.

He silently debated the best way to get her alone. Perhaps he could suggest that Eben take O'Connell on a tour of the engine room, while he fixed Miss Ryan a cup of coffee. She must have been bored by all the masculine conversation. Like any member of the fairer sex, she'd appreciate a bit of flattering attention.

"Well, I'm not so certain I understand," Gavin admitted a little too loudly, bringing the center of attention back to himself. "How can you be positive that Hegel can't prove what he claims? Maybe his civil action is an honest attempt to secure what he feels rightfully belongs to him."

"Honest?" Eben nearly shouted. He took the pencil stuck behind his ear and threw it down on the map. "That'll be the day."

Nell slipped down from the stool and moved to stand beside Ross. He bent his head and stepped closer, enjoying the delicate floral fragrance that lingered about her.

"What do you mean by that?" she asked Eben.

"I mean," said Eben, "that Hegel is known for his diabolical tricks."

"Give me an example," she encouraged.

He scratched his head and thought for a moment. "Well, for instance, when he worked the Emerson Mine, he timed the sinking of his shafts and the placing of his crosscuts to stay always just a level above the workings of the nearby Rosemary. That meant that the water in the Emerson would seep down into the deeper neighboring mine, forcing its owner to pump out Hegel's water without costing the dirty rascal a penny."

"But is that illegal?" she asked doubtfully.

"No," Ross admitted. "Just shrewd and unprincipled."

"You can't convict a man for being clever," she said in dismissal. She walked over to look at the outspread map. "Sounds like you're going to have to convince the jury that the vein of ore you've been following originates here at the Glamorgan. I'd think that for two experts in geology that would be an easy matter to prove." She looked up pointedly at Ross. "If it really does."

He followed her to the desk and stood beside her. "It's not quite that simple, angel eyes," he explained. "Veins don't always run continuously from the surface down. More often than not, they're broken or faulted." He pulled over a chart, unrolled it, and pointed to its jagged, uneven lines. "Sometimes, they're cut off by worthless rock, only to show up again farther below. That's what Hegel insists has happened at the Forrester. A vein leadin' down from the surface was lost near the vertical wall of his mine. In his complaint, he's pleadin' that the vein we're working in the Glamorgan is a geological continuation of the Forrester's."

"And that's a bunch of poppycock!" said Eben. His blue eyes glittered with outrage.

"The judge who granted the restraining order didn't think so," Gavin pointed out calmly.

Nell turned to her fellow attorney. "A restraining order?"

"All minin' activities in the Glamorgan and the Forrester have been enjoined by Judge Curry," Ross told her. He removed his eyeglasses and placed them in his shirt pocket. "Until the rights for the copper ore have been established in court, neither I nor Hegel will be allowed to work our claims. His Montana Copper Purchasing Corporation can afford to sit back and wait it out. I'm not so fortunate."

Ross didn't add that every penny he had and every one he could borrow was tied up in the Glamorgan. Everything he'd managed to save during the grueling years he'd worked for other companies as a mining engineer was invested in his mine. There was no way he could continue to keep men on his payroll or make the payments on the expensive equipment he'd bought on credit without continuing his mining operations, even if it meant doing so illegally. Either he worked his claim or the Glamorgan would go belly up.

"How long has your mine been shut down?" Nell asked in surprise.

"We stopped work on the eleventh of June," he hedged. That much was true. What he didn't tell her was that he'd secretly resumed mining operations two days after her brother's accident.

"But Sean died on the eighteenth. Why was he down in the mine despite the injunction?"

"Your brother was a shift boss. As I told you before, he was merely conductin' a routine check on the timberin'," Ross said in a tone of quiet conviction meant to soothe an inquisitive female.

He didn't want her thinking that anything was out of the ordinary at the Glamorgan Mine. Hell, the last thing he needed was Miss Elinor Ryan poking around at the twelve-hundred-foot level.

Nell could sense Morgan's guarded reaction. "I'd like to see the place where Sean died," she said coolly.

His brows snapped together at her soft-spoken demand, and she raised her hand, palm outward, in an attempt to placate him. "I'm not threatening to sue you, Mr. Morgan. I'm merely making a polite request. Considering you're a client of my uncle's firm, surely that's not too much to ask. Anything I learn down there will be confidential."

Eben Pearce stared at her with wide, stricken eyes. "There's nothing to learn, Miss Ryan."

"Whether or not Nell will discover anything, I strongly suggest that she be granted her wish," Gavin said with a sneer. He shoved his hands in his trouser pockets, rocked back on his heels, and looked at Morgan with unconcealed disdain. "Since her brother was accidentally killed in your mine, I think she has the right to find out as much as possible about his death. What could it hurt for you to take her down there, if only to satisfy the fears of a grieving sister?"

"You're supposed to be *my* lawyer, O'Connell," Morgan bit out. "I'd like to think you're puttin' my best interests first and foremost."

Gavin turned white at the slur on his professional integrity. Before he could answer in kind, Nell hurried over and placed a hand on his sleeve in a gesture of conciliation. She had no intention of causing a ruckus, thereby destroying her friend's already shaky relationship with the man who'd hired him. It would be devastating for Gavin to have to go back home and explain to his father that he'd been fired by the owner of the Glamorgan Mine before he'd even made his opening statement to the jury.

"Let's table my wishes for the moment, gentle-men," she said. "Considering how very gallantly Mr. Morgan came to my rescue yesterday afternoon, I can hardly begrudge him his understandable reti-cence about a death that occurred on his property. I hope that, before I return to Boston, the two of us can reach a mutually acceptable solution."

A smile hovered at the corner of Morgan's mouth as he met her pleading gaze. "I'm willin' to spend as much time as it takes to sort things out with you, Miss Ryan. For a start, why don't I fix you a cup of coffee? We can talk while Eben takes Mr. O'Connell on a tour of the engine room."

"Yessiree, boss," Pearce said in wholehearted agreement. He immediately headed for the door. "Come on, O'Connell. I'll show you how the sig-nals for our new electric bell system work."

With a worried frown, Gavin met Nell's gaze. "I don't think . . ."

"Go ahead," she insisted. "The more you learn about the Glamorgan, the better you can prepare your defense."

"That's an excellent suggestion," said Morgan. He looked over at his superintendent and added, "You can show him the skip and the ore bin as well. Take all the time you need. Miss Ryan and I will just relax and get to know each other a little better."

Before following Eben out of the office, Gavin glanced back at Nell. "If you're sure?" he said doubtfully.

She gave him a cheerful wave. "I'll be fine."

The moment the door closed behind them, she turned to Morgan. "We should have no problem furthering our acquaintance, if you'll promise not to address me as angel eyes."

Placing his hand over his heart, he groaned in feigned regret. "Did that meanin'less term slip out again? I swear, I won't bore you with another trite endearment for the rest of the mornin'."

She gazed up into green eyes aglow with an engaging humor. The man had more inborn charm than a snake-oil peddler. She thought she'd been fleeced by the cleverest bamboozler in the country, but Charleton, on his best day, couldn't have begun to compete with the natural, effortless magnetism of the handsome male who stood before her.

She raised her eyebrows and affected her most condescending manner. "I suspect there isn't a lady in Butte who'd accuse you of being boring, Mr. Morgan."

His grin widened. "Now there's that beguilin' Irish blarney I've heard so much about." He gestured toward the door with a flourish. "The coffeepot's on the stove in Eben's office. Please allow me."

She ignored his suave attempt to take her elbow and marched ahead of him to the door. "I don't need your help walking into another room, sir. I'm a strong, healthy woman."

"I can see that," he murmured in a voice pulsing with sensuous male admiration. He quickly followed Nell to the door, reached around her, and swung it open.

Refusing to acknowledge his provocative remark, she swept past him in dignified silence.

Chapter 5

"**S**it down and make yourself comfortable," Ross told Nell, "while I fix us a fresh batch of coffee."

In the corner of the front office was an old potbellied stove with a dented blue-and-white-speckled coffeepot sitting on top. He stuffed a wadded piece of newspaper and a couple of chunks of wood inside the stove, lit a fire, and slammed the cast-iron door shut. Then he ground the roasted beans in a little hand mill, filled the pot with fresh water from a large crock, and placed it on the stove.

While he worked, she wandered across the room to a bench shoved up against the wall which resembled a decrepit church pew. She set her handbag on the wooden seat, then perched on its gouged edge, as straight and regal as a monarch on her throne.

"You really needn't go to all this trouble," she told him. She removed her black gloves and placed them carefully atop her bag. "Gavin and I are planning to stop at a restaurant for dinner when we leave here."

From a shelf on the wall, Ross pulled down two blue ironstone mugs, one chipped, one cracked, and set them on Eben's cluttered desktop. Then he propped his butt against the edge of the desk and folded his arms across his chest, prepared just to enjoy the sight of her while he waited for the water to boil.

"Which restaurant?"

"I don't know. I think Gavin has something special in mind."

She glanced down at the front page of the Butte *Miner* that lay on the seat beside her. Eben had brought the newspaper to the office that morning to share the scathing article denouncing the previous day's riot as a terrible disgrace. According to the news story, the town had garnered some pretty shameful notoriety on all the front pages across the country.

She looked up to meet Ross's gaze. "I want to thank you again, Mr. Morgan, for coming to my aid yesterday afternoon. Afterward at the boardinghouse, I was too rattled to express my appreciation properly. But I want you to know that I honestly believe you saved my life."

"I don't think you believe that at all, Nell."

"Of course I do."

"Prove it," he countered.

She stared up at him from under the brim of her veiled hat. When she'd first arrived at the mine office that morning, she'd lifted the black netting and folded it back over the flat crown. He had a clear view of her lovely face, wide-eyed now in astonishment. "I beg your pardon?"

"If you really believed I saved your life," he explained, trying not to grin at her shocked expression, "you wouldn't still be callin' me Mr. Morgan."

A sudden smile played at the corners of her mouth. "You're a very persistent man, Ross."

"Ah, you see? You said it, and your tongue didn't turn black, your nose didn't grow long, and your hair didn't fall out."

She burst out laughing, and the sound reminded him of the musical tinkling of silver chimes. His heart thrummed an accompanying rhythm, beating out the bass line like a snare drum. It took every bit of his willpower not to cross the room and take her in his arms.

"You're a very audacious, persistent man," she amended.

"Now that's a matter of opinion. Some folks in this minin' camp might agree with you, but not my friends."

"Well, I'm sure no one's ever accused you of being shy and retiring."

"You're right on that score," he agreed. "But I've found that you have to reach out and take what you want in life. Cowerin' silently in the background never got a man anywhere. Or any woman."

"Do you mean it never got a woman anywhere either, or it never got any man a woman?"

Ross grinned. "You ask questions just like a lawyer. I bet you're darn good at interrogatin' witnesses."

"I am," she said. "But in court, the witness is required to answer the question, not evade it with personal remarks about the attorney."

"Good thing we're not in court," he quipped. He went over to the stove, picked up the coffeepot with a folded cloth, and carried it to the desk. Pouring the hot brew into the cups, he added in apology, "I can't offer you any cream, but we've got lots of sugar."

"Thank you, but I drink it plain." She cocked her head toward the *Miner.* "Did you read this morning's paper? Two men lost their lives in the riot. I understand that the culprits involved blew up a halfbox of dynamite in front of the Columbia saloon. It was lucky more people weren't killed."

"The editorial condemned both sides. But the weight of the blame lies squarely on the shoulders of the men who put up those APA letters."

"I don't agree," she shot back. "The Cornish miners had a right to express themselves without fear of reprisal. Our freedom of speech is one of our most cherished possessions."

He shook his head in surprise at the proud woman from Boston. He'd expected anyone with the name of Ryan to rally to the side of the Green.

Ross was Welsh by ancestry, Protestant by birth, and Republican by choice, and yet he was the one defending those bullheaded Micks, while she was siding with the Cornishmen.

He carried the mug of coffee over and handed it to her. "Those Cousin Jacks knew what they were doin' when they put up that orange shield in the middle of the holiday bunting. They were just beggin' for trouble."

"They were certainly using poor judgment," she conceded as she took the hot cup. "That much, I'll agree with. But resorting to violence is never the answer."

"Never?" Ross shoved the newspaper out of the way and sat down beside her. He propped an elbow on the back of the bench and reached out to touch a strand of chestnut hair that had escaped her tight chignon. The silken lock dangled in front of her ear, presenting a nearly irresistible temptation for any male over the age of fourteen.

She turned her shoulders to face him. The mug was poised in her right hand like a Colt revolver. Ross was suddenly aware of the steaming liquid that nearly sloshed over its chipped blue edge. He froze, his fingers a scarce inch from her head.

"Well, almost never," she admitted. Her expressive eyes glowed with a mischievous warning: he was flirting with instant retaliation.

His glance swept over the supple curves displayed by her stylish gown, then back up to meet her gaze, twinkling now in playful devilment. She was absolutely the most desirable woman he'd ever met.

He ignored the loaded weapon in her hand and grinned like a madman in the face of danger. "If someone's foolish enough to wave a red flag in front of a bull, that someone shouldn't be surprised at the violent reaction of the beast, once she's gotten his attention."

Nell bent her head and sipped the coffee, her hat brim hiding her flustered reaction to his words. His fingertips traced a line as light as thistledown along the nape of her neck, and a current of energy surged through her like a jolt of electricity. She was tingling with excitement. She felt the insistent pressure of his forefinger beneath her chin and reluctantly lowered the cup. When he brought her face up to meet his gaze, his green eyes were shimmering pools of desire.

"Miss Elinor Ryan," he said in a low, hoarse voice. "I'd like nothin' better than to further our acquaintance." He slid the pad of his thumb across the cleft of her chin and then up to follow the horizontal seam of her lips.

She opened her mouth to admonish him for such imprudent behavior. His thumb slipped inside, the edge of his square-cut nail bumping gently against a front tooth. Without a moment's hesitation, he slid his thumb between the twin rows of her teeth and swept along the sensitive edge of her tongue. The unexpected penetration was bewitchingly erotic. Mesmerized, she clutched the coffee mug in both hands and watched him bend closer, till she could feel his cool breath on her face and smell the spicy scent of his shaving cream.

"And I can't think of a better way to get to know each other than this," he murmured. With her chin trapped in his hand, he moved his thumb aside and covered her open mouth with his lips.

In spite of all her resolutions to the contrary, Nell responded to his kiss. Her tongue met his invasion eagerly. As he slanted his head and adjusted his mouth to hers, she leaned toward him, longing to return the pressure of his kiss, yet all the while conscious of the hot coffee she held tightly in her hands.

She tore her mouth away, breathless. "I'm liable to spill it all over you," she warned.

"I'll chance it," said Morgan, his lips moving softly against her cheek. He placed quick, light kisses behind her earlobe and down the side of her neck. A thrill of shivering delight coursed through her.

"I'm not so adventurous," she whispered back. She wondered in distraction if he could hear her heart banging against her ribs. His tongue flicked across the pulse that throbbed at the base of her throat, and she was nearly certain of it.

"Don't worry," he assured her. "I won't make any sudden moves." As if to prove his words, he slowly stroked the back of her neck with his long fingers while he traced the inner shell of her ear with his moist tongue.

Nell could feel an enervating warmth seep through her as he continued his thorough and unhurried exploration. Sighing with pleasure, she surrendered to the moment and turned her head to meet his kiss.

He pried the mug from her fingers and set it beside the newspaper on the bench seat behind him. Then he took her in his arms and captured her lips with his. As his tongue traversed the cavern of her mouth, his hand moved with hypnotic deliberation over her rib cage. Nell's breasts grew heavy and lushly sensitive, as though yearning for his touch.

With a whimper of confusion at the overpowering feelings that rocketed through her body, she tried to pull away. Morgan held her fast in his embrace without a hint of effort. He ignored her spurt of resistance and continued the passionate kiss, while his fingers moved relentlessly upward toward the twin mounds of his forbidden goal. Alarmed by his obvious intention, she grasped his large hand and squeezed hard in an attempt to drag him to a halt. At that overt signal, any proper gentleman would have ceased such improper advances.

She'd been correct from the start. Rossiter Morgan was no gentleman, proper or otherwise.

He didn't stop.

He cupped her breast in his palm, and the pressure of his touch burned right through the jacket, shirtwaist, and corset she wore as though the layers of material were melting away. Sexual desire, which had been slowly uncurling within her, like a drugged sleeper who's just been awakened after years of dreamless slumber, was now fully aroused and charging through her nervous system. Physical and emotional needs she'd ruthlessly denied, even to herself, swirled through the dark cave of emptiness inside her.

This was wrong. This wasn't decent.

But oh, dear God, it felt so good to be held in his arms. To be stroked in such a comforting fashion. To have assuaged, if only for a moment, the cold ache of loneliness that was her constant companion.

Nell released the grip she had on his hand and raised her own to his shoulder. She arched her back, shamelessly giving him tacit permission to continue. He gently palmed the pliant breasts uplifted by the stiff whalebones of her corset. It was nigh impossible to keep from purring with enjoyment.

Ross raised his mouth from hers and met her languid gaze. Her dark brown eyes, soft and dreamy with sensual arousal, were half hidden beneath lowered lids. Her full lips opened slightly as her breathing grew deeper, heavier. He watched the play of emotions on her face while he caressed her with all the tender skill he possessed. She responded to his touch with unabashed pleasure, rubbing against him like a kitten begging to be petted. Whatever her lawyer friend might think, Nell definitely was not a frigid woman, although she tried her darnedest to appear that way.

Hot male lust throbbed and pulsed through every inch of Ross's taut body. His voice was raspy with need. "Don't be in such a hurry to go back to Boston, little doll," he urged. "Give me a chance to—"

The sound of footsteps on the gravel outside penetrated his nearly total absorption with the delectable creature in his arms. He immediately released her and pulled away. Returning the chipped mug to her grasp, he propped one ankle on the opposite knee, casually covered his swollen crotch with the folded newspaper in his hand, and lounged back against the bench in seeming detachment.

O'Connell barged into the room with Eben at his heels. "I've seen enough mining equipment for one day," the lawyer growled. He looked at Nell, who sat quietly sipping her coffee. "Are you ready to leave?"

She peeped up at her colleague from under her long lashes. Her cheeks bloomed the color of spring roses. "Yes."

Ross stood and took the cup from her trembling hands. Then he helped her up from the settle and handed her her gloves and bag. Her lips were flushed and swollen from his kisses. She dragged her eyes up to meet his gaze, and it was clearly all she could do to keep from hiding her face in her hands in mortification. When it came to dissembling, the lady attorney was clearly no expert.

O'Connell moved closer. A scowl marred his finely chiseled features. "Is anything wrong?"

"No," she murmured. "Let's go." As she pulled on her gloves, she turned to Eben and offered a tremulous smile. "Mr. Pearce, it's been good visiting with you this morning. If I don't see you before I leave for home, thank you again for all your help."

Eben glanced at Ross and then back to their lovely visitor. "I just wish I could have been more helpful, ma'am. And that your visit to Butte had been made under happier circumstances. Have a safe journey."

"You'll see Miss Ryan again," Ross said with complete confidence.

She stared up at him, a mixture of surprise and hope in her eyes. "Then you've changed your mind about letting me go down into your mine?"

"No."

She couldn't keep the disgruntlement from her voice. "I'm scheduled to leave in two days, Mr. Morgan. If you feel differently before then, please let me know." She lifted the veil up over the curved brim of her hat and brought it down to cover her flushed face. "If not, I'll thank you now for your time and any inconvenience I may have caused you. Good-by."

"Good-by, Nell," said Ross.

He hoped she'd offer her hand, but she gave him a distant nod instead. Behind the crisscross of fine black netting, her eyes glittered with anger. O'Connell took her elbow, and together they moved toward the door. Eben leaped to open it for them, and the two attorneys departed.

Ross allowed himself the indulgence of a slow, self-satisfied grin. Whistling under his breath, he picked up the cracked mug of coffee sitting on Eben's desk and headed back to his own office.

No need to thank me, angel eyes. Nothin' in my life was ever less inconvenient.

That afternoon, Nell went to the Western Union telegraph office alone. She and Gavin had visited over a long luncheon, discussing possible strategies he could employ in the upcoming trial. She'd been appalled to learn that he had no plans to bring in expert witnesses to testify to the fact that the disputed vein of copper originated on the site of the Glamorgan Mine. Gavin had dismissed the idea out of hand, saying he wasn't certain a disinterested mining engineer would find that it did.

Afterward, he'd offered to escort her back to her boardinghouse, but she'd insisted that he return to his hotel room where he could concentrate on drafting his client's defense reply and his counterclaim against the plaintiff. She'd scolded Gavin for his unwarranted delay in preparing and filing the papers. He'd shrugged with indifference and headed down the street, as though he hadn't a care in the world.

Her friend's lackadaisical attitude toward his work had always irritated Nell. He'd been given the best education, along with all the finer things in life, and yet he never seemed to show any spark of real interest in his profession. Perhaps because she'd had to struggle so hard to get there, each time she appeared before the bar she was filled with a sense of both profound responsibility and high exhilaration. She was disappointed at Gavin's uninspired plans for the Glamorgan's defense. But if he refused to take her advice, that was his decision. And if he lost the mining rights to the opposing party, it'd be his career damaged, not hers. How the lawsuit was finally settled wasn't her concern.

As she entered the tiny telegraph office, she realized she was frowning in chagrin. It wasn't over her colleague's lack of commitment, however, but the presumptuous mine owner who'd hired him. During the meal, she'd forced herself not to think about what had happened between her and Ross Morgan that morning. The memory of her shocking behavior had surfaced the minute Gavin departed. What had come over her to make her act like such a wanton, love-starved female?

A young clerk, with a felt visor on his head and long black cuff guards protecting his spanking white shirtsleeves, greeted her with a cheerful smile at the counter window. No more than eighteen, he wore an official-looking badge on his striped vest that read, "Shamus Killian, Telegraph Agent."

He waited politely while she stood at the narrow counter in front of him and wrote her message to Cormac Ryan. She wanted to let her uncle know that she'd arrived in Butte on the Fourth of July and was safe in spite of the now notorious APA Riot. She added that she'd be returning home as quickly as possible. For the sake of the genial Mr. Killian, she refrained from including the comment that the so-called treasure city of the Rockies was nothing more than a festering blister on the rump of Creation.

Killian glanced at her writing to make certain he could read it, prior to starting the transmittal of the telegram. Dismayed, he stared up at her before he'd even read the entire message. "Were you caught in that awful rumpus yesterday, ma'am?"

She looked into his round blue eyes and read the sincere concern there. "I was trapped right in the middle of it," she told him, trying hard not to show her disgust for his hometown.

"Miss Nell Ryan?" he questioned in surprise when he'd finished reading her missive. "Why, we just received a wire for you. I was about to send a messenger over to the Thornton Hotel with it."

She took the dispatch, then paid him for her own, asking him to wait until she'd read the one she'd received before sending hers. She walked over to a ladder-back chair that stood in front of the room's only window and sat down. After tearing open the envelope, she scanned the telegram. It was from her uncle, just as she'd expected. But the astonishing news it contained wasn't nearly so predictable. She read it again, unable to believe her eyes. And then reread it a third time, still refusing to credit its contents.

RECEIVED MORGAN'S WIRE THIS AM STOP GLAD
TO HEAR YOU'RE SAFE STOP HE REQUESTS YOU BE
ASSIGNED AS HIS PRIVATE COUNSEL STOP REMAIN
IN BUTTE UNTIL THE CASE IS SETTLED STOP GIVE
GAVIN MY BEST STOP UNCLE CORMAC

Nell sprang to her feet, staring wildly at the yellow paper clutched in her hand. Morgan had telegraphed Ryan, Sheehy, and O'Connell to ask that she be appointed to his case. The rat! The conniving, despicable, egotistical rat! When she'd been at his office that morning, he'd already planned to request that she be assigned to help Gavin with the lawsuit. But the wily mine owner didn't dare say so. Not and attempt to seduce her too. Well, maybe not seduce, but certainly fondle and kiss in a very scandalous manner.

She stomped back over to the counter window, this time making no attempt to hide her scowl. "I'd like to send a different telegram," she told the friendly clerk. "Throw the first one away."

With a look of curiosity, he handed her a fresh piece of paper. She dashed off the message and shoved it toward him.

GLAMORGAN CASE COULD GO ON FOR MONTHS STOP NO WISH TO REMAIN IN THIS GODFORSAKEN PERCH OF SATAN A MOMENT LONGER THAN NEC-ESSARY STOP ASSIGN SOMEONE ELSE STOP NELL

The clerk read her scribbled message and then looked up at her in baffled disapproval. Nell glared into his reproachful eyes and tapped her index finger on the counter impatiently.

"Send it just as it's written. And don't misspell *Godforsaken*," she warned him.

She watched with suspicion as he tapped out the dots and dashes of the Morse code on the sending key with lightning speed, uncertain if he'd dare to change her insulting words. Just how much integrity did a telegraph operator have, anyway?

"I'm not staying at the Thornton," she told him when he'd finished. "Please have the answer delivered to Kuusinen's Boardinghouse. I know it's far too late to expect anything from Massachusetts this evening. I'll be back in the morning, if I haven't received a reply by then."

"Yes, ma'am," he meekly agreed as she stalked out the door.

Nell charged down Granite Street toward the trolley stop, her thoughts whirling. What conceit the man had, to think she'd want to remain here in this outpost of barbarism as his legal counselor.

She'd planned to make one last try at having Gavin or Eben Pearce assist her in going down into the Glamorgan. But now she sincerely doubted that there was any gross negligence of safety involved in the accident that killed her brother. Ross Morgan was far too concerned with the day-to-day running of his precious mine to allow slipshod habits of his employees to go by unnoticed. Inspection of the place where Sean had died no longer seemed necessary.

After meeting Morgan, she'd had to revise her preconceived notions about him, though only slightly. He might be a greedy copper baron, just as she'd expected, and an overconfident lady-killer to boot, but he didn't strike her as being a careless fool.

She cringed inwardly, recalling the shameless way she'd allowed him to touch her. How could she ever face him again? Heaven save her, she couldn't. The more space she put between her and that philanderer, the better off she'd be. Several thousand miles sounded like just the right amount of territory.

Come what may, in two more days, she'd be on that Northern Pacific train leaving Butte.

Chapter 6

❧━━━◦◦◦━━━❧

As Nell stepped into Hertta's big dining room that evening and saw the double row of male boarders seated at the table, she once again considered moving to the Thornton Hotel where Gavin was staying. But from the moment she crossed the threshold, everyone treated her with respect and kindness. She was deeply moved by the men's bashful but sincere expressions of sympathy when Hertta introduced her as Sean Ryan's sister.

Nell slipped into the chair her landlady indicated and looked down the table where more than twenty-five stalwart men sat eating. If she remained at Kuusinen's, she would be able to talk to people who'd known Sean. Who'd worked and played and fought alongside him during his last weeks. For that reason alone, she was willing to stay on at the boardinghouse for two more days, regardless of the presence of the irritating Rossiter Morgan. He wasn't going to run her out of Kuusinen's any easier than he was going to succeed in keeping her in Butte to help with the defense of his blasted mine.

She looked across the enormous dining table laden with platters of summer sausages, jellied veal, baked ham, salted salmon, sliced roast beef, and tall stacks of rye, barley, and pumpernickel bread to where Morgan sat beside a youngster who could only be his son. Although she hadn't seen Ross since he'd kissed and mauled her so expertly that morning, she'd been prepared to encounter him at supper. After all, he was a fellow boarder. What she hadn't been prepared for was the exact miniature of Ross who now sat across from her.

Shocked, Nell stared at the boy whom Morgan had failed to mention. She narrowed her eyes thoughtfully, wondering why he'd been so circumspect. Had it been a mere oversight, or did he have something to hide? Like the existence of a wife, perhaps?

The boy was a small replica of his father: blond, green-eyed, athletic, and handsome. He'd also been lucky enough to inherit his sire's natural charm and breezy manner. There was a dusting of light brown specks on the boy's nose, yet Nell couldn't imagine Ross Morgan's tanned visage with freckles—not even in childhood. Perhaps the boy had inherited them from his mother. What else, if anything, had she bequeathed her son? And where, exactly, was the missing wife and mother?

"Nell," Ross said without a hint of embarrassment, "I want you to meet my boy, Luke."

She smiled at the lad uneasily. Perhaps Morgan was a widower, and she was merely jumping to conclusions. One way or the other, she had to find out. "Have you and your parents lived at Kuusinen's long?"

"My dad and I've been stayin' here since last September," Luke told her. "Ever since we came to Butte." He plopped a spoonful of mashed potatoes on his plate and handed the large brown crockery bowl to Eben Pearce on his right, before looking up to meet her gaze with an enchanting sideways grin.

Ignoring the heat of a flush at her mounting suspicions, Nell blurted out the question uppermost in her mind. "And your mother? Where is she? It must be lonely for the two of you without a woman to look after your needs."

Nell could feel the older Morgan's gaze pinned on her in disapproval. She met his cold green eyes, daring him to deny what she knew to be true: all men were philanderers at heart. She refused to acknowledge his unspoken warning that she was treading on dangerous ground. If there actually was a wife, she had no intention of telling the boy about his father's latest indiscretion, but, of course, Morgan didn't know *what* she was capable of blabbing out. Let the deceitful husband squirm a little.

Ignoring Morgan's baleful glare, she smiled at Luke and pressed onward. "Did you leave your mother in Colorado?"

"My mom's dead," the boy answered. There wasn't a trace of sorrow in his clear green eyes.

Nell lifted her brows in embarrassment at the simple, direct statement. She could guess what Morgan was thinking now. Served *her* right for being so evil-minded.

"I'm . . . I'm sorry, Luke. Forgive me for . . ." She glanced at the boy's father in peeved contrition, unable to say the odious word. *Prying.* She was thoroughly ashamed of her own tactlessness.

Morgan spoke through a false smile and clenched teeth. "Luke was barely two when his mother died. He doesn't remember her. And I've been looking out for my own needs for some time now. I sure don't need a woman questioning my every move."

His eyes glinted with anger. He knew she'd assumed that he was an unfaithful husband, and he wasn't a bit happy about it. His chilly expression made her feel petty and mean-spirited. She'd blundered into a very sensitive area, that was apparent.

It was also apparent she'd made an addlepated fool of herself. Fudge! She didn't usually jump to conclusions. Through preparations for lengthy and complex trials, she'd learned never to assume anything. It saved an attorney a lot of unhappy surprises during cross-examinations. But when it came to dealing with Ross Morgan, she found herself repeatedly doing the opposite of everything she firmly believed in.

Kalle Kuusinen was seated at the head of the table on Nell's immediate right. His bushy eyebrows drew

together in a ferocious scowl at Morgan's incivility
toward their newest guest.

"Mighty nice to have a lady at our table," the
burly Finn boomed out to no one in particular as
he passed her the gravy boat.

Nell rewarded her self-elected champion with a
hesitant smile. "Thank you, sir," she said quietly.

She'd met the owner of the boardinghouse that
morning at breakfast. Hertta's husband was a great
bear of a man with massive forearms and hands
like oversized paws. Beside his colossal frame, his
robust, big boned wife looked a mere slip of a girl.

"You're velcome, ma'am," Kalle said with a jocu-
lar wink. He nodded his head toward her plate. "Go
on and eat your supper and don't be bothered by
anyt'ing t'at overeducated mucker from Colorado
has to say. He's been a vidower for too long. Lost
any reputed charm he had vith ta ladies years ago.
T'at is, if he ever really had any to start vith."

Nell ignored Eben's muffled snort of laughter and
ladled the brown gravy over her potatoes in sheep-
ish concentration. Outside of Hertta and the two
adolescent Finnish girls who scurried in and out
of the dining room with huge platters of food, she
was the only woman present. Gavin had been right.
Of the boardinghouse's fifty paying residents, Nell
was the sole female.

"How old are you, Luke?" she asked, trying to
smooth over the awkward lull that had settled at
their end of the table.

"I'm ten, ma'am."

"Are you enjoying your summer vacation?"

"Yes'm. I've got a job as a newsboy. I hawk papers
first thing in the mornin'. Then me and my pals go
down to Bell Creek to the swimmin' hole in the
afternoon." He grinned impishly. "After that, we
usually wander around town."

"Just be careful where you're wanderin'," his
father instructed. "You roam into Dublin Gulch
once too often, and you're going to come home

with somethin' a whole lot worse than that shiner
you got last month."

"Aw, you should've seen the other kid, Dad."
Luke shrugged in unconscious imitation of Morgan's
carefree ways. The youth was big for his age, with a
huskiness that promised one day to rival his father's
impressive physique.

"I'll bet you gave him a good belt or two," Kalle
said with a hearty belly laugh.

The man on Nell's left looked up from the thick
slab of Finnish bread he was buttering. "Hit ta ot'er
guy first," Gus Mikkola offered succinctly. "Ask
questions later."

Luke's father nodded his head in placid agreement. "Don't fret about the greenhorn who takes
the time to remove his coat and hat. It's the cowboy who leaves 'em on that you've got to worry
about."

"Your pop's right," Eben added, his blue eyes
serious. He brushed the crumbs from his thick red
mustache as he looked down at Luke. "And staying
out of Dublin Gulch in the first place is a whole
lot smarter than having to fight you way back out
again."

"What is Dublin Gulch?" asked Nell. She was
appalled at their cavalier attitude toward physical violence. Apparently brawls were an everyday
occurrence, despite all their disclaimers about yesterday's riot. Hadn't any of them heard of law and
order, for mercy's sake?

"Oh, that's where the Micks live," Luke cheerfully explained between forkfuls of mashed potatoes.

"Careful what you say, son," Morgan cautioned.
A playful grin hovered at the corner of his mouth
as he looked across at Nell. "Miss Ryan's one of
'em."

The youth's eyes grew wide. He stared down at
his plate and swallowed with a noisy gulp. Then he
wrinkled his freckled nose and looked up to meet
her gaze with the winsome smile of a young angel

who'd accidentally tumbled from a cloud. Or been kicked off.

"I get along with just about everybody, ma'am. Unless they try to take a poke at me first."

Nell laughed in delight at his graceful recovery. "I promise not to try, Luke. Word of honor. I wouldn't want to go back home to Boston with a shiner."

"Geez, I'd never hit a girl," Luke assured her in all sincerity. "No matter what she did." He glanced at Morgan out of the corner of his eye and made a comical grimace. "My dad would beat the tar out of me."

The bond of love between father and son was so apparent, Nell was certain that striking a female was one of the few things Luke *would* get a whipping for. The pride in Morgan's eyes when he smiled at the boy was unmistakable.

"Is Dublin Gulch the only place that's dangerous?" she asked her supper companions.

"Meaderville's verse," Gus answered shyly.

Nell remembered Eben's attempt to explain the various sections of the copper camp on their trolley ride the day before. There were Walkerville, Dogtown, Seldom Seen, Chicken Flats, Centerville, Hungry Hill, Corktown, and Parrot Flats that she could recall. The ethnic diversity of the city's suburbs had been too much to master all at once. "You mean the area north of the city? What makes that place so hazardous?"

"Italians," said Gus around a mouthful of bread and butter. Blushing bright red from all the attention, he speared a piece of ham from the platter going by, then reached for a jar of pickled herring without offering her any further explanation. To the other diners, his acerbic reply seemed to cover it all.

"Italians?"

Ross watched with amusement as she looked in mystification from one male to the other. He could sit and stare at Miss Elinor Ryan for hours and never get bored. In no hurry for the meal to end, he sat back in contentment and waited for someone else to explain Gus's cryptic warning. He wondered if she'd already learned that he'd telegraphed her uncle early that morning. Probably, since she'd been shooting darts at him with those gorgeous peepers from the moment she'd sat down. It'd been a trifle high-handed of him, but it was the only way he could think of to keep her from leaving for Boston in two short days.

Coming to her rescue once again, Kalle jabbed his fork toward Luke's head. "Here in Finn Town, no one's going to give ta boy a second glance. But t'at yellow mop of his vould stand out in Meaderville like a candle flame in an abandoned stope."

"Don't worry, Miss Ryan," Luke piped up happily. "You can go anywhere you want. No one would hurt you."

Ross propped his elbows on the table and folded his hands in front of his mouth to hide the smile he couldn't contain. Nell's deep brown eyes were enormous as she looked from one to the other of her new neighbors with dawning awareness. From his and Luke's golden-brown curls, to Kalle Kuusinen's sandy, thinning pate, to Gus Mikkola's flaxen locks, their heads were all fair. Eben's burnished copper was the only exception, and he was far from being brunet.

"Because of my dark hair?" she questioned. The worry on her delicate features conveyed her thoughts. She was suddenly wondering just how safe an Irish brunet *was* living in Finn Town.

Unable to remain deadpan a moment longer, Ross gave up and grinned outright. "What my son means, Miss Ryan, is that there isn't a male in Silver Bow County that'd harm a hair on your dainty head, whether you were a blond, a brunet, or a redhead. A beautiful woman is welcome anywhere, but nowhere more than in a minin' camp."

Nell refused to give Morgan the satisfaction of responding to such impertinent flattery. "But the

boys from rival sections routinely engage in fisticuffs?" she continued, as though he'd never spoken.
"Is that it?"

Morgan ruffled Luke's curls affectionately. "You
grow up tough in Butte," he said with understated
simplicity, "or you don't grow up at all."

Whatever his flaws, the presumptuous man was
a caring father. Nell shifted uneasily in her chair.
She realized with acute discomfort how much she
would love to have a son like Luke. There were no
small children in the Ryan family. Uncle Cormac
and Aunt Lydia were childless, and at Sean's death,
their branch of the family line had come to an abrupt
end. That evening, the unhappy thought oppressed
Nell more than usual. Family ties were extremely
important to her. They were the bastions against the
outside world from which she must hide her terrible
secret.

For fourteen years, she'd told herself that she
didn't want to get married. She didn't want
to experience the hurt that was the inevitable
result of wedded life. Gazing at Luke's sun-
kissed face across the table, she recognized the
sharp pang of regret she'd refused to conscious-
ly acknowledge. She would never have children
of her own. Even if she changed her mind about
the idiotic myth of romantic love, she'd never
marry.

She couldn't.

It was as simple as that.

"Your brother was a real scrapper, ma'am," Kalle
Kuusinen told Nell as he mopped up the last of the
gravy on his plate with a crust of rye bread. "I vent
vith him to ta Clipper Shades one evening after getting off verk. Ve had to fight our vay out of t'ere, by
golly."

"You were a friend of Sean's?" Nell couldn't keep
the pleasure from her voice.

"Oh, sure. Gus and I vere on ta same shift vith
him. Everyone liked your brother."

"For a sawed-off Irish runt, Ryan vas a good egg," Mikkola added with a gentle smile that belied his critical words. "He vas learning all he could from us about shaft timbering and sinking operations. He took to ta dangerous verk like a flea to a dog."

Her brother had been several inches taller than Nell. She'd never considered him a runt. But compared to the Herculean Finns, he must have seemed small of stature indeed.

"Where's the Clipper Shades located?" she asked curiously. "Maybe I could go by there just to see the building."

"That wouldn't be a good idea," Morgan interjected in a tone of finality. When she frowned at him in annoyance, he added, without any attempt to soften his edict, "It's an infamous dive in the wrong part of town. Sean shouldn't have been frequentin' the Clipper Shades in the first place. Don't you go anywhere near it."

She tipped her chin up, piqued at what his nasty remark implied. Her brother had been a fine young man. He might have gone into a notorious saloon on a lark or a dare, but he certainly hadn't visited seedy establishments on a regular basis. She glared at Morgan through narrowed eyes, unable to put her thoughts into words in front of the others, yet hoping he could read the antagonism in her cold glance.

"Your brother often spoke of you, Miss Ryan," said Eben. "He was always bragging about the older sister who'd raised him after his mom died. He was very proud of your being a lady attorney and working with your uncle in his law firm."

"Thank you, Mr. Pearce." At the nostalgic remark, Nell could feel the sudden tears burning her eyes and quickly blinked them away.

"Sean played checkers with me in the evenin'," Luke added ingenuously. The youngster seemed to sense Nell's need to hear every detail of her brother's life in the copper camp. "He told me all about

Boston, where you stayed with your uncle and aunt, and about how you lived with your mom in Bar Harbor before that."

"And did you win at checkers?" she asked with a tender smile. "After Sean turned twelve, I never won another game with him."

"A few times. And I really did beat him," Luke assured her. "He didn't just let me win 'cause I was a kid. I hate that."

"Tell you what," Eben offered, "I'll play you tonight, and I promise to beat the pants off you."

"If you're willin' to put your money where your mouth is," the boy shot back, "I'm ready to bet two bits a game that you'll be the one leavin' the room without the shirt on your back."

Everyone around Luke laughed in good-natured camaraderie at his grown-up retort.

At that moment, Hertta swept by, followed by one of the serving girls, who carried an enormous lacquer tray loaded down with the evening's dessert. The landlady plopped a large plate of cookies in front of her husband. Kalle looked up and grinned at Hertta with pride. Then he held the dish out toward Nell so she could choose one of the golden-brown pastries.

"My vife makes the best *Finska kakor* in Butte," he told Nell. "By golly, my Hertta's the best cook in the whole damn verld."

Hertta smiled lovingly at her large husband in return and then continued on along the table, briskly reaching over the broad shoulders of the men to set down the plates pilled high with the crescent-shaped cookies.

Nell bit into the tender dough to find it filled with sweetened apricots. The Finnish cake was as delicious as it smelled.

Watching Hertta bustle around the long table, Nell was amazed at how joyous the housewife seemed to be, in spite of the hard work involved in feeding and caring for fifty bachelors. The

vivacious woman seemed to radiate a boundless energy. Absently, Nell looked down at the
rich, sweet pastry in her hand that seemed to
symbolize the bond of obvious affection, both
physical and emotional, between the Finnish husband and wife. Could a married couple really be as happy as the Kuusinens seemed to
be?

When she looked up, she found Morgan watching her. Nell's breath caught in her throat at the
unconcealed hunger in his intense green eyes. As
her gaze entangled in his, the vision of him bare-
chested and stropping a razor returned to haunt her.
What would it be like to be married to someone
so unapologetically male, so unashamedly aggressive? Someone like him? Would he hold her in his
arms each day the way he'd held her that morning?
Touch her even more intimately, as they lay side by
side in bed at night? The stirrings of desire that his
caresses had aroused curled through her once again,
like a banked fire suddenly exploding into flame.
She looked away, certain he was able to read in her
eyes the memory of that forbidden pleasure.

Staunchly, Nell repressed her flight of fancy.
Hertta's happiness was only a charade, put on for
the sake of her roomers. No doubt, Kalle's glowing
pride in his wife was merely for show as well, perhaps to keep the other men at a distance from his
attractive spouse.

Nell knew better than to believe in the fairy tale of
marital bliss. No bride lived happily ever after. Men
were either wastrels like her father, who couldn't be
trusted to stay; scoundrels like Charleton Blevins,
who seduced a female solely for her money; or
greedy, power-grasping businessmen—like those
she'd dealt with in her uncle's law firm—who
cheated on their wives without compunction.

No, she didn't need a man. And she didn't want
one. She was satisfied with her life just the way it
was.

Though for custom's sake she resided with her aunt and uncle, Nell earned a good living and enjoyed the nicer things in life. Thanks to Cormac Ryan's wealth and his wife's social prestige, Nell moved in the finest circles of Boston's Irish Catholic community. But she knew, all too well, that it was only through emotional and financial independence that she was safe from the anguish of abandonment. If she wasn't tremendously happy, still she wasn't miserable either. She was meeting life on its own terms. Innately suspicious and skeptical, she understood the human condition with all its follies and foibles. After all, it was her shrewd understanding of her fellow man that had made her such a success as an attorney.

Luke's words interrupted her pensive thoughts. "Dad, can I be excused?"

"May I," Morgan replied automatically, his gaze still fastened on Nell.

Luke grinned. "Since you've finished everything in sight, Dad, you've got my permission to leave the table."

Morgan turned to cuff his son playfully on the shoulder, and Luke dodged it with the natural agility of a ten-year-old. In less than two seconds, he'd reached the dining room door and turned to look back at his father expectantly.

"Go on. Get out of here," Morgan said with a chuckle, "before I put you to work washin' the dishes."

In a flash, the youngster disappeared into the hallway. Up and down the table, the diners were shoving back their chairs and starting to leave.

"If you've finished your meal, Mr. Morgan," Nell blurted out a trifle too loudly, "I wonder if I might have a word with you?"

Every man within earshot paused to listen. Caught with a cookie halfway to his open mouth, Eben peered at her with startled interest, while Kalle cocked his balding head and pursed his lips to keep from grinning. At the far end of the table, Hertta stopped mid-stride and waited with unabashed curiosity for the mine owner's answer.

Undaunted by their inquisitive audience, Morgan smiled in unexpected pleasure. "Certainly, Miss Ryan."

He won't be pleased for long, Nell thought with satisfaction. She nodded politely to the other residents as Morgan hurried around the end of the table to assist her.

"We can visit in the parlor," he said. He pulled her chair out with the smooth grace of a top waiter in an expensive restaurant.

"Let's walk out onto the front porch," she suggested in a much lower tone. Once on her feet, she turned and favored him with a look of cool civility. "We'll have more privacy there. I'd like to speak to you alone."

His grin was positively wicked. "You took the words right out of my mouth, little darlin'."

Chapter 7

Ross followed behind Nell Ryan as she marched out of the dining room and through the entryway to the Kuusinens' front door. Shoulders back, head high, she purposely kept three steps ahead of him. The view of her straight, slim back proved almost as fetching as the delightful sight of her across the dinner table. It wasn't any wonder he'd been admiring her all evening. Dressed in a black satin skirt and gray silk blouse, she had the cool, sophisticated elegance of a Parisian fashion model. And the unyielding posture of a British colonel.

She was a pistol, all right.

She was also mad as blue blazes, and it didn't take a college education to figure out why. He had a hunch he was about to receive a stinging lecture on his peremptory ways. Well, he'd do his damnedest to appear properly chastised. But it wasn't going to be easy.

So far, he was enjoying every minute of it. He'd have to be blind not to appreciate the sight of her hips swaying enticingly beneath the stylish skirt. He was tempted to reach out and give her a good smack on the bottom for the naughty way she'd behaved at supper. That might take some of the starch out of her.

She deserved a caustic sermon herself on the error of jumping to nasty conclusions. The moment she'd met his son, she'd assumed Ross was a married man out for an adulterous fling. She'd believed the worst

91

of him and had promptly set about trying to prove what a deceitful cad he was by cross-examining Luke.

With a toss of her head, Nell graciously allowed Ross to hold the screen door open for her as she glided out onto the verandah that ran across the entire front of the large frame building. She moved to the porch railing, where she came to an abrupt halt and spun around to face him.

She looked him up and down with the patent revulsion of a housewife who's just discovered a cockroach in her flour bin. When she finally spoke, the ice in her voice would have frozen a weaker man's blood.

"Mr. Morgan, I'm sure it won't surprise you to learn that I received a wire from Boston today. A Western Union telegram from Cormac Ryan, to be precise." She leaned toward him and curled her lips in a patronizing sneer. "You know, one of the senior partners of Ryan, Sheehy, and O'Connell? The firm that happens to be representing you in your current lawsuit?"

"No, that doesn't surprise me."

With her sparkling eyes and her flushed cheeks, she was a sight to behold. He longed to take her upstairs to his room and let her continue scolding him to her heart's content while he slowly undressed her. After which, he'd offer his profuse apologies in the most physical way possible. With iron resolution, he schooled his features, lest they betray his lecherous thoughts.

Luckily, she didn't seem to have a clue as to what he was thinking. She waited in silence as two men came out of the house, politely lifted their hats, and descended the porch steps. When they headed up the sidewalk to the nearby trolley stop, she resumed the harangue with single-minded concentration.

"Then it won't astonish you to hear that my uncle has ordered me to remain in Butte indefinitely to help Gavin O'Connell defend your interests in court?"

"Nope, that doesn't surprise me either."

"I should think not," she grated, "since you're the one who requested it." She clenched her fists and took a belligerent step toward him. "Let's stop this ridiculous farce, Mr. Morgan, and get down to plain facts. Just who do you think you are, that you can pull strings and have me kept here against my wishes? This morning, I asked you for a small favor, a simple request to go down into your wretched mine. Would you accommodate me then?"

He started to speak, but she answered for him.

"Oh, no! You couldn't find it in that stunted, weaselly heart of yours to extend a token of sympathy to Sean Ryan's bereaved sister." Her soprano voice rose a full octave higher than usual as she strove to control her Irish temper. "You could, however, display the unmitigated gall to wire my uncle and request that I be appointed your legal counselor."

Ross walked past her to the porch railing, where he turned and leaned his rear end against the wooden balustrade. He folded his arms, patiently waiting for her to get it all out of her system. There was no sense trying to explain anything to a woman caught in the throes of a temper tantrum. If he'd learned anything in his four and a half years of marriage, he'd learned that.

She whirled and glowered at him. "You have a very fine attorney in Gavin O'Connell," she continued, scarcely pausing for breath. "He comes with the best of credentials. He's eminently qualified to represent the interests of the Glamorgan Mine."

"Now, that's somethin' I'm not so sure of, sugarplum. O'Connell hasn't impressed me with his legal know-how since the first day he stepped off the train sportin' his pin-striped suit and his forty-dollar gold watch. He's delayed filin' my counterclaim for nearly two weeks. I have to assume that either he needs some help completin' what is evidently a staggerin' amount of paperwork or he's just plain incompetent. Which one is it?"

"Neither, and you know it," she snapped back.

"Then he should have had the papers filed by now. That right?"

She looked down and carefully brushed an imaginary piece of lint from the lustrous black satin skirt. Her costume was far too classy for supper at a boardinghouse, but not a man at the table would have dreamed of voicing a criticism. It was clear she had a taste for pretty clothes and didn't hesitate to indulge her whims. It was also obvious she didn't want to admit that O'Connell had dropped the ball. Hell, that fancy, dude lawyer hadn't picked it up in the first place.

Twin spots of red stained her cheeks as she lifted her eyes to meet his. She answered with sullen reluctance. "After we had lunch together this afternoon, Gavin left me to return to his hotel room and complete the necessary papers. I'm going to look over the pleadings he's drawn up tomorrow morning— just for my own edification, of course. Then he'll see that they're filed at the district court in the afternoon."

Ross smiled in satisfaction at the news. "That's exactly why I wired your uncle to suggest that you stay and work with O'Connell. I could tell from the questions you asked about apex laws and minin' geology that you'd be an asset. You'll make a real difference in this case, Miss Ryan."

They were interrupted again, this time by a group of five miners who strolled out onto the verandah. Nattily dressed in frock coats, spit-shined shoes, and derby hats, they were ready to embark on a night of drinking, gambling, and wenching. Each man tipped his hat to Nell with a wide smile and wished them both a pleasant evening before he departed.

Mollified by Ross's flattering explanation, Nell moved to the railing and stood beside him. The boardinghouse was built on the slope of a steep hill.

She braced her palm against one of the porch's painted wooden columns and gazed down in abstraction at the street below, where the Finns were hurrying to catch the trolley car that waited at the corner.

"When I was at your office this morning," she said, "I asked a few simple questions that any lawyer would have brought up." She shrugged in modest self-deprecation. "I was merely satisfying my natural curiosity. But I know next to nothing about present mining laws, previous apex litigation, or past appeals to appellate courts. And familiarity with any precedents already set in the determination of similar cases, either on the state or the federal level, will be vital.

"My firm has handled mining suits in the past, but I was never involved with any of them. That's Bryce O'Connell's field of expertise. So I've nothing to offer you as private counsel that Gavin hasn't already thought of—or won't in the near future under the guidance of his brilliant father."

Morgan wasn't easily dissuaded. "Sure you have. For one thing, angel eyes, you can offer your enthusiastic support. You showed more interest in the Glamorgan Mine this mornin' than O'Connell has shown in the entire two weeks he's been here.

"Besides," he added magnanimously, "I can teach you all the basic terms of minin' and geology you'll need in order to help with the trial."

Nell tilted her head and studied Morgan from the corner of her eye. Something just didn't ring true.

She wasn't used to having a man she'd only just met accept her as a competent attorney. Usually she had to prove her ability every step of the way, and always in the past, it had been done under Uncle Cormac's protective wing. In the beginning, she'd been given only the simplest tasks at the law firm. She quickly found that the drawing of deeds, bonds, and mortgages required limited technical skill, once she'd caught the knack of it. Later, she was assigned wills and some probate practice to handle on her own. But in any litigated case, she'd worked under her uncle's direction and then only as his assistant. No client of Ryan, Sheehy, and O'Connell had ever been willing to let a lawyer in petticoats go before the bar as his sole legal representative.

Nell wasn't bitter. It was the way of the world, and she accepted it. Just being allowed to practice law as her uncle's assistant was far more than most women ever achieved. Of the few females in the country who had won the right to plead before the courts, nearly all of them were married to lawyers and worked side by side with their husbands.

No, she didn't resent the opposite sex for its unconscious and often unthinking prejudice, but she did have an innate dislike of being manipulated by anyone, male or female. She suspected that was exactly what Ross Morgan was trying to do.

"I don't know," she said in her most helpless, little girl voice. "It sounds awfully difficult. You'd have to be very knowledgeable, as well as being a wonderful instructor, to teach me all that complicated stuff."

Morgan took the bait, just as she'd expected. He puffed up like a peacock. Lord, if he had feathers, he'd be preening them.

"I'm willin' to spend all the time it takes, punkin, for you to understand the elementary principles of minin' copper," he drawled.

"You're very generous with your time, sir." She had to look down and fidget with the large buckle on her patent leather belt to keep from smirking. Heavens to Betsy, what inordinate male pride!

"Why, I'm certain it'd be far too difficult," she avowed with a sigh of dismay. "I'd just never understand such complex information."

Like the conceited ass he was, Morgan waltzed right into her trap. "No one would expect you to master anythin' more than a few simple terms."

"And you'd be willing to spend hours and hours trying to instill them in my illogical female brain?"

He still hadn't caught on. He smiled in overweening generosity. "I'll give you all the time you need, little darlin'."

Exasperated, she gripped the porch railing with both hands. She couldn't decide whether to laugh in his handsome face or slap the fatuous smile off it.

Trying hard not to give his hilarity away, Ross propped one hand beside hers on the balustrade and fought the urge to burst into laughter. He'd caught on to her game of playing the brainless female with her first simpering disclaimer. He leaned closer and breathed in the tantalizing fragrance of gardenias. She was as bright as she was beautiful. Though he dared not show it, he was delighted that Cormac Ryan had ordered Nell to remain in Butte. It was the only way to keep her within arm's reach. If she stayed—and it looked as if she didn't have any choice—he wouldn't be able to fire Gavin O'Connell as he'd been seriously considering. That meant he'd have to work twice as hard supervising the preparations for the trial. Nell had admitted that she didn't know much about mining litigation, and he sure as hell couldn't leave his legal defense in the hands of that incompetent Harvard dandy. If he were smart, he'd send them both packing and hire another firm. Christ, he was really letting his crotch rule his brains on this one. Never in his life had he been so all-fired taken with a woman.

At thirty-one, Nell Ryan was in full bloom. She was like an open flower, dew-touched and drenched in its own delicate perfume. A surge of desire flooded his veins as he relished the spiraling tension between them. He'd purposely goaded her, enjoying the way she'd pretended to consider his offer to tutor her, all the while behaving like a mindless doll. He planned on giving her some lessons, all right. But the only thing they'd have in common with copper mining was the sinking of a shaft. The muscles of his groin tautened in primal anticipation.

Damn it, he was on fire.

And she was like ice.

He could sense her innate distrust of him, a distrust that seemed to come from deep in her soul. He wondered who had hurt her so badly that every male thereafter was immediately suspect. How long would it take to break down the barriers she'd built against the outside world?

Hell, he probably shouldn't even try. She was a pampered Eastern filly, who'd never be happy living in the West. Still, the court battle between the Glamorgan and the Forrester could drag on for months. He'd never be able to hold out against her charms for long. Why attempt the impossible in the first place?

She stared down at her hands as though pondering his generous offer. "Would you really be able to devote all that time to my studies, Mr. Morgan?" she baited in a sugary tone. "We'd have to meet frequently."

"Every day and twice on Sunday," he assured her. "Teachin' a girl anything of an intellectual nature has to be harder than drillin' into solid granite."

Livid, Nell looked up in time to catch the flash of the aggravating man's crooked grin before he managed to control his hilarity. But his eyes continued to sparkle with amusement. Amusement at her expense. He'd been wise to her playacting all along. Ironically, that only made her angrier. She clenched her jaw and glared at him, silently daring him to continue his obnoxious teasing.

Morgan reached out and lightly traced the line of her shoulder with his fingertips, moving from the seam of her puffed sleeve to rest at the base of her throat. With smooth, lingering expertise, he drew a tiny circle below the high-standing collar of her blouse. She could feel the heat of his touch through the gray peau de soie. It was as though he were stroking her bare skin.

"Since you're goin' to be stayin' in Butte for a while, Miss Ryan," he coaxed, "why don't we try to get along with each other?"

Despite her fury, Nell's body reacted instantaneously to the sensuous caress. The pulse in her throat throbbed wildly beneath the pressure of his fingertips. As though in unconscious memory of the way he'd fondled her that morning, her breasts grew fuller, their crests suddenly erect and tight with need.

He met her startled gaze. The sure knowledge of her response to his touch lit up the golden flecks in his emerald eyes. Slowly, seductively, he lowered his lids and stared at her lips for a long, breathless moment. With one hand still curved about her throat, he reached out with the other to draw her nearer.

Nell shoved his arm aside and sprang out of his embrace. She took one large step backward, widening the distance between them in instinctive self-preservation.

"I know why you schemed to keep me here," she told him. She drew a deep breath and tried to control the telltale shaking of her voice. "And it's not because you think I can help Gavin with the lawsuit."

Morgan pushed away from the porch railing to tower above her. "You're right, Nell," he said in a thick, raspy voice. "I admit it. I want you. I'm burnin' up with it."

"Well, you can burn in hell for all I care," she whispered. "If you think I'm going to let a practiced womanizer seduce me, you're in for a big surprise."

"I'm not a womanizer." His words were clipped and short. He took a menacing step closer. It was all she could do to hold her ground and not retreat before his ferocious scowl.

Nell sniffed in caustic disbelief. She started to leave, refusing to spar with him any further. He caught her neatly around the waist and slammed her up against him.

"Your misguided attempts to prove my debauchery at supper were entirely uncalled for," he said in a low, angry voice. "In the future, my son is not to be used as a pawn in our relationship."

"We have no relationship, and I'll say whatever I like to your son or anyone else."

"You try to draw Luke into your dirty-minded little interrogations again, and I'll give you the paddlin' your daddy should have given you—but obviously failed to do. And if I spank you, Miss Ryan, you won't sit down for a week."

Aghast, Nell glared at him. "If you dare to lay one finger on me, Mr. Morgan, I'll have the police lock you up for assault and battery. And if you don't believe I'll press charges, just try me."

Ross looked down into her big brown eyes, blazing now with wrath and fear. Jesus, she was driving him frigging crazy. He'd never so much as threatened a woman, let alone struck one. With his size and strength, he'd always been careful not to hurt a member of the weaker sex accidentally. Just an inadvertent bump with his elbow in the middle of the night could break a ladylove's fine-boned nose.

Why in the hell had he said that to her? Every time he tried to woo this irascible female, she got her hackles up. This time he'd responded to her sharp tongue like a damn fool. And so much for trying to intimidate her.

He could feel her breasts smashed against his chest, lush and warm and enticing. Beneath her fancy skirt, her long legs were pressed against the tautening muscles of his thighs. A fire exploded deep in his groin. The anger pumping through his veins quickly turned to raging carnal need.

He released her before she became aware of his arousal through the rustling black satin. "I'm sorry, Nell," he told her in a hoarse whisper. "I didn't mean to frighten you."

"Well, good, because you didn't."

Once free, she wobbled for a moment on shaky legs. He reached out to steady her, and her fingers trembled visibly as she tried to shove his hand away. When he wouldn't be denied, she placed her slender fingers in his and grudgingly accepted his aid with an air of bruised dignity.

She lowered her lids, and the long lashes lay like dark brushes on her pale cheeks. Her smooth brow furrowed in contrition. "I'm sorry too, for what I said to Luke. I was wrong to question your son about his mother, and I apologize. I won't do anything so heedless again."

He squeezed her fingers in a brief salute to her courage. "Thank you for that."

Lifting her chin, Nell met his eyes as she stubbornly withdrew her hand. "If you'll excuse me, I'm going to go to bed now. It's been a long and exhausting day."

The wariness in her gaze told him she wasn't ready to listen to anything more he had to say that night. He nodded and spoke with all the tenderness with which he longed to surround her. "I'll see you in the mornin'."

Left alone on the porch, Ross reached inside the front pocket of his shirt and pulled out a fine Havana cigar. He didn't smoke often, but tonight he needed the tobacco's calming effect on his raw nerves. Striking a match, he lit the cigar and drew a deep breath through its aromatic length.

Then he leaned his shoulder against a porch column and stared absently out at the gathering dusk. Summer days were long in Montana, but here and there, lights began to twinkle out on the flat below the city.

What was the reason for this irresistible, nearly uncontrollable attraction to a spinster lawyer with the body of a houri and the heart of a shrew? Miss Elinor Margaret Ryan wasn't like any female he'd hankered after before. She was certainly nothing like his deceased wife, who'd been a skinny, pale-eyed blond without an interest in anything but the gratification of her own wishes.

Immediately after graduation, he'd married the chic New York debutante, whom he'd met at a party during his last year at Columbia. She'd pursued him. He'd been flattered by her open avowal that she found him incredibly attractive. It wasn't just talk. She backed up her words with a sexual aggressiveness he'd never expected in a woman. As a green buckaroo from Colorado, he'd never had it so hot and wild.

Wilhelmina Van Deist Morgan accompanied her groom to his native state, where their son was born three years later. She hated the West. It was too open and empty. She also confessed that she'd never liked sex all that well either. What she'd offered so freely before the wedding, she found every excuse to avoid once he'd slipped that gold ring on her finger.

Their increasingly unhappy marriage had been marked by her sulks and tantrums when he was with her, relieved by periods of calm when he went on extended trips for his engineering jobs and left her and Luke in Denver with his parents.

Willie resented his long absences and the occupation that required them, though she'd known full well when she'd married him that he was a mining engineer. She claimed he was driven by a ruthless ambition and a love for his work that didn't leave room in his mind or his heart for anyone. She'd threatened to leave him and the child and go back to New York alone. Before she could make good her threat, she was killed in a buggy accident. Luke was only a toddler when it happened. Sometimes Ross wondered if the boy could remember her screaming that she hated them both for keeping her there in that loathsome place.

He'd buried his wife with the cold realization that he should never have married her in the first place. His second mistake was bringing her out West. He'd been a young fool to think a spoiled Eastern socialite could adapt to the rigors of the frontier. Life in a mining camp was far too hard for a delicate female.

As he puffed on the cigar, his thoughts turned to the beautiful creature getting ready for bed upstairs. She was probably down on her knees right now, praying to God that she wouldn't have to stay in Butte any longer than two more days.

Hell's fire, he couldn't blame her. He'd behaved like a brute—arrogant, insensitive, and heavy-handed. When he was around her, all his reputed charm with the ladies disappeared like a cage dropping down an open shaft. In the short time she'd been there, she'd succeeded in reducing him to a rutting caveman with systematic and appalling ease.

He should wire Cormac Ryan in the morning that he was hiring another law firm and let the lady attorney go on back to Boston with her incompetent colleague. If he were using the intelligence the good Lord gave him, that's exactly what he'd do.

Ross took one last puff and threw the cigar butt into the nearby lilac bush. He should put her on the train himself, bag, baggage, and big, brown, angel eyes.

But he wouldn't.

Now that he'd found her, now that he'd kissed her, now that he'd breathed in the intoxicating scent of gardenias in her hair and tasted the honeyed warmth of her sweet mouth, he had no intention of letting Nell Ryan get away.

Chapter 8

Nell was sitting at the breakfast table when the Western Union messenger arrived at the front door of Kuusinen's Boardinghouse. Hertta, who'd gone to answer the jangling bell, carried the distinctive envelope into the kitchen and placed it beside Nell's plate.

"T'is just came for you," the landlady said with a worried frown. She absently patted the thick flaxen braid that crowned her head and spoke with an air of gloom that was out of keeping with her usual buoyant nature. "I hope it's not bad news. I never got a telegram t'at vasn't an awful surprise."

Nell popped the last forkful of the *pannukakku* into her mouth and eyed the missive with sleepy-eyed complacency. That morning she'd discovered for the first time the wonderful taste of a Finnish oven pancake topped with a generous mound of fresh strawberries.

"Don't worry, Hertta." Nell's voice rang with optimism. "This is one telegram that's no surprise. I'm expecting it to be very good news, indeed." With a smile of certainty, she snatched up the envelope and tore it open.

But Hertta had been right.

The contents were a terrible surprise.

GODFORSAKEN NO EXCUSE STOP REMAIN TILL GLAMORGAN CASE IS SETTLED STOP PURCHASE ANYTHING NEEDED AND CHARGE TO FIRM STOP

LAW BOOKS AND CLOTHES HAVE BEEN SHIPPED
STOP I EXPECT YOU TO WIN STOP UNCLE CORMAC

Nell sprang up, the paper clutched in her hand.
She waved it in the air like a wild woman. "I can't
believe this! I just can't believe it!"

"I can believe it," Hertta said, with pessimistic conviction. "T'ose dreadful t'ings alvays bring
bad news." She plopped down next to Nell at the
long trestle table covered with the morning's dirty
dishes. "Now take a deep breath and tell me vhat's
so terrible."

Nell sank back down on the bench, still staring at
the telegram. Dazed, she handed it to the landlady.

"My uncle has ordered me to remain in this hellish place indefinitely. He wants me to help Mr.
O'Connell represent the Glamorgan Mine in court.
I was planning on leaving tomorrow! My clothes are
all packed and ready to go."

"Looks like you're going to have to unpack t'em.
Ta bedroom is yours for as long as you need it,
Nellie. I'll charge you ta same rate I charged Sean.
T'ere's a list of men who've requested a single room,
but t'ey'll be villing to continue sleeping in one of ta
dormitory bedrooms so you can stay on here. T'ey
don't need t'cir privacy half as much as you do."

Nell tried to focus on Hertta's sensible suggestion, but the astonishing dispatch she'd just received
made it impossible to think straight. The whole turn
of events was unbelievable! She'd been certain her
uncle would wire her this morning to say he was
sending someone else to Montana to work with
Gavin. Why in the world had Uncle Cormac made
such an unexpected and unlikely decision? He'd
placed the selfish demands of a egocentric client
over the personal wishes of his own niece, whom
he professed to love like a daughter.

What had that conniving Ross Morgan said in
his telegram that had influenced her uncle to deny
her request and grant his? She'd always thought

Cormac Ryan was the exception that proved the rule as far as the rapacious greed of the male members of the species was concerned. Now she wasn't so certain.

"I . . . I can't stay here," she told her new friend in muddled confusion. "The court case could take weeks . . . months."

"And vhy couldn't you stay at my boardinghouse for an entire year, if you wanted to?" Hertta demanded.

"With fifty unmarried miners?"

"And a mine owner. And his young son, his superintendent, my husband, and me. Vhat's vrong vith t'at? Ve'll be one big family. You'll have lots of adopted brothers to look out for you. Finnish men are so shy, you'll be lucky if t'ey say five verds to you ta whole time you're here."

Nell shook her head doubtfully. "But you're so busy with the other boarders. Having a solitary female to look after would be adding one more unnecessary chore."

"Nonsense." Hertta patted Nell's hand. "It vill be fun having you to talk to. Kalle's a vonderful husband, but I miss gossiping about vomen's t'ings. Men never pay any attention to ta newest styles or ta latest display of yard goods in ta stores. Or anyt'ing else t'at really matters."

Nell smiled at the thought of the big Finn miner staring in perplexity through a shop's front window at the latest, most outlandish fashions in women's apparel.

"When do you ever get a chance to sit and gossip, Hertta? You're busy twenty-four hours a day."

It was no exaggeration. The boardinghouse was open and running around the clock. Miners were either coming off or going on shifts. That meant that Hertta and her two serving girls, Maija and Fetsi, were up at four each morning to serve breakfast and prepare a lunch pail for every boarder. In

addition, the dining table, which could easily seat
twenty-five hearty men, was always being laid or
cleared. Immediately after supper, substantial evening snacks were set out. These were removed only
to be replaced by hot meals for the miners coming back from afternoon shift, followed by those
from graveyard. It was an exhausting routine. Only
someone as robust as Hertta could have kept it
up.

"Ve'll visit at breakfast every morning," said the
landlady. "By ta time you're up and dressed, I'll be
ready to sit down and take a few minutes off. And in
ta evenings after supper, ve can gossip vhile ve relax
for a bit in ta parlor." Her dark blue eyes twinkled
with an impish light. "T'at is, if you're not too busy
spooning vith Ross on ta front porch."

Nell scowled, remembering Ross's offer to teach
her everything she'd need to know about mining
for the coming trial. "If I am with Mr. Morgan, we
won't be doing anything so romantic as courting. I
don't like that man. He's too self-serving by half.
It's all his fault I'm stuck in this uncivilized place.
He wired my uncle demanding that I stay on."

Hertta propped her chin in one work-roughened
hand and met Nell's gaze with an air of calm consideration. "Staying in Butte doesn't have to be all
t'at terrible, Nellie. Don't let ta other day's row
between ta Orangemen and ta Irish mislead you.
Once you get to know ta people here, you'll find
t'em amazingly free of prejudice. T'ey'll accept you
for vhat you are, not for who your parents vere or
vhat language your grandpa and grandma spoke."

Nell lowered her eyes, embarrassed to think she'd
appeared so snobbish. Aside from the day-to-day
battle of being a female attorney in the male world
of jurisprudence, she'd had to struggle against class
consciousness all her life. Her adolescence in Bar
Harbor had taught her how vast the chasm was that
separated the daughter of an Irish mother employed
at the inn and the debutantes who spent summer

holidays there with their families. But that lesson wasn't nearly as painful as what had lain in store for her as an adult, when she went to live with her uncle and aunt.

In Boston, the Brahmins ruled polite society with a near-religious fervor. Because her ancestors hadn't crossed the Atlantic on the *Mayflower*, she'd never been allowed to mingle as an equal with the Protestant upper crust. Nor would she ever be. The keen-eyed and practical Yankee businessmen might leer at her suggestively from across a crowded ballroom or try to pinch her bottom in a darkened hallway, but their haughty wives made it as cold and clear as the ice carvings on their magnificent banquet tables that Nell was merely a laboring girl of questionable descent.

Hertta stacked the table's dirty silverware on top of the breakfast plates and rose to her feet. Shaking her head in warning, she continued her advice as she carried the dishes to the sink. "You vill find t'at many of ta people here go by nicknames, Nellie. It's not considered polite to ask a man vhat surname he vas born vith. In ta mining camp, you succeed or fail on your own merit. It's vhat you do right here, right now—not vhat you accomplished or failed at somevhere else—t'at counts."

"I'm sorry, Hertta," said Nell contritely. "I didn't mean to hurt your feelings." She gathered up her own utensils and plate and carried them to the counter. Then she looked around for an apron to put over her dove-gray morning dress.

"You didn't." Hertta pointed to a large, clean dish towel hanging on a wooden rack nearby. She poured steaming water from a kettle into the large sink, added soap, and ran cold water from the tap.

"My father vas a miner, just like Kalle," she told Nell. "Vhen I go uptown, I hold my head high. I feel proud to be ta daughter and vife of mining men. I'm as good as anyone, even ta vealthy matrons on ta Vest Side in t'eir fancy fur coats, or t'eir spoiled daughters driving around town in t'eir private carriages. I know it, and so do t'ey."

Aware that both of the serving girls were upstairs making beds and dusting, Nell wanted to give her busy friend a helping hand. She tied the white linen toweling around her waist and began scraping the breakfast plates.

"You can't blame Ross for trying to keep you here," Hertta said as she started to wash the dishes. "Ta outcome of t'at trial means everyt'ing to him. I overheard Eben tell my husband last veek t'at Ross vill be completely ruined if ta verdict doesn't go his vay."

At supper, Nell had learned that Kalle was the head foreman in charge of timbering at the Glamorgan. It seemed that both of the Kuusinens had a deep loyalty to its owner.

"From what I understand," Nell said thoughtfully, "Morgan chances losing all rights to remove ore from the Glamorgan. It'll be shut down permanently if Felix Hegel proves that the contested vein of copper originates in his Forrester Mine." She shrugged in explicit disinterest. "But if that happens, Mr. Morgan can always work the ore on his other properties."

"He doesn't have other properties," clarified Hertta. "Every nickel he owns is tied up in ta mansion he's building on Park Street or in t'at one mine. He's in debt up to his ears for ta machinery. If it's closed down, Ross vill be destroyed."

"That's not my problem," Nell replied with stubborn persistence as she dried the plates and stacked them on the countertop.

"Isn't it?" Lifting her brows, Hertta stared at Nell in wonder. "I thought lawyers vere supposed to be concerned about t'eir client's velfare."

Nell wrinkled her nose in unhappy agreement. "You're right, of course. The well-being of Mr. Morgan's finances has suddenly become my primary concern."

"T'at's probably only fitting, Nellie, because I t'ink you've become his first consideration. Or at least his most exasperating problem. Ta Colorado Cougar isn't used to having a pretty lady turn down his invitation to supper at a fancy restaurant." Glancing sideways at her female boarder, she mugged in lighthearted drollery. "And I don't t'ink he's ever asked out a homely one."

"Why do people refer to Ross Morgan as a cougar?"

"I don't know. Maybe it has somet'ing to do vith his ability to land on his feet." Hertta grinned down at the soapy water, her dimples flashing. "Or maybe it's because he has ta hunting instincts of a big cat."

Lifting the stack of blue-and-white plates to an empty spot on the pantry shelf, Nell spoke over her shoulder. "Or maybe it's because he's so good at being downright pussyfooted and sneaky."

Hertta tipped her face toward the ceiling and burst out laughing. "T'at poor man's really got his verk cut out for him."

Later that morning, Nell shopped for a new hat to replace the one that had been ruined during the riot. She'd decided that her low spirits needed a boost. If anything could cheer her up, it'd be shopping. Uncle Cormac had advised her to purchase what she needed and have it billed to Ryan, Sheehy, and O'Connell. Consequently, she was browsing in La Mode Chapeau, the most expensive millinery boutique in the city. She hoped the charge would be added to Morgan's statement of account.

Item: One lady's bonnet.

She smiled to herself, imagining his surprise, then scowled in consternation. Given his presumptuous ways, he'd be pleased to learn he was buying her a hat, especially a costly one. She found the thought disturbing. On further reflection, she decided she'd stand the expense of this particular headpiece herself.

The store had the sophisticated atmosphere of Boston's finest haute couture shops. A quiet saleswoman in subdued clothing remained in the background, available for immediate assistance should the patron desire it.

While the clerk hovered, Nell tried on one hat after another. There was a stunning English felt, called the Windsor, trimmed with bows, rosettes of velvet, a wide silk ribbon, and three feather tips. But the saleslady advised her with unruffled serenity that it came in brown and ecru only. No black. The Empress, however, was available in black silk and velvet, with a jet edging, fancy puffed crown, two dyed-black ostrich feathers—half plumes, of course—plus ebony bows and rosettes of satin ribbon. When she placed the awesome creation on top of her head, it seemed to rise skyward like the Tower of Babel. Definitely not a wise choice.

Standing before a large mirror, she tried on a jaunty flat-crowned black felt aptly named the Toreador. She cocked her head this way and that, as she debated the effect of its jetted feather and pin.

"Go ahead. Get it," a feminine voice urged. "It was made for you."

In the looking glass, she met the gaze of a stunning brunet, who stood just behind her.

She returned the young woman's engaging smile. "Do you think so? It's not too plain?"

"Oh, no! Its simple lines are perfect for you." The newcomer contemplated the hat in the looking glass with the critical air of an expert. "It allows your gorgeous hair to be seen and not overshadowed by all the gewgaws."

"I think you're right," Nell mused, "though my hair's far from gorgeous. I'd give anything to have your magnificent ebony locks."

The stranger's dark eyes sparkled. "I sure as heck think you're wrong," she contradicted with a plucky grin, "but I'm not going to fight over it."

"Then thank you for the compliment." Nell turned and thrust out her gloved fingers. "My name's Elinor Ryan. I just arrived on the train the other day."

"Miss Letitia Howard," the lady answered. "Welcome to Butte." She grasped Nell's hand and shook it with the unabashed friendliness of youth.

The vivacious woman was somewhere in her early twenties. Slender and lithesome, she was dressed in the very last word in fashion. Her brightly flowered promenade gown and matching parasol of lavender and white made Nell, in her dark walking suit, look like a somber black crow.

"You have a keen eye for hats," said Nell. "It usually takes me hours, while I try on every headpiece in the place before I can make up my mind. And then as soon as I walk out the door, I decide I've made the wrong choice and should have taken the runner-up instead."

Letitia giggled sympathetically. "It's easy when the hat's on someone else's head."

She removed her lilac bonnet and tossed it on a display case close by. Twirling around to face the mirror once again, she plopped a yellow straw gypsy decorated with silk blossoms on top of her coal-black waves. She pursed her lips in a comical moue at her own reflection as she tied the wide silk ribbon under her chin in a large bow.

"Those daisies are sure to attract bumblebees," she said. She rolled her eyes upward dramatically. "There's nothing that makes me more teeth-chattering nervous than looking like a walking flower garden in the summertime."

Nell laughed in frank enjoyment of the girl's high spirits. "I'll tell you what. Let's take turns trying them on and giving each other some honest advice. No being polite, now, just the plain, gospel truth."

"It's a deal," Letitia agreed. She untied the yellow bow, yanked off the bonnet, and pitched it aside with carefree abandon.

The saleslady hurried over to snatch up her abused merchandise. With a disdainful sniff, she dusted it off and returned it to its proper place. She glared at Letitia through narrowed eyes, then smiled ingratiatingly at Nell. Resuming her spot behind the counter, the thin, gray-haired woman stood with her hands clasped in front of her, as though in silent prayer for her young customer to be a little more careful with the expensive goods.

The pair of shoppers spent the next thirty minutes in happy exploration, trying on one piece of headgear after another. Beribboned straw boaters, forward-tilted felt hats bristling with feathers, bonnets with hanging gardens of flowers spilling over their brims, toques in velvet, braided pillboxes, enormous picture hats called Marlboroughs after the famous duchess who once wore them, and silk turbans with great clusters of plumes—nothing was overlooked. The two ladies kept their bargain. Each offered the other her ruthlessly frank opinion. It was no easy task for two discerning and outspoken females, but each eventually settled on what she believed was precisely the right choice.

After Letitia had paid her bill, she thanked Nell profusely for her help, said a warm good-by, and started to leave.

"Don't go just yet," Nell begged. "I'd like to invite you to have lunch with me this afternoon at the Thornton Hotel. There's someone I want you to meet." She smiled beseechingly as she leaned closer to speak in a lower tone.

Across the counter, the pinch-faced salesclerk, who'd glowered at Letitia the entire time they'd been trying on hats, had to look the other way or admit she was plainly eavesdropping.

"My friend's a lawyer from Boston," Nell continued in a near-whisper, "and a newly arrived stranger just like me. He's also a handsome bachelor."

Letitia grew deathly serious. "Thank you for the kind invitation, Miss Ryan, but I couldn't accept." Her lovely features suddenly wistful, she reached out and touched the gold braid on Nell's sleeve in an impulsive gesture fraught with some unexplained sorrow. "You can't know what your offer of friendship means to me."

"Then perhaps another time," Nell suggested in confusion. The young woman's lighthearted demeanor had changed to gloomy preoccupation so swiftly, she was certain she'd said something to upset her. Though what, she couldn't imagine.

"No, I'm afraid not." Letitia's eyes swam with tears. Her lower lip trembled. She gripped the handle of her parasol in her lavender-gloved fingers as if she were standing in the path of a windstorm and was afraid the sunshade would be blown away. And herself along with it. "What a kind . . . kind lady you are," she whispered. "For a few minutes, you made me forget . . ."

Without saying what it was she'd forgotten, Miss Howard spun on her heel and left the shop.

Mystified, Nell paid for the pert felt hat she'd chosen and turned to go. She blinked in astonishment at the sight before her.

There in the open doorway stood Ross Morgan. He was dressed in a black suit, white shirt, and striped silk necktie. If the khaki work clothes and tight-fitting Levi's he'd previously worn had accentuated his hard-edged virility, the severe cut of the expensive jacket and trousers now brought his aura of wealth and power to new and unnerving heights. Beneath that outer layer of easygoing Western charm was an inner core of steely determination, keen-eyed perceptiveness, and razor-sharp cunning. He'd like her to think he was just some misplaced cowboy from Colorado. She knew better. Seeing him in the stark, conservative clothes of a prosperous businessman, she recognized him for exactly what he was. A ruthless copper baron.

With one muscular shoulder propped against the jamb and his arms folded across his chest, he waited for her with irritating complacency. He must have spotted her through the store's plate-glass window. From the gloating smirk on his face, she deduced that she wasn't the only person in Butte to receive a telegram from the East Coast that morning.

Nell swallowed the lump of nervousness in her throat, then lifted her chin in open defiance. If he thought she was going to surrender gracefully to his vile machinations, he was wrong. Dead wrong. Oh, she'd stay and work with Gavin on the lawsuit, just as she'd been ordered. But she planned on having as little to do, personally, with their avaricious, scheming, and opportunistic client as possible. Morgan could relay his wishes in the matter of his legal defense to Gavin. Gavin could then repeat them to her. There was no reason she had to give Mr. Overbearing Morgan anything more than the polite time of day.

For reasons she refused to explore, the aggressive mine owner with the physique of a Viking and the guile of a vandal unsettled her like no other man she'd ever known. She wasn't attracted to him. Good Lord, no. Nor did she want to be held in those powerful arms ever again. Not in a pig's eye.

It was just that he had a way of getting her all flustered and breathless every time he got too near. She needed a wide space between her and that intimidating, golden-haired male. It had something to do with their personal chemistry, she imagined. Like being oversensitive to certain foods. That's why she grew flushed and achy whenever he touched her. And why her heart was banging against her sternum, right now, like a judge's gavel pounding for order in a noisy courtroom.

The man was poison to her nervous system. Plain and simple.

She met his confident gaze across the length of the millinery shop, from where his gold-flecked eyes had pinned her to the spot with revolting ease. A slow, lazy smile curved up the corners of his mouth as he patiently waited for her to come to him. Like a trapped prisoner forced to run the gauntlet, she braced herself and started for the door. And freedom.

Chapter 9

Ross watched Nell Ryan sweep across the hat shop's Oriental carpet with the hauteur of a Mandarin empress. She favored her lowly subject with a frosty smile.

"Looking for a new bonnet, Mr. Morgan?" she quipped as she attempted to glide past him and out the door.

At the last moment, he stepped in front of her, effectively blocking her escape. "This store's too rich for my blood, honeybunch. Besides, I don't look all that great in feathers and ribbons. They clash with my five o'clock shadow."

He reached politely for the hatbox.

She jerked it away.

He reached for it again.

"I can carry it myself, thank you," she snapped, unwisely clutching the parcel's gold-braided handle to her chest. The round pink box dangled in front of him, presenting an irresistible temptation.

"I'll carry if for you," he insisted. Undaunted by the disturbing proximity of her breasts or the mulish set of her chin, he started to pry the cord out of her fingers. Hell, she might as well get used to his autocratic ways from the beginning. He'd been taught to behave like a gentleman, and by God, that's what he was going to do, whether Nell reciprocated and acted like a lady or not.

They struggled for a moment, but the outcome was never in doubt. With a graceful flutter of her gloved hands, she released the braided cord as though assigning a package delivery to a bellboy.

"Thank you, sir. You can take that to Kuusinen's Boardinghouse for me. I have a pressing engagement right now. Good day." She scooted out the door and started down the busy street.

He was right beside her. "*We* have a pressin' engagement, angel eyes. I'm joinin' you and O'Connell for lunch. I was just on my way to the Thornton when I saw you through the window."

"This is a business meeting," she said curtly. She glanced at his suit coat and trousers with disdain. "There was no need to get all dressed up. You're not invited."

He nodded courteously to a stout lady and her plump daughter, who stood in front of a Greek grocery store eyeing the phyllo pastry, then slipped his hand beneath Nell's elbow, pleased despite her show of belligerence. Apparently, she'd given up reprimanding him for the use of pet names. He was making some headway, at least. Sooner or later, he was bound to hit on one she liked.

The street was crowded with people. He had to guide her around a tight knot of shoppers surging toward a clanging trolley. Along the curb, horses and buggies stood waiting for their owners.

"I've invited myself," he told her, "since the business to be discussed is mine."

"But the strategies to be decided upon are mine and Gavin's. As your legal counselors, we'll make the necessary decisions and then discuss the pros and cons with you before setting them in motion."

She stopped in the middle of the sidewalk and glared at him. "I realize you're lacking in any ability to understand subtle nuances, Mr. Morgan. Otherwise, you'd never have pulled the despicable, conniving trick you did and then dared to approach me on the street as though there was nothing but sweet accord between us. Or are you just ignorant?" She paused for breath. When she continued, her voice was filled with trenchant sarcasm. "You do know that my uncle has insisted that I remain here and assist Gavin *against my wishes*?"

He tried to look reasonably concerned at the display of fireworks. But with her eyes shooting sparks of anger and her vivid coloring heightened, she was so damn beautiful he wanted to smile in pure enjoyment instead. This hot-tempered spinster was definitely not a woman with ice in her veins, no matter what she wanted a man to think. She was filled with passion. But that zest for life had once left her open and vulnerable. She'd been hurt, and hurt badly. She needed to be shown that intimacy with a man could be good. Good? Jesus, with her it'd be downright glorious. He'd have to go a whole lot slower than he was used to, but he was more than willing to give her all the time she needed. It was going to take patience, and plenty of it. He could feel his body already tightening in anticipation. Hell's fire, if he didn't keep a strong rein on his baser impulses, he might just go a little loco in the meantime.

Ross affected his most conciliatory manner. "Yes, ma'am, I know that you're stayin' on. Cormac Ryan wired me this morning. He said you'd give me your best legal advice. He sounded confident that you could win my case."

With an exasperated toss of her head, Nell turned and continued up the walk. He matched her stride for furious stride. They passed two elderly Chinese laundrymen who stood in front of a washy-washy house, enjoying the midday sunshine while they smoked their long-stemmed pipes.

"Whether we can win your suit remains to be seen," she said succinctly. "But win or lose, you'll be charged for every single expenditure I'm forced to incur while I'm kept here in this devil's playground."

"That sounds fair enough," agreed Ross immediately. "Is that what's in the box?" he teased. "A business outlay?"

She peeked up slyly at him from beneath her long

lashes. "Why not? If I hadn't been caught in that hullabaloo yesterday, I wouldn't have ruined my best bonnet."

"The riot was my fault?" he protested. "I never realized I was the cause of all that commotion." He stopped and held the rose-colored hatbox out in front of him with sham apprehension. "Was it expensive?"

"Very." At his look of stark terror, she laughed in spite of her testy mood. "You needn't worry, Mr. Morgan. This one I'm paying for myself. However, if any more hats are destroyed, you're footing the bill. So consider yourself forewarned."

He sighed with mock relief. "Thanks for the warnin', doll face. I'll set up a budget for bonnets as soon as I get back to my office."

Ross steered her past the street where the worst of the fray had taken place, certain that the sight of the rubble and broken windows would add to her already cantankerous frame of mind. The Thornton Hotel was on Broadway, but he decided a round-about walk would give him a chance to mollify her anger before they joined up with O'Connell. He couldn't blame her for being upset. He'd gone over her head, wiring her uncle like that. But he'd been positive that if he made the suggestion for her to remain and help with his lawsuit, she'd have given him a flat refusal without even taking the time to think it over.

"Did you have a nice mornin' shoppin'?" he asked in an attempt to divert her thoughts to something more pleasant.

"Yes, I did. In fact, I made a new acquaintance," she told him, frowning in sudden perplexity. "But my offer of friendship was refused."

That surprised him. He couldn't imagine anyone spurning the chance to be Nell's friend. "What happened?"

"I don't know," she admitted with a rueful smile. "I must have said something dreadfully wrong."

"To a male or female?" Ross didn't add that she had a very independent way about her that might get the hackles up on a man less patient than himself.

"To a very beautiful young lady named Miss Letitia Howard. We met while trying on hats and had a wonderful time giving each other advice. But when I invited her to join Gavin and me at the Thornton, she acted as if I'd insulted her." Nell slowed, deep in thought. "No, not insulted, exactly. It was more like I'd hurt her feelings. Why, she nearly started to cry when I offered to meet her for lunch another time. I can understand someone not wanting to further her acquaintance with me—but weeping about the very suggestion? It didn't make any sense."

A suspicion formed in Ross's mind. "What did this young lady look like, aside from being pretty?"

"Oh, pretty isn't a strong enough word," Nell said with conviction as she resumed her energetic pace. "Dazzling, vivacious, entrancing—those terms are more accurate. She had a marvelous head of pitch-black hair, eyes to match, and a perfect complexion." Nell glanced down at her somber mourning clothes. "I guess she decided from my outfit that I wouldn't be a very interesting person to know. It's too bad. I'd hoped to introduce her to Gavin."

That last bit of news warmed Ross's heart. He was delighted to learn that Nell didn't return O'Connell's affections. If she was looking for an eligible female to introduce to her colleague, then she wasn't hiding any tender feelings for him herself.

His earlier suspicions, however, had just been confirmed. The attractive woman Nell had met in the millinery shop was Lottie Luscious. He'd seen her coming out of the store. They'd even exchanged a quiet smile of greeting. Though he'd never heard her last name before, they knew each other well enough. He'd purchased her services more than a few times.

Apparently, for all her knowledge of the legal profession, Nell was unaware of the opportunities available in a career that women had pursued for centuries. A little warning might be in order, since Butte had a population of whores running close to a thousand in a red-light district that rivaled San Francisco's notorious Barbary Coast. Lottie worked in one of the ornate bagnios that catered to the camp's millionaire mine owners and their playboy sons.

He waited for a pair of housewives to pass by, their straw baskets, filled with fresh vegetables, swinging on their arms. Once the women were a safe distance away, he drew Nell a little closer.

"Your new acquaintance refused your offer of fellowship, sweetheart, because she couldn't accept it," he explained as circumspectly as possible. "Although you were unaware of it, she knew full well you shouldn't be seen with her. In fact, she should never have spoken to you in the first place. Take a word to the wise and be a little more careful who you invite to lunch. Lot . . . ah, Miss Howard is a workin' girl. The minin' camp's full of 'em."

Nell blinked at him in confusion. At the uncomfortable pause that followed, he realized he'd have to spell it out for her.

"Lottie works on the line."

Hell, if that wasn't putting it bluntly, what was? But she still didn't catch on.

"I didn't realize there were so many factories in Butte that employed women," said Nell with a shrug of indifference, "but I've no prejudice against the laboring class. Why, back home, society ladies give me the cold shoulder because I work in my uncle's firm. I would have explained that to Miss Howard, had I realized what she was worried about. There's certainly no harm in two working girls having lunch together."

Ross stopped in his tracks. He searched her brown eyes for some sign she was joking. At the smug complacency he found there instead, he couldn't help himself. He howled with mirth. Clearly bewildered, Nell stiffened in chagrin. Afraid she'd take off down the street in a snit, he slipped his arm around her slender waist and held her in place beside him while he struggled to contain his laughter.

"Sugarplum," he said between chuckles, "you might both be workin' women, but you're in two diametrically opposed professions. You uphold the law. She breaks it. Miss Howard, otherwise known around our copper camp as Lottie Luscious, is one of the light ladies who follow the heavy money. She works in a fancy parlor up on Mercury Street that boasts more fine French furniture than many of the millionaires' mansions over on the West Side."

Realization dawned. With a muffled groan of embarrassment, Nell broke free of his hold and charged up the sidewalk, her adorable nose stuck in the air, her rosy cheeks flaming. Scarcely a minute later, she stopped, whirled, and stared at him. Her eyes were enormous with mounting suspicion.

"How is it that you can recognize Miss Howard from the brief description I gave you? You might be thinking of the wrong female entirely."

Ross stopped chuckling. If she hadn't figured it out by now, he sure as hell had no intention of explaining it to her. "It's gettin' close to noon," he said. He took her elbow and hurried her past an Afghan tamale peddler, who'd stopped calling out his wares to watch them curiously. "We'd better hustle or O'Connell will think we've forgotten him. After lunch, I want to take you to see the house I'm buildin'."

In spite of Nell's resolution to remain as aloof as possible from Rossiter Morgan, she soon discovered that her evenings were inevitably spent in his company. At their meeting with Gavin, the three concluded that the first order of business, after asking for an immediate postponement of the court date, was to file Morgan's response and counterclaim. Nell had then gone over the notes Gavin had jotted down for his opening arguments. She found herself more confused than ever over her partner's seeming lack of a cohesive strategy. When she tried to discuss various alternatives, such as bringing in expert witnesses from other mining towns or drawing up detailed geological charts to be submitted as evidence, he told her it'd be a waste of time and money.

She didn't agree, but there was a lot she had to learn about the mines of Butte before she could prove her point. Once she'd accepted the fact that she was going to remain in the camp until the lawsuit was settled, she decided to surrender to the inevitable stay and all it entailed—including working closely with Ross—as gracefully as she could. So against her better judgment, she felt compelled to accept his offer to tutor her in the basics of mining.

His first suggestion was that they study together in his office at the Glamorgan after his usual work hours were over. She refused, saying it wouldn't be wise to spend so much time in each other's company without the presence of a third party. People might talk. Perhaps if Eben would agree to join them . . .

But Morgan insisted that his mine superintendent had more important things to do than play chaperone to two adults over thirty. Since her room at the boardinghouse was as out of the question as his, they finally settled on working in Hertta's big parlor. Every night after supper, Morgan commandeered the library table in one corner. Nell learned that Luke had done his homework there during the winter months. Recently it had been the site of an ongoing checkers tournament. Now, Morgan hauled maps and charts home from his office and spread them out on the smooth oak surface.

None of the other residents complained. Each evening, however, Morgan and Nell were sur-

rounded by a spellbound audience. The day shift
miners would cluster about the large drawing room,
ostensibly to relax and visit with one another. Few of
the men said a word. But they listened to Morgan's
explanations of the science of mining with silent
fascination, nodding in agreement when they felt
he'd made an important point, shaking their heads
when they thought he'd failed to mention something
crucial.

Only Kalle Kuusinen, Gus Mikkola, and Eben
Pearce were outgoing enough actually to offer
any advice. But these three frequently felt called
upon to share with Nell their own interpretation
of Morgan's words, especially if they thought his
explanations weren't clear or concise enough for an
illogical female brain. By the end of the week, it was
becoming apparent, even to Nell, that holding the
lessons in the parlor wasn't going to work.

On their fourth consecutive evening of study,
Ross drew a diagram on a sheet of paper in front
of her. "In the Glamorgan, as in all Butte mines,
a level is established every one hundred feet," he
pointed out. "A tunnel is then started in a horizontal direction outward from the original descending
shaft."

"It's called a drift," Kalle added with a cheerful
grin.

Morgan scowled at the unsolicited help and continued. "Along the floor of the drift, tracks are laid
for ore cars, which shuttle the ore from the point of
excavation to the station—"

"Vhere ta ore is hoisted to ta surface in a cage,"
concluded Gus from his spot directly across the narrow table.

Eben, who'd just come into the room, leaned
over Nell's shoulder and scanned Morgan's drawing with a critical eye. He pulled up a chair and
sat down next to her. "Tell her about the stoping
process next, boss," he suggested. He brushed his
fingertips across his coppery mustache thoughtful-

ly. "She'll want to learn how the men do the drilling
and the dynamiting."

Morgan laid down his pencil in frustration. He
seemed about to address a few pithy remarks on
keeping quiet to his mine superintendent, when
Luke came into the room, followed single file by
two of his friends. The boys padded across the rug
on bare feet, plopped down on the red horsehair settee, and calmly stared at the grown-ups.

Deep in thought, Nell glanced up to smile at the
youngsters and then looked back at the sketch in
front of her. In less than a second, she swiveled
around and gaped in shock at the trio of youths.
Their hair had been shaved to a quarter-inch of
their pink scalps. All three heads, originally covered with thick, blond locks, now resembled fuzzy
billiard balls.

"Luke," she cried, "what happened?" She rose
from her seat and covered her mouth in horror,
certain that, in spite of his father's warnings, the
fearless ten-year-old had strayed into Dublin Gulch
once too often. And this time, instead of a shiner,
he'd returned minus his beautiful golden hair. She
clenched her fists, furious at such inhumane treatment, even when it had probably been perpetrated
by youngsters no older than he.

"Who did this to you?" she demanded.

Locking his hands behind his neck, Morgan leaned
back in his chair and stretched his long legs out in
front of him. He had put on a fresh change of work
clothes before coming to the supper table. The khaki
pants outlined his massive thighs, while the rolled-
up sleeves of his shirt displayed powerful forearms
covered with golden-brown hair.

"Looks like the boys got a livery stable haircut
today," he stated calmly.

"Merciful heavens," she gasped, dumbfounded
at his lack of concern. "What kind of a haircut is
that?"

"It's a baldyshine, Miss Ryan," Luke informed

her with a crooked grin. He rubbed his hand self-consciously over his crown, where an old scar from a past injury was now plainly visible. "We got it at Dobson's Livery. They gave it to us for nothin'."

"I should hope so!"

She turned and met Morgan's mirthful gaze. "Every spring, the animals that are kept at the livery stables are sheared of their heavy winter coats," he explained. "This year the shearin's late because we had such a long, cold spring."

She was aghast. "They shear the boys too?"

"It's sort of a Butte ritual," he said. It was clear he was finding it hard not to laugh out loud at her horrified reaction. "The hostlers at the stable cut the thick horsehair with clippers that are powered by a big wheel attached to a bellows. All the boys take turns helpin' spin it. In return for their labor, they get a free haircut."

"Can Birdie and Shoelace stay the night?" Luke asked his father. "They're afraid to go home."

"Our ma's gonna whip us for sure, Mr. Morgan," Birdie piped up, seemingly as untroubled as his crony. "She warned us last year that we wouldn't be able to sit down for a week if we ever got a baldyshine again."

Nell had learned that the two Saarelainen brothers, who lived with their large family in a white frame house only two doors away from the Kuusinens, were known throughout the neighborhood only by their nicknames. It had taken some persistent prying on her part to learn their given names.

"If your mother told you not to get a livery stable haircut, Heikki, why on earth did you and Pentti do it?"

"They had to, ma'am," Luke offered.

"Ya, we had to," Pentti agreed. He flashed her a victorious, gap-toothed grin.

"Had to?"

"If we didn't get a baldyshine," Heikki told her with an air of total vindication, "we wouldn't be able to show our faces around the camp for the rest of the summer. Not until all the other guys' hair grew out."

"I see," Nell said softly. Speechless, she sat back down beside Morgan. When it came to barbaric male rituals, she didn't see at all, but she wasn't about to admit it. She was surrounded by a throng of hulking, barrel-chested men, all of whom seemed to think that what the boys had done was perfectly normal and natural. With a sigh, she picked up the list of mining terms from the table, trying to focus on the new words she'd learned that evening.

At that moment, Hertta burst into the room. "Snacks are ready," she sang out to the men.

The parlor was quickly emptied as the miners and Eben, with the three scalped boys on their heels, headed for the dining room. Each evening, sliced loaves of barley, pumpernickel and rye, cold meats, pickled herring, chilled salmon, hard-boiled eggs, cheeses, and *pulla*—Finnish coffee cake—were laid out on the dining table along with cups of yogurt called *viili*, sprinkled with sugar and cinnamon.

In the deserted drawing room, Morgan took the sheet of paper from Nell's fingers and laid it on the cluttered tabletop. "Let's quit for tonight," he suggested. "I think we've worked long enough."

He took her hand, turned it palm upward in his own, and slowly traced her lifeline with the tip of his forefinger, studying it as though searching for the answer to some complicated riddle.

"We didn't get very far this evening," she apologized. She cleared her throat nervously as she fought to ignore the tingling sensations that coursed through her body at his feathery touch. "With . . . with all these interruptions, I'll never be ready to go to trial."

He met her gaze with a look of unruffled serenity. A faint smile touched his lips. "You're a fast learner, sweetheart. You'll be ready."

Nell shook her head. "Not fast enough. We're

going to have to find another place to study. One where we're not constantly interrupted by all your well-meaning friends."

"We can always move to the mine office."

The thought of working alone with Morgan on his own turf was still too threatening to Nell. It was why she'd refused to consider the suggestion in the first place.

"I have a better idea," she said. "Gavin rented a small office on Montana Street this afternoon so that he and I can have a place to work." Remembering how she'd had to meet with Gavin every day at the Thornton, she wrinkled her nose in dissatisfaction. "Working in the lobby of his hotel definitely has its limitations."

Ross smiled as he squeezed her fingers encouragingly. "If it's proper for you to be alone with O'Connell in the office durin' the daytime, there's no real reason why we can't study together there in the early evenin'."

"If we leave the shade up on the window and remain in full view of the street, it would be proper, yes," Nell agreed. "But how wise it would be, I'm not so sure. I've known Gavin for many years. I trust him completely." She lifted her brows, pleading for Morgan's understanding. "I met you only a few days ago."

He reached out and followed the curve of her cheek with the tip of his finger. His deep baritone vibrated with tender reassurance. "I'd never force you to do anythin' against your will, little doll. By now, you've got to have learned that much about me."

Nell knew he spoke the truth, though her heart was racing so fast she was nearly breathless. It wasn't his brute strength that frightened her. It was his captivating charm that posed such a threat to her peace of mind.

"Except for keeping me here against my wishes in the first place," she corrected.

Laughter flickered over his features at her pert retort. "That goes without sayin'," he admitted. The amusement in his eyes slowly faded, replaced by a look of naked hunger. "I had to keep you here, angel eyes. You were plannin' on leavin' in two days, and there was no way I could have followed you back to Boston. Not until the trial was over."

"You're wasting your time, Mr. Morgan," she said. She wet her lips and swallowed convulsively, knowing the trembling of her voice had put the lie to her words.

"You're wrong," he replied with absolute conviction. "No matter what happens between us, darlin', I'm not wastin' my time. And I'll do my damnedest to make sure I'm not wastin' yours."

She lowered her lids and stared down at their clasped hands, uncertain what to say. Afraid to say anything.

The silence between them was filled with a terrible poignancy—an unspoken promise of an intimacy that time and space would never sunder. It was as though Ross were touching her, caressing her, loving her in his thoughts, and those thoughts were being transmitted straight from his mind to hers.

From his soul to hers.

Nell felt her heart pause and stagger before resuming its thunderous beat. Surely in the breathless quiet, he could hear the pounding as it reverberated wildly against her ribs. She'd never been so attuned to anyone. Or so terrified. Or so enraptured.

What was this singular fascination she had with this one male? In the company of every other man, she thought of herself, first and foremost, as an attorney—and a good one. With Morgan, she was overwhelmingly, intoxicatingly female.

He spoke at last, breaking the tense stillness with a soft chuckle. "Thank you for springin' to Luke's defense this evenin'. I couldn't help but notice you were ready to draw someone's cork when you thought he'd been purposely mistreated."

She laughed in embarrassment at her overdramatic reaction to Luke's haircut and bent her head, wanting to hide her face from his view. "As if I really could," she scoffed.

"The thought was there, sweetheart, and that's what counts. You don't really think I'd stand for anyone harmin' Luke, do you?"

Nell looked up to meet Ross's questioning gaze. A need to know his deepest secrets, his past disappointments, his future hopes, blossomed within her. She longed to ask him what Luke's mother had been like. She wondered how long Ross had grieved for her. She wondered what the woman had looked like, certain she must have been very beautiful.

"No," she said quietly, "you'd never allow anyone to hurt Luke. If there's one thing I have learned about you in these seven short days, it's that you are a wonderful father."

"I don't know about that," he answered with honesty. "But I can promise you one thing, Nell. I take care of my own."

The gold flecks in his green eyes shimmered like firelight as he moved even closer. He framed her face with his strong hands, tipped his head to one side, and kissed her. It was a kiss of incredible sweetness, a sweetness that seeped like a healing balm into Nell's tortured soul. With an inner sigh of surrender, she covered his hands with her own and leaned forward to return the pressure of his lips.

She opened her mouth, accepting the invasion of his tongue, even as she realized with a shiver of apprehension exactly what he'd *not* pledged. He'd vowed only that he wouldn't force her to do anything against her will. He hadn't said a word about not trying to seduce her. May heaven save her, she prayed, as she boldly met the soft warmth of his tongue with her own, for she was no longer certain she could save herself.

"Come on, you guys, the food's ready," Eben

called from the doorway. "Oops," he added, as he realized what he'd just interrupted.

Nell jerked back against the hard wooden chair. She stiffened and rose to her feet, and Morgan rose with her.

"You're goin' to have to learn to knock, Mr. Pearce," Ross said with an unabashed grin. "Or I'm goin' to be lookin' for another mine superintendent."

Eben's teeth flashed white beneath his great handlebar mustache. "But the door was wide open, boss," he pointed out.

"Next time, I'll make certain it's closed."

"There won't be a next time," Nell stated. "Good night, gentlemen." Rigid with mortification, she swished past Eben, heading straight for the stairway and the safety of her room.

Chapter 10

"So do you endorse the wearin' of bloomers or not?" Ross persisted. He looked down at the top of Nell's bent head and bit the inside of his cheek to keep from smiling.

Refusing to answer or even look up, she gripped the pencil in her clenched fingers and continued to focus her attention on the book that lay open in front of her.

Ross stood at the side of the map table where she sat studying. From his position above her, he could see the fine carving on the two large tortoiseshell combs that held her chestnut hair in place on top of her head. The thick waves were drawn up and back to display her ears and neck in the fashionable coiffure the ladies called a pompadour. He wondered how long it would be before she allowed him to remove those combs and let her long hair fall like a silken curtain about her bare shoulders.

Bracing both hands on the table's scarred surface, he leaned closer to her in friendly, but undeniable, persuasion.

"Well, do you?"

She cocked her head and looked up from the textbook he'd brought for her to study just that afternoon. For the last twenty minutes, she'd been trying to concentrate on the concise explanation of the smelting process he'd underlined for her. Her brown eyes flashed with annoyance as she stared at him in obvious frustration. Realizing he wouldn't be satisfied until she responded to his question, she reluctantly put down her pencil.

"Just because I said I disagreed with that article in the *Ladies' Home Journal* about the New Woman," she clarified, "it doesn't necessarily follow that I think every female in the country should go around all day long in knickerbockers." She tried to keep the peevishness out of her voice, but didn't quite succeed. "Bloomers were designed years ago so that women could enjoy the pleasure of riding a bicycle. Why everyone wants to equate the belief in women's rights with the wearing of bloomers, I haven't yet been able to figure out."

"But you have worn them?" He bent forward, tipped his head slightly to one side, and nuzzled her ear. When he probed the delicate shell with his tongue, she shivered in automatic response.

Laughing softly at his unflappable perseverance, she pulled her head away. She leaned back against the chair's wooden slats and tried to hold him at arm's length by the impossible means of one slender hand braced against his chest.

"Yes, I've worn bloomers," she admitted. "And don't pretend to be so shocked. Wellesley has a fine sports program, including a modern auditorium where we were taught the importance of vigorous exercise."

Ross grinned. "Now that's a sight I'd like to see. A gaggle of nubile young ladies rompin' around a gymnasium in scandalous attire."

"Bloomers are not scandalous! Why do people always overreact to such a commonsense approach to clothing? In the future, as women enter professions previously closed to them, they're going to have to adopt a more practical way of dressing."

"Such as?" he prodded. He wrapped his fingers about the ruffled cuff at her wrist and started to pull her slowly toward him.

Nell flushed and jerked her arm away. "Never mind. You're only trying to provoke me. I have to concentrate on these chapters you marked for me to read." She picked up her pencil and circled a phrase on the page in front of her. Her dark lashes fanned out across her cheeks as she sought to hide her discomfort at the thought of discussing the particulars of intimate female apparel with a man.

They'd been working at the law office on Montana Street since late afternoon. Earlier in the week, he and Eben had brought an old map table over from the Glamorgan and set it up in the back of the tiny office so that the large geological charts, showing the disputed veins of copper, could be rolled out and studied. It was just about time for Ross and Nell to return to the boardinghouse, where they'd make an ample supper from Hertta's late-evening snacks. Gavin had been with them earlier, but as usual he'd departed the moment he felt he could sneak away without Nell fussing at him for quitting so soon.

From what others had told him, Ross knew that in the balmy July evenings the dandified Easterner regularly frequented the burlesque houses that were open twenty-four hours a day, every day of the week. It seemed O'Connell had developed a penchant for gambling and whores since discovering that Butte had plenty of both and no legal restrictions on either—at least none that couldn't be circumvented by a well-placed bribe to the right official. No one seemed to be sure which pastime had higher priority on O'Connell's summer itinerary. The word around the mining camp was that he'd be better off sticking to the sporting women, however. Their charges were controlled by the going rate. With a stack of twenty-dollar gold pieces the standard fee just to get into a friendly game, faro and poker were said to be costing him dearly.

"Come on, punkin," Ross insisted, "tell me what you consider practical attire for women." Unwilling to let Nell ignore him and return to her studies, he sank down on the chair beside her with single-minded determination. He caught the wisp of reddish-brown hair that dangled in front of her right ear, enjoying its silkiness between his thumb and forefinger.

She was right. He was deliberately trying to provoke her. She took everything so seriously, as though life itself were some thorny problem to be analyzed and resolved. And she was so doggone certain that he held the usual conservative male views on women's rights, it didn't take much prodding to get her riled up and on the defensive.

This time, however, she ignored his bait, refusing even to look up at him. He tugged the pencil from her fingers and tossed it aside. Placing his hands on her elbows, he resolutely turned her to face him.

"I've never had a real, live feminist explain it to me before," he pleaded. "I saw Mrs. Stanton once at a New York train station when the suffragettes were travelin' to one of their conventions. She looked like somebody's plump, gray-haired grandmother. I didn't go near any of them, though. Everyone assured me they were a bunch of unbalanced cranks."

Nell's dark brows drew together in an exasperated frown. She folded her arms and eyed him speculatively. They'd been arguing over a topic that had been the hub of conversation at the boardinghouse for nearly a week now. The latest edition of a popular women's magazine had featured a cover story on what everyone in the country was currently referring to as the New Woman. In the article, which was pompously titled "Let Us Go Back," the author bemoaned the disappearance of the old-fashioned virtues and the emergence of what he labeled "club women," who actually played cards for money under the excuse of socializing or—worse yet— engaging in charity work. Feminists were accused of trying to ape men in their fight for what, in their neurotic caterwauling, they called "reform dress." What man, asked the writer, did not prefer to see

members of the gentler sex display traditional feminine modesty in their appearance?

Nell had let slip her radical views one evening
at supper when Eben had asked Ross if he'd read
the article. A horrified silence had descended on
the Kuusinens' dining table when she remarked to
everyone within earshot that women shouldn't have
to please men by dressing like frothy nitwits. The
tough Finn miners had stopped shoveling the food
into their mouths and stared at her as if she'd just
declared she was running for the presidency of the
United States.

"By *practical*," Nell said now with an exaggerated
sigh, goaded at last into responding to Morgan's persistent gibes, "I don't mean that women should go
around wearing trousers like men. I mean improved
undergarments, fewer petticoats, no corsets, and
shorter skirts."

Ross feigned shock as he stroked her smooth
cheek with his fingertips. "How short? Above the
ankles?"

"Two or three inches shorter, at least," she
snapped. She jerked her head away as though his
touch had burned her. "There's no reason our hems
need to drag on the ground, for heaven's sake. We
ought to be able to participate in tennis and bicy-
cling and golf without injuring ourselves."

"Tennis, bikin', and golf," he mused, " . . . and no
corsets." He shook his head in wonder. "My, oh,
my. What a world! I only wish I could live to see
the day."

"Humph," she sniffed. "The day might come sooner than you think, Mr. Morgan."

The wide roller shade on the front window had
been pulled down late in the afternoon to block the
glare of the setting sun. At the time he'd drawn
the blind, Ross had also quietly locked the door
and turned on the room's two gaslight lamps. As
daylight faded, the office had gradually become suf-
fused in their soft, golden glow. Sitting with her

back to the entrance, Nell had forgotten they were safely screened from view.

Ross was fully aware of it. He ran his hands up her arms, skimming the puffed sleeves of her ivory shirtwaist, to rest them lightly on her slim shoulders. In the afternoon's warmth, she'd removed the jacket of her black suit and hung it on the back of her chair.

He questioned her in a tone of mild disbelief. "Surely you've never done any of those things, angel eyes?"

She smiled triumphantly. "As a matter of fact, I own a bicycle. One of the new ones with pneumatic tires. And when I ride it, I wear a divided skirt."

"No!" he exclaimed, as though nearly overcome with astonishment. "All over Boston?" His thumbs rested at the base of her throat, and he drew small circles on the satiny material that covered her delicate collarbone.

Her chin came up in a gesture of pugnacious self-defense. It was obvious she'd had many an argument with her uncle and aunt on that score. "Wherever I want," she declared. The light in her expressive eyes clearly dared him to criticize such unbounded audacity.

He slid one hand up to cup her stubborn jaw. "You never cease to amaze me, Miss Ryan," he said in a properly scandalized tone. He lowered his head and covered her lips with his open mouth.

This time, rather than pull away, she met his tongue with her own, readjusting slightly to allow him greater access, just as he'd taught her. Then she followed his example and crossed the threshold of his teeth with her moist tongue to traverse the welcoming cavern of his mouth. He issued a low rumble of encouragement and praise deep in his chest, telling her without words how pleasing her kiss was to him.

Along with the lessons in mining technology, they'd been exploring the delightful art of kissing

for the past five evenings. What she wasn't aware of,
however, was that they were about to enter the second phase of her instruction, and it wasn't going to
center around the study of reverberatory furnaces.

Whoever her previous admirers had been, they'd
done a mighty poor job of teaching her how to
spoon. At first, she'd grown stiff and tense each
time he'd started to kiss her. He'd suspected, from
the beginning, that it would take patience on his
part. He hadn't dreamed just how much. Or how
marvelously erotic the slow pace would prove. On
their way home in the private carriage he'd hired,
he'd lured her a tiny step further each evening along
the path of sensuality he'd charted for them.

Little by little, he was building a need within
her for his kisses and his touch. But while he was
fanning the low-banked flames of passion within
her, Ross blazed with desire. Whenever they were
alone together, he was in a constant state of sexual
arousal. Like a case of dynamite with all the fuses
lit, he was going to explode in one thunderous roar.
It was only a matter of time. Stolen kisses in the
privacy of a darkened coach were not enough. He
wouldn't be satisfied until he held her warm and
naked in his arms, until he'd explored every inch
of her supple body, until he'd buried his hot flesh
in hers and brought them both to that moment of
supreme conflagration when the entire world would
disintegrate around them.

Continuing the kiss, Ross slid his arm around
her waist and moved slowly to his feet, bringing
her with him, drawing her closer. At each stage
along the way, he'd lost no opportunity to heighten
the carnal tension between them. He'd used every
possible excuse to stroke her hair, her cheek, her
hands, until gradually she became used to his touch,
like a baby bird that has to be coaxed and cajoled
into letting its captor pet it. Now, at last, he'd succeeded in bringing her to the point where he could
take her in his arms, hold her pressed against the

full length of his body, and kiss her like a lover.

Nell ignored the small voice of reason that whispered inside her head, warning her to stop this dangerous behavior. She slipped her arms around Ross's neck instead, and returned his voluptuous kiss. At her uninhibited response, he pulled her even tighter, till she could feel the sharp protrusion of his hipbone, the corded muscles of his thighs, and the unmistakable evidence of his male erection.

This *had* to stop.

In just a few more minutes, she *would* stop.

From the very beginning, she'd had no intention of carrying their dalliance any further than a few pleasant kisses, and that only to satisfy her curiosity. Back home, she'd smoothly and skillfully fended off pot-bellied bankers and stout-bodied merchants armed with their equally plump wallets. The knowledge that a man had a wife, along with a passel of kids, waiting for him at the end of the day made it easy for her to forgo an invitation to a private supper and the romantic assignation it always implied.

But from practically the first day she'd met Ross Morgan, Nell had wondered what it would be like to have a harmless flirtation with this magnificent male.

He'd cooperated fully. Why, it had been as though he'd read her thoughts. He'd lured her on, offering her sweet busses and innocent touches like harmless candy treats, till she discovered, too late, that she was addicted to them. The more she kissed him, the more she craved the taste of his lips. The more she allowed him to touch her, the more she yearned for his embrace. Away from him, she was tormented by an insatiable longing that was almost, but never quite, satisfied when he held her in his arms. So she kept returning for more. There was no explanation for this madness, except that it was some kind of wild, wicked insanity carried like mountain fever on the cool Montana night air.

She could feel his hands moving up and down her back in steady, soothing strokes as he kissed her. Then he cupped her bottom in his palms and lifted her up against his hardened manhood. A searing ache swept through her groin to spread in shimmering sensations across her abdomen and down her thighs. With it came the nearly undeniable need to flatten her body against his muscular frame, limb to limb, belly against belly, skin against skin, until there wasn't an iota of space between them. Until she was part of him, and he was part of her.

Shocked at the urgency of her feelings, she pulled her mouth away, gasping for breath. "Ross," she whispered, "we shouldn't . . ." She turned her face aside, as she braced her hands against his shoulders and tried to push him away. "We shouldn't be doing this."

He didn't answer. He traced a path of moral destruction down her neck with his questing tongue. With his even teeth, he gently nipped the smooth skin above the frill of her stand-up collar. Still holding the juncture of her legs tight against the crotch of his worn Levi's with one hand, he caught the back of her head in his strong fingers and turned her face to his once again. He silenced her protests with his lips as he resumed the kiss, his tongue probing and withdrawing in erotic persuasion. His hips moved ever so slightly against hers, tantalizing and enticing, until she was quivering in uncontrollable excitement.

Without warning, he broke the kiss and let her slide slowly down his hard, sinewy body in a movement that seemed to sap Nell of every ounce of high-minded resolution. His heavy-lidded gaze impaled her. She could feel her breathing constrict high in her chest as she stared at him in mesmerized enchantment. Then he leaned his flanks against the edge of the map table, spread his legs, and drew her between his thighs. His hands shifted from her derriere upward to encase her rib cage, his thumbs bracketing the soft, malleable sides of her breasts. Lowering his head, he nipped tenderly along the underside of her jaw and the bare column of her neck above her ruffled collar. Sparks of white-hot desire shot through Nell's veins. God, God, God, she was on fire. Beneath the ivory sateen of her shirtwaist, her breasts grew swollen and hard, their tips erect and aching for his touch.

"Ross . . ." She panted in breathless confusion. She threaded her fingers through the thick, golden hair at the nape of his neck, trying frantically to understand why her flesh and bones were doing exactly what her mind was warning her against. "Ross, I can't think."

"Then don't."

He cupped her breasts in his palms and bent his head to cover the crest of one full globe with his open mouth. She could feel the heat of his tongue through the satiny material and held her breath in startled dismay. Dear Lord, what must he think of her?

She wore no corset.

The only garments beneath the ivory blouse were a lacy silk chemise and a camisole of sheerest chiffon. He had to be shocked beyond measure at the wantonness he'd just discovered.

Ross wasn't shocked.

He'd realized several evenings before, as he kissed her and held her close in the cab of the hired coach, that she sometimes didn't wear a corset. Thank God for the radical feminists who railed against such binding and unhealthy underwear. He caressed her pliant breast with his mouth and rubbed his stubbled cheek against its softness, for once in complete agreement with the sisterhood of suffragettes. He tugged at the tail of Nell's blouse, pulling it free from the waistband of her black skirt. Before she had a chance to reflect on the wisdom of such a provocative move, he slipped his hand beneath her diaphanous chemise and caressed the cool smoothness of her bare skin.

Ross heard the startled intake of her breath. Her rib cage rose and fell beneath his fingers in tempo with the thudding beat of his heart. Slowly, inexorably, he pushed the soft material of her shirtwaist and lingerie up her silken torso. She started to step backward in protest or confusion. He held her in place between his legs with the unyielding pressure of his thighs.

Wait, darlin', wait. Give me a chance to show you how good it can feel.

She grew still, as though she'd heard his unspoken plea. Ross lifted his head from her breast and gazed into thick-lashed eyes wide with wariness and an awakening sensuality. Then she lowered her lids in tacit permission.

Her chemise was edged in deep, pointed lace; the camisole was as fine and delicate as cobwebs. A fleeting smile crossed his lips. He realized with satisfaction that Miss Elinor Ryan, prim, unmarried attorney from Boston, indulged in lingerie as sybaritic and uninhibited as any a pagan love goddess would have chosen.

He forced himself to move slowly, afraid he might tear the gossamer finery in his urgent, driving need. Carefully, lingeringly, he slid the hem of her blouse, along with the frothy chiffon and fragile silk, above her breasts, till her round pink nipples were revealed to his sight.

Sweet Jesus, she was beautiful.

Ross felt as though he'd been kicked by a mine mule right square on the breastbone and had the holy stuffing knocked out of him. Drawing in a quick draft of air, he reveled in the intoxicating scent of gardenias, as all the muscles and nerves of his body tautened and sang with vibrant sexual energy.

Her fine-grained skin was almost translucent, the blue veins leading to the aureoles faintly visible in the mellow glow of the gaslight. Holding the bunched material of her upper garments captured in his hands, he lifted Nell up before him, bringing her naked breasts to his mouth and worshipping her incredible beauty with his lips and tongue. Ross suckled her with all the tender reverence he felt, willing her to accept the ecstasy he yearned to give.

Don't fight me, baby. Don't fight me. Let it happen.

Nell whimpered deep in her throat: little, plaintive sounds of delight and submission. She could feel him tug on her engorged breasts with his lips, making them swing in gentle rhythm with his movements. Borne on an ever-rising tide, unremitting breakers of sensual pleasure surged through her, sweeping away all rational thought as he drew each hardened nipple into his moist, warm mouth and flicked his tongue back and forth across its tight crest in exquisite seduction.

Her head drooped forward in graceful lassitude. The sight of him suckling her sent an enervating fever radiating from the core of her femininity outward to the furthermost tips of her fingers and toes. Consumed by a languor she'd never known before, she rested her hands on his upper arms and surrendered herself to his tutelage. Nell could feel the bunch and coil of his muscles beneath the plaid flannel shirt as he held her up in front of him as easily as if she were the little doll he called her.

Through the haze of sexual lethargy, she heard someone knocking as though from a great distance away. With supreme effort, she tried to focus her attention on the world beyond the two of them and the incredible sensations in which she was drowning.

Ross reacted instantly. Before she'd become fully aware of the noise outside, he'd already set her on her feet and was tucking the lacy hems back into the waistband of her skirt and smoothing her garments in place.

"Miss Ryan," a stranger's voice called through the closed door. "Are you there? It's the police, ma'am. I need to be speaking with you."

Dazed, Nell turned her head and stared at the entrance, as though expecting the peace officer to enter at once.

"Here," Ross said in a quiet, urgent voice, "put your jacket on and button it up. No one will know your shirtwaist is wrinkled." He held up the black suit jacket for her to slip on. Once she'd thrust her arms into the sleeves, he spun her around and fastened the row of brass buttons down the front with swift efficiency.

"You sit down and take a deep breath," he told her with a nod toward the chair, "while I go open the door."

"Is it locked?" she asked in confusion.

"Yes."

By the time he'd exchanged a brief greeting with the policeman, Nell was seated at the map table, her head bent over the open textbook. She turned and rose as the two men crossed the room. The warmth of a blush tinted her neck and cheeks with a rosy glow. As she moved with slow, deliberate grace to meet them, her eyes glittered with suppressed desire. Her lips, swollen from his kisses, curved up in a tremulous, forced smile of welcome for their unexpected visitor. Ross wondered if he'd ever get used to her electrifying beauty.

The officer, dressed in the uniform of the Butte police force, took off his cap and placed it under his arm. In his mid-forties, he had a thatch of graying black hair and an enormous, bristling mustache. If he was shocked to find an unmarried woman alone with a man behind a locked door, he gave no inkling, though his blue eyes twinkled in male understanding when he glanced at Ross.

"I'm Officer Barry Quinn, ma'am," he told her with consummate politeness. "Sure, and I'm sorry to be bothering you so late in the day now. But there's a prisoner at the jail that needs a lawyer. She says she's wanting you to defend her. And it's a good defense she'll be needing, too, I'm thinking."

"A . . . a lady?" Nell asked.

Quinn squinted and rubbed his chin. "Well, as to her being a lady or no, I'll not be saying. But Lottie Howard has just been arrested for theft. She's being booked for felony robbery right now. She begged me to ask you to come as quickly as possible."

"Certainly, officer. I'll come right away."

"I'll take you there," said Ross. He stepped closer, making it apparent he had no intention of allowing her to go without him. "Our coach was just arriving out front when I let Officer Quinn in."

Her mouth drawn into a tight line, Nell glanced away, then forced herself to meet his steady gaze. By now, she'd had time to regain her composure. She'd also had time to start feeling guilty. And to start placing blame.

"Very well," she agreed reluctantly.

"In that case," Quinn said, putting on his hat, "I'll be heading along home now. I was just going off duty when I agreed to give you Lottie's message." He touched the brim of his hat and left.

Without a word, Ross waited for Nell to gather her handbag, hat, and gloves. Then he took her elbow and guided her out to the waiting carriage. He helped her up the step to the cab, called directions to the driver, and joined her inside. When he tried to sit down next to her, she immediately moved to the opposite seat.

"Nell . . ." he began the moment the coach lurched forward.

"Don't say it, Morgan," she interrupted, her stilted words raw with a deep, inner pain. "Don't try to apologize. You don't have to explain anything. The fact that you had the foresight and the confidence to lock the office door conveys it all." She met his gaze, her eyes narrowed with anger and mortification. "How could you be so sure?"

"I wasn't, sweetheart," he admitted huskily. "I only hoped."

Her chin jerked up as though he'd slapped her. "This must never happen again," she said. "I want your promise on that."

He shook his head slowly. "Nell, you know I can't make that promise. Good Lord, girl, I've wanted you from the moment I met you. Surely you know that."

"Then I shall arrange it so we're never alone together. When Gavin leaves the office in the afternoon, I'll have him escort me back to the boardinghouse." Tearing her gaze from his, she looked down at her lap, where she clutched her things with whitened fingers. She removed the hatpin from her bonnet, placed the confection of black feathers and silk rosettes on top of her head, and replaced the pin with an angry jab.

Ross leaned forward and rested his elbows on his knees. His words were hoarse and urgent.. "Nell, don't do this."

"I mean it, Morgan." She pulled on her black kid gloves with quick, furious little tugs. "Either I have your solemn oath that nothing like this will ever happen again, or I swear to God, we'll never be alone together for as much as a second."

"You don't mean it," he contradicted. "If you can't be honest with me, at least be honest with yourself. You crave the touch of my hands on your flesh for the same reason you enjoy the feel of those silken undies on your naked skin. You're filled with sensual passion."

She shot him a killing glance. "My body, yes," she hissed, "but not my mind. Not my intellect. Only my foolish emotions."

"Trust your emotions, Nell."

"I can't!"

They stared at each other in stubborn silence. Suddenly, her eyes pooled with moisture, and a single teardrop slid down her cheek. It was the closest she'd come to divulging the sorrow he'd sensed she kept hidden deep in her heart.

"I'm not him, little girl," he told her softly. "Who-ever that blackhearted bastard was who hurt you so badly, I'm not him."

She sank back against the seat, clearly stricken by his insight into her private secrets. For a fleet-ing second, he glimpsed an almost childlike fear of discovery in her eyes. Then she smiled with bitter irony. "For someone who's not a bastard, you're cer-tainly behaving like one."

He raised his open palms in surrender. "All right, darlin', all right. I've rushed you along too fast. I'll slow down. You have my word."

"Very well," she agreed, looking out the window into the dark street, as if she couldn't stand the sight of him. "I'll accept your promise. We'll continue to work together. But don't worry about pushing me along too fast, because the two of us aren't going anywhere."

"Nell, look at me," he commanded.

Without turning her head, she moved her eyes to meet his.

"I know you're upset about what happened between us this evenin'. But you're so goddamn beautiful, I couldn't help myself."

Her head snapped around. She leaned toward him, rigid with fury. "Don't say that," she nearly shouted. "It's bad enough that you continue to use those trite endearments all the time. Don't try to manipulate me with your conniving flattery. You'll find I'm not as easy to fool as some lovestruck young girl."

Ross leaned back against the leather seat, regard-ing her thoughtfully. In her burst of spleen, she'd given away far more than she realized. "If you've ever looked in a mirror, Miss Ryan," he said with quiet gravity, "you know darn well you're beauti-ful. To say so can hardly be considered connivin' flattery."

But she'd recognized her error. She sat across from him for the rest of the ride to the city jail in stiff-backed silence. Wondering, no doubt, just how much of her past she'd disclosed with her outburst of temper. And why on earth had Letitia Howard asked for her as a legal counselor?

Chapter 11

***

The madam wasn't at all what Nell had expected. A woman who ran a bawdy house was supposed to be grossly fat, with an enormous white bosom that spilled over the top of her stained gown, bleached hair that resembled mildewed straw, and a garishly painted face with a cigarette hanging from her scarlet lips. Nell asked herself why she'd ever believed such a thing. She'd never met a prostitute in her life until she came to Butte. Back in Massachusetts, ladies of the night didn't attempt to retain the costly legal services of Ryan, Sheehy, and O'Connell.

But the attractive woman who stood in the open doorway of the big brick house on Mercury Street was neither overweight nor stained with cosmetics. Tall and slim, with strawberry-blond hair, intelligent blue eyes, and faultless posture, she was attired in a stunning pink-and-white morning gown that could have come directly from Paris. She welcomed Nell and her escort into the bordello with a graceful gesture of her manicured hand.

"Y'all come on in," she said in a rich, contralto voice. She was in her mid-forties and spoke with an unhurried Southern accent. The huskiness was probably from years of smoking, Nell decided, though there wasn't a cigarette in sight. That and the carmine fingernails were the only things about the procuress that fulfilled her expectations. The mint julep drawl was in all likelihood counterfeit.

"I'm Althea Grigsby," the woman continued, once they stood inside the spacious entryway and she'd closed the door behind them. "It's nice t' meet you, Miss Ryan. Lottie's told me how kind you've been t' her." Mrs. Grigsby offered her hand in a polite but not overly friendly gesture, and Nell shook it.

Over her hostess's shoulder, she could read a lacquered sign which hung on the blue-and-white-striped wallpaper.

The Magnolia Blossom
Home of the Most Beautiful Girls
in the World

The madam turned her attention on her other visitor. "Ross," she cooed. On her lips, his name was two syllables long and steeped in the essence of crushed magnolia petals. She favored him with a coy smile of recognition.

"Thea," he replied with a perfunctory nod. "It's good of you to let us come."

Mrs. Grigsby lifted her eyebrows and shrugged, as though to declare, "Whyever not? You've been here plenty o' times before." With a hint of amusement lighting her eyes, she turned and led the way through a pair of sliding double doors that stood open to an adjoining room. "Now that you're here, y'all might as well come on into the parlor and sit down," she called over her shoulder. "I had Juniper Jess run up t' tell Lottie you'd arrived when we heard the bell ring. This early in the day, I knew it had to be you. That's why I answered the door myself."

The parlor was even more of a shock to Nell than its owner. Decorated in exquisite taste, it could have been the drawing room of one of Boston's wealthiest shipping magnates, though it wasn't done in Hepplewhite or Chippendale, but in a pleasing mixture of Louis Quatorze and Empire. Not garish reproductions either, but graceful furniture that could easily have passed for genuine antiques. White and gold and pale blue predominated, with touches of coral.

At Mrs. Grigsby's invitation, Nell sank down on a satin couch and looked around in amazement at the yards and yards of ice-blue drapery that swathed the tall windows on two sides of the room. From the high ceiling hung an enormous bronze chandelier that would have taken a maid an entire afternoon to dust and polish. She decided belatedly that the intricate knob and key plate on the massive front door really had been solid silver, after all.

Women who worked in this type of establishment were commonly referred to as soiled doves. Yet in her unadorned gray walking suit, she was the one who looked like a plain, drab pigeon, while the proprietress resembled a brilliant flamingo. With an inner grimace, Nell wondered why she'd decided to wear her most businesslike outfit. But she already knew the answer. She'd garbed herself for this excursion like a Puritan about to ferry the River Styx to rescue a lost soul.

"I'm originally from New Orleans," Mrs. Grigsby explained with undiluted Rebel pride, as Nell gawked openly at the room and its contents. "That's where I learned my trade. I always loved the beautiful homes in the Old Quarter. When I was successful enough t' furnish my own place the way I wanted to, I did it just like some o' the mansions I'd seen."

"It's a lovely room," Nell said lamely, unwilling to ask how the woman had managed to get so much as a peek inside the homes of the wealthy. She gulped, scarcely able to believe they were talking about the decor of a brothel like two housewives admiring a fine set of china. Or that its owner had serenely referred to her early years of pandering as *learning her trade.*

Mrs. Grigsby, who'd remained standing at Morgan's side, swooped up a cigar case from a 'spindle-legged table, opened the carved ivory lid, and offered its contents to her male guest. "Ross, honey," she coaxed, "wouldn't you like a pana-tela?"

"No, thanks."

She snapped the box shut with a complacent shrug. Nell had never seen Morgan smoke. Apparently, Althea Grigsby knew him much better than she.

"Well, then, I'll leave you two alone for a few minutes," their hostess said. She absently fluffed the rows of gathered Chantilly lace that adorned her gown's big puffed sleeves just below the elbows. "There are a few things I need t' take care of this morning. We had a busy time of it last night. Lottie will be down in a moment, I'm sure." She left the room in a swirl of pink silk and white lace.

With his hands shoved into his trouser pockets, Morgan prowled across the room's thick Persian rug, clearly ill at ease. He could have found a place to sit down without much effort. The room was filled with available spots. There was a love seat and two parlor chairs upholstered in blue satin with gilded white wood to match the sofa, as well as half a dozen or so smaller reception chairs. The large drawing room was obviously meant to accommo-date a crowd.

Like Nell, Morgan had also chosen to wear a somber color that morning. The finely tailored black suit fit his broad shoulders and narrow hips to per-fection. He'd ruthlessly combed his golden-brown hair back from his brow in an attempt to conquer its natural waves. In the costly business clothes and slicked-back hairstyle, he was the quintessen-tial millionaire copper baron. He should have taken the cigar. It would have added to the image of self-serving male greed he portrayed.

She hadn't missed the fact that the comely Mrs. Grigsby and the prosperous mine owner were already acquainted. How well, Nell couldn't guess and didn't want to find out. She'd been a naive idiot not to have realized why Morgan had so quickly and accurately identified the lovely young woman in the millinery shop as Lottie Luscious.

Not that she cared one whit.

Ross propped his elbow on the fireplace mantel and stared at the angry Miss Ryan, sitting as stiff and straight as a bishop's wife on Thea's fancy settee. He wondered how in the hell he'd ever square himself with her after this debacle was over. Since the night they'd gone to see Lottie in the basement of the city jail two weeks ago, Nell had barely spoken to him.

The lovely harlot had been so relieved to see them, she'd burst into tears when they walked up to the cell where she'd been kept since being arrested. She'd reached through the bars and clutched their hands in spontaneous and uninhibited joy before the jailer, who'd been hovering nearby, had put an immediate stop to any further physical contact.

It hadn't taken Nell longer than the blink of an eye to figure out that Ross and Miss Howard had been previously introduced. She'd canceled the cozy evenings of study in the law office forthwith.

He'd tried to smooth things over with Nell several times since then. It had been like trying to romance a drift of solid granite. Hell, he could hardly come right out and apologize for having frequented a whorehouse on a regular basis up until she'd arrived in Butte.

Somehow, he didn't think she'd be impressed with the fact that he hadn't lain with a woman since the day he met her. It wasn't something you blurted out across the boardinghouse supper table. And damn it to hell and back, that was about the only time he got to see her anymore. They were never alone together for longer than a few minutes at a time. Just when she'd started to bloom under his slow, careful tutoring, this brouhaha had erupted and taken the two of them all the way back to square one. Nell had closed up like a tight little rosebud. All he was likely to get now, should he reach for her, was the sharp prick of a thorn. Or a bite on the hand from her even white teeth. Well, that scenario had its possibilities, he admitted, barely able to keep from grinning at the mental image he'd conjured up.

Lottie had been released from jail four days after her arrest, thanks to Nell, who'd been present at the arraignment as her defense attorney, and to Thea, who'd sent Juniper Jess with the money to post bail. Now, ten days later, Nell had come to the brothel to question Lottie. This would be the final chance to review the incidents leading up to the charges filed against her prior to her appearance before the magistrate that afternoon. Ross intended to go with them to the Silver Bow Courthouse for the preliminary hearing—no matter what Nell said.

When he'd first learned that Nell actually planned to visit the parlor house that morning, he'd tried to talk her out of it. She'd remained intransigent, so he'd insisted on taking her there. During the ride in the hack, she'd delivered a scathing tirade, informing him with ear-curling frankness that his presence as her escort was completely uninvited, unnecessary, and unwanted.

"There was no need for you to come with me this morning," Nell fired at him from her place on the sofa, as though she could read his thoughts. She tapped her slender fingers on the black handbag resting in her lap with unconcealed annoyance. "I told you at breakfast I planned on taking a trolley to the corner of Main and Galena and then simply asking directions to the Magnolia Blossom from there."

He nearly exploded again at the thought of it— just as he'd done earlier that day in Hertta's kitchen. His fury had been fueled by a very real fear for her safety. He'd informed her in no uncertain terms that the mining camp's red-light district was one hell of a place for a virtuous woman to go walking. Even in the morning. Once the sun went down, it was a preacher's nightmare. Galena Street was crowded with men, young and old, who wandered up and down the line, past girls of all races and creeds boldly soliciting from doorways and open windows.

"You shouldn't have come here at all," he retorted, "and you goddamn well know it."

"I need to question my client about several matters," she told him with an aggrieved toss of her head. "If I'm going to build an adequate defense, I have to gather as much information as possible, including the knowledge of Miss Howard's working environment and her . . . ah, fellow workers."

Ross couldn't keep from snorting in derision. "Don't try to bluff me, angel eyes. There was no need for you to see the Blossom firsthand. Lottie could have met you at your office on Montana and answered all your questions there."

From the corner of her eye, Nell could see Morgan standing in front of the brick fireplace, with one shoulder propped against the marble mantelpiece and his sinewy arms folded across his chest. He was glaring at her in ferocious disapproval.

"Had I realized you were so familiar with this establishment and its occupants," she retaliated with icy scorn, "I could have saved myself some time and simply questioned you."

Before he could answer, a delicate, auburn-haired creature in a lime-green boudoir gown peeked into the room. "Oh, hi, Colorado!" she called with a plucky grin. "You're here bright and early."

Morgan straightened and took a small step forward. "Hello, Jess," he said. He scowled and fiddled with the knot of his black neck scarf as though it were suddenly too tight.

The girl, who looked no more than eighteen or nineteen, started to enter the room, then saw Nell on the sofa and halted. Hesitating, she stood just inside the doorway, apparently too shy to intrude, though how anyone in her profession could be bashful was beyond Nell's ken.

"Serious business about Lottie, huh?" Jess said to Morgan, raising her dark, penciled brows for emphasis. Her pale green eyes matched her flowing bedroom apparel to perfection. If she were a celebrated actress on the stage, she couldn't have been lovelier. So far, it seemed the sign on the entry wall was one hundred percent correct.

Morgan nodded to her in silent agreement.

"Well, I'll see you later," Jess added with a guileless shrug of her shoulders. As though suddenly aware of the implications of what she'd just said, she burst into a high-pitched giggle, then winked impishly and scurried away.

Nell refused to meet his eyes. She knew Morgan was watching her smallest reaction with his usual shrewd regard. He probably *would* see Juniper Jess later. To tell the truth and shame the devil, he seemed to be on intimate terms with everyone in the place.

"Nell . . ." he began in a coaxing tone.

"Miss Ryan, I'm so glad you're here," Lottie called with relief as she came through the open sliding doors. "Hello, Ross," she added with a wan smile before sitting down on the cushion beside Nell. "Thanks for coming today. Both of you." She clasped her hands together on her lap, inhaled audibly, and then released her breath with a ragged sigh. "Oh, lordy, I'm a bundle of nerves this morning. I've never been hauled into court before. Thea always takes care of everything with the police. They leave us alone as long as they get their protection fees on a regular basis."

She met Nell's gaze, and a worried crease appeared between her ebony brows. "I dressed just like you told me to, ma'am. One of the other girls even helped me with my hair. Ye gads, I hope I look okay."

Nell patted her client's hand in reassurance. "If that's your most conservative dress, then it will have to do." She'd hoped for something in charcoal or navy, but the teal-blue was becoming without being gaudy or vulgar. Thankfully, Lottie's marvelous black tresses were pulled into a tight, schoolteacher's bun at the back of her neck. "Your hair is perfect," Nell added. She smiled encouragingly. "I can't believe you got all those wonderful curls smashed down so effectively. However, that bonnet will have to go."

Lottie reached up and gingerly touched her wide-brimmed hat's fantastic array of shimmering teal and emerald peacock feathers. "But it matches my dress," she exclaimed. "And I sure as heck don't own anything less colorful."

Nell pondered for a moment on the wisdom of allowing Lottie to arrive at the courthouse looking so vivacious. She wanted the young woman to appear lovely. That wouldn't hurt in a nearly all-male environment. But a *penitent* lovely. A flamboyant coquette wouldn't make the right impression on that irascible judge they'd met on the day of the arraignment. Reaching up to her own head, Nell withdrew a hatpin and lifted down the flat-crowned felt she was wearing. "Here, put this on," she suggested. "It's plain, but it'll serve our purposes much better."

Clearly dismayed, Lottie rolled her eyes at Morgan, who'd crossed the room and sat down on a nearby armchair. "Gray with teal?" she said. "I don't think—"

"Do as Miss Ryan says," he ordered with unconscious authority. "She's only tryin' to help you." At his words, Lottie reluctantly complied.

"What will you wear, Miss Ryan?" she asked, suddenly aware of Nell's plight. Neither of them could appear at the hearing without some type of head covering, any more than they could go uptown without their gloves and handbags. Some things just weren't done. Not even by trollops and lady lawyers.

"Since we don't have time to return to my boardinghouse, it looks like I'm going to be wearing your bonnet." Nell looked down at the brilliant peacock feathers and smiled wryly.

Lottie was incredulous. "Won't everyone guess that we switched? After all, your suit will match the hat I'm wearing, and my gown will go with your bonnet."

Chuckling ruefully, Nell placed the feathered headpiece atop her own smooth chignon. "Every woman present—and there'll be mighty few of those—will know exactly what we did. But the magistrate won't have a clue, mark my words. The only male in the entire courtroom who'll know of our subterfuge is Mr. Morgan, and that's only because he's seen us make the exchange."

"Now, I resent that comment," he drawled goodnaturedly. The charm of his lazy, sideways grin was irresistible. "I may look like a simpleminded mucker from the Comstock, but I'm not color blind."

Lottie gave a peal of laughter. "You two are the least simpleminded people I know," she protested. "That's why you make such a natural pair. Sorta like the King and Queen of Hearts."

"Why, thank you, Lottie," Morgan replied. He turned his head to meet Nell's startled gaze, and his green eyes glinted with more than just amusement. His deep voice was low and taunting. "I kinda feel the same way myself."

"Letitia, I want to go over what happened one more time before we leave for the hearing," Nell stated abruptly, ignoring the warmth of his steady regard and the answering thrum of her heart. "But first, I want to give you a chance to reconsider having me represent you in court. I'm not a criminal attorney, as I've already pointed out several times. I've worked alongside my uncle in corporate law as his assistant. I've never defended anyone in a criminal trial. You'd be much better off to retain a counselor with some experience in that field."

"No, ma'am, I wouldn't," Lottie announced with conviction. "You're the only lawyer I'd trust. What man would do anything more than collect his fee? That is, if I could even find one willing to represent me, let alone someone who believed I was truly innocent."

"All right, if it's what you want, I'll do my best to defend you. Now, let's go over again all the events leading up to the night you were arrested. I know you were in the train station because you planned to leave Butte that evening. Aside from Lucas Dills, had you told anyone what you were going to do? Think carefully. It's important."

Lottie's slim shoulders drooped in discouragement. "No, ma'am, I never said a word to a single soul but that lousy, two-bit gambler. Not even Thea."

"Why not?"

"I didn't want anyone trying to persuade me to stay. I just wanted to up and leave it all behind. The only reason I even told Lucky was that I was so blasted excited. I couldn't keep it from spilling out of me. I had to tell someone or burst."

"Had you seen Mr. Dills before that evening?"

"Oh, sure. Lucky was one of my regular customers. I thought he was sweet on me. Shows how much I know about men." Her words were filled with self-mockery.

"I see," said Nell thoughtfully, attempting to approach the subject of bawdy-house patrons with the same matter-of-fact attitude as Lottie. But the presence of the virile man sitting across from them didn't help her sense of dispassionate objectivity. "Would you have had trouble leaving the Magnolia Blossom, if you'd told any of the other girls?"

"No."

"Would Mrs. Grigsby have tried to keep you here by force?"

Lottie shrugged. "I don't think so. It's just that quitting this line of work doesn't happen too often."

She placed one hand beside her mouth and whispered dramatically. "The money's too dang good."

"Then what made you decide to give it up?"

"You, ma'am."

"Me?"

"Yes'm. That day you were so kind to me in the La Mode Chapeau, I came straight back here and bawled my eyes out. Since I started working on the line, no one decent like you has ever treated me so all-fired nice. I decided then and there, I was going home and start all over with a clean slate."

Nell was deeply moved by the girl's words. "Where's home, Letitia?"

"Des Moines. My sister still lives there. I was going to stay with Fanny and her husband till I got settled and could support myself."

"What were you goin' to do for a livin'?" Morgan asked curiously.

Lottie's black eyes sparkled. "Open a hat shop with the money I'd saved. Miss Ryan gave me the idea when she said I had a special talent for choosing the right bonnet."

"That brings us to the funds you had on your person when you were arrested," Nell said. "A thousand dollars is an enormous amount for anyone to be carrying around with her."

"I earned that money, Miss Ryan," Lottie cried. "Every penny of it!" Her slender hand flew to her throat in dismay. She was clearly frightened that her savings might never be returned to her. "I've worked here at the Magnolia Blossom for three and a half years."

Nell couldn't keep the pessimism from her voice. "It's going to be awfully hard to convince the judge at the hearing today that you accumulated a thousand dollars in such a short time."

The stunning brunet clenched her fists in frustration. Her words were laced with bitter sarcasm. "I don't know why, for Pete's sake. Everybody knows where I live and what I've been doing to earn it.

Heck, in this mining camp, any worn-out floozy can make sixty dollars a night, easy."

Morgan quietly intervened. "Did you tell Lucas Dills how much you were taking to Des Moines with you?"

"Yes, and I could cut my tongue out for blabbing like that," she moaned. "But he was always giving me pretty compliments and calling me sugar. He's a good-looker too, dressed to the nines, and real friendly-like. Never a mean word. A sweet-talking smoothie, if you know the type."

Nell knew the type all too well, but made no comment. "Tell me exactly what happened at the depot."

"I was just about to buy my ticket when Officer Quinn came up and asked to see my handbag. When he didn't find but a few dollars, he asked me to hand over the small satchel I was carrying. It was plenty heavy 'cause it was filled with twenty-dollar gold pieces. The moment Quinn took it, I knew I was in trouble. He took one look inside and said he was arresting me for stealing from Lucas Dills. He said Lucky claimed he'd won a thousand dollars in a poker game the evening before, and that I'd agreed to hold it for him overnight, till he could put it safely in a bank. It seems Lucky had gone to the police station earlier that evening and accused me of trying to leave town with his winnings."

Morgan leaned forward in his seat, his arms braced on his knees. "Did anyone see you with the thousand before that time, Lottie?"

She frowned and shook her head. "Nobody. Not a blessed soul. I even kept it a secret from Juniper Jess and Buffy." She looked up at Nell and smiled sadly. "They're my best friends."

"Did you write to your sister to tell her you were coming?" Nell asked with a measure of hope.

Lottie moved back slightly on the sofa cushion and wrapped her arms around her waist, as though in physical pain. She lowered her lashes to hide her thoughts. "No."

Nell persisted, quiet but firm. "You sent her a telegram, didn't you?"

Lottie's gaze flew to meet her attorney's narrowed eyes. "I don't want Fanny involved in this! I'd rather go to prison for twenty years than have my sister suffer the shame of admitting in public that she's related to a whore."

"Did you tell her about the money and your plan to open a millinery store?"

"It don't make a bit of difference what I told her. She's too timid and shy to appear in court, anyway. Besides, her husband is a Methodist minister. That would just about take the cake, wouldn't it? A preacher's wife appearing on the witness stand to defend a harlot!" Lottie clamped her jaws shut and pursed her lips in obstinate refusal.

"Your sister may not feel that way about it," Morgan suggested. "Did you notify her of your arrest?"

The young woman shook her head. "I had Jess send a telegram for me while I was still in jail, saying I'd changed my mind after all. Fanny doesn't know about my trouble. And that's the way I want it to stay."

"Her appearance in court could be the only thing standing between you and a verdict of guilty," Nell warned.

"I don't want my sister to know anything about this mess."

Nell decided to accede to her client's request, at least for the time being. If the judge at the preliminary hearing found there was enough evidence to hold Lottie to answer the charges, she might have to go against the young woman's wishes—for her own best interest.

"Well, Miss Howard," Nell said, "as it stands now, this is what we're up against." She ticked off the points on her gloved fingers. "Number one, nobody—other than Fanny—can verify your claim that you were going home, because you told no one except Dills about your plans. Two, nobody can confirm that you actually had that much money, because you kept it a secret. And three, you hadn't as yet purchased the ticket to Iowa, so we can't even use that as evidence of your intentions to return to the bosom of your family and seek a better way of life. For all we can prove, you might have been heading for Seattle or Denver. Or San Francisco and the Barbary Coast."

"It ain't good, is it?" Lottie asked in a hoarse whisper. A solitary tear rolled down her pale cheek.

"It sounds like it's going to be your word against the gambler's," Morgan answered quietly. He met Nell's gaze as though hoping she'd contradict him.

"And who in the Sam Hill is going to believe me?" Lottie wailed. She buried her face in her trembling hands.

"I believe you," Nell said. "If we can't convince the judge of your innocence at the hearing today, then we'll just have to convince the jury at the trial." She rose from the blue satin sofa and looked from one worried person to the other with calm resolution. "Now let's go uptown to the courthouse and meet with that magistrate."

Chapter 12

"**D**on't be discouraged," Hertta said complacently. She poured a dipper full of water on the large heated stones before climbing the shallow stairs to place a bucket of hot water on the wooden platform beside Nell. "Just because t'at idiot Judge Long ruled t'at Lottie Howard has to stand trial doesn't mean she von't get a fair one. Ta people in t'is mining camp von't hold her profession against her."

"I find that hard to believe," replied Nell, gasping for breath as the steam ascended toward the pine ceiling above them in billowing clouds. Despite all her efforts, the magistrate had ruled at the preliminary hearing that there was enough evidence to hold Lottie to answer the charge of grand theft. "The twelve men on that jury will probably sit in judgment of my client as though not one of them has ever done anything to feel guilty about. Righteous men are notorious for their public pillorying of fallen women. Yet they or their fellow man are the ones responsible for her degradation in the first place. You can be sure Lottie's initial descent into her present state of ill repute took place in a very private setting, so the man's own willing participation could be kept a secret."

Hertta splashed another dipper of hot water on the sauna stones that had been placed on top of the wood-burning iron stove. The steam burst forth in a hissing vapor.

Soaked with perspiration, Nell blinked, gasped

again, and then moaned out loud, certain she could
hear the warmed blood rushing through her veins.
"Don't you think that's a little too much heat?" she
queried. "I feel like I'm being boiled alive. Bless us
and save us, I keep looking around for the canni-
bals."

Tossing the long flaxen braid that dangled in front
of her bare breast back over her shoulder, Hertta
smiled serenely. "Ta sauna can't be too hot, Nellie.
I'm trying to keep ta temperature a little bit lower
for your sake." She sat down on the wooden bench
and handed her guest a lump of soft soap and a
rough cotton cloth.

The two women were in the small frame building
attached to the back of Kuusinen's Boardinghouse.
Hertta had explained to Nell that it was called a
sauna in Finnish, although the other residents of
the copper camp referred to it with ignorant and
scornful derision as a "Finn bath." The landlady had
shown Nell how to use the sauna the first week she'd
arrived in Butte. Since the male residents took over
the bathhouse every Saturday night without fail,
and Kalle and his wife used it together every Friday
after supper, Nell had begun the ritual of bathing
in the sauna on Sunday evenings. Maija, Fetsi, and
Hertta would sometimes join her, if they were able
to squeeze time away from their household chores.
The serving girls spoke little English. They would
simply smile and beam at Nell through the steamy
mist in companionable Finnish silence. When the
landlady bathed with her, she and Hertta would
sit on one of the wooden benches that resembled
bleachers and gossip like a pair of old crones. Hertta
had once explained that her and Kalle's unusual
talkativeness stemmed from the fact that both their
mothers hailed from the province of Karelia, whose
people were known to be notorious chatterboxes in
a country where taciturnity was a way of life.

Nell soon learned that the Finns, who were bashful to a fault in every other aspect of their life,

thought nothing of being seen in their natural state while using the sauna. It wasn't long before she overcame her innate shyness with the other women, whose matter-of-fact acceptance of the human body as something everyone has and certainly nothing to be embarrassed about, quickly put her at ease. Hertta assured her that mixed bathing of adults, other than members of a family, never took place. Still, Nell fretted about the accidental intrusion of some unsuspecting man. So in deference to her guest's worries, Hertta made a large, handwritten sign in Finnish, which Nell could place on the outer door of the dressing room, to ensure complete privacy from the male boarders and still allow the other ladies to join her at their convenience. Before long, everyone at Kuusinen's knew that on Sunday nights the sauna was reserved for ladies only.

"What I have to do," Nell continued, as her thoughts returned to Lottie's upcoming trial, "is convince those twelve good men and true that Letitia Howard had made an irrevocable decision to reform her life just before she was arrested on those trumped-up charges. If the jury can be convinced that she was, indeed, going back home to her sister in Iowa, it will be that much easier to convince them that she was carrying money that she herself had earned." Absently, Nell gathered the wet strands of her loosened hair into one thick clump behind her neck and then let it fall free down her back. She recalled with chagrin the beautiful girl's adamant refusal to involve her sister, Fanny. "However tainted that money might be," Nell added tersely, "it wasn't stolen from some cheating, lying, sonofagun gambler."

"You can convince them, if anyone can," Hertta said. Her fair skin glistened with moisture. Although her big-boned frame glowed with health, her usual boundless energy appeared slowly to dissipate. That wasn't surprising. Nell had discovered that, as the radiant heat of the sauna walls began to penetrate her taut muscles, it brought with it a feeling of complete relaxation.

Tilting her head back, she draped the wet washcloth over her nose and breathed through it. "How can you say that?" she asked in a muffled voice, enjoying the languorous sensation of total well-being that engulfed her. She felt as though she were floating on a warm, puffy cloud. "You've never even seen me in court."

Through the swirling vapor, Hertta's twin dimples flashed at Nell. "I've seen you enough to know t'at you can do anyt'ing you want to do."

"Hmm, I wish I could agree with you." Nell dipped the soap into the bucket of hot water and lathered the cotton cloth. "Somehow, I don't think I'll feel quite that invincible before the magistrate. Especially in a criminal trial. And without my Uncle Cormac sitting right beside me."

After Nell had scrubbed herself, Hertta poured hot water over the top of her bent head. In the process of bathing Finnish style, pails of water were splashed over the bathers, over the wooden platforms and stairs, over just about everything. Nell could feel her flushed skin tingling as Hertta threw more water on the red-hot stones. The temperature spiraled upward with the steam.

"How is your verk for Ross going?" Hertta asked, settling back down on the bench beside Nell.

"Fair," she answered truthfully. "We succeeded in getting a lengthy postponement of the court date. That means we'll at least have more time to get ready."

What she didn't say was that she and Gavin had bumped heads repeatedly in their preparations for the coming apex litigation. Time and again, she'd been forced to appeal to Ross Morgan for a final decision, since her colleague never seemed to concur with any of her suggestions. On each occasion, after listening thoughtfully to both of their arguments, Morgan had sided with Nell. She'd been certain he'd balk at the idea of a further postponement, especially considering the fact that all mining at the Glamorgan was enjoined till after the case was settled. To her surprise, he'd gone along with her wishes. It was also decided that they'd bring in expert witnesses to testify on behalf of the Glamorgan and its owner, just as she'd wanted to do from the very beginning. Once he'd heard her explanation of their possible importance, Morgan had immediately telegraphed a professor at the Columbia School of Mines. Dr. Adolph Gunter had agreed to come to Butte and make an assessment of the copper mine. They were expecting his arrival within two weeks. Another consultant, Morris Yandel, was an acquaintance of Morgan's from earlier days, when they'd worked together as mining engineers. Yandel was coming from the mine fields of Coeur d'Alene to survey the Glamorgan and render his opinion to the court.

When Gavin had heard Ross's decision, he'd been furious. Nell suspected it was her partner's injured pride, rather than any real belief it was a mistake in legal strategy, that had made him so angry. But her friend had gone off in a huff that afternoon, leaving Morgan to escort her back to their boardinghouse.

Lately, Nell had found herself in Ross Morgan's company more and more often. What was worse, he was beginning to show up in her dreams. Night after night, he kissed and touched her intimately, just as he'd done on the evening Lottie Howard was arrested. All too frequently Nell awoke in her darkened bedroom, tortured by desire. Even during the daytime, she was racked with an ever-increasing sense of physical and emotional frustration. Confused by the emptiness and lack of fulfillment that seemed to gnaw at her continuously, she discovered, to her horror, that it took no more than his brushing up against her to leave her aching for his touch. The thought of Morgan holding Lottie or Juniper Jess or that sophisticated madam from New Orleans in his arms, naked and writhing with pleasure, was driving her to the brink of insanity. How often had he returned to that notorious bagnio on Mercury Street since the day he'd accompanied her there two weeks ago?

"Hertta," she began awkwardly, "does a man have a need to be with a woman . . . ah, that is, to sleep with a woman . . . frequently?"

The married lady's cornflower-blue eyes glowed with merriment. "I suppose you mean an able-bodied man in his early t'irties?"

Nell's gaze dropped to the washcloth clutched in her hands. "Well, more or less."

"Ya," came Hertta's simple reply.

"Even if he feels nothing for the female? If all that drives him is his own personal motives, whatever they might be?"

"I t'ink for a man, sometimes all t'at does drive him is his physical needs. Unless marriage is in ta picture, he can't satisfy t'at need vith a respectable girl vithout compromising her reputation. So he consorts vith vomen who verk in parlor houses, until he meets someone who means a whole lot more to him t'an just satisfying his fleshly desires."

"Can't he do without it, until he meets her?"

"For a vhile, I'm sure he can. But if a man t'inks he's not going to marry, at least in ta near future, I suspect he'd be pretty uncomfortable denying his sexual needs for veeks, months, even years at a time."

Nell wiped away the droplets of sweat that stood above her top lip, while she silently digested that intriguing piece of information.

"Don't be too hard on Ross," Hertta urged with irritating composure. "If he patronized ta Magnolia Blossom on a regular basis, he did no more t'an ta other bachelors in t'is mining camp. As you've surely noticed, t'ere's a real scarcity of vomenfolk. Add to t'at ta fact t'at no man of honor vould ruin an innocent girl, and it's no vonder Venus Alley is such a t'riving concern."

Nell purposely diverted the topic of conversation, unwilling to discuss any further Ross's familiarity with the copper camp's red-light district and its sporting women. "This hell-raising town never sleeps, does it?" she asked with a chuckle. "When I first arrived, I thought it was the ugliest, meanest place on the face of the earth. Little by little, I've become fascinated by its people. I've never seen such a diversity of nationalities crowded together, all living and working at such a frenetic pace."

She'd seen mobs of men, some still in their sturdy miner's clothes, crowding day and night into the saloons and gaming establishments, where they played at faro, craps, stud poker, and roulette. But gambling and prostitution weren't the city's only pastimes. In the last few days, Nell had seen posters advertising a new feature attraction at the Comique Theater. Her curiosity to see a burlesque house had been piqued by the blatant advertisements of the latest variety show, starring Eddie Foy and Eva Tanguay, nailed to the camp's tall board fences and along the walls of its commercial buildings. If there was one thing Nell loved, it was a stage performance of any kind.

Hertta handed her a bundle of birch leaves tied up with twine. Following the landlady's example, Nell dipped the *vihta* into a pail of hot water and let it drip onto the hot rocks, where the drops sizzled and popped, releasing a sweet, pungent, aromatic steam. She struck herself lightly with the bouquet of leaves, till her lobster-pink skin, already aglow with the intense heat, was stinging pleasurably.

Then Hertta descended the steps and went into the small outer room, where they'd shed their clothes and left them in neat piles. She brought back a pail of cold water and splashed it over Nell, who screamed and laughed in startled delight. "You Finns are the craziest people in the world," Nell protested through gulps of vaporous air. But the water actually felt warm on her overheated skin.

"Ya, ya, we are t'at," Hertta agreed, just before she poured a second bucketful over herself. "And ta cleanest, too. Now if ve vere back in Finland, ve'd be jumping in ta ice-cold lake or rolling in a snowbank. Here, ve have to settle for a tub of cold vater."

Despite her yelps of surprise, Nell thoroughly enjoyed the sauna. Near the platform stood a big wooden tub filled with cold water in which she'd soon be immersing herself. Then after wrapping up in a warm robe, she'd scoot up the back stairs to her room and sleep through the night as soundly as a baby. She'd decided that she'd never felt so clean as after her Sunday evening ritual. When she went home to Boston, she was going to explore the possibility of building a little bathhouse at the back of Uncle Cormac's spacious lot. Aunt Lydia would be scandalized at first, but once she'd learned what a marvelous thing a sauna was, Nell was certain she'd change her mind.

"Have you seen the posters for the comedy show at the Comique?" she asked her friend with studied nonchalance. She wondered if Hertta would be shocked to learn that she wanted to visit a music hall.

"How could I miss t'em? T'ey are all over town."

"I thought it might be fun to see Eddie Foy," Nell mused out loud, hoping Hertta would offer to go with her. "He's supposed to be terribly clever. They call him the prince of comedy. I mentioned it to Gavin yesterday, but he wasn't a bit interested. The show's only going to be in Butte two nights. I know I couldn't go there alone."

"Vhy don't you ask Ross to take you?"

Startled, Nell looked into her landlady's intelligent eyes. "I couldn't do that!"

"Vhy not? My bet is t'at he'd take you to ta Arctic Circle, if you told him you vanted to see ta Eskimos."

"Well, I just couldn't ask him, that's all."

"T'en I guess you'll never know vhat you missed," replied Hertta with seeming indifference.

Nell couldn't help but feel there was a deeper meaning to Hertta's words. Springing to her feet, Nell made her way carefully down the slippery wooden steps and climbed into the big oaken tub filled with cold water. She dunked her entire body, head and all, beneath the surface, determined to erase the memory of Rossiter Morgan's fiery kisses, or drown herself trying.

Ross adjusted his wire-rimmed spectacles further up on the bridge of his nose and leaned over Nell's shoulder. She was seated at his drafting table on a tall three-legged stool. From his spot directly behind her, he pointed to a jagged line that ran down the length of the survey map. "There's the vein we found in June. Here's our station at the twelve-hundred foot level. And here's the outer wall of the Glamorgan."

"I see," she said. She traced the heavy black mark with the tip of her slender finger. "I've been carefully reading the books my uncle sent out for Gavin and me to study. Mineral law, as confirmed by the federal statutes of '66 and '72, gives the locator of a vein or lode the right to follow it, with all its dips, angles, and variations, downward to any depth beyond the sidelines, provided that its top or apex is enclosed within the boundaries of the surface location."

"These lines form the perimeter of the Forrester's claim," he pointed out, his lips almost grazing her ear. Ross breathed in the scent of gardenias that lingered in her thick mahogany hair and willed himself to concentrate on the grid in front of them. Inch by inch, he'd broken down the barrier that had separated them for over five weeks. It'd been like hacking through a ten-foot wall of bedrock with an ice pick. Only a few days ago, he'd succeeded for the first time in luring her to his office at the

Glamorgan without the accompanying presence of her constant companion, Gavin O'Connell. Ross sure as hell wasn't about to ruin his chances now by some foolish misstep.

"Unfortunately," she said softly, as though thinking out loud, "the apex law also presupposes that a simple mineral vein remains sandwiched between two walls of rock like a piece of salami in a roll. That's something your charts indicate isn't always the case."

"In Butte," he explained, "as in Coeur d'Alene and Grass Valley, there's a combination of geological conditions at the surface that allow various types of entry, even though fissure veins predominate. Tunnelin', mill, and placer minin' only increase the likelihood of lawsuits."

He braced his open palm on the drafting stand and studied the porcelain skin that covered the delicate bones of her face. Her long lashes cast a fringed shadow on her smooth cheek as she pored over the document in front of her. The dark mole just above her upper lip enhanced the creaminess of her perfect complexion. Once again, he was reminded of a nymph from paradise.

Damn it to hell, he was getting mighty tired of waking up at night with her name on his lips and his rigid staff swollen and aching to pleasure her. He wanted her there in his bed beside him. And if he had anything to say about it, the celibate life he was presently leading was going to come to a screeching halt.

Seemingly unaware of his scrutiny, she picked up a pencil and rolled it back and forth between her fingers. "A lot is going to depend on the legal definition of terms such as *vein*, *lode*, and *ledge*. If a vein leading down from the surface of the Forrester is lost near its vertical wall, and a similar vein of identical ore, which you've been mining in the Glamorgan, is found to be directly below or on one side of the Forrester's vein, is it a geological continuation of the adjoining claim or a completely separate vein? Rather a complex issue, really. That's why I want those consultants you've contacted to take the stand as expert witnesses. The jury will listen to geologists and mining engineers brought in from the outside much more objectively than they'll listen to you and Felix Hegel each try to defend your personal right to mine the same vein of ore."

She tapped the point of the pencil on the chart thoughtfully. "What we have to do is make all the technical questions about vein structure and formation crystal clear to the members of the jury. We need to keep our explanations simple, concise, and easily understood. We want to make it evident, even to an uneducated layman, that the vein you were mining in June begins on the Glamorgan's surface claim, regardless of where it ends."

They were interrupted by a knock on the office door. At Ross's answering call, Eben Pearce opened it and looked in. "How about a cup of coffee and a little something to eat for you two?" he asked. Beneath his handlebar mustache, a contagious grin creased his freckled face.

Ross straightened and stretched lazily. They'd been studying various documents for the last two hours. "Sounds like a good idea. Nell, how about it?"

She slipped off the stool and shook out the folds of her dark brown walking dress. "I could use a break," she agreed, rubbing the small of her back.

As he removed his eyeglasses and placed them in his shirt pocket, Ross wondered if she was wearing a corset that morning. Its stiff whaleboning would cause a great deal of discomfort to anyone bending over a worktable for very long. He considered offering to massage her aching muscles, but immediately thought better of it. To bring any relief, the binding undergarment would have to be removed first. He'd made some headway in the last few days, but not that much.

Eben disappeared, only to return a few minutes later with a cracked lacquer tray that held their lunch. He placed it on the corner of the littered oak desk that stood by the window. "Making any progress?" he asked.

"Well, I think I've finally convinced my legal counselor of the legitimacy of my claim," Ross declared. He thrust his chin forward, hooked his thumbs in his belt, and rocked back and forth on the soles of his miner's tie boots in his best imitation of an egotistical and filthy-rich copper king.

Nell pursed her lips, refusing to laugh at his clowning. "You convinced me of that four weeks ago, when you first explained how to read a topographical map. What we have to figure out now is how to persuade the men on the jury."

She plopped down on the dilapidated wicker-back chair that stood beside Morgan's desk and gazed up at the tall, athletically built man. Dressed in khaki work shirt and trousers, he was the image of the golden-haired conqueror who invaded her dreams with increasing regularity and seduced her with such effortless skill. As he'd leaned over her at the map table, she'd longed to rest her head against his muscular chest and learn, once again, what it was like to be held, safe and secure, within the haven of his strong arms. In his presence, she was conscious of every movement he made, as though her soul was tied to his, like the tail on a kite.

"We can't do anything on an empty stomach," Morgan said. "Let's relax and forget about my legal problems while we eat."

"I've got to check on the pump equipment at the eleven-hundred-foot level, boss. It's been acting up again," said Eben. At Nell's look of surprise, he added quickly, "Even though we're not blasting right now, we still have to keep pumping the water out or the lower levels will be flooded. Well, enjoy your lunch." Eben left, closing the door behind him.

Morgan handed Nell an unfamiliar type
and placed a steaming mug of coffee for he
edge of his desk. Then he pulled his own
chair next to hers and sat down.

"What's this?" she asked. She turned the golden-
brown rectangle around, looking it over in dubious
curiosity.

"It's called a pasty," he told her. "The name
rhymes with *nasty*, but it's anythin' but foul tastin'.
It's a Cornish meat pie, angel eyes. You can eat it cold
like this or hot from the oven. The Cousin Jacks take
them down into the mines in their tin lunch buckets.
They call them 'letters from home.' "

She inhaled the pasty's delicious aroma, nibbled
cautiously on the edge, and then took a tentative
bite. It tasted absolutely wonderful. "Heavens, it's
marvelous," she exclaimed around a mouthful of
food. She looked at the strange pastry in her hand
with heightened appreciation. "What's in it?"

"Diced beef, potatoes, and onions wrapped up
and baked in a pie dough. Eben probably bought
these from one of the miners' wives, who had some
extras to sell this mornin'."

"Mm," she said. She licked her lips to catch the
flavorful crumbs. "We never had anything like this
in Bar Harbor."

"How old were you when you moved to Boston?"

"Actually, I was born there. My mother, my
brother, and I went to stay in my uncle's cottage
on Frenchman's Bay when my father left for the
Colorado goldfields. After Momma passed away,
Sean and I returned to Boston to live with Uncle
Cormac and Aunt Lydia. I was seventeen at the
time."

"Is that when you became so interested in wom-
en's rights? When your aunt and uncle refused to
let you bicycle around Boston in your bloomers?"
There was a playful rumble in his deep voice. His
emerald eyes sparkled with deviltry. With a sharp

pang of relief, she realized just how much she'd missed his teasing and how good it felt to be the recipient of his outrageous baiting.

"I attended my first suffrage rally while I was at Wellesley Female Seminary." She tipped her nose in the air and pretended to be hurt and upset. "Why? Does the idea of equal rights for women make you feel threatened?"

"Not in the least, punkin," he told her with a wicked grin. "I'd love to reach a plateau of equality with the opposite sex. Then I could stay home and let a woman support me." He brushed the crumbs from his fingers and picked up his cracked coffee mug. "Did you go on to law school after Wellesley?"

Her mouth full of pasty, she shook her head.

"I wondered why you'd never mentioned any prestigious institution," he added. "O'Connell blurted out that he'd graduated from Harvard Law practically the moment he stepped down from the train."

"After graduation from college, I read the law under my uncle's guidance. I worked as a legal apprentice for him until I passed the examination for the bar. At twenty-five, I joined the firm of Ryan, Sheehy, and O'Connell as Uncle Cormac's assistant."

Ross propped one ankle on the opposite knee and cautiously continued his interrogation. "What's your aunt like?"

"Lydia Ryan is plump and giggly and hasn't an independent thought in her pretty head," Nell answered without a hint of sarcasm. "When Momma died, she took my brother and me into her home and into her very generous heart. She was unfailingly kind to us in the years that followed. Sean and I were treated as though we were the children my uncle and aunt never had."

"I'm sure they were both very proud of you."

Nell's enormous brown eyes twinkled mischievously. "Not always. Aunt Lydia was clearly disappointed that I didn't want to mingle with Boston's Irish upper crust as a society debutante. But Uncle Cormac couldn't have been prouder. He supported my decision to study law almost from the moment I mentioned the idea. Last year, I even assisted him before the Supreme Court of Massachusetts."

"I'm impressed," Ross told her with quiet sincerity.

He waited, hoping she'd go on. He was listening for some clue to explain her extreme wariness toward the male gender. Her aunt sounded like the type of woman who placed all her hopes and dreams in her spouse and children, without any lofty aspirations of her own. She sure as hell didn't sound like a man-hater. He wondered if it had been Nell's mother who'd taught her to distrust the opposite sex.

Clearly pleased by his words of praise, she peeked at him over the brim of her coffee cup. Then she set it down on the scarred desktop. She smoothed the front of her flared skirt in that nervous way she had just before she dropped a bombshell. He waited in fascination.

She didn't disappoint him.

"Ross, would you take me to the Comique Theater one evening to see Eddie Foy?"

He tried desperately to hide his exhilaration at the thought of taking her anywhere. "Oh, I don't know," he drawled with slow consideration, as though having to mull over such a shocking request. "Don't you think that place is a little too scandalous for a lady lawyer?"

"I don't think so at all," she contradicted. Her mouth puckered up as if she'd been eating lemons. The sudden bloom on her cheeks put the lie to her words. "I've seen the posters around town advertising the new comedy act just in from Seattle. It sounds perfectly respectable to me."

"Concert saloons aren't generally considered all that respectable," he warned. "Especially not that one. But I'll tell you what, little darlin'. If you're so willin' to chance bein' seen goin' in there by some upright pillar of this community, I'll take you to the Comique on Friday night."

"Great!"

He put up his hand to caution her. "But it'll cost you."

"Oh, I'm perfectly willing to pay my own way. And yours too," she offered magnanimously. She leaned forward in her chair and bestowed a smile radiant enough, at that short distance, to blind a man.

"Well, you are certainly one liberated female," he said with a grin. He leaned back in his worn leather desk chair, locked his hands behind his neck, and stared at her in mock amazement. "But that's not the payment I was thinkin' of, buttercup. In return for my investment of time and energy, not to mention the risk of losin' my fine reputation, I'd like the honor of your presence at a picnic on Saturday."

"Okay," she blithely agreed. All of a sudden, the sunny smile faded as her eyes narrowed in suspicion. "Who's going to be at this picnic?"

"You and me."

She scowled and started to shake her head.

"No picnic, no Comique," he proclaimed in a voice of implacable determination. "And no comedy show starrin' the one and only Mr. Eddie Foy."

She pressed the tips of her fingers against her lips, as though to keep from blurting out the wrong answer. She studied him, her worried gaze moving over his set features and his posture of deliberate indifference. To his delight, her shoulders drooped in surrender. Well, sonofagun, who'd have thought the prim little spinster had a taste for slapstick?

"All right," she acceded in a cross whisper. "What time will we leave for the Comique?"

"I'll have a hired coach pick us up at Kuusinen's at eight." Before she had a chance to change her mind, he rose from his chair. "Now we'd better get back to work. O'Connell will be joining us shortly."

That night, Ross lay in bed and stared up at the ceiling. He could hear Luke's gentle snore from across the room, where the ten-year-old slept on a narrow cot. His son was a bundle of energy during the day and dead to the world at night. They'd shared a room at the boardinghouse since arriving in Butte, but it wouldn't be long before they'd move into the big house he was building for them on Park Street. Although he looked forward to having the privacy of his own bedroom, and better yet, the luxury of his own parlor and kitchen, he wasn't all that anxious to move out from under the roof he shared with his beautiful legal counselor. He'd been able to see her every evening at supper, even when she was spitting-nails mad at him. Now that he'd nearly bridged the chasm that separated them, he was in no great hurry to leave Kuusinen's. Hell, he could hardly wait for Friday night and their first real outing as a courting couple. It was about time they quit arguing and got on with the romancing.

Miss Elinor Ryan was a bundle of contradictions. What other female attorney would have agreed to represent a strumpet in a public trial? By doing so, Nell would expose herself to innuendo and ridicule. He'd heard her tell Miss Howard that she believed her story, and had sounded as if she meant it. Ross himself doubted Lottie was actually telling the truth.

His concern didn't lie with Lottie, however, but with Nell. It seemed to him that, somewhere in her past, Nell had purposely repressed all the feelings of sexuality that were an inherent part of her nature. He was certain those passionate feelings were still there, just beneath the cool facade she struggled so hard to maintain. He wondered, once again, if her mother had taught her, as a young girl, to deny her sexuality as something evil or dirty. That would explain her skittishness whenever he got too near her.

He thought about the letter on the table beside his bed. It had just arrived that morning from Denver. His mother had written several pages of lighthearted news and ended with a plea for him to bring Luke for a visit, if only for a few weeks. Unlike Nell, Ross had inherited his own mother's open enjoyment of life's pleasures and her frank appreciation of the world's sensual beauty.

He grinned at the crack in the moonlit plaster above him, remembering how shocked he'd pretended to be at Nell's request to visit the Comique. His mother, Clarissa Corneille, had been employed as a burlesque actress and singer in a Central City music hall when she met and married Lloyd Morgan. She'd brought her gaiety and vivacity to everything she did. Ross's childhood home rang with merriment and love. Though he'd clashed with his irascible father time and again as he was growing up, his mother had always smoothed things over with her nonjudgmental and sometimes comic ways, exerting a softening influence on her crusty, hard-nosed husband.

Lloyd Morgan was the reason Ross couldn't go home. Not until the Glamorgan mining rights were settled in his favor. His father was of the old-fashioned school, who thought mining was done by intuition and the seat of your pants, not by book learning. He stood staunchly against unions or any mollycoddling of his miners. When Ross had returned from Columbia, he'd tried to change some of the conservative practices in his father's silver mines. But the older man refused to take any advice, saying it was merely useless theory. The two exchanged bitter words. Neither would swallow his pride and apologize. After that, Ross had worked as a mining engineer for other companies until he'd built up enough savings and credit to purchase the Glamorgan. He was going to prove to his father that he could be a success in mining. He was going to become a self-made millionaire just as Lloyd Morgan had.

Not seeing his sprightly mother had been the hardest part of Ross's self-imposed exile from Colorado after that final skirmish with his father. He owed it to Luke to make amends and take the boy to visit his grandparents. But Ross wasn't going to return to his childhood home as a failure. His pride wouldn't let him. Only when Ross succeeded in his lawsuit and established the Glamorgan as one of the richest copper mines in the world would he return home.

Whether he succeeded depended in a large measure on the elusive and exasperating female whom he planned to seduce that coming weekend. At the thought of his intentions, his heart thumped against his ribs like a drum roll for an opening curtain. He'd already laid his plans for the coming Saturday afternoon, complete with flowers, wine, food, and a great big blanket.

And through her dramatic retelling of countless variety acts, his spirited mother had taught him the value of one of life's most important strategies: the wow finish.

Chapter 13

❧

The audience on the main floor went wild the moment Eva Tanguay exploded onto the stage. Hoots, whistles, and maddened applause shook the rafters. Nell had never witnessed such an uninhibited display of male appreciation for the opposite sex.

And on this particular occasion, *sex* was the right word to use. The famous variety show star literally raced out of the wings, screaming her theme song. "I don't care! I don't care!" she belted out at the top of her very adequate lungs. She bounded from one corner of the stage scenery to the other, filled with some turbulent, frenetic, sensual energy.

It was clear to Nell that the blond sex bomb truly *didn't* care.

Dressed in a costume that shimmered, sparkled, glittered, and gleamed, the effervescent songstress was covered from shoulders to hips in scarlet and jet bugles and swaying gold fringe. Her criminally gorgeous legs were displayed for all eyes to see, covered only by sheer silk stockings. She tore around the stage, her curvaceous hips wiggling, her large breasts bouncing, her long legs kicking, her derriere shimmying, as she screeched the words of her brassy song in a soprano voice loud enough to fill every corner of the concert hall.

Mesmerized, Nell reached for her wineglass without taking her eyes off the jolting performance. She sipped the chilled champagne in the hopes it would cool her heated cheeks. Morgan had been right. The

Comique Theater was much too scandalous for a prim and proper lady from Boston. But to tell the truth and shame the devil, this spinster lady was enjoying every raucous minute of it.

The moment she set her long-stemmed glass back on the table, Ross splashed more champagne into it. Tearing her gaze away from the crazy antics on stage, she met his deep green eyes. Their gold-flecked depths were glimmering with laughter.

"Oh, no," she said, almost as an afterthought. She fluttered her fingers over the bubbling glass in a gesture of belated concern. "I've had too much already."

"It's Friday night," he coaxed. "Let's enjoy ourselves."

Turning her head so she could speak directly into his ear and be heard more easily over the shrill caterwauling, she smiled shyly and admitted, "I am."

"I guessed," he replied. His firm lips quirked in amusement. He bent his head and dropped a light kiss on her brow. The buss was almost fraternal, meant more to put her at ease than to be seductive. But a feeling of delicious anticipation swept through Nell, bringing with it a slightly breathless excitement. He slipped his arm around her shoulders and squeezed her comfortably. His long fingers played idly with the black velvet bow that decorated the shoulder of her gray silk blouse. Alarmingly aware of his presence, she tried to focus once more on the stage below.

They were sitting side by side at a table for two in one of the Comique's private boxes. The theater was two stories high. On the first floor, strewn with sawdust, were the regular customers. Most of them were miners and their lady friends, who sat at tables of four or more. Scantily clad waitresses, carrying great trays balanced on their uplifted palms, brought them round after round of liquid refreshments. Tall mugs of beer seemed to be the preferred drink, although hard liquor was also available. Morgan had asked for a whiskey, straight up with a beer chaser, when he'd ordered the champagne for Nell.

The second floor of the concert saloon was really a gallery that encircled the auditorium. It contained separate compartments that looked down onto the stage. When they'd first arrived at the brick building on South Main Street, Ross had hurried Nell into the theater through a back entrance off the alley and hustled her quickly up the stairs and into the private stall.

"Thanks for bringing me in the back way," she told him now with a throaty giggle. She put her fingers to her lips in surprise at her unladylike behavior. She wasn't used to drinking spirits, and the champagne was going to her head. As she turned to look at him, her cheek grazed the rough wool of his dark brown jacket. "I don't think anyone saw me, least of all some upright pillar of the community." Relaxed by the hilarity of the previous act and the soothing effect of the imported French wine, she allowed herself to enjoy the wonderful feel of his sinewy arm about her. Tingles of pleasure caromed through her nervous system. Despite the lulling effects of the alcohol, she was filled with a tightly coiled tension that demanded immediate release. She felt like a jack-in-the box ready to pop out of its prison.

"No one saw you, sugarplum," Morgan reassured her. "I made certain of that. But you'd be surprised how many supposedly upright gentlemen have ascended those same stairs." He chuckled, and the sound reverberated softly against Nell's shoulder. "There's a good reason why these boxes have mesh screens across the front of them. Probably more than a few of the camp's wealthy playboys are here tonight."

"To see Eddie Foy?" she asked wryly, trying not to smile.

"Of course," he answered with a questioning lift of one golden-brown eyebrow. "Who else?" Beneath their thick lashes, his eyes glittered with humor.

Earlier, Ross had explained that various pastoral scenes were painted on the front of the wire screen, ensuring that no one on the main floor could see the town's bluebloods in the gallery boxes above. This clever decorating scheme afforded complete anonymity to the theater's wealthy patrons, while allowing them to enjoy both the show and the capering of the less inhibited hoi polloi.

"When I asked you to bring me here, I had forgotten the 'Electrifying Hoyden' was also on the playbill," she explained with a hint of apology. "Believe me, I never saw anything like this back in Keith's Theater in Boston."

She didn't want him to think the variety shows she'd attended before offered anything other than decent family entertainment. What was referred to on their billboards as "Polite Vaudeville," with a program that contained no swearwords or jokes to offend the ladies, was always delivered as promised.

Morgan bent his head and lightly grazed her temple with his lips. "I'm sure you didn't, punkin." His words were filled with a teasing warmth that seemed to imply he wouldn't care if she'd seen a striptease dancer at a carnival sideshow. Or been one, for that matter.

Light-headed, Nell leaned back on her escort's supporting arm and turned her attention to the rollicking performance on stage. The dynamic singer had burst into a strident rendition of "It's Been Done Before but Never the Way I Do It." Nell gasped in shock at the risqué lyrics. She should have brought a fan. If she couldn't have cooled the warmth of her blush with its counterfeit breeze, at least she could have hidden her reddened cheeks behind its outspread folds.

Ross stroked the nape of her beautiful neck above

her ruffled collar, delighting in the feel of her smooth skin against his hot fingers. Desire raked through him, tightening the muscles in his groin and playing havoc with his attempt to remain composed and almost brotherly. His attention was riveted not on the buxom blond gyrating about on center stage, but on Nell. It had been the same way through all the previous acts. There had been three acrobatic jugglers, an Irish baritone who warbled several sentimental ballads, followed by two comedians in blackface who danced and chattered and beat each other over the head with gusto in a one-act skit. Along with the rest of the audience, she'd burst into laughter at each ridiculous pratfall or bitingly clever piece of dialogue.

Ross hadn't paid the slightest heed to any of them. His lustful thoughts raced ahead to the coming afternoon, when he would take Nell in his arms and bring to a culmination this endless yearning to possess her. He'd wanted her so badly and for so long, he'd almost come to accept the constant ache of sexual frustration as part of his everyday life. Since the end of his unhappy marriage at the death of his wife eight years before, he hadn't gone without sex for more than two weeks at a time. Until Nell had arrived on the scene. Tomorrow would bring, at last, an end to this self-inflicted torture—forever, he hoped. Instinctively, he knew that their mating would bind her to him as nothing else could. And with each passing day, he'd become more and more convinced that no other woman would ever satisfy the deep, soul-wrenching need that Nell had created inside him.

Eva Tanguay completed her act to thunderous applause. The curtain was lowered, and the gaslights went up in the theater. A brief intermission was announced before the main attraction would begin.

"I hope you're not sorry you came," said Ross. He traced the delicate line of her jaw with his fingertips in a movement meant to soothe and reassure her. "The shows at the Comique can sometimes get a little randy. Burlesque performers just naturally play to their audience. They know from previous engagements that they can get away with a lot more double entendres in San Francisco or Butte than in cities like Pittsburgh, Minneapolis, and Portland. One-liners that bring howls at the Palace in Chicago fall flat in Duluth."

"I'm not offended," Nell replied. "Momma had a very earthy sense of humor. Her parents were simple farmers, both born on the Old Sod. There was nothing highbrow or pretentious about them."

"You think your mother would have enjoyed this evenin's performance?" he asked in amazement.

She laughed at his obvious surprise. "Quite frankly, she'd have loved it. But how do you come to know so much about show business?"

"My mother was an actress with a travelin' stage company when she met my dad. She was performin' in a Central City concert saloon at the time. She still brags that she was makin' over two hundred dollars a week."

"How fascinating!" Nell turned in his embrace to look up at him. "Was she talented?"

"Accordin' to her very immodest recollections, she was the most popular singer and dancer in the Colorado goldfields at the time she gave it all up to get married. She used to entertain me with bits of knockabout when I was just a pipsqueak."

Nell's velvety brown eyes grew wide with curiosity. "What's knockabout?"

"That's when comedians drive home their jokes by battin' each other all over the stage. My mother claims rather cynically that nothin' inspires such immediate and spontaneous laughter from the audience as seein' mayhem and misfortune befall some other hapless human bein'."

They were interrupted by a discreet tap from the hallway. Morgan rose and moved to the door, where he pushed back a small slide. A waitress placed an ice bucket containing another bottle of champagne on the narrow shelf attached to the door.

When they'd first arrived, Nell had been startled to see him close the door to their private box and slide shut the iron bolt located on the inside. She'd learned from Morgan that the girls who served the stalls in the gallery through the shuttered portholes were given red tickets by their customers. These were later redeemed by the owner for the waitresses' very generous commissions. To her surprise, these same young ladies, attired in evening dresses so short the straps of their garters showed above their black net stockings, jumped up on the main floor tables between acts to sing and dance. They were inevitably showered with gold and silver coins by the appreciative, mostly male, audience.

"You shouldn't have ordered another bottle," she scolded Morgan, as he carried the ice bucket over and set it on the floor at his feet next to the first one. "I'm already feeling a little dizzy, and you said we had to leave early tomorrow morning for the picnic."

"Just sip it slowly," he encouraged. "You'll be fine. There's plenty of time to enjoy your champagne. The headliner act is still to come."

The dissonant wail of Turkish music floated up to the gallery, and they turned their attention back to the show. The musical extravaganza starring Eddie Foy was set in a harem. It was a parody of the tale of Ali Baba and the Forty Thieves. Foy was brilliant. Thin, elfish, and graceful, the comic star had a large, mobile mouth made up with greasepaint to look even wider. For the night's performance, he wore a black pirate's wig. His pantomiming and eccentric dancing were done with wide-eyed and wondering innocence. Entranced, Nell leaned against Morgan, undisturbed by the fact that he was sliding his hand up and down her arm in a series of long, lingering caresses that sent rivulets of sweet sensation coursing through her already overstimulated nervous system.

"I wanted to see Foy last year in his musical based on the story of Sinbad," she told him in an attempt to school her thoughts. "The reviews said it was wonderful. But I really shouldn't have come tonight. I'm still supposed to be in mourning."

"Sean would have been the first person to disagree with you, sweetheart. Life is for the livin', and he knew that. I think he grew to love this hellfire minin' camp with all its warts and wrinkles. In fact, Sean and I came to the Comique to see that Sinbad musical when it played here last winter. He wouldn't begrudge you this evenin' out. And I have a feelin' it's been a mighty long time since you've enjoyed a good laugh."

Nell squeezed Morgan's hand in appreciation. "You always know the right thing to say, don't you? I think you must have a little bit of the Irish in you. You're just not admitting it."

He nuzzled her ear. The soft tickle of his warm breath caused a jolt of pleasure to ricochet through her bloodstream. His words were tinged with amusement. " 'Fraid not, doll. My dad's a Welshman. And Mom's always insisted her parents were French. Since my grandfolks have both gone to their final reward, who's to challenge her?"

Nell cocked her head and studied the strong angle of his jaw. "So that's where you get all that natural charm. From your Gallic ancestors."

He lightly touched his lips to hers in a kiss of honeyed flirtation. "I didn't realize you found me so charmin'. Hold on to that thought, and we'll continue this conversation when the show's over."

Everyone in the cast was on stage for the finale when Eva Tanguay did her notorious Dance of the Seven Veils. Nell was certain that the only thing the "I Don't Care Girl" wore, other than those flimsy pieces of gauze that she tantalizingly removed one by one, was the jeweled headpiece in her fuzzy yellow hair. The saucy, impudent dancer stopped barely in time to avoid arrest for indecent exposure. Just as her poster bills always promised, the audience was electrified.

When the curtain went down for the last time, Nell stirred reluctantly. With her head resting on Ross's shoulder, she'd felt so content within the curve of his arm she could have stayed there forever. He'd entwined his fingers with hers and brought them to rest on his corded thigh. Beneath the sensitive pads of her fingertips, she could feel the hard mass of muscle through the brown wool trousers.

"I'm sorry it's over," she admitted with a sigh. She started to rise, but he held her in place beside him.

"There's no hurry to leave, darlin'. I want to give the crowd time to disperse before we use the stairs. Our coach will be waitin' for us in the alley whenever we go down." He brought her hand to his mouth and gently kissed each fingertip.

A thrill of delight ran the entire length of Nell's body at the sensuous touch of his lips. "Did . . . did you enjoy the performance?" she asked breathlessly.

"Mm, every second of it," he murmured. He slid both arms around her and drew her to him.

Nell braced one hand against his massive chest. Under his dark brown jacket, he was wearing a white shirt with ruffles down the front. She gripped the linen frill between her fingers. "You didn't seem to be watching the show," she said, in one last attempt to distract him. "Not even the dazzling Miss Tanguay."

The husky rasp of his deep voice seemed to damn Eva Tanguay to oblivion. "I've seen her before."

Ross kissed Nell's smooth temple, her fluttering eyelids, the bridge of her nose, as he pulled her closer. He moved his hands in gentle, seductive caresses across her back and shoulders, then captured her narrow waist between his palms. Sliding his hands upward, he bracketed the sides of her breasts with his thumbs.

Hot spurs of desire raked through him as she arched her back, not merely allowing him to continue, but silently urging him on. He cupped her lush breasts in his hands, his thumbs rubbing against the round pink nipples hidden beneath the cool silk of her blouse. She sighed with pleasure, slid her hands around his neck, and lifted her mouth to his. The fragrant scent of gardenias swirled around them.

Ross bent his head and captured her lips in a passionate kiss. He thrust his tongue inside her open mouth to explore it with fierce possession, while he continued to shape and mold the voluptuous globes of her breasts. Breaking the kiss, he drew back to study her perfect features. His gaze moved from her finely arched brows to her delicate lids to her full mouth in a slow, lingering salute to her beauty, as he drank in the sight of her.

Her lips trembled. "I missed you," she confessed.

Although they'd seen each other nearly every day for the past six weeks, he knew exactly what she meant. "Oh, sweetheart," he rasped in a voice thick with need, "not half as much as I missed you."

He bent his head and nuzzled her breasts. His hands explored her body, sliding over the tantalizing curves of her hips and across the flat plane of her stomach. Nell's head fell back. He traced a line of rapacious hunger up the column of her exposed neck with his feverish tongue. He longed to pull her down to the floor with him and feast on her beautiful, naked body, devouring her with his mouth, nipping her gently with his teeth, tasting her with his tongue. Talons of raw, primal lust ripped through him, and he was suddenly afraid he'd lose control and frighten her with his unbridled sexual ardor.

He pulled away, instead. His heart battered against his ribs, pumping the blood in hot gushes through his veins. "We'd better get out of here," he said hoarsely, "while I can still walk."

He rose to his feet and drew her up beside him. He started to guide her to the door, then stopped, and turned her toward him. Cupping her bottom, he lifted her up against his thighs and rocked her gently back and forth across his hardened staff. A low groan tore from deep in his throat. Sweet, sweet Jesus, he'd *never* get enough of her.

"I thought you said we had to go," she whispered in confusion. She squirmed in his arms, and he wasn't sure she even knew what she was doing to his honorable resolutions.

The unrelieved ache in his tautened groin was pure male agony. He nibbled on her lower lip, then flicked the tip of his tongue across the dark mole above her mouth before calling into play his iron willpower. "We do. I guess I just wanted to torture myself a little more." He set her on her feet, his hands at her waist to steady her. "Come on, angel eyes. Let's go find our coach."

Chapter 14

The Tie Lang Noodle Palace was in the heart of Chinatown. Two stories high, it had a tiled pagoda roof and two gilded red dragons at the door. Nell found herself on Morgan's arm, actually clinging to him for support as they entered the Celestial establishment.

It was scarce wonder that she couldn't stand on her own two feet. She was fully and gloriously aroused. Beneath the pearl-gray peau de soie of her shirtwaist, her breasts were swollen and aching for his touch. She worried that the other customers might be able to tell, just from looking at her, that she throbbed with sexual tension. Surely they could see that her lips were bruised and swollen from Morgan's kisses. The warmth of a flush heated her cheeks, while her heart pounded and her lungs struggled to accommodate her mortifying shortness of breath. She was certain her heightened coloring would give away her scandalous thoughts to anyone who glanced in her direction.

She'd assumed when they left the Comique Theater that they were going directly back to the boardinghouse. Morgan hadn't told her any differently until they descended from their hired hack in front of the noodle parlor. During the ride there, he'd continued his provocative exploration of her body with a thoroughness that had left her trembling—and longing for more. He even dared to slip his hand beneath her skirt and learn the feel of her stockinged legs from the calf all the way up to the lacy frills on her French silk knickers.

Shocked at his boldness, she clamped her thighs together and tried to push his questing fingers away. Since his hand was caught beneath her petticoats, he became entangled in the layers of embroidered cotton lawn. He'd laughed softly, refusing to help, while she tried to wrestle his hand and forearm out from under the voluminous folds of her black satin skirt. They both wound up stretched out full-length on the seat, with her lying on top of him. In the end, the only thing that had stopped his indecent behavior was the vehicle pulling to a halt. Then he'd swung her down from the cab of the coach as if there wasn't a thing to be embarrassed about and informed her with his cocksure grin that they were going to share an after-theater supper with a few friends.

By that time, she was in such a state of fevered sensitivity, she all but fell into his arms. He caught her and twirled her high in the air before setting her down on her shaky limbs. Heavens to Betsy, how could she possibly walk into a restaurant and calmly order a meal when every inch of her was vibrating with sensual excitement? He was trying to drive her crazy.

The moment they stepped inside the noodle parlor, a middle-aged Chinese man, wearing a high-collared silk jacket and baggy pants, came up to them. He pressed his palms together in front of his thin chest and bowed graciously. An ebony silk skullcap adorned his blue-black hair, which was braided in a long queue that fell all the way down his back. His shiny jet eyes beamed at them through huge, round spectacles. "Mistah Molgan," he said with a broad smile. "How velly nice to see you again."

"Thank you, Lee." Ross slipped his arm around Nell's waist and drew her closer to him. "Angel eyes, I'd like you to meet Mr. Yipp. He owns this noodle palace, along with several washy-washy places, a joss house, a fan-tan parlor, and probably half of Chinatown as well."

Nell held out her hand and smiled. Lee Yipp took it in his graceful brown fingers and bowed low once again. "Miss Angel Eyes, I am honoh you have come to my humble restaulant." Straightening, he waved his arm in a flourish of welcome. "Come light this way, please. You have fliends al'eady waiting for you at youh table."

Nell had never seen anything like the Tie Lang Noodle Palace. Great globe lanterns of blue and yellow and green swung from the ceiling, providing a rainbow of light to the huge room. The faint smell of incense mingled pleasantly with the delectable aroma of roasted pork and fried rice. On the papered walls hung grotesque masks of demon gods, bearded, horned, gilded in gold, and splotched with ebony and scarlet. Enormous scimitars, decorated with giant peacock feathers, were crossed in menacing formation above the doorways. The restaurant was packed with people. It looked as though half of Butte was there that night.

As the owner led the way, Morgan placed his hand on the small of Nell's back and gently guided her toward a table at the far corner of the room. They'd taken only a few steps when a feminine voice called out to him.

"Hey, Colorado! What's your hurry? Come over here and say hello."

In a booth by the wall sat Juniper Jess and Lottie Luscious. Both women were dressed in magnificent gowns of watered silk, with matching velvet trim and lace ruffles. Seated beside them were two young men of obvious means, attired in expensively tailored evening wear. Nell realized, without explanation, that they were the sons of wealthy mine owners. Morgan shook hands with the men, whom he seemed to know. He placed his hand protectively on Nell's shoulder as he introduced her.

She recognized the name of the younger. Fred Burwell had thrown himself a party on his twenty-first birthday to the tune of thirty thousand dollars. It had been written up in the Butte *Miner* with a long list of the society belles and their well-to-do escorts who'd attended, including detailed descriptions of the ladies' ravishing costumes. No one seemed the least perturbed that the sandy-haired play-boy's present party included two stunning ladies of questionable repute.

Juniper Jess looked up at Morgan with a gaze of adoration. She was wearing pale green again, the exact shade of those beautiful, bedroom eyes she used with such professional skill. Her lower lip edged out in a tempting pout as she batted her lashes at him shamelessly. "I haven't seen you for a long time, Colorado," she simpered.

A feeling of relief flooded Nell at the ingenuous admission and all it implied.

The girl's attractive escort wrapped his arm around her narrow waist, hauled her up against his youthful frame, and planted a noisy smack on her cheek. "What are you making sheep's eyes at the Cougar for," Burwell complained good-naturedly. "I'll buy you anything you want. Just name it."

Lottie giggled. "What Jessie wants isn't for sale." She twirled the stem of her wineglass between her fingers and looked from Nell to Ross. She winked at them slyly. "On top of that, he's already spoken for."

"You have a knack for hittin' the nail right on the head, Lottie," admitted Morgan. Nell could hear the warmth of laughter in his voice.

She thought it best to redirect the conversation before her relationship with her handsome client became a subject of common gossip. "I'd like you to stop by my office one afternoon next week, Miss Howard. I want to go over some points in your testimony for the coming trial. I've decided I'm going to put you on the stand."

What she didn't tell the girl was that she'd also decided it was imperative they contact her sister in Des Moines. It could mean the difference between an acquittal and years in prison. She was going to broach the idea once more with Lottie. If she remained dead set against it, Nell intended to ignore her client's wishes and contact Fanny herself.

"Yes, ma'am," Lottie said. "I'll be there on Monday." The stricken look that swept across her lovely features reminded everyone just how precarious Letitia Howard's future really was.

Nell felt a similar pang of concern. Had she been an overconfident fool when she'd agreed to defend the woman against such serious charges? Lottie had insisted that she wanted Nell to defend her. Nell prayed to God Lottie wouldn't suffer because of her female attorney's lack of experience in criminal law.

"I think Miss Ryan and I had better go find our table," Morgan said to the group. "Our friends are waitin' for us." With his hand still pressed lightly against Nell's shoulder blade, he guided her behind Lee Yipp, who'd stood nearby, waiting for them.

One of the things that Nell had come to enjoy about the copper camp was the lack of pretension among its varied inhabitants. She'd learned from Hertta that it was the fashion for Butte residents to go to a noodle parlor after a ball or show. Tonight, the Tie Lang was filled with West Side millionaires and high-society matriarchs, along with Cabbage Patch panhandlers and Galena Street trollops. As the two of them made their way through the maze of crowded tables, Ross was greeted by animated waves from painted demireps straight out of the red-light district, and sophisticated debutantes whose pictures appeared regularly in the society pages. It was apparent that the ladies of the mining camp had a special spot in their hearts for Rossiter Morgan.

Nell could easily understand their captivation. No

doubt, they were attracted to his easygoing charm, dazzled by his athletic physique, intrigued by his educated ways, and fascinated by his drive and ambition—not to mention his reputed wealth. Painfully obvious, as well, was the fact that Ross was completely at ease with members of the opposite sex. Nell's heart sank at the realization that he'd probably enjoyed discreet liaisons with some of the lovelier ones.

"Boss, I'm over here," Eben Pearce called above the noise. He stood in front of his chair, waving to them. At the table sat Hertta and Kalle Kuusinen, smiling broadly.

Eben hurried to pull out a chair for Nell next to his, while Ross hovered over her until she was seated. "Hertta and Kalle just arrived a few minutes ago," Eben announced with a welcoming smile. He turned to his employer. "Mr. Yipp said you'd already ordered dinner for us."

Morgan sat down beside Nell. "Yes, I spoke with Lee yesterday about the menu." She looked at him in surprise, realizing just how much he'd taken for granted. "The food here is the best Cantonese in Butte. In all of Montana, for that matter."

"How vas ta show?" Hertta asked them, as a waiter in black silk pajamas brought a bottle of wine to the table for Ross to examine.

"Wonderful!" Nell exclaimed. She was determined to put her worries over the trial and her suspicious thoughts about Ross from her mind and enjoy the evening. "The musical was straight out of the Arabian Nights, complete with dancing harem girls and singing Barbary pirates. I've never seen anything so exotic and colorful."

"Foy's great," Eben agreed enthusiastically. "Tomorrow's his last night in town. I'm going to try to see the show before he leaves."

"Be prepared for a thrill," she warned him with a teasing smile. "Eva Tanguay does her infamous Dance of the Seven Veils."

"Great balls of fire!" Eben stared at her in aston-ishment. Cocking one eyebrow, he twirled the ends of his handlebar mustache like a villain in a melo-drama. "I thought that act was outlawed back in Philadelphia."

She laughed at the look of wicked anticipation on his freckled face. "I don't know about Philadelphia, but it certainly wasn't allowed in my hometown."

"Ah, banned in Boston," he replied with his boy-ish grin. "This gets better and better."

"I warned Nell that in this hell-raisin' minin' camp the show would be a little hotter than she was used to," said Ross. His green eyes twin-kled with mischief, telling her just how much he'd enjoyed watching her shocked reaction to the naughty jokes.

Gradually, a murmur from the crowd of diners could be heard rumbling through the restaurant. People at nearby tables craned their heads to see whose arrival had created such a stir.

"Looks like the temperature's heating up in here," Eben said with a chortle. "We're gonna think we're sitting in the Kuusinens' Finnish bath before the night's over." He glanced at Ross and then lifted his glass of beer to Nell in a gallant salute. "Here's to your happiness, Miss Ryan."

By that time, the waiter had poured Nell's wine. She lifted the goblet and returned Eben's toast. "And to yours, Mr. Pearce." She smiled across the table at Hertta and Kalle. "To all my new friends."

The hubbub in the room grew louder. Nell couldn't help but turn and rubberneck, right along with the rest of the customers. It seemed a group of performers from the variety show were being seated at a table close to the front. A cluster of waiters partly obscured the view. When they moved, Nell realized what all the fuss was about. Eddie Foy and Eva Tanguay were among the newly arrived dinner party.

Morgan didn't bother to look around. He took

Nell's hand in his and absently played with her fingers. At his touch, the sexual tension, which had cooled slightly during the business of greeting everyone, coiled through her once more. Nell was astonished at the turbulent response he could evoke with such a slight caress.

Just then the waiters started coming, two and three at a time. They brought great silver platters of chicken with almonds and snow peas, roast pork with Chinese cabbage, pepper steak and egg rolls, fried rice with shrimp, wonton, sweet-sour pork with pineapple, bowls of egg-drop soup, and pots of hot tea.

Nell had never before tried to eat with chopsticks. She picked them up and eyed them warily.

"Hold them like this, sugarplum," Ross advised as he demonstrated the correct way to use them.

Her first attempt was disastrous. She giggled as the wonton slipped back on top of the fried rice with a soft plop.

"We can get forks," he said, his eyes alight with fond amusement. He looked around for a waiter.

She gave a determined shake of her head and gripped the chopsticks even tighter. "No, no. If everyone else can manage these oversized toothpicks, so can I."

"T'at's ta spirit, Nellie," Hertta called from across the table. "It alvays tastes better vhen you eat it ta vay it's meant to be eaten." Both the Finnish landlady and her husband were wielding the ivory sticks with practiced ease, making it clear they were frequent patrons of the Tie Lang.

Nell picked up a snow pea and transported it with painstaking care toward her open mouth, this time with greater success. She almost had the food to her lips when it slipped off the chopsticks.

"Here, darlin'," Ross said with a chuckle. "At this rate, you're liable to starve to death." He caught her chin in his hand and turned her face toward him. "Open that pretty little mouth."

She obliged with unthinking acquiescence, and he fed her a shrimp. Reacting instinctively, she stuck out her tongue to catch the pink shellfish before it could slip away. This time she was triumphant.

Their eyes met over the poised chopsticks. The message in his smoldering gaze reminded her of the first time he'd kissed her. That day, on the floor of the mercantile store, he'd told her he wanted to taste her all over. Suddenly, she thought she understood exactly what he'd meant. Lowering her lashes to hide the feeling of breathless alarm that threatened to smother her, she purposely chewed and swallowed.

He leaned over and kissed her sticky lips. "I suppose now you're ready to give up and send for a fork," he teased.

But Nell refused to be defeated by the awkward eating utensils. She kept trying, and with each new victory, her friends cheered her.

They were interrupted in the middle of a round of applause. Eva Tanguay charged up to their table as though she'd been hurled at them by one of the show's acrobatic jugglers. The three men automatically rose to their feet. Without pausing to greet anyone else, the buxom singer threw her arms around Ross.

"You big, handsome lout," she boomed. "Why didn't you come to see my show?" She was dressed in a gold-beaded evening gown cut low enough to display the magnificent bosom she now pressed up against Morgan's broad chest.

"I did see it," he told her. He disengaged Eva's manicured hands from around his neck and held her out in front of him. "I was there at your performance tonight."

Scowling, Eva pulled her hands away and propped them on her ample hips. "Then why didn't you come to my dressing room afterward?"

"I had another engagement," he replied quietly.

For the first time, Eva seemed to be aware of the

people who sat at Morgan's table and were staring up at them in silent fascination. Her glance swept around the circle, passing right over Nell, as though the brunet in the somber clothes couldn't possibly be Ross's companion for the evening. Then as the others were each eliminated in turn, the variety star's cold blue eyes snaked back to rest on Nell in a glare of pure hatred.

"Who's the little pigeon?" she asked Ross with a haughty flip of her head. Her glance took in Nell's gray shirtwaist and black satin skirt with unconcealed disgust.

For the first time in her life, Elinor Ryan felt the green-eyed monster of jealousy take possession of her soul. God, how she detested that loud, vulgar, fuzzy-haired blond. Lifting her chin, Nell stiffened in her seat and met the woman's challenging stare. A faint recollection of reading newspaper stories about Miss Tanguay's vicious cat fights came to mind, but Nell was determined not to be the one to crumple and look away.

"The lady is my lawyer," answered Ross. There was a steel-edged warning in his softly spoken words. It was clear he had no intention of introducing the famous performer to any of his guests, let alone his female companion.

"But I was planning on painting the town red tonight, honey," Eva whined without a hint of subtlety. She smoothed her scarlet fingertips across his broad chest in crass supplication. Nell could barely keep from snorting in disgust. Next to Juniper Jess's polished enticement, Miss Tanguay had all the finesse of a Cabbage Patch slattern.

"I hope you enjoy the evenin'," Morgan replied with glacial politeness. He glanced pointedly at Eben and Kalle, who were still standing in front of their chairs. "Now I think my friends should return to their dinner before it gets cold."

Eva spoke through clenched teeth. "By all means. Don't let me interrupt your meal."

She had no sooner flounced off than a slim, good-looking man in a black tuxedo approached their table. This time, no one stood. The stranger ignored the complete absence of any welcome and brashly placed himself between Nell and Eben's chairs.

"Well, Morgan, it looks like you've upset Miss Tanguay," he remarked. His words, spoken with a crisp, educated Eastern accent, were addressed to Ross, but his gray eyes were fastened on Nell. He appraised her with the lingering glance of a connoisseur.

"Eva will recover by the time she reaches the show's next stop," Ross replied in a tone of unruffled boredom. He picked up a platter and piled more shrimp on Nell's plate.

"I haven't as yet met your beautiful counselor," the uninvited visitor added. He inclined his head of thick brown hair toward Nell and smiled ingratiatingly.

Ross leaned back in his chair and folded his arms across his chest. "What's the hurry? You'll meet both my attorneys soon enough in court."

Undaunted by the icy reception, the man shrugged with consummate charm. "Why not now, since I'm here?" He didn't wait any longer for a formal introduction. "May I take the liberty of introducing myself, Miss Ryan? I'm Felix Hegel."

It was the first time Nell had met the copper king who'd brought the restraining order against the Glamorgan. He was reputed to be a millionaire many times over. Hegel owned not only the Forrester, but several other mining properties, as well as the Montana Copper Purchasing Corporation with its many smelters. He was nearly as tall as Ross, though not so muscular in build.

She immediately extended her hand. "Mr. Hegel, how are you?" She smiled warmly, thrilled at the opportunity to show Ross Morgan that he wasn't the only person in the world who was attractive to the opposite gender. She'd had her fill of watching

half the female population of Butte throw themselves at his feet without a hint of regard for the
feelings of the lady at his side.

Hegel squeezed her fingers and then retained
them in a gesture of blatant flirtation. "Call me
Felix, Miss Ryan. We don't stand on ceremony
around this rustic encampment. I wouldn't know
how to react to someone addressing me so formally."
He leaned closer and spoke in a theatrical whisper. "I
hope your uncongenial client hasn't blackened my
good name too badly. I long for the opportunity to
show you that I'm not nearly the ogre these people
have painted."

She made no attempt to retrieve her hand from
his firm clasp. "I don't remember anyone using the
word *ogre*, Felix," she cooed. She peeped up at him
from under her lashes in a clumsy imitation of Juniper Jess's coy expertise. "I try to leave my legal
animosities on the front steps of the courthouse and
not carry them into my personal life. So please call
me Nell."

"Then perhaps you'll honor me by attending my
gala birthday celebration next month, Nell. Most of
this town's society lions will be there. I'll introduce
you to Butte's finer element."

Before she could answer, Morgan's chair scraped
across the tiled floor as he rose to his feet. Although
Nell was turned away from him, she could feel the
hostility that suddenly swirled around them. She
recalled the primitive brawl that had taken place
the first day she'd arrived, and realized the two men
were only a hair's breadth away from stepping out
into the alley. If they did, they wouldn't engage in
a gentlemen's sporting bout of fisticuffs. It'd be an
eye-gouging, kidney-punching, head-banging fight
that wouldn't end till one of them had beaten the
other senseless.

Ross laid his hand possessively on her shoulder.
She could feel the controlled tension in his strong
fingers. "Miss Ryan has a previous commitment,"

he informed Hegel tersely. "She won't be able to accept."

"But I didn't even mention the date," his adversary protested with a knowing smirk, never taking his pale eyes off Nell.

"Mr. Hegel . . ." she began apologetically in an attempt to gain some control of the situation.

Morgan interrupted her. "My attorney's time is completely engaged, Hegel. You can return her hand to her now. She'll need it to finish her supper."

Nell's Irish temper started to rise. Apparently, it was all right if he flirted with every woman in town under fifty, but she wasn't allowed a single admirer of her own. The two men towered over her in an ominous battle of male wills. To contradict Ross now would be like tossing a match on a kerosene-soaked pile of wood chips. But to give in to his arrogant, dominating ways, as though she were some brainless doll unable to make her own decisions, would set a precedent for all future disagreements between them.

Felix Hegel waited for her answer with urbane charm. Reluctantly, she tugged her fingers out of his grasp and smiled a polite dismissal. "It was a pleasure to meet you, sir. If you'll be so kind as to send me an invitation with the actual date, I'll check my calendar. Should I already have a previous commitment, then I'll see you again in court, as Mr. Morgan has so graciously pointed out."

The others at the table tried to smooth over the whole incident once Hegel moved away, but Nell sensed Ross's lingering fury. His playfulness of a few minutes before had disappeared. He smiled briefly at Kalle's jokes and Eben's attempted raillery as the two men valiantly tried to restore the convivial mood. Although he remained politely attentive to Nell, his rigid posture and granite jaw radiated his fierce displeasure at her consorting with his enemy.

The rest of the party bantered about the coming

election for the site of the state capital, with Kalle and Hertta supporting the city of Anaconda and Eben vociferously behind Helena. From there, they moved on to politics in general. Nell learned that the Irish miners were Democrats, while their rivals, the Cornishmen, usually voted for the Grand Old Party, as did most of the wealthy copper barons.

"Vhat about you, Nellie?" Hertta asked. "If you could vote, vhat party vould you choose?"

"The one that supported women's suffrage," she answered without hesitation.

"But if you *could* vote, you'd already have the suffrage," Eben pointed out. "So come on, stick your neck out and make a choice."

Nell pursed her lips thoughtfully. "Since I'm not a propertied person with a large bank account, I guess I'd have to go along with my fellow Irishmen and vote Democratic." She turned to the contentious man beside her with an apologetic smile, hoping to coax him into a sunnier mood. "What about you, Mr. Morgan?"

"I'm Republican," he said curtly. He rose to his feet and loomed over her. "If you're ready, Miss Ryan, I'll escort you home."

She hesitated, looking across the table at Kalle and Hertta for some sign of guidance. She'd never seen Ross so angry. He'd usually been relaxed, even devil-may-care in her presence. Now he seemed so large and forbidding, she grabbed her crystal goblet and took a last, quick swallow of wine before answering. "Perhaps the Kuusinens can take me back to the boardinghouse with them."

He placed a hand on the back of her chair. His quiet words had the ring of absolute authority. "I'll see you home, Nell."

No one at the table questioned his decision.

"Good-by, Nellie," Hertta said with a smile. Her deep blue eyes glowed with sisterly encouragement. "I'll see you in ta morning."

Nell breathed a little easier. Mrs. Kuusinen had

known Ross for some time, and she didn't look the least bit worried about her female boarder's safety.

Bravely laying her napkin beside her plate, Nell said good night to her friends with all the serene composure she could muster, while her heart thumped a frantic alarm to her worried brain. With a fake smile of tranquillity pinned to her lips, she allowed Morgan to guide her to the door. Heavens to Betsy, she had nothing to be afraid of. After all, what could he do to her, besides deliver a scathing lecture she had no intention of paying the least heed to?

With his hand firmly on Nell's elbow, Ross hurried her out of the noodle parlor before anyone even noticed they were leaving. Not pausing to waste a syllable in needless argument, he helped her into the waiting coach and gave instructions to the driver. Then he climbed in beside her, effectively trapping her in the corner she'd so foolishly chosen.

"If you think—" Nell began in a frigid tone the moment the hired hack started to move.

Ross pulled her to him before she could utter another sound. "Don't say a word," he warned softly. "Before you dig yourself in any deeper, little girl, there's somethin' I'm goin' to teach you."

He slipped one hand behind her neck and slanted his lips across hers. It was a bruising kiss of total male ownership. His tongue ruthlessly invaded her mouth without waiting for any hint of invitation. He pressed her back against the seat's cool leather, pinning her with his greater strength, while he slid his hands over her slender shoulders and down her upper arms. She tried to turn her head away, but he wouldn't allow it. He deliberately covered her full breasts with his outspread fingers, imprisoning her with masterful insolence. He wanted to make certain she realized just how helpless she was at that moment. And how furious she'd made him.

When he'd seen her batting her big brown eyes at Hegel, he'd been ready to pick the sonofabitch up and fling him across the room. If the ass had been foolish enough to regain his feet, Ross would have gladly beaten him to a bloody pulp. That aggressive energy surged through him still, transformed now from the primal need to assert territorial dominance to the rapacious desire to take complete possession of his prize.

Unable to make anything but choked little squeaks in the back of her throat, Nell pushed against his chest in a futile attempt to dislodge him. When that failed, she tried to wriggle away, but her skirt was caught beneath her, and only served to increase her imprisonment. She grabbed a hank of his hair and jerked painfully. He had to reach up and slowly but inexorably squeeze her wrist until she was forced to let go.

Impressed by her show of courage, he purposefully eased the aura of violence, reminding himself of her lack of experience when it came to games between men and women. He sure as hell didn't want her terrified that she was about to lose her virginity in the bouncing cab of a hired hack.

Gentling the pressure of his lips, Ross pulled her blouse until it was free of her skirt's waistband and his fingers touched her bare skin. Then he broke the kiss and drew back. He met her velvety eyes, wide with confusion and awakening desire. Even in the darkened coach, lit only by the moonlight that streamed in through the window glass, he could see her bite her lower lip to keep it from trembling. With his gaze entrapping hers, he slid his fingertips beneath her silken chemise and lightly stroked her nipples. She jerked in convulsive reaction and then shivered beneath his touch as she gave a low sigh of surrender.

"Oh, Ross . . ." she whispered.

He pushed her loosened clothing upward to reveal her bare breasts. Her agitated breathing caused those perfect, silken globes to rise and fall in irresistible temptation. A groan of raw, sexual hunger was torn from deep inside him. Bending his head, he laved her nipples till their crests were tight buds of arousal against his tongue. He could feel her fingers tangle in his hair, but this time in a shy, feminine signal that urged him onward.

Moving her with him, he sat back on the coach seat and lifted her onto his lap. The firm curve of her buttocks pressed against his turgid rod and filled him with a deep, soul-satisfying pleasure. He eased her over his arm till her head was tipped back, exposing the curve of her throat and lifting her lush breasts upward toward his waiting mouth. He paused in fascination at her sensuous beauty.

She was a love goddess come down from some erotic, mystical paradise to tease and torment him. He'd gladly take all the delicious torture she chose to inflict on her willing victim. But he wasn't about to allow another living male to be enticed by her incredible allure. The memory of Felix Hegel holding her graceful fingers in his sweaty palm fueled Ross's raging need to claim her as his own.

"I want you, Nell," he said, his low voice thick with desire. "This waitin' has just about driven me insane, but it's goin' to come to a sweet, sudden end."

He cupped her breast and covered the top of its swollen fullness with his open mouth. As he suckled her, he moved his hand downward, over the satin folds of her skirt and under its hem. She tried to sit up straight as his fingers slid along her stockinged leg, but there was no way she could gain the needed leverage.

She was wearing silk drawers. The deep rows of frilly lace at the knees brushed against his fingertips, and a searing jolt of white-hot lust spread through his body. He palmed her stomach, covered by the gossamer fabric, and then found the narrow ribbon that fastened her underwear. With a quick tug, he released the bow holding the two nearly separate leg pieces together at the waist and slipped his hand inside the opened crotch.

The moment Nell felt his warm fingers on her bare abdomen, she knew exactly what he intended to teach her. A feeling of overwhelming sexual excitement shimmered through her tense body, part anger, part frantic, uncontrollable need for him. It was what she'd yearned for all evening—to have him hold her in his arms and touch her intimately. Her emotions whipsawed crazily, with jealousy, desire, frustration, and wrath all mixed up together.

He lifted his head from her breast and traced a trail of fire up her neck with his tongue. "Open your legs for me, angel," he urged softly in her ear. He cupped her mound in his hand, his fingertips brushing through the tightly matted curls. "Don't be afraid, darlin'. I won't enter you, I promise. I'm just going to touch you."

She obeyed. There wasn't any other choice. The pulsating sensation that unfolded within her at his caress, like a flower starting to blossom, took complete control of her body. She couldn't have stopped what was happening inside her anymore than she could have kept a rosebud from blooming.

With his burning gaze locked to hers, Ross stroked the delicate folds of her womanhood. Embarrassed at the shocking intimacy, she lowered her lids, but he wouldn't allow her to hide what she was feeling.

"Look at me, Nell," he ordered hoarsely. "I want to see your eyes when you reach fulfillment. I want to see into your very soul."

He set an unhurried pace. She could feel the slick moisture that sprang up at the fiery touch of his fingers and the honeyed enticement of his words. All the erotic tension that had ricocheted through her during the evening was now centered in the sensitive, engorged tissues at the very core of her femininity. He played with her gently, teasingly, rhythmically, till Nell thought her pounding heart would burst. He seemed to know the instant she'd reached the point where the slightest stroke brought mindless shafts of pleasure lancing through her. With loving expertise, he took her through the elusive door of female orgasm, covering her mouth with his firm lips to muffle the plaintive sob of her release.

Nell's heart raced wildly out of control as she took in deep drafts of air. In the aftermath of ecstasy, she was vaguely aware that Ross efficiently retied the ribbons of her drawers, pulled down her petticoat and skirt, and smoothed their wrinkled folds into place. Then he cuddled her in his arms, his lips tracing tender, reassuring kisses on her temple and cheek.

"How did you get to be so sweet?" he questioned her with a soft chuckle of male victory. "I'm going to devour you like a man eating a pomegranate."

Wrapped in a delicious languor, Nell rested her head against his broad chest and listened to his quickened heartbeat. Her fingers lay against the dark wool that covered his upper arm. She leisurely stroked the rough fabric, relishing the feel of muscles bunching beneath her touch. Slowly, she lifted her heavy lids and found him gazing down at her with an expression of unutterable tenderness.

"Is that what you wanted to teach me?" she asked, her husky words dreamy and faraway.

A smile skipped around the corners of his sensual lips. "No, angel eyes. That was just my way of gettin' your attention. The lesson for your edification this evenin' is that you should never play games unless you're sure you know all the rules."

"The first one being?"

"I'm a very possessive lover."

"And the second?"

Although he spoke in a soft tone, there was an edge of iron-willed determination in his words.

"Don't ever flirt with Felix Hegel again."

There was an *or else* implicit in his warning, but she didn't ask him to explain further. She wasn't certain she really wanted to know.

Chapter 15

It was a glorious Saturday morning, the last one in August. The celebrated Montana sky was a breathtaking dome of deepest azure. A light breeze blew puffy white clouds ahead of them and ruffled the golden fringe on the surrey's canopy top as Nell and Ross headed up into the foothills of the Highland Mountains. They were climbing quickly, leaving far behind all trace of the stark gallows frames, the ugly, belching smelters, and the staid Victorian buildings of the copper camp.

The rolling grassland was golden in the sunshine. Deep coulees cut across the open prairie. Bushes grew along the ravines in thickets, their dark green leaves a lush backdrop for wild currants, gooseberries, and hawthorn berries. Intoxicated by the pure mountain air, Nell fought the insane temptation to burst into one of the scandalous songs they'd heard the night before. Her high spirits were partly due to the lingering effects of Mr. Foy's musical extravaganza. But her elation was also stirred by the knowledge that the magnificent vista before her was the last vestige of her country's Western frontier.

Off in the distance, a great herd of cattle ambled across the undulating hills. She leaned out of the buggy in excitement when she realized that the animals were being moved by honest-to-goodness cowboys mounted on their working cowponies. Except for glimpses from a Pullman car window, until that moment all she'd seen of cattle ranching were the few ranch owners who came into Butte infrequently on business. And they were usually dressed in ordinary suits, even if they did wear ten-gallon hats and high-heeled boots.

"Careful, darlin'," Ross warned her with a slow, lazy chuckle. His eyes glinted with wry amusement as he pushed his wide-brimmed hat back on his head. "If you lean out any further to catch a peek at those cowpokes, you're goin' to tumble right off and land in a patch of prickly pear."

She turned to him with a curious smile. "What's that?"

"Cactus. You'll get acquainted with its finer points real fast if you fall in the stuff." He motioned to her with a jerk of his head. "Come over here and sit beside me, honeybunch. You've been hunkerin' over there on the end of the seat long enough."

With the reins held firmly in his strong hands, he sat relaxed, making it look easy to control the spirited team. She knew that wasn't so. Under Ross's expert guidance, however, the lively pair had the manners and presence of the finest carriage horses in Boston.

She affected an air of bored disinterest as she scooted to the center of the buggy's front seat, careful to leave a modest distance between his muscled leg and the deep blue muslin of her summer gown. Ross wore a plaid shirt with its sleeves rolled up, revealing his powerful forearms. The indigo denim of his Levi's was molded to his lean flanks and massive thighs. She avoided looking at him as much as possible without appearing to be unnecessarily rude or painfully shy. Heaven save her, she *had* to keep her eyes on the scenery. The sight of all that potent male virility had a drastic effect on her usually steady heartbeat.

She lifted the small bouquet of flowers she held in her hand and breathed in their perfume. "I was just trying to see a little of the countryside," she told him with an air of ennui. "When I'm back in Boston, people will ask me what Montana is like, and I'll want to be able to tell them I've seen more of it than one wild and woolly mining town."

Secretly, she was thrilled to be bowling along at a spanking pace in one of the sweetest surreys she'd ever seen, seated beside the most dynamic man she'd ever known. They were traveling through a setting that would have made a jaded world traveler breathless. She kept her thoughts to herself, however. She wasn't about to tell Ross Morgan how pleased she was to be in his company. He was bold enough without her encouragement.

Earlier that morning, she'd tried to talk her way out of going on the picnic at all. Actually, she'd attempted, at first, to sleep her way out of it. Ross had told her during an intermission at the Comique Theater that they were to leave by seven at the latest. She was still in bed at six-thirty, when he pounded on her door. She refused to respond to such cavalier treatment, so he sent Hertta in to wake her up. The landlady had left the door slightly ajar. He called to Nell from the hallway that if she wasn't up in five minutes, he'd come into her bedroom and get her ready to go, if he had to dress her himself. That had got her up and moving.

Sleepy-eyed, she'd joined him for breakfast in the boardinghouse's big kitchen. She refused to meet his gaze, mortified at the memory of what had happened in the carriage the previous night. She'd been so tired when she'd climbed into bed, she'd fallen asleep the moment her head touched the pillow. Now, in the morning light, everything came back with perfect and humiliating clarity. She couldn't possibly spend the entire day alone in Morgan's company after the liberties he'd taken with her in the hired hack. The fact that she'd *allowed* him those liberties only made it worse. She could have kicked herself for being such a fool. Her brains must have gone on a holiday.

"Where's Luke?" she inquired with a sullen pout, her eyes glued to the Finnish pancake in front of her. "I wanted to ask him if he'd like to go along on the picnic. Maybe he and his friends could join us." She knew the ten-year-old had stayed overnight with the Saarelainen brothers, who lived next door. That stratagem had given his father the freedom to attend a party till all hours at the Tie Lang Noodle Palace, as well as the time to attempt a seduction of his female companion on their way home.

Ross smiled amiably. He looked so clear-eyed and refreshed, she could have kicked him. "Why, sugarplum, if I'd known you wanted to bring the boys on this outin', I'd have asked them for you. As it is, the three were out diggin' worms in the backyard at five o'clock this mornin'. They left to go fishin' at Bell Creek nearly two hours ago."

"I'm not sure I'm up to this jaunt," she complained peevishly. She set her coffee cup down and pushed her untouched breakfast aside. Holding her head in her hands, she massaged her temples with dramatic exaggeration. "I drank too much champagne last night. I'm probably going to have a terrible headache. I warned you I wasn't used to imbibing spirits."

"You're just a little tired," he told her bracingly. "You didn't have enough liquor to put a canary under the table." He picked up her dish and slid the blueberry-covered *pannukakku* she'd ignored onto his empty plate. "All you need is some fresh air and good food," he continued as he poured melted butter on top of his second generous serving of pancake. "And maybe a little hair of the dog that bit you."

"Vell, I like t'at," Hertta scolded in mock displeasure. "Vhat's vrong with ta food in front of you, may I ask?" Bustling around the long trestle table, she refilled his coffee cup and then reached for Nell's.

Ross winked at his ill-tempered breakfast partner and flashed his lazy grin. "Now don't get yourself in a dither, Mrs. Kuusinen. We're all aware that you're the best cook in Butte. I just want the little dolly here to know that I'm not goin' to take her on an all-day outin' without feedin' her properly."

"Why don't you come along with us, Hertta?" Nell peeked at Morgan from under the cover of her hands, expecting him to show some sign of consternation.

But he was no fool. He beamed as though he were wondering why he hadn't thought of inviting Hertta himself. "Yes, why don't you join us?" he asked. His grin widened and a look of unruffled good humor spread across his handsome face.

"Pooh, you two stop being so silly and get on out of here." She flapped her striped apron at them like a farmer's wife shooing chickens from her garden. "I'm not going to horn in on your picnic. Anyway, I vill be leaving to do ta grocery shopping very shortly."

Nell realized with disgust that Ross had remembered Hertta's habit of buying the boardinghouse's food supplies for the entire week on Saturday mornings. He'd known there wasn't the slightest danger that she'd accept his invitation.

The moment breakfast was over, Ross had whisked Nell outside, where a surrey and team stood waiting. The sight of the lovely rig, painted a dark green with gold striping to match the canopy's fringe, and the two perfectly matched chestnut trotters harnessed in front, made her disheartened spirits soar. A trip to the countryside in such a darling carriage would be a rare treat.

But she remembered all too well what had happened the last time she was alone with Rossiter Morgan. For a woman who'd vowed never to have another romantic relationship with a man, she'd come disastrously close to losing every hard-won measure of emotional independence she'd gained in the years since her tragic affair with Charleton Blevins. Men couldn't be trusted. Plain and simple.

Just because this particular male had all the honeyed charm of a traveling tinker didn't change that basic truth one iota.

"I don't think I should be going on this excursion with you," she told him from the vantage point of the wide front porch. "Especially alone. I'm sorry I ever promised to go. I don't think it's proper."

He took her elbow and hustled her down the stairs to the surrey before she had a chance to dig in her heels. "Too bad you've had a change of heart, little girl," he said without a hint of sympathy. "But since I've already taken you to the Comique, it's too late for you to back out of our agreement now. A bargain's a bargain. And goin' on a picnic with your beau isn't half as improper as that show we saw together last night." He moved even closer and leered at her suggestively.

She jerked her arm out of his grasp. "You're not my beau," she informed him with a scowl. "And it wasn't the variety show I was thinking of. Besides, you kept me out so late, I'm overtired. I'm afraid I wouldn't be very good company. We'll have to postpone this jaunt to some other time."

"You can sleep on the way," he said. "Don't feel you have to chatter every minute. I like a woman who knows when to be quiet." He tossed her up into the buggy, climbed onto the seat beside her, and placed a nosegay of rosebuds, violets, and lilies of the valley in her hand. Then he whistled sharply to the team, and they were off.

Nell hadn't chattered during the ride, but she hadn't fallen asleep either. Nor did she come down with a headache as she'd predicted. She was far too busy enjoying the landscape as they drove into the wooded uplands to remember she was supposed to be tired and cranky. They made several stops along the way to stretch their legs and rest the horses. By noon they reached a shady glen beside a bubbling stream. Along its banks were stands of river birches, alders, and aspens, their leaves rustling in the gentle wind.

Ross pulled the team to a halt beneath a spreading willow tree that must have been close to a hundred years old. Sunlight glistened here and there through its branches, bathing the August grass that encircled its massive trunk in brilliant splotches of gold and brown. Drifts of wild sunflowers danced in the nearby meadow. All around them was a forest of lodgepole pine and Douglas fir, with limber pine and alpine fir on the higher elevations.

"What a beautiful place," she exclaimed. Enchanted, she looked around in sincere appreciation. "It's a perfect spot for a picnic."

Ross jumped down from the buggy and reached up to help her descend. "I thought you'd like it here."

He didn't clasp her politely by the waist when he lifted her down from the high, four-wheeled vehicle. And he didn't immediately set her on the ground as good manners dictated. With his arms wrapped shamelessly around her hips, he held her pressed against his powerful body, her shoulders well above his broad ones, her bosom dangerously close to his upturned face. Grinning wickedly, he twirled her in a dizzying circle.

Caught by surprise, she grabbed his shoulders and squealed in protest. "Put me down!"

"Okay, sugarplum." He let her slide slowly down the long, hard length of his tall frame till their eyes were on the same level and her toes didn't quite touch the ground. "Give me a kiss and I will," he promised.

"No," she declared in her coolest lawyerlike manner. "Going on a picnic was the whole bargain. Kissing was never mentioned once."

"Heck, I'll throw in the kissin' for nothin'. I won't even charge you for it."

She stared into his eyes, alight with deviltry, and felt an answering call to cast aside all inhibitions and

join him in an afternoon of spontaneous, childlike
play. She quickly stifled the foolish notion, determined to remain aloof, poised, and even a trace
frigid, if need be. His lighthearted demeanor didn't
fool her one bit. She knew where this was leading.
Heavens to Betsy, she hadn't just fallen off a turnip
wagon.

"No."

"You don't get down till I get my kiss," he warned
her cheerfully. He squeezed her tighter, pressing her
abdomen against his flat stomach in flagrant violation of the proprieties.

She lifted her chin and tried to stare him out of
countenance. "How long do you think you can hold
me like this?" she asked derisively.

"All day if I have to."

She scoffed at the very idea. "You'd get awfully
hungry."

"I had a big breakfast. I ate yours too. Remember?"

"Oh, very well," she conceded, unable to resist
for a moment longer the stirrings of pleasure that
spread like wildfire through her veins. The feel of
his corded thighs burned through the crushed layers of blue muslin and ivory lawn. Her gaze drifted
to his mouth. "One kiss."

"One kiss," he agreed.

She waited with outward serenity for him to lean
toward her and press his firm lips against hers.
Instead, he just looked at her in happy expectation.
She returned his sunny gaze in bemusement.

"I'm waitin'," he reminded her blithely, when she
made no move.

Flabbergasted, she pointed to herself and lifted
her brows in a silent, wide-eyed question.

He nodded. "You can kiss me anytime you're
ready, angel eyes. That is, if you think a Yankee
spinster lawyer could ever be any good at spoonin'."

Those were fighting words, and Nell accepted the
challenge. She was going to give Mr. Popularity a

kiss that would make his socks roll up and down. And that was *all* he was going to get. One single, solitary kiss for the entire afternoon.

First, she lifted off her straw bonnet and let it dangle down her back on its broad satin ribbon. Then she removed his high-crowned Stetson and casually tossed it on the ground. Framing his cheeks with her palms, she tipped her head to one side. She leaned closer, then stopped, her lips mere inches from his.

"I'm not getting too heavy, am I?" she taunted. "I wouldn't want you to drop me right in the middle of my big smooch."

"I won't drop you," he promised. "No matter how heavy you are or how excited I get."

At his provocative gibe, she tightened her hold on his face and smashed her lips against his. Beneath the fierce pressure she exerted, his mouth opened in complacent invitation. Nell thrust her tongue inside, sweeping the warm moist cavern, daring him to join her in a flirtatious dance of enticement. Thanks to him, she'd come a long way in her kissing technique since she'd first arrived in Butte. The evenings of study at her office on Montana Street hadn't been wasted. She put everything she'd learned into that sizzling kiss.

He didn't drop her, but he certainly got excited. She could feel the hard bulge of his male arousal pressed against the juncture of her thighs. She'd succeeded in tantalizing him, just as she'd intended. But her plan to torment her brash companion didn't work quite the way she'd expected. For there was an aching emptiness deep inside her now that could only be eased by his touch.

All the physical longing he'd nurtured within her the night before came crashing back like a tempestuous storm she'd so foolishly thought was spent and blown. She inhaled the lingering spice of his shaving soap and fought the inexplicable urge to unbutton his cotton shirt and bury her fingertips in the thick mat of golden-brown hair that curled just below his collarbone. She wanted to rub her cheek against his bare chest and drown herself in the marvelous male scent of him. Awed and wary, she wondered what had come over her. It was only one kiss. What was this strange power he exerted so effortlessly?

Bewildered by her cartwheeling emotions, she drew back and met his smoldering eyes. The sure knowledge of her foolhardy self-entrapment shone in their gold-flecked depths.

"You . . . ah . . ." She cleared her throat and started again. "You said you'd put me down after . . ."

"Yes, ma'am," he said and immediately set her on her feet.

Nell felt a stab of acute disappointment as he stepped away from her. She avoided his shrewd gaze, determined to keep her unladylike thoughts well-hidden. Pretending an air of calm civility, she looked over at the surrey. "We'd better get the things unloaded," she announced with a carefree smile.

Together, Nell and Ross spread a dark green lap robe in the shade beneath the giant willow. While she unpacked the wicker basket, he unhitched the two mares and led them down to the water. Then he hobbled the snorting, snickering, affectionate pair so they could graze nearby.

"You thought of everything," she told him when he returned to join her on the soft wool blanket. "After last night's marvelous food, it's a wonder we can even think of eating."

"I ordered that basket of goodies from the Meaderville Bakery. When I explained that we were plannin' to dine outdoors, the Italian proprietor promised to fix us an *alfresco* meal fit for a copper king."

Ross helped her set out the sumptuous feast. There were assorted cheeses, imported olives, a loaf of French bread, salami, and slices of roast beef, as well as fresh strawberries and green grapes. For dessert, there was a small tin of white, crescent-shaped cookies.

"I hope you're hungry," said Nell. Thoroughly impressed by her escort's largesse, she sat back and surveyed the generous array. "We have enough food to feed an entire shift of starving miners."

Ross removed the cork from a bottle of wine and poured it into two crystal goblets. He handed one to her and set the other on the grass nearby. "Before we eat, we're goin' to enjoy an outdoor concert."

Nell laughed and looked around at the picturesque setting, as though half expecting a group of musicians to appear from the trees. "Where's the band?"

"Right here." He lifted his trumpet from its case with a flourish, and the horn's shiny brass glittered in a patch of bright sunshine. She hadn't even noticed the brown leather box on the floor of the buggy's back seat.

"What do I do for my share of the entertainment?" she asked enthusiastically.

"You get to be the audience, buttercup. Just sip your wine, relax, and listen while I serenade you."

Until that moment, Nell had forgotten entirely that Ross played an instrument. "I haven't seen you with your trumpet since the Fourth of July," she said with a smile of anticipation.

"That's because I haven't played a note since the parade." He fingered the valves and adjusted the tuning slide. "I had to tell the other members of the band that I wouldn't be able to practice with them until after the lawsuit was settled."

Nell realized that, instead of playing with the Boston and Montana Band, he'd been spending his evenings tutoring her in mining technology. But his lack of practice didn't show. He went from one song to another, the timbre of the clear notes brilliant and incisive. It was an impressive display of talent. With smooth virtuosity, he played all the songs they'd heard in the variety show at the Comique. The clever vaudeville performers had added their own risqué lyrics to many of the familiar old melodies. The memory of their irreverent words brought a grin of unmaidenly delight, which she made no attempt to hide.

Ross was sitting cross-legged on the green blanket, looking for all the world like a golden-haired snake charmer. Seated directly in front of him, she listened in rapt fascination. His last piece was a scintillating rendition of the musical's sultry harem dance.

While he played, Nell held one hand to her face in imitation of a dancing girl's veil. She peeked over her fingers and rolled her eyes suggestively. When he finished, she set down her empty glass and applauded wildly. "Bravo! Bravo!"

"Thank you, darlin'. Thank you." He stood and, with arms spread wide, bowed over and over again like a wily burlesque entertainer milking his audience for the very last bit of applause.

"Encore, encore," she begged.

"Maybe later." He bent down and laid the horn back in its velvet-lined case. "Right now we're goin' to indulge in what's considered an absolute prerequisite on every Montana picnic."

"What's that?"

"We're goin' wadin'."

She looked at the stream, sparkling and gurgling in the summer sunlight. "I don't know," she said doubtfully. "We'd have to take our shoes off."

"Most people usually do when they go wadin'."

"You'd have to turn your back while I removed my stockings." She clasped her hands together on her lap, just like the prim old maid she was, and peered up at him suspiciously.

Beneath their thick lashes, his green eyes lit up with wicked merriment. His lips quirked in a roguish smile. "Only if you insisted."

"I would. I do!"

"Yes, ma'am." He plopped back down on the blanket and proceeded to pull off his tall Western boots and wool socks, then started to roll up his Levi's. Nell turned so her back was presented to him and quickly removed her black patent shoes, dark stockings, and garters.

She hadn't gone wading since she'd left Bar Harbor. The prospect sounded delightful. With the hems of her embroidered muslin frock and two layers of petticoats gathered up in one hand, she padded barefoot down the grassy bank and waded out, till the clear, rushing water almost reached the knees of her frilly knickers.

"Don't slip," he warned her, his deep voice filled with the impudent hope that she'd do just that. In less than a minute, he'd joined her in the splashing stream. "If you fall and get wet, you'll have to hang that pretty dress and petticoat on those kinnikinnick bushes over there to dry. And I didn't bring along an extra blanket to wrap you up in." He tucked his thumbs in his belt and grinned like the unrepentant rakehell he was. "But for another one of those Yankee kisses, I'd give you the shirt off my back."

"Don't worry, I know how to go wading," she assured him with a haughty lift of her chin. "I used to live at the seashore. I even know how to swim."

He looked at her in astonishment. "You're kiddin'."

She could tell that this time she'd really impressed him. "I told you I was a liberated woman," she replied. She made no attempt to hide her pride in such a daring accomplishment.

"Well, hot damn," he said and took a step toward her. "Let's go swimmin'."

She moved backward in quick retreat. "Not without a proper bathing costume, I won't! Besides, this water's freezing." In her hurry, her bare heel slipped on a smooth rock. She teetered dangerously, and his arm came around her like a band of steel. He bent toward her, his luminous gaze fastened on her mouth.

She laughed and turned her face aside to avoid his lips. "You don't expect me to kiss you after that infamous Turkish music, do you?" she teased. "I know who you were thinking of when you played it."

"Who?" he baited. A wolfish look flashed across his rugged features.

"Who else but Eva Tanguay?"

"As a matter of fact, you're dead wrong," said Ross. "I thought of harem music the first moment I saw you."

Astonished, she leaned back against his arm and searched his eyes. He could read the disbelief in her quizzical gaze. Her lips were slightly parted in an intrigued smile. "Whyever did you do that?"

"Because you looked like you stepped right out of a seraglio," he murmured, pulling her closer. He studied the inviting fullness of her lips and the exotic beauty of the dark mole against her creamy complexion.

"What?" she exclaimed in mystification. "I don't follow your logic. Or is there any?"

Ross nuzzled her ear and gently bit the soft, sensitive lobe before answering with a chuckle. "It's a matter of history, punkin. When those Spanish soldiers were stranded on the shores of Ireland at the time of the Armada, there must have been a Moor or two among them. And one of those dark-eyed infidels was your great-great-great-great granddaddy."

"How ridiculously fanciful!" she mocked with a jeering laugh. "What else did you think of when you first met me?"

"A Muslim paradise."

His green eyes burned with an electrifying intensity. Nell sobered in the space of a heartbeat and lowered her lids in flushed confusion.

He answered her unspoken question with a fiery kiss that threatened to sweep away the last remnants of her control. She shivered in his arms, clinging to him like the Mohammedan love nymph he'd implied she resembled.

He ended the kiss with obvious reluctance. "Let's have lunch," he said, his voice thick and raspy. "You didn't have anything to eat at breakfast. You must be starvin'."

After the meal and a second glass of wine, Nell stretched out on the blanket, completely relaxed and a little light-headed. She tried not to giggle like a schoolgirl when Ross insisted on feeding her a cluster of grapes in imitation of a Roman gladiator at his last orgy. Not to be outdone, she sat up beside him and lifted a plump green grape to his lips. He took it with a greedy thrust of his tongue and then nibbled on her fingertips as well. After that, they took turns dipping the strawberries in powdered sugar and feeding them to each other.

Ross held a juicy, ripe strawberry to Nell's sultry mouth and watched her bite it in half with her even white teeth. A jolt of red-hot desire shot straight through him. He felt as though he'd been impaled on a lance of flame and nearly groaned out loud with the exquisite torment of it.

Leaning closer, he kissed her sugary lips with gluttonous relish. "Mm, sweetheart," he murmured. "You taste as wonderful as you look. I knew you'd be delicious, the moment I laid eyes on you."

At the sure knowledge of what he planned to do next, Ross's heart hammered wildly against his ribs. But he was determined to hold himself in check. The last thing he wanted was to stampede her. He was certain that under her cautious exterior Nell hid a passionate, sensual nature. In their evenings of study together, she'd made no secret of her love for tantalizing perfumes and beautiful clothes. She'd confided that she dreamed of visiting Paris and Rome or sailing to some faraway tropical isle. Her drive to fill her life completely with work seemed to be motivated by some strange need to keep all men at bay while she punished herself with a self-inflicted isolation, as though atoning for past sins. What she'd done to feel so guilty about, he couldn't

imagine and didn't really care. He knew her character was as pure and unsullied as a child's.

Ross took Nell in his arms and kissed her deeply,
passionately, trying to tell her without words how
he yearned to pleasure her. Moving slowly, so as
not to startle her into retreating behind that practiced wall of indifference, he slid his hands over her
voluptuous curves, getting her used to the feel of
his touch. One by one, he removed the pins from
her gorgeous hair. The thick tresses fell around her
slender shoulders like a curtain of mahogany satin,
and he buried his fingers in their silken depths. The
scent of gardenias filled his nostrils.

His breathing quickened and deepened, as talons
of hot male lust sank deep into his abdomen, thighs,
and groin, threatening to rip apart his mask of calm
control. Carefully, purposefully, Ross ignored the
spurs of raw, primal need that raked through his
covetous body as he ignited and nurtured the passion within her. Easing her down to the blanket, he
stroked her slim shoulders and straight back with
increasing ardor, then caressed her lush breasts and
rounded buttocks, intent on bringing the flame of
desire to a raging blaze.

He crooned to her softly, telling her how beautiful she was and how much he needed her, while
he unbuttoned the bodice of her dress and tugged
on the narrow ribbon that fastened her lacy chemise. He suckled her swollen breasts and slipped
his hand beneath her light muslin gown and the
layers of gauzy petticoat. When he untied the ribbons on her cotton drawers, she stiffened in sudden
alarm.

"Wait, Ross," she croaked, a hint of panic in her
shaky voice. "There's something I have to tell you.
Something you don't know about me."

He lifted his mouth from the sweet heaven of
her silken body and met her anguished gaze. Her
delicate features were creased with worry. "Sweetheart," he teased with a soft laugh, "I already know

you're an Irish Papist Democrat. There can't possibly be anything worse to add."

"I'm not a virgin," she blurted out.

"Neither am I, darlin'," he admitted with a low growl of mock-apology. "So I guess we have something in common after all."

Nell looked up into his heavy-lidded gaze and found complete reassurance. He hadn't batted an eyelash at her shameful confession.

With their gazes locked, he slipped his hand inside the opening of her knickers and caressed the most intimate part of her body. He spread her delicate folds, the pads of his strong fingers rubbing gently across the engorged tissues of her womanhood, enticing Nell to set aside her false pride and listen to her heart. All the hidden desires she'd tried so desperately to deny filled her being, her very soul. The spiritual longing for a life mate to cherish and adore was even stronger than the physical passion that flowed through her veins. Tears blurred her eyes as she realized she was shaking with emotions she thought she'd never know.

Nell could feel the fullness between her thighs as his fingers eased inside her. She was moist and slick, her body responding to the building pressure he created with the steady, throbbing rhythm of his touch. Never before had she felt this primeval need to belong to another, a need that seemed to spiral up from the very core of her being. Apart from him, she was incomplete. Together, they were one. Two halves made whole.

The insatiable desire he'd built within her during the evenings they'd spent together and the erotic intimacy they'd shared last night, coupled with the tenderness he now showed after hearing her terrible secret, swept away all doubts. She wanted him to make love to her. She wanted to accept the joy and pleasure he was offering, all the while knowing that she would never be the same again. She would have the memory of their coupling to cherish in the empty, barren years ahead, when the aching loneliness would once more become a living presence in her heart.

Nell slid her fingers in the tangled waves of his golden hair and pulled his head down to hers in wanton female enticement. "What if someone comes?" she whispered against his lips.

"There isn't a soul in ten miles, darlin'."

Grateful they were both still barefoot, Ross quickly shed his Levi's and drawers. He knew Nell would never undress completely in the open countryside, no matter how much he tried to convince her that they wouldn't be interrupted. For their first time together, he'd have to go along with her feminine reticence. Later, he'd have the pleasure of exploring her nubile body at his leisure in a comfortable bed. Hell, he'd have the rest of his life to memorize every silken, supple inch of her.

Ross throbbed with a wild sexual frustration that had tortured him all summer long. At times during the past weeks, he'd been afraid he'd go plain loco and try to take her by force like some rutting stallion. The muscles of his groin clutched and tautened with primal excitement as he knelt between her slender white legs, pushed her gown and petticoat up to her hips, and gently lifted her knees. There was no need to remove her dainty knickers. Unfastened, the two nearly separate leg pieces opened wide, revealing the cloud of mahogany curls that covered her soft female core.

His heart stalled at the sight of her. She was so damn lovely, so unbelievably perfect. His hand shook as he reached out to touch her. Beneath his loving caress, her delicate folds grew swollen and slick with arousal. He stroked the fragile petals of her womanhood with tender care, longing to taste her, but unsure if she'd react with pleasure or shock. What had her previous lover taught her? Whoever the bastard was, he'd certainly left her crippled with feelings of shame and guilt about the most precious

gift a man and woman could share. But that was all
over. Ross had no intention of letting her return to
Boston and that fool idiot's arms.

"Touch me, sweetheart," he urged with a groan.

Timidly, she placed her fingers on his turgid staff.
He was surprised at the shy, hesitant awkwardness
of her movements. Knowing he was unusually well-
endowed, he wondered if the sight of his erection
had startled her. He covered her hand with his,
showing her how to stroke him, letting her get comfortable with his naked male virility.

That proved a mistake. The past weeks of unfulfilled need, when he'd kissed and petted her without seeking his own satisfaction, had left him nearly
crazed with desire. Even though he quickly took her
hand away, it was too late.

"Darlin', I can't wait any longer," he gasped in
hoarse apology. He cupped her buttocks in his hands
and lifted her to him. With a powerful thrust of his
hips, he drove his manhood deep inside her.

She cried out in pain at the same instant he realized that he'd entered the tightest passage he'd ever
encountered. He stopped, frozen with surprise, his
engorged staff wedged inside her sweet, constricting
warmth, his weight braced on his hands to keep from
crushing her ribs. With iron self-control, he forced
himself to remain absolutely still.

"Jesus, Nell! You've done this before?"

Her frightened voice trembled pathetically. "Yes."

"How many times?"

"Once."

"How long ago?"

"When I was seventeen."

"Jesus H. Christ!"

Ross was racked with remorse. If he'd known she
was so inexperienced, he'd have gone much, much
slower. But it was too late. He was fully embedded
in her tender flesh. With her eyes shut tight, she lay
totally passive beneath him—in shock, no doubt,
from his swift, forceful entry.

He propped his elbows on either side of her head and gathered the thick locks of her gardenia-scented hair in his fists. He kissed her smooth neck and the soft underside of her jaw with all the aching tenderness he felt. "For Christ's sake, darlin', you should have told me," he whispered hoarsely in her ear.

"I did!" she cried in confusion. "And you don't need to keep swearing about it." She started to move beneath him—in agitation, not passion—as though she were trying to buck him off.

"Wait," he cautioned. "Stay still." But it was too late.

"Oh, baby, I'm sorry," he moaned. His whole body shook with the force of his ejaculation.

She lay perfectly still, her face turned aside to avoid his gaze, while he withdrew as slowly and carefully as he should have entered. He used his clean white handkerchief to gently wipe away the traces of his spilled seed, then retied the ribbons of her drawers and smoothed her petticoat and gown. Lying back down beside her, Ross took her in his arms. She turned her head to stare at him in hurt silence, her velvety brown eyes enormous with distrust and dismay and, of course, bitter disappointment.

Christ, he'd bungled it.

Under the mistaken assumption that at thirty-one and no longer a virgin, she must be at least moderately experienced, he'd moved far too fast, leaving her unsatisfied and filled with regret. He'd been overwhelmed by his nearly frantic drive to possess her. Damn it to hell, he'd acted as impulsive and impatient as a sixteen-year-old kid with his first girl. Never in his life had he lost control like that.

"Just give me a few minutes to catch my breath, love," he said, "and I'll do it right. Next time, I'll make it good for you."

"There'll be no next time," she corrected in a hollow voice. She shoved his arm aside and rose to her feet. Turning her back to him, she fastened the buttons of her gown. "Please take me home."

Ross moved to stand behind her and placed his hands lightly on her stiff shoulders. "Nell, don't do this," he pleaded. "We can't leave here like this."

"Take me home!" Her strident words were filled with a mounting panic, as though she were afraid he would force her to do it all over again. She pulled out of his grasp, knelt down, and started packing the picnic basket with quick, jerky movements.

Baffled by her violent reaction, he stood watching, naked from the waist down, as she methodically wrapped up the leftover food and stored it away. He understood her dissatisfaction, but not her fear. "Sweetheart," he began, "you're makin' a mistake."

"I've already made my mistake," she said, refusing to look at him. "But it's not going to happen again."

He took a step toward her, and she jumped in fright.

"All right," he said in soft reassurance. "Let's go home. We've got a long ride ahead of us. We can talk this out on the way back."

Chapter 16

"I'm all done with my packin', Dad."

Ross laid a folded shirt atop the stack on his rumpled bed and looked over at his son. "You sure you got everything? Better check that bureau again, just to be certain."

Whistling softly under his breath, Luke turned to look into his dresser drawers for the third time that evening. He was clearly excited about the move to their new home and the prospect of having his own bedroom. Just the day before, the furniture Ross had ordered from San Francisco had been transferred from the warehouse, where it had been stored all summer, into the completed mansion on Park Street. In the morning, a rented livery wagon would be hauling the last of their personal belongings from the boardinghouse in Finn Town to the affluent West Side.

They both stopped their work when they heard the sound of footsteps and the rustle of starched petticoats. Ross immediately recognized the light, hurried tread coming down the hall. He straightened and looked across the room to see Nell appear in the open doorway, a worried frown on her delicate features.

It had been four days since they'd gone into the Highland Mountains together. Four long days since he'd held her in his arms and worshipped her beautiful body with his. He hadn't had the chance to tell her how much that afternoon meant to him or how deeply troubled he was by her present elusive behavior. Since they'd returned to the boardinghouse, she'd made certain she was never alone with him.

Just that evening, he'd tried to coax her into stepping out onto the front porch with him after supper. She'd been as recalcitrant as a homesick mine mule. Now, at last, it seemed she was ready to put her juvenile evasiveness aside and talk to him like a mature woman.

Ross smiled at her with relief. "Don't be shy," he told her, his voice husky with suppressed elation. "Come in and join us. You can supervise the packin'. We could use some female advice."

Nell glanced down at the brown box tied with white string she held in her hands and lifted her eyes to meet his gaze once more. She tried to ignore the accelerated beat of her heart at the sight of him. He was wearing faded Levi's that hugged his sinewy legs like a second skin. His green cotton shirt was partly unbuttoned, revealing a luxuriant mass of golden-brown hair on his chest. His large, well-muscled frame seemed to fill the small bedroom he shared with his son.

"Hertta asked me to bring these up to you," Nell told him with a defensive tilt of her chin. "She made some *pepparkakor* for you as a housewarming gift."

"Oh, great!" exclaimed Luke, glancing back at Nell over his shoulder. "I love Mrs. Kuusinen's gingersnaps." He slammed the bureau's bottom drawer shut, straightened, and turned to grin at Nell in unabashed welcome.

She walked slowly into the room and laid the cardboard box down beside Ross's folded shirts. The wonderful aroma of warm cookie dough mixed with cinnamon, nutmeg, and ginger swirled around them. "I see you're almost packed," she said to the younger Morgan. "I was going to ask if I could help."

"Thanks, but I'm all done," Luke replied. "We'll

be takin' our things over to our new house tomorrow."

Hesitantly, she glanced about the cluttered room. Their belongings had been shoved haphazardly into emptied hardware barrels, wooden apple crates, and grocery cartons. Several fishing poles were jammed upright into one barrel, alongside books and wrinkled piles of their white flannel combinations. Her attention was drawn to a picture frame that lay beside an open tackle box on top of a crate. She picked it up and studied it silently.

"That's my mom," Luke explained. Going over to stand beside her, he pointed to the sepia-tinted figures in the heavy brass frame. "That's my dad, and that's me."

"Your mother was very beautiful," she said softly. There was a nearly imperceptible catch in her voice. "What was her name?"

"Wilhelmina Morgan, but Dad called her Willie." Luke shrugged with the unquestioning acceptance of a ten-year-old. "I don't really remember her, though."

Nell met the boy's ingenuous gaze. The dusting of golden-brown freckles on the bright, innocent face caught at her heart. "I can see the resemblance around your eyes," she told him truthfully. "The three of you made a very handsome family." With a trembling smile, she blinked back the tears that blurred her vision, praying that Luke's father wouldn't notice.

Ross scooped up a stack of plaid flannel shirts from his bed, walked to a partly filled crate near the doorway, and dropped them inside. "Luke, you go on downstairs and see what Mrs. Kuusinen's put out for evenin' snacks," he suggested with an encouraging smile. "I'll finish up the packin'."

"Okay, Dad."

Luke moved past Ross, who now stood with both booted feet planted firmly in front of the open doorway, and headed into the hall. Without taking his gaze off Nell, Ross reached for the knob and closed the bedroom door behind him.

She stared at Ross with wide, tormented eyes. Dressed in a dark blue gown with a prim little white lace collar, she looked like a reproachful, and somewhat frightened, angel. With her lips pursed tightly shut as though determined not to say another word, she laid the picture back down beside the fishing gear and tried to edge around him.

He caught her elbow and held her firmly in place. "You're not goin' anywhere, sugarplum, until we have a talk. You can't keep avoidin' me forever. And you can't pretend that nothin's happened between us. I know I rushed you along too fast, darlin'. I take full responsibility for everything that happened. But I can't apologize for something I wanted so badly and sure as hell don't regret."

"There's no need for an apology," she whispered. She swallowed convulsively and lowered her lashes, as though mortified even to speak of their lovemaking. "I'm the one to blame. I allowed my emotions to rule my head, but it's not going to happen again." Her gaze drifted back to the photo, and a scowl creased her forehead.

"*Why* won't it happen again?" Ross demanded, trying to understand the reasons behind her decision. "Because you think I might still be in love with my wife?" Incredulous, he looked at the photograph and then back to her downcast features. The idea couldn't have been crazier, but maybe it was his fault she didn't realize that. He'd never talked to her about his former spouse because he didn't want to speak ill of his son's mother. And he'd given the picture to Luke simply because he thought the boy should have some visual link to his past.

Nell jerked her elbow away. She raised her chin and stared at Ross with what she hoped would pass for smug disinterest. Until she'd seen the picture, she hadn't dared to ask him about the woman who'd played such an important role in his life. But now, after seeing the chic, willowy blonde who'd peered at the camera with such a knowing, self-assured smile, Nell was tortured by the stark realization of her own inadequacy. A torrent of jealousy swept through her.

Her heart ached as she remembered their love-making and how dissatisfied he'd been with her awkward performance. He'd cursed in disappointment, not once but three times! Heavens to Betsy, what had he hoped for from a lonely old maid? She couldn't compete with the cool sophistication of Wilhelmina Morgan. Or the skilled expertise of women like Lottie Luscious and Juniper Jess. He hadn't the right to expect it of her. Even so, she remembered the look of dismay in his eyes when he'd discovered her to be woefully inept.

"*Are* you still in love with your wife?" she asked with a jaunty smile. Despite her pathetic attempt to be flippant, her voice cracked.

Ross shook his head emphatically. He was deadly serious. "I don't think I was ever in love with Willie. Infatuated, maybe. Certainly flattered that a high-society New York debutante would fall for a rough-and-ready minin' engineer from Colorado. But Willie was never happy. I used to believe it was my fault because I brought her out West. But she wouldn't have been content anywhere. She was the kind of woman who was never satisfied with her life, always wantin' something she couldn't have. Believe me, Nell, her ghost will never come between us."

Somberly, Nell read the sincerity in his eyes. No, it wasn't his dead wife who rose like an insurmountable barrier between them. It was the ghosts of Nell's past.

"There's far more standing between us than your feelings for your deceased wife," she told him quietly. "What happened last Saturday must be forgotten, Ross. It was not only foolish but also professionally unethical."

He grasped her shoulders and drew her nearer. She felt the tension in his fingers as they clamped about her upper arms in a punishing grip. His eyes glittered with angry sparks of green and gold.

"Nell, I don't believe you mean that! You can't expect me to act as though you're nothing more than my legal counselor. We can't deny our feelings, sweetheart. Christ, I've never felt this way about a woman before. Never. You're a part of me now. And you're going to be a part of my life in the years to come. What we have is far too precious to throw away. And I sure as hell am not givin' you up without a fight."

She tried to break free, but he wouldn't let her. So she lashed out at him, saying the only thing she could think of to make him release her. "I wasn't all that moved by the experience, so don't waste your time making plans for the future. *There won't be a next time.*"

"Don't try to tell me you didn't respond to my touch," he warned with a low growl. "I know better." He bent his head till their faces were only inches apart and she could feel his warm breath on her lips. "You were burning for me, angel. You were aching for me as much as I ached for you. Why won't you admit it?"

"I'll admit what's between us is lust," she cried. "Nothing more than a primitive, physical need."

He shook his head as though he couldn't believe she would tell such a lie. "You're wrong, sweetheart. I've experienced lust before. I've been about as primitive and physical as a man can be. And last Saturday afternoon, when I lay on that blanket beside you and took you in my arms, when we became one flesh, one body, that wasn't mere lust that joined us together, but something far deeper, something that's going to bind us to each other for the rest of our lives." Before she could utter a word of denial, he brought his lips against hers in a bruising, possessive kiss.

The feel of his strong arms enfolding her sent a jolt of breathless desire through Nell. It took every bit of her willpower to remain absolutely passive. Some foolish, wanton part of her longed to wrap her arms around his neck, bury her fingers in his thick golden hair, and return his kiss. She yearned to accept what he offered so freely, to give what he boldly demanded. But her skepticism and pride, fueled by years of bitter self-recrimination, refused to listen to the childish, timeworn fairy tale of two people living happily ever after.

In spite of the intoxicating warmth of his mouth, of the wonderful feel of his tongue stroking hers, of the seductive pressure of his corded thighs and the hard bulge of his arousal against her willing body, she refused to respond. She simply waited for him to realize that this time his practiced charms weren't going to work.

When he drew back to search her eyes, she ignored the searing need that had burned her with his touch and forced herself to speak with frigid detachment. "If you persist in this unwelcome behavior, I'll have no choice but to return to Boston at once. And quite frankly, I'm not sure Gavin would have much of a chance of winning your lawsuit without my assistance. I certainly don't think it would be fair for me to leave right now."

Ross realized with a sinking heart that he was making no headway. Frustrated at her stubborn refusal to listen to reason, he made no attempt to hide his anger. "To hell with O'Connell!" he snapped. "That bastard hasn't given you one goddamn bit of help. I wouldn't be surprised if he's been takin' money from Hegel since the day he got here."

"That's not fair!" Nell protested. "Don't make accusations unless you have some kind of proof to back them up." She raised her eyebrows in affronted innocence, but the telltale red that stained her cheeks betrayed her own suspicions about her partner.

Ross grinned derisively. "That little weasel plans to attend Hegel's friggin' birthday party. What other proof do I need?"

"That's hardly evidence of unethical behavior," she scoffed. "I've been invited there myself."

At the cold realization that her loyalty might be as tenuous as Gavin's, Ross released her and stepped away. He clenched his jaw and bit back an expletive. When he could trust himself to speak, his words were low, taut, and edged with a scarcely veiled threat. "Do you intend to go?"

"I haven't made up my mind yet. But if I do attend Felix Hegel's ball, it won't prove that I'm taking bribes from him or anyone else." She braced her hands on her hips and foolishly attempted to take the offensive. "Furthermore, you have absolutely no right to question me about it. My personal life is my own business."

"Since your private intrigues could blow my minin' rights to hell and back, I'm makin' your personal life my business from now on, doll face. And don't be fooled by Hegel's smooth Eastern charm. You may think all he wants is a light flirtation, but I know better. As he waltzes you around his ballroom, he'll be lookin' into your big brown eyes and imaginin' your naked body in his bed."

She slapped him so hard his head snapped sideways with the force of the blow. "Not everyone's as base and despicable as you, Mr. Morgan," she hissed.

Ross grabbed both her wrists. "You push me any further, little girl, and I'll toss you on that bed over there and teach you just how base and despicable I can be when I put my mind to it." Struggling to gain control of his white-hot anger, he released her and stepped away. He favored her with a mocking grin as he waved his arm toward the door in a gallant flourish. "Now if you don't mind, Miss Ryan, I have some packin' to do."

"Mind?" she grated out scornfully. Her dark eyes

were enormous in her pale face. "I'm delighted to know you'll be moving out in the morning. It will save me from having to find another place to live." She turned on her heel, threw open the door, and fled the room.

"You came, after all, Miss Ryan. I'm so pleased that your colleague was able to talk you into attending my little party." Felix Hegel took her gloved hand and smiled a warm welcome.

"It wasn't easy," Gavin admitted. A grin of triumph flashed beneath his thin brown mustache. He stood at Nell's side, a picture of male splendor in his formal evening dress. Like their handsome host, he was attired in white tie and tails. "I had to threaten Nell with dire consequences," he added conspiratorially, "though I hadn't a clue as to what those consequences would be."

"The important thing is that you're here, my dear." Hegel squeezed her fingers and then retained them in his grasp, just as he'd done that evening at the Tie Lang Noodle Palace.

Nell awarded him with an answering smile, flattered by his obvious pleasure at seeing her again. Hegel had made his way straight toward her the moment she'd entered the ballroom of his elegant, colonial-style mansion. "When I was informed that I'd miss the gala of the fall season if I didn't come tonight, I had no choice but to accept your gracious invitation."

She hadn't wanted to come, pleading that she was still in mourning. But Gavin's persistence had finally worn her down. Her friend had pointed out that it'd been three months since Sean's death. It was the middle of September and time for her to move to the next stage of grieving. Reluctantly, she'd begun to put aside her costumes of black and gray and wear the deep browns and blues of half mourning considered appropriate for the loss of a sibling.

No one had lifted an eyebrow in criticism. She'd

found that on this furthermost edge of civilization, sudden and unexpected death had been such a frequent visitor in its short, violent history that nobody expected the living to forgo the immediate pleasures of the world in order to honor the dear departed. A sense of dispassionate fatalism set the tenor for the Devil's Throne, as the local inhabitants cynically called their mining camp.

A cluster of giggling debutantes in their lovely organza pastels swarmed nearby like a flock of gay songbirds. The girls followed Hegel's every move with bright-eyed animation. It was clear they were eagerly waiting to surround their tall, slim, and very rich host the moment Nell and her escort moved on.

"I understand congratulations are in order," said Hegel. Without a glance at the bevy of young ladies in their colorful gowns, he drew Nell's hand under his arm and started toward the dance floor. "I was told that you scored quite a victory in court yesterday."

"Nell was magnificent," Gavin boasted with pride.

"Thank you kindly, sir," Nell said with proper humility, as she lowered her lids and dipped a quick curtsy. The neckline of her bodice was cut low, revealing the shadow of her cleavage and exposing her bare shoulders. The full-skirted gown's enormous puffed sleeves were edged with deep ecru lace at the elbows, while a wide black velvet bow decorated the front of the bronzed satin dress.

"It was my first criminal case," she told Hegel in explanation, "and I can assure you there's nothing sweeter than success."

"You deserved it," Gavin insisted.

Hegel shot Nell a glance of sincere admiration. "Your pretty young client must have been very grateful. I was told that your defense strategy was brilliant."

"Miss Howard's thanks should go entirely to her

sister," Nell admitted with honesty. "If Mrs. Woakes
hadn't traveled all the way from Iowa to take the
witness stand on her sister's behalf, I'm not sure I
could have pulled off such a coup."

Gavin chuckled. "Lottie Luscious's brother-in-law
didn't hurt either."

"Mr. Woakes appeared in court alongside his
spouse, I take it?" Hegel inquired. His gray eyes
shone with amusement.

"Yes, and it's pretty hard to discredit the testimony of a Methodist minister's wife," Nell said,
fighting to keep back a giggle, "especially when
the clergyman is sitting in the courtroom with his
Bible on his lap, listening to every word that's being
said."

"Even if the unfortunate defendant is a sporting
girl," Gavin added with a loud crack of laughter.

Nell laughed right along with the two men. She
recalled with satisfaction the look of horror on Lucas
Dills's face when she'd called Fanny Woakes to the
stand as her key witness. Not only had Lottie's sister
testified that she'd received a telegram eight days
before Lottie had been arrested, she'd produced the
wrinkled missive as well. In the wire, Lottie had
informed her older sister that she was coming home
to Des Moines to start a hat shop with the thousand
dollars she'd saved.

As Nell had succinctly pointed out to the gentlemen of the jury, that was a full week before the date
designated by Mr. Lucas Dills in cross-examination
as the night on which he'd given the defendant the
money to hold for him. The very same night he'd
supposedly won it in a poker game. She added that
she knew he'd been nicknamed Lucky, but even
that fascinating sobriquet didn't explain how Miss
Howard could have known an entire week ahead of
time that he'd win exactly one thousand dollars at
a game of chance and then promptly give it to her
for safekeeping.

"Nell's final arguments were a legal masterpiece,"

Gavin added as they came to a halt on the edge of the dance floor. "God knows, she pulled out every stop, from placing the blame for Lottie's initial fall from grace on some unknown and perverted member of the so-called stronger sex to playing on the jury's sympathy for the penitent girl's intention to leave her unhappy profession and start a new life. Nell even quoted Scripture at the close. She reminded her captivated listeners of the tragic woman who'd been brought before the Savior, a poor soul of the same afflicted lifestyle as Miss Howard's, and how the Master had turned on her accusers. When Nell likened the prosecutor to the hypocrites who'd wanted to stone the pitiful sinner, a hush fell over the crowded courtroom. I swear, you could have heard the ticking of the clock on the wall. Even Judge Long had tears streaming down his cheeks by the time she was done. The jury acquitted Miss Howard after not more than a minute of deliberations."

Hegel reluctantly released her hand from his arm. "I want to hear more about your triumph in court, Miss Ryan. Unfortunately," he apologized, "I can't remain with you right now. I must greet all my guests before I can enjoy the ball. But O'Connell can introduce you around. There are a lot of people anxious to meet you. You've become a cause célèbre among the women of Butte. Enjoy the festivities. I'll come back to claim a waltz before the night is over." He started to move away and then paused. "And thank you for not holding my own success at the hearing earlier this week against me. The continuance really was necessary in order for my attorneys to prepare an adequate response to the counterclaims you filed on behalf of Ross Morgan."

Scowling, Nell glanced at Gavin, then met Hegel's silvery gaze with somber composure. "I tried my best to avoid a delay for my client's sake. As long as the right to mine his own ore is enjoined by the court, another postponement only places a further hardship on Mr. Morgan. Naturally, I have no wish to continue this discussion any longer."

She could have added that the two expert witnesses they'd brought to Butte had finally given up and returned to their homes. The added expense and inconvenience of bringing them back in another month would have to be met by Morgan. But she had no intention of giving Hegel any information that could be used against them. She didn't want his attorneys to file another motion for continuance in the hope of forcing Ross to the wall.

"The Forrester suffers the same fate as the Glamorgan, Miss Ryan," purred Hegel with an injured air. "I too am unable to mine my copper. I was just wise enough not to put all my eggs in one basket. Now if you'll excuse me?"

"We shouldn't have come here," Nell said to Gavin the moment their host had moved away.

"For crying out loud, don't be so silly." His handsome features twisted into a scowl of exasperation. "Come on, there's a lot of folks that want to meet you. Let's forget about our unfortunate client's troubles and enjoy the party."

The ballroom was filled with copper millionaires, their wives, and their patently over indulged offspring. Hegel was very popular with the society matrons and their daughters, who arrived smothered in diamonds and expensive furs.

Nell was treated like a celebrity. Everyone crowded around her, offering their sincere congratulations on her recent success. No one seemed the least disturbed that she was a female lawyer or that she'd actually defended a prostitute. Indeed, even the youngest belles were familiar with the details of the case and asked her questions that would never have been whispered in a Boston drawing room. Unlike the Back Bay aristocrats, the people of the mining camp had a get-rich-quick attitude that spilled over into their personal relationships. An unassuming democracy ran through both their

248   KATHLEEN HARRINGTON

business and social transactions. The wealthy guests
displayed an unquestioning tolerance of their fellow
man, seldom bothering to make any pretenses or
strike affected poses. It was a delightful change from
Nell's experience with the stratified, class-conscious
Bostonians.

She danced every dance. Waltzes, shottisches,
mazurkas, polkas, even a cakewalk and a taran-
tella. Nell tried to forget the ache in her heart that
had become her constant companion since that tragic Saturday afternoon two weeks ago, when she'd
foolishly surrendered to her physical needs and her
emotional hunger with such devastating results.

She told herself to forget the past and enjoy the
party. After all, there was no need to worry that
she'd unexpectedly spot a tall, golden-haired figure among the whirling dancers. Rossiter Morgan
would disdain making an uninvited appearance in
his enemy's camp. But he'd know by morning—if he
didn't already—that his two attorneys had attended Felix Hegel's fortieth birthday celebration. She'd
known when she decided to come that she'd be
lighting a fast-burning fuse to a keg of dynamite.

After their bitter confrontation in his bedroom,
she'd expected Ross to fire her or Gavin. To her surprise, he hadn't. Instead, he'd treated her with a cool,
businesslike decorum—exactly as she'd demanded.
She'd been on pins and needles ever since. It was a
relief, Nell told herself as she was led off the dance
floor, to know that after tonight the chasm between
her and Ross could never be bridged.

"I'm here for that dance you promised me," Hegel
said as he appeared at her elbow. He swept her out
onto the floor and twirled her gracefully around the
room. The band was playing a Strauss waltz, one of
Nell's favorites.

Felix Hegel was a superb dancer. He was also
an accomplished flirt. "Thank you for making this
birthday the most memorable ever," he said. "If you
hadn't come tonight, I would have been inconsol-

able." He held her a little tighter than good manners allowed. She could feel his strong arm press against her corseted figure in brash familiarity.

"Surely one of the beautiful young ladies present this evening could have consoled you," she protested with a laugh.

"I'm afraid not, Nell. I've thought about no one but you since the evening we met. When I saw you in court last Monday at the hearing, I wanted to walk over to your table and sit down beside you." He smiled disarmingly. "My lawyers wouldn't hear of it."

She shook her head in charmed disbelief. "I should think not! That would have come as quite a shock to the magistrate, not to mention my client."

"Your client didn't seem too happy the last time I saw him," Felix observed.

Nell sobered at once. "I'm afraid that subject is off limits."

Hegel shrugged as though it were a matter of no consequence and turned the conversation to a lighter topic.

When they finished the waltz, he guided her to the punch table and filled a cup for her. Side by side, they wandered over to a tall window, which had been left slightly ajar to admit the cold night air. The ballroom was growing warm with the press of the crowd, even though, outside, the temperature had dropped below freezing.

"You look very lovely tonight, my dear," he said. "I'm happy to see you've put away your black weeds. I hope you've come to look upon your brother's untimely death with some measure of acceptance." He paused before adding, "Even though it was surrounded by such mystery."

"Mystery?" Nell's heart squeezed painfully.

Felix set her punch cup on a nearby plant stand. Taking both her hands, he stepped a little closer, bent his dark head, and searched her eyes with compassion. "Surely you were aware that Sean Ryan's body was removed from the Glamorgan in the middle of the night, even though the mine had been placed under injunction a week before? No one should have been down there at all—not at any level. Nor was there a single whistle blown to alert the camp of an accident. A cloud of secrecy surrounded the entire episode. Even at the funeral, the mourners were asking one another just what had happened. No one seemed to have the full story."

Nell swallowed to ease the ache in her constricted throat. She'd learned that at any kind of disaster in the Butte mines, every whistle in the camp blew to alert the populace. Her words came out in a rusty croak. "I was told that Sean was down at the twelve-hundred-foot level on a routine inspection of the timbering."

Felix drew nearer. His eyes were filled with sympathy and doubt. "My dear girl . . ." he said softly and then stopped, as though uncertain whether to go on. He smiled and began again in a tone of cheerful encouragement "Nell, why don't you put this tragedy behind you? Nothing you could say or do now would bring Sean back to life."

Nell's lower lip trembled. Her eyes filled with tears. She frowned and looked away, gazing at the glorious ballroom crowded with handsome people. They were chattering, laughing, flirting, and dancing in happy abandon. The thought of her brother's life snuffed out at so tender an age filled her with renewed anguish. She lowered her head and, with her gloved fingers, furtively wiped away the tears that ran down her cheeks.

"I have to go now," she said simply. There was no need to offer her host any reason for her early departure. It was surely apparent on her tearstained face.

"May I see you again?" Felix asked.

Nell looked up and met his eyes, surprised at the quiet intensity of his words. "No," she said kindly. "Not if you mean what I think you mean. Until this trial is over, I can't be seen in your company."

His plea was tinged with gentle humor. "You're being seen with me right now."

She remained completely serious. "In the middle of a crowded ballroom, yes. But I really shouldn't be here in your home at all. Now I'd better go find Gavin."

She moved to leave, and Hegel caught hold of her arm, just between the edge her elbow-length glove and the lace of her puffed satin sleeve. His fingers were warm against her bare skin. "Wait, Nell." He stared into her eyes for a long moment before he continued. "I'm a very wealthy man, my dear."

A wry smile lifted the corners of her mouth. Amusement at such a typical male ploy softened her words. "The answer is still no."

Impatiently, he waved his hand. "You don't even know the question." He paused, and then resumed in a hushed tone. "Should I win this case, Miss Ryan, I could afford to be very, very generous."

Nell stood stock-still, astounded at what he was hinting. She tried to keep the disgust from her voice when she was finally able answer him. "How generous is that, sir?"

"Twenty thousand dollars could buy you a lot of pretty new ball gowns, my dear girl."

Aghast at such a bold-faced attempt to bribe her, Nell glared at him. "I don't sell out to the highest bidder, Mr. Hegel," she said through clenched teeth. "So you can take your money and . . . and . . ."

She turned on her heel and left.

Nell listened to the geologist drone on. She shifted slightly in her hard wooden chair in an effort to get more comfortable and tried to ignore the clouds of pungent cigar smoke that drifted about the room. Hegel's attorney, Shelton Broply, had been questioning his first witness for the last two hours in a tedious barrage of unrelated questions. It was nearly impossible to tell in which direction the lawyer was heading. She was tempted to believe he didn't have one. She knew better.

Broply was smooth—a polished professional who looked completely at ease in the courtroom. Handsome, dignified, and polite, he had a slightly incredulous air about him that seemed to ask the honorable gentlemen of the jury what ever had happened to law and order, to decency and fair play, to man's respect for his fellow man? But if his theatrical effects were meant to impress the jurist seated behind the bench, they were wasted.

Judge Otis Curry sat slumped back in his swivel chair, his feet propped up on the desk in front of him, and snored. The bearded magistrate had no idea what was going on in his own courtroom. Nell had the unhappy suspicion that no one else did either.

Beside her at the counsel table sat Gavin O'Connell. On his other side was Ross Morgan, listening to every word of the garbled, rambling testimony with an intent scowl. He was probably the only person in the room who could follow the confusing litany being offered in several languages, German and French included, which touched on physics, surveying, mineralogy, metallurgy, geology, chemistry, assaying, mathematics, and mining engineering. Every once in a while, Ross would jot down a note and shove it in front of Gavin. Her legal partner would invariably glance down at the scribbled message and then shrug his shoulders in an ineffectual gesture of acknowledgment.

Nell couldn't get over the feeling that she'd walked into someone else's dream. Only this dream was rapidly turning into a nightmare. Nothing had gone right since the day of the postponement hearing almost two months ago. She'd hoped to avoid another lengthy delay, knowing that every week that passed without a settlement would bring Morgan closer to ruin. Until the injunction was lifted, he wouldn't be able to mine his ore, driving him further and further into debt and eventual bankruptcy. But

Judge Curry hadn't bothered to consider the undue hardship placed on the owner of the Glamorgan Mine. The magistrate had granted the petitioner's motion for continuance with the snide implication that it was merely a matter of routine, and Nell and her co-counsel were foolish to have tried to contest it. At the time, she'd had the uncomfortable sensation that the postponement and the continued court injunction had both been foregone conclusions.

Now she was certain of it.

It had taken three weeks to impanel a jury. Despite Gavin's lack of assistance, she'd tried to ensure a selection of men who couldn't be bribed outright, or subtly influenced by Felix Hegel's status and power. But the judge wouldn't even allow her to ask the prospective jurors, many of obvious Irish descent, if they held prejudices against mine owners who employed Finnish or Cornish miners.

Hegel's counselors challenged any man who looked the least bit honest and forthright. Judge Curry hadn't uttered a word of remonstrance as, among the five of them, they managed to throw out every ranch owner and cowboy on the jury panel. Until that point, she hadn't realized that the magistrate himself must be in Hegel's pocket.

Strangely, Morgan had taken the setbacks with calm, almost cheerful, deliberation. When she'd apologized profusely for her failure he'd taken her hand in his and tenderly assured her that he knew she'd done her best. In truth, she'd been far more upset over the trial's postponement than he had been.

Judge Curry's lack of attention to the present witness that morning wasn't unusual. Generally, he stared out the window in preoccupation whenever anyone, except himself, was speaking. Every once in a while, he'd stir just long enough to turn his shaggy gray head and send a stream of tobacco juice into a brass cuspidor placed strategically nearby.

He hadn't even appeared to be listening during the opening statement.

Finally, Shelton Broply began winding up the questioning of his expert geologist. "And so would you say, Mr. Harlech, that the testimony of a retired professor from Columbia, who's been trained in Heidelberg and has never even worked in a Western copper mine, should be considered irrelevant?"

Nell sprang to her feet. "I object, Your Honor. Insufficient foundation. Mr. Broply is asking for an opinion on the expertise of a witness whose credentials haven't even been presented to the court yet."

Curry barely stirred. "Objection overruled."

"Exception!" protested Nell.

The judge swung his feet down from the desktop and stared at Nell with icy regard. From the beginning, he'd made no bones about the fact that he resented her very presence in his courtroom. Unlike the fair-minded Judge Long, who'd presided at Letitia Howard's trial, Curry had rudely questioned Nell's qualifications to stand before the bench. She'd informed him at the hearing that she was as qualified as any other attorney in the room, unless she had to pass a special bar examination just to practice before *him*. They both knew that, like all the other Eastern lawyers involved in the present mining litigation, Nell's credentials had been verified and recorded before she'd been allowed to appear in the Silver Bow District Court.

Curry glared down at her now with an unblinking, reptilian stare. "The exception is noted, madam," he said. His gravelly voice dripped with sarcasm, making the title sound as if she were the procuress in a cheap bagnio on Galena Street.

"Your Honor, with all due respect, I'd like to request that you don't address me as *madam*," she bit out in a clipped tone, "unless you call the opposing attorneys *sir*."

The judge leaned forward, his horny hands clasped together on the top of his bench. "And

just what would you like me to call you, my dear?"
he inquired in a patronizing tone.

Nell fought to control her temper. She smiled
brightly, trying to give the jury the impression that
she thought of the judge as a benevolent father figure. "My name is Miss Ryan, Your Honor. But if you
can't remember that, I'll happily respond to the title
of Counselor."

Gavin touched her elbow in warning, and Nell
sank back down in her chair. The last thing she
needed was to be cited for contempt of court.

Curry nodded to the bald-headed man on the witness stand. "You may proceed."

As though on cue, Harlech straightened up tall
in his chair, looked over at the jury, and addressed
them in a clear, ringing voice. "In my opinion, far
too many so called experts come out here from their
university towers in the East and try to render judg-
ments based on faulty geological precepts that originated in Europe. These self-professed experts lack
the workingman's basic knowledge of mining in our
own beloved Rocky Mountains. I myself learned the
trade in the silver mines of the Comstock Lode in
the Sierra Nevada, where I started as a nipper."

Broply had rehearsed his witness well. The
middle-aged Harlech sounded sincere and likable.
He'd answered questions promptly and candidly,
with just the proper touch of humility. No posturing,
no bombastic exaggerations. Despite the amazing
array of technical verbiage, he oozed down-home
accessibility, stressing his Western roots and tapping
into the jurymen's natural suspicion of outsiders.

"And would you explain what exactly a nipper is, sir, in case there's someone from the East
Coast here in the courtroom who doesn't understand that term?" Broply whirled to face Gavin
and Nell, making it all too clear to whom he was
referring.

Harlech addressed the jury, who sat listening in
rapt attention, although every man in the place knew

precisely what the term meant. "A nipper is a boy who's responsible for the tools. Among other things, he picks up the miners' dull or damaged steel drills and replaces them with sharpened ones. Every level has its own nipper. I was twelve years old when I made my first trip down in a cage." He grinned wryly, leaned toward the jury box, and said in a confiding tone, "By George, I thought my heart was going to stop before the cage did." Every man on the jury returned his smile, as each one recalled his own terrifying first experience. "As any hardened miner knows," Harlech added, "book learning behind the ivy-covered walls of Eastern colleges can never replace the Westerner's school of hard knocks."

When Gavin didn't stir in his chair, Nell rose. "Your Honor, I object to this line of questioning. I fail to follow the esteemed counselor's need to dwell on East versus West, as though we're here to root for our alma mater's debating society. Or the significance of the first cage ride of a twelve-year-old boy down into a silver mine. Is all this really relevant?"

Broply grinned. He spread his hands in a gesture of meek surrender, implying that she'd made an unwarranted attack upon his professional integrity and he was far too much of a gentleman to strike back at an hysterical female. "I'm just trying to establish my witness's credibility."

"We've already acknowledged Mr. Harlech's status as a learned geologist," Nell replied with an equally ingratiating smile. She wasn't going to let him push her into the role of a razor-tongued shrew. "We don't need to hear his life story or his home-grown philosophies."

Curry rapped his gavel. "Objection denied."

"Exception," said Nell. She struggled to hide her mounting frustration. "May counsel approach sidebar?"

"Why certainly, my dear," Curry responded with the enduring patience of a doting grandfather addressing a disruptive two-year-old. "Mr. Court Reporter, please join us at the side-bar."

Shelton Broply, trying hard to suppress a smirk, accompanied Nell and the court reporter to the far side of the bench, well out of hearing range of the curious jury.

"With all due respect, Your Honor," Nell said in a strained whisper, "I move for a mistrial on the grounds that your intense personal dislike of me will prevent my client from receiving a fair trial."

Curry stared at her through bleary eyes. The rank odor of chewing tobacco combined with the fumes of alcohol nearly staggered her. "Let me make it clear to you, madam, that you are not going to run my district court of law and equity the way you took over Judge Long's state court of common law. I've heard all about you and your flashy, high-binder ways. If you think you can bat those brown eyes and twist *me* around your little finger, you're mistaken. You are to behave with ladylike decorum in my courtroom, Miss Ryan, or you'll find yourself cited for contempt."

Nell should have kept her mouth shut, but she didn't. "I trust that means that the esteemed counsel for the petitioner is expected to exhibit his most gentlemanly and decorous manners as well," she said sweetly.

There was a flicker in the judge's watery blue gaze that disappeared as quickly as it came. But Nell had read its meaning in that short, intense instant. Curry persisted in calling her madam because he wished she *were* some tart he could buy in a brothel. It was the only way a rum-soaked old goat like him could ever have a decent woman like her, and they both knew it. That made him angry and mean-spirited and very dangerous.

"I find your attitude toward me extremely upsetting, Your Honor," she persisted, trying to control her rage. "How can you have formed such a low

opinion of me on such brief acquaintance? I respect-
fully suggest that your prejudice against me is based
on the fact that I am a woman, and that it will influence your judgment during the entire course of this
trial."

"Don't get fresh with me, Counselor," Curry
snarled. He was furious at her incisive accusation.
"Your motion is denied. Is there anything else you
want to put on the record? No? Then let's get on
with this trial, madam."

As she started to leave, Broply leaned closer to
Nell and whispered in her ear. "Aren't you in a little over your head, beautiful?" He flashed her the
toothsome smile of a shark.

She turned slightly, so no one else in the room
could read her lips, and whispered back, "Go to
hell."

Pinning a smile of complete satisfaction on her
face for the benefit of the jury, Nell returned to
the counsel table with a confident step. Inwardly,
she was shaking with fury. A fury she had to control, if she was going to project an attitude of polite
obedience and humble deference to that jackass of a
judge. Otherwise, she ran the risk of having the jury
suspect her of being just another conniving Boston
lawyer, too clever for her own good.

She glanced at the other counsel table on the way
back to her seat. Felix Hegel and his four other attorneys were staring at her with supercilious
grins pasted below their well-trimmed mustaches.
They were all dark-haired, attractive men attired in
superbly tailored suits. In her Newport walking outfit, Nell felt as gauche as if she'd chosen her costume
from the Sears and Roebuck catalogue.

Beneath the protection of the tabletop, she
clenched her hands into tight fists. Letitia Howard's
acquittal had been a fluke. Nell's first foray alone
in court, with a sympathetic judge, a vivacious
underdog defendant, and a fascinated jury made
up mostly of cowmen and merchants, had given her

484

a false confidence in her own ability. The opposing counsel was right. She *was* in over her head.

What had Uncle Cormac been thinking when he'd insisted that she take on this difficult case? She'd always worked in his shadow. Surely he'd known what kind of vile harassment she might endure as the only female standing before the bar in this hellish outpost of Creation. Perhaps he'd felt that Gavin would protect her. Her law partner was sitting there in silent abstraction, as though this whole blessed farce had nothing whatsoever to do with him. Heaven save her, when Cormac Ryan had cut the leading strings, he'd done it with a vengeance. She was learning just how much her uncle had protected her from this type of churlish mistreatment.

"If you're finished, Mr. Broply," Judge Curry said, "the witness can stand down." He paused and looked at Nell. "Unless Miss Ryan wishes to cross-examine."

She rose and forced a smile. "Not at this time, Your Honor."

Curry banged his gavel. "Then we'll adjourn for lunch and reconvene in two hours."

The three representatives of the Glamorgan Mine sat alone in the emptied courtroom. Ross pushed back his chair and came around to face Nell across the narrow table. He braced his palms on the polished surface and leaned toward her.

"What's goin' on?" he asked quietly.

"His Honor is a vicious toad." She propped her elbows on the tabletop and stared down in misery.

"Nell," cautioned Gavin, "you can't snap back at the judge like that. The jury will think you don't respect him."

"I don't!"

"Well, for crying out loud, you'd better try to hide it," he warned, "or the fine gentlemen of the jury will turn against us." His chair scraped across the planked floor as he jumped to his feet in agitation. "And from now on, whatever happens, our client here had better stay in his seat. I had to grab hold of Morgan's arm to restrain him when Curry was ripping out at you." Gavin turned to Ross with an expression of horror. "For Christ's sake, I thought you were going to leap out of your chair, reach over Curry's bench, and throttle the daylights out of him."

"If that bastard keeps talkin' nasty to Nell," Ross said, "I'm goin' to pick him up and toss him out that window."

"Ross!" Nell cried. "No matter what the judge says to me, don't you dare utter a sound!" She searched his hawkish features. "Promise me that!"

Ross made no such commitment. He met her frightened gaze with unflinching resolution.

"I'll stay calm," she promised. "I won't lose my temper again."

"Can you keep from doin' that?" he asked doubtfully. He straightened and shoved his hands in his trouser pockets, studying her with a thoughtful frown. His tawny hair curled in unruly waves that just brushed the top of his starched white collar. The black business suit he wore was tailored to fit his large frame with crisp perfection. Next to Ross's uncompromising masculinity, Hegel and his dapper attorneys resembled a sextet of gelded choirboys.

Nell gathered up the loose papers scattered across the tabletop and straightened them into a neat stack. She knew that since Hegel's birthday celebration, Ross had suffered second thoughts about the loyalty of both his lawyers. Now he was beginning to question their competence as well. And with good reason. She wondered why he didn't fire them on the spot and seek new counsel. Then she looked up into his determined eyes and knew the answer. He wanted it all. Her *and* his damn copper mine. What was astounding was that he didn't seem to realize he was doomed to lose them both.

"It's not going to be easy to maintain my composure," she admitted ruefully. "Curry is out to destroy

us. Maybe it's his personal animosity toward me.
Maybe it's something more. But he's going to try
to break me. He wants me to lose control in front
of the jury. If I start screaming in sheer frustration,
he'll nail me to the wall."

"Can we get another judge?"

"No," Gavin interjected.

"Then what do we do?" Ross asked, looking from
one to the other.

"If Curry persists in this gross travesty of justice,
our only hope will be an appeal," she said. She met
her client's eyes with total honesty. "We'll have to
build a record for the appellate court."

"In the meantime, Nell," Gavin complained, "let
me do the objecting, okay? I don't seem to set Curry off the way you do."

"Well then, for God's sake, get on your feet and
object!" Nell's voice rose in aggravation. "Don't just
sit there and let Broply walk all over us."

"Let's get some lunch," Ross said evenly. He came
around the side of the table to pull out her chair.

Dejectedly, she shook her head and waved him
away. "You two go on. I'm not hungry. I'll stay here
and go over Dr. Gunter's report one more time."

"Nell, you've got to eat," Ross insisted. The timbre of his deep voice was filled with quiet gravity.
His strong jaw hardened in silent concern.

Slowly, she stood and met his gaze, reading the
uneasiness etched on his rugged features. He'd left
unsaid the very noticeable fact that she'd been
steadily losing weight. For the past two months,
she'd barely slept. She'd had no appetite. Worry
over the trial preparations had been only part of
the reason for her distress, and they both knew
it. After he and Luke had moved into the mansion on Park Street, she'd seen Ross at the District
Courthouse or in brief meetings at her office, with
Gavin always present.

The aching loneliness inside her was a raw wound
that wouldn't heal.

"Come on, Nell," Gavin interposed with forced cheerfulness. "You'll feel better with some food in you."

Ross took her elbow and led her down the center aisle of the courtroom toward the entrance, with Gavin following immediately behind.

"What did Broply say to you?" Ross asked softly.

She gave him a blithe smile and lied without hesitation. "The counselor for the petitioner complimented me on how nice I looked today."

"That shyster had better watch his step," Ross said, and the harshness of his tone was like the low rumble of thunder just before the storm. "Broply's no goddamn judge. If he says one smart-mouthed thing to you, I'll break his friggin' neck."

Nell woke from a fretful sleep and lit the gas lamp beside her bed. The alarm clock on the marble-topped nightstand showed three in the morning. She got up and wearily pulled on her heavy dressing robe and fuzzy slippers. Sitting down at her small desk, she resumed her work on the three-dimensional model of the Glamorgan she'd started during the long, restless nights waiting for the trial to begin.

The scale model she was building out of papier-mâché and smooth wooden sticks was a precise replica of the diagrams and charts she'd studied with Ross that summer. When it was finished, it would show in detail the tunnels, ore chambers, shafts, and surrounding formations of the Glamorgan Mine. She hoped to use it as an exhibit. With the help of Dr. Adolph Gunter, the retired professor from Columbia who was to be their star witness, she intended to demonstrate that the rich veins of copper that Hegel claimed for the Forrester actually apexed on the Glamorgan site.

Her colleague's behavior continued to worry her. She wondered if his lack of effort during the trial was only another example of his lackadaisical attitude toward his work or if it indicated something much more unprofessional. On the carriage ride home from Hegel's ball, she'd told him of their host's attempt at bribery. Gavin hadn't shown the least bit of surprise or anger.

"We are, after all, in a wide-open mining camp on the outer fringe of civilization," he'd pointed out with cool detachment. "You shouldn't be too shocked at Hegel's attempt to corrupt a smooth Boston lawyer, even if the lawyer is a lady."

She'd stared at Gavin, seated across from her in the hack, in uncomfortable silence. She took pride in her ability to judge a person's character. Now she wasn't so sure she was using her common sense. Did she believe in her law partner's integrity merely because she *wanted* to believe he was incorruptible?

Gavin's reaction to Hegel's statements about Sean's fatal accident was far more explosive, however. He pointed out to her that, even though Ross had shown them extensive charts, maps, and diagrams of the Glamorgan, neither one of them had ever been allowed to go down in the mine.

Nell refused to place any credence in Felix Hegel's unsubstantiated implications. After offering his phony sympathy over her brother's mysterious death, the copper baron had immediately turned around and tried to bribe her. How could she take a scoundrel's word over that of the man she'd come to care about so deeply?

As she worked, Nell recalled the dream that had disturbed her slumber. Like every other one she'd had for the past two months, it was of Ross. No matter how she tried, she couldn't break the bond he'd forged with their mating. His kisses, his caresses haunted her. She longed to go to him and beg him to hold her in his sheltering arms. Their happy, summertime conversations, when she'd tried to study and he'd teased her with devilish persistence, ran through her head like familiar bedtime stories.

In the quiet stillness of the night, memories of past betrayals rose up to haunt her. When her father had abandoned them and then died in Leadville, Nell's widowed mother had supported her children as best she could on her meager earnings. Yet, despite the fact that Jack Ryan had left his family in his lust for gold, Nell had continued to idolize her father right up until that day she was working in her uncle's office as his legal assistant. Strictly by accident, she'd come across the letter Uncle Cormac had received at the time of his younger brother's death. As a young girl, Nell had been told her father was killed in a saloon fight. What she learned from that forgotten letter was that her father had, in fact, been shot to death on the second floor of that establishment in a drunken altercation over a harlot.

The feelings of abandonment and betrayal she'd denied throughout her childhood surfaced nearly to destroy her. It had been no wonder she'd fallen for Charleton's smooth, practiced lies. She'd have believed any man who'd courted her with such sugared flatteries. For at seventeen, she was longing, *starving*, for the male love and attention she'd never received from her own father. She'd been easy pickings for Blevins, who'd discovered her through her mother's obituary. After talking her out of all the savings that Maude Ryan had left her children, Charleton had made love to an infatuated Nell only once—the night before he disappeared with the money.

The consummation was hurried, mechanical, and unfulfilling, carried out, no doubt, merely to ensure her silence out of shame. In her youthful ignorance, Nell hadn't even realized what was happening until it was nearly over. For her experienced seducer, it was all a charade, enacted not out of sexual need, but from the desire for money. The same lust that had driven her father to leave his family.

Greed and sex were the two appetites that drove the human male. And Nell had learned, to her sorrow, that a man would use any means at his disposal to achieve them.

Knowing she had to get some sleep, she pushed the replica of the Glamorgan aside. She crossed the room and stopped to gaze down at the empty brass bed. With a soft cry of despair, she dropped to her knees and buried her face in her hands.

Dear God, what was to become of her? Despite everything she'd learned about men, she still hadn't been able to stop herself.

She'd fallen in love with Ross Morgan.

Chapter 17

Snowflakes drifted down in lazy swirls to settle on the roofs and treetops, across the darkened yards and alleyways. Ross looked up at the big frame boardinghouse, his thoughts filled with the elusive enchantress who lodged there. Ignoring the chill of the frosty night air, he stood on the sidewalk and gazed up at the lit windows of the three-story home. The golden light from the gas lamps streamed out across the winter lawn, making its blanket of white twinkle like diamonds. He'd left his son in the care of Mrs. Rooney, the housekeeper he'd hired to run their fine new home on Park Street. That evening he had come to Finn Town with one intention in mind. He was going to resolve the affliction that had tormented him for far too long.

It had to come to an end. This insatiable, unfulfilled yearning for Nell. The recurring questions about her loyalty. In the courtroom, she seemed to be doing her absolute best to defend the Glamorgan mining rights. Yet as the trial proceeded, he saw the chances for a favorable verdict growing slimmer and slimmer. Was it the judge who was sabotaging his court battle, as Nell had suggested, or was it the two lawyers who were suppose to be representing him? Deep in his soul, he couldn't believe Nell capable of such unethical behavior. Yet the ugly suspicions haunted him. He was a man stretched on a rack, torn by doubt and desire.

Whenever the two of them were together, the very air crackled with unspoken longing, so electric, so palpable that others nearby would fall silent and gaze from one to the other in stricken self-consciousness.

He wanted Nell with a fine, keen-edged hunger. Like the steel-blue blade of a hunting knife, that hunger had carved out a hollow spot in the furthermost recesses of his soul. There was no other woman who could ever fill the emptiness inside him. No other man would ever love her the way he did. She belonged to him. It was time for her to accept that.

Ross had grown almost used to being in a state of constant sexual frustration. Almost, but not quite. That evening, as he'd contemplated spending another night in his lonely bed, he'd decided he wasn't waiting any longer.

After their argument the night before he'd left Kuusinen's, he'd tried several more times to reason with Nell. But they were never alone together, and any attempts at reconciliation were doomed from the start. When Ross demanded to know why she'd gone to Hegel's ball against his wishes, she claimed he'd pushed her into it. He tried to explain how treacherous it looked for his attorney to be waltzing around a ballroom floor in the arms of his opponent. He didn't add that he'd felt utterly defeated by her disloyalty. She wouldn't have listened anyway. Nell seemed so distraught each time he tried to resolve their misunderstandings, Ross finally allowed her to keep him at arm's length for fear she'd bolt and run back to Boston. It soon became clear that words alone wouldn't settle the differences between them. So he'd been patient, hoping that, if she remained in Butte, she'd eventually come to him of her own accord. Christ, it was evident to everyone around them that they were made for each other. He'd mistakenly believed it would be only a matter of time before she'd see that too.

It was now the first week in November. Two full months had passed since the summer afternoon they'd spent together in that shady mountain meadow. Nell showed no more intention of admitting how much she wanted him now than she had on that glorious picnic day.

His patience had worn out. Tonight, the need for her far outweighed the doubts that still afflicted him. Ross started up Kuusinen's steep porch steps, determined to bring the uncertainty to an end, once and for all.

He was positive that Felix Hegel had attempted to bribe Nell, though she'd never indicated by a single word that he'd tried. The owner of the Forrester Mine had the ethics of a robber baron. Ross knew the greedy bastard would never pass up the chance to dangle a large sum of money in front of her pretty nose, any more than he'd fail to try to tempt Gavin O'Connell. Hegel's birthday celebration had afforded the wily sonofabitch a perfect opportunity to impress both of the Glamorgan attorneys with his millions. Ross hadn't attended the gala, but plenty of his acquaintances had been at the affair. He knew that, though Nell had danced all evening, she'd waltzed only once with Hegel. After speaking with her host briefly at the punch table, she'd left the party in Gavin's company.

The trial had been in progress less than a week when Ross acknowledged to himself that O'Connell had succumbed to the temptation of Hegel's gold. What Ross didn't know was how much money the copper king had offered him. And whether Nell had taken it too.

His legal counselors weren't the only ones hiding secrets. Despite the injunction, Ross had never halted work in the Glamorgan. A week after the mining of the disputed vein had been enjoined by the court, Sean Ryan was killed by a falling timber. When Ross and Eben found his body at the twelve-hundred-foot level, they heard the blasting that had caught Sean's attention and had sent him exploring along the entire length of the abandoned stope. The unmistakable sound of dynamiting meant that mining operations were under way in the nearby Forrester. Without factual evidence, Ross knew it would be useless to ask Judge Curry for a court order to inspect Hegel's property. So he had made the decision, then and there, to ignore the injunction against the Glamorgan and proceed to mine his own copper in secret. He'd struck a bargain with the owner of an abandoned mine site near the Glamorgan. For a substantial fee, Deke McAllister had agreed to begin bogus operations in the Patty May. Working under the cover of darkness, Ross moved his ore through a connecting crosscut and lifted it up the Patty May's mine shaft to the surface. From there, the copper was hauled to a smelter, whose owner wasn't prone to ask too many questions if the profits were large enough. Although there were plenty of Butte miners who realized what was going on, none felt compelled to notify the law. Felix Hegel had made a lot of enemies in the copper camp. Ross had kept the covert operations hidden from his own lawyers, certain they'd refuse to go along with the illegal scheme. For that same reason, he'd never allowed either one of them to descend into his mine.

Shaking off his reverie, Ross entered the boardinghouse. He bypassed the crowded parlor and dining room filled with miners and went straight to the back of the home, where he found Hertta alone in her large kitchen. She was seated at the long trestle table, copying a recipe. The wonderful smell of fresh-baked Finnish coffee bread filled the warm room.

When she heard him enter, she looked up and smiled a cheerful welcome. "Ross! You're just in time for evening snacks. T'ey are already laid out on ta dining room table. I took ta *pulla* out of ta oven only a few minutes ago. Go help yourself before it disappears."

He shook his head, so taut with unreleased tension he could barely return her smile. "I came to see Nell."

Hertta cocked her white-blond head to one side and propped her rosy cheek against her hand. The trace of a smile lingered around the corners of her pursed lips. "It's Sunday evening," she dutifully pointed out. Her words were soft and chiding, but her china-blue eyes sparkled with mischief. "You know vhere Nell alvays spends her Sunday evenings."

"I know." He made no attempt to hide his intentions.

Her intelligent gaze never wavered from his. She laid her pencil on top of the paper written in her native language and rose to her feet. "I'll tell ta girls t'ey are not to use ta sauna t'is evening vhen t'ey are t'rough vith t'eir chores. Ta men already know it's off limits tonight. You von't be disturbed. I'll see to it."

Ross headed for the side door that led from the kitchen to the Finnish bath. "This is one I owe you, Hertta," he called over his shoulder. "Go buy yourself that new stove you've been wantin'."

"As if I could be bribed," she scolded. "Save your money and buy your sveetheart a vedding ring." He could hear her laughter all the way out the door.

In the bathhouse's small dressing room, Ross quickly shed his clothes and hung them on the metal hooks that lined a rough pine board. He grabbed a folded towel from the stack of clean ones and entered the sauna. The sight that met his eyes lit a bonfire inside him.

Nell was stretched out on her stomach atop a wooden bench along the far wall, a white towel spread beneath her for a cushion. She was naked, right down to her dainty pink toes. Her eyes were closed, the thick chestnut lashes fanning out across her fine-grained skin. Her flushed cheek was cradled on her folded arms. In the light of the glowing sauna fire, her smooth back and round buttocks glistened like ivory satin.

With his heart hammering against his rib cage like a compressed air drill boring into solid rock, he bent and poured a dipperful of water on the red-hot stones. The water sizzled and spurted, rising toward the pine ceiling in drifts of aromatic steam. His own body heat soared too.

"Let's not get it *too* hot in here tonight," she complained in an indolent voice without even opening her eyes. "You ladies are always trying to cook me alive."

Ross tossed his towel on a nearby bench and padded closer to the heavenly vision that shimmered before him. Every nerve ending in his body throbbed with licentious need, as the muscles in his groin tightened in primal anticipation.

The bath was a haven of sweet self-indulgence. If he'd entered a paradise of hedonism, he couldn't have been more engulfed in a sense of unapologetic physical gratification. He had stumbled upon the garden of earthly delights. The nymph of his dreams lay waiting for him on her couch.

Too lethargic to open her eyes, Nell half dozed in a mood of complete relaxation. It seemed as though the brief time she spent in the bathhouse was the only part of her week in which she felt truly at peace anymore.

She lay prone on a fluffy towel, her thoughts drifting to Ross as they always did when she wasn't concentrating on that horrible charade of a trial. Steam wafted about her in vaporous puffs. Surrounded by the sweet fragrance of balsam, she could have been floating on a soft bed of pine boughs in some forest primeval. When she'd heard someone enter the room, she'd assumed from the silence that it was either Maija or Fetsi. She knew it couldn't be

Hertta. Her loquacious landlady would never just stand there saying nothing.

But whichever shy serving girl it was, the newcomer didn't venture over and sit down on the wooden platform beside Nell. After splashing water onto the hot rocks to send a sizzling vapor spraying upward along with the room's temperature, whoever it was just stood there in aloof contemplation.

The Finnish penchant for taciturnity was, by now, something Nell had come to accept without question. At Kuusinen's Boardinghouse, she was always the one to carry the conversation forward.

"You finished your work early," she commented, still not bothering to open her heavy lids. She waited for the usual one-syllable answer.

There was no reply. The atmosphere in the sauna grew heavy with silence. Suddenly, Nell realized who stood beside her. She felt his presence as surely as if he'd reached out and touched her. Her eyes flew open.

Ross was less than an arm's reach away.

Stark naked.

Fully aroused.

She'd never dreamed any human being could look so magnificent. Or so unconsciously predatory. The tendons of his long limbs were thick with brawn. His shoulders were broad, the upper arms bulging with male power. A mat of golden-brown hair covered the well-defined pectorals on his deep chest, then trailed in a narrow band across an abdomen ridged with muscles to form a wiry nest around his hardened manhood. Her captivated gaze swept downward over the massive thighs and well-formed calves. The sight of his bare feet, braced slightly apart, brought back the image of him at their picnic, when he'd playfully invited her to go swimming. Startled by the depth of feeling that memory provoked, she looked up to study his rugged features framed by the thick waves of golden hair. The unconcealed hunger that burned in his eyes took her breath away.

He was lethal male aggression held on a tight
rein.

Despite the aura of ferocity that had invaded
the sauna, a delicious languor curled through
Nell, making it nearly impossible to move. She
couldn't have fled the room had she wished. She
was consumed with an awareness of her own body's
fine-boned fragility in comparison to his masculine
bulk. For the first time in her life, she understood
the complete trust that a female had to have in her
mate.

"You picked the wrong evening," she said huskily,
unable to lift her cheek from her arms. "Sunday is
ladies' night."

His deep voice flowed over her like molten passion. "Not this Sunday, angel eyes. Tonight's our
night."

"Maija or Fetsi could walk in any minute," she
warned him in a hoarse whisper. "If they see you
in all your glory, they might not want to leave."

His expression was as solemn as hers. "No one
else is goin' to join us, little doll. I have Hertta's
word on that."

In one fluid movement, he stepped over to the
bench and crouched down beside her. His fingers
stroked a line of fire along her spine. His strong
hand curved over the twin hills of her buttocks
and then slid between her legs to caress the sensitive skin of her inner thigh. Gasping, Nell raised
up on her elbows in automatic reaction to the shock
of his touch. As she turned toward him, he slid his
fingers across her upper leg and over the curve of
her hip.

His gaze swept over her, lingering for uncounted
moments on her exposed breasts. "My God, you're
beautiful," he said thickly.

"So are you," she whispered back, too overcome
to consider dissembling.

A wicked glow lit his eyes. He cupped her cheek
in his hand, bent his head, and covered her mouth

with his. As he kissed her, he gently eased her back down on the bench, until she lay supine on the soft towel. Then he broke the kiss to rise and sit on the edge of the platform beside her. His gaze moved over her slowly, exploring with bold admiration every inch of the curves and valleys of her nude form.

Nell's body glistened with moisture. She'd just finished pouring a bucket of icy water over herself before he'd come in, and her unbound hair clung to her neck and shoulders in shiny, wet strands. Droplets of water beaded her top lip.

"It's too hot in here for this," she said with a throaty laugh. In spite of the disclaimer, she reached up and rested her fingers at the base of his neck. Her thumbs rubbed against his collarbone in an unconscious ploy of female seduction.

His suffocated voice was raw with need. "It's going to get a whole lot hotter before we're through."

He caressed her, running his hands over her moist skin. He cupped her breast, bent his head, and teased the nipple with his tongue until the pink crest was tight and puckered with desire. Then he drew the fullness of her engorged breast into his mouth, making it swing gently as he suckled her. Shards of ecstasy exploded inside Nell. As he laved the other breast, she moaned out loud with pleasure. In response to her frank admission of delight, he nipped her gently with his teeth before taking her into his mouth.

She smoothed her palms over his upper arms and shoulders, learning the marvelous feel of his bare skin, the thick bulge of his muscles.

He lifted his tawny head and pinned her with a rapacious gaze. He had the lean, ravenous look of a hunting cat about him, and she knew, without a doubt, why he'd been likened to a cougar.

"I gave up waitin'," he told her. "For the past two months, I've lain awake at night, prayin' the next day you'd come to tell me that this torture had gone on long enough. That you needed me just half as much as I needed you." A smile of bittersweet irony curved up the corners of his sensuous lips. "I never dreamed you'd be so goddamn stubborn, Irish, or I'd have done this eight weeks ago."

She framed his face with her hands. "Every night, I've awakened in the darkness, dreaming of you. Over and over, I found myself asking if this longing would ever end."

His answer was a low rumble. "Not in our lifetime, angel."

Ross slid his hand down the smooth plane of her stomach to curve his fingers over her soft mound. He gently parted the puff of mahogany curls that guarded her fragile petals. He turned his face into her hand and ran his tongue back and forth across the crease of her palm, matching the movement of his fingers as he stroked her in a slow, seductive tempo. An involuntary shiver ran the length of her supple body. He took his own sweet time, building up the need in her, till her hips were arching upward in rhythmic response to the pleasure he gave so freely. He wanted her in a state of wild, uncontrollable arousal. He purposely brought her to the brink of mindless excitement and then stopped. She whimpered in confusion as she sucked in a long, ragged breath.

"Come on, little darlin'," he said. He rose to his feet and bent over her. "We're goin' to splash around for a while in that big barrel over there."

Dazed, she looked up and met his gaze. Her wide brown eyes were luminous with sexual desire as she put her arms around his neck in unquestioning compliance. He lifted her up in his arms and carried her to the copper-hooped cask of cold water. The wooden container, large enough to accommodate several bathers, resembled an enormous wine vat that had been split down the middle. To their overheated bodies, the cool water would feel pleasantly warm and refreshing.

Ross stepped over the tub's edge and set her on her bare fanny. Sinking down beside her on the smooth oak bottom, he slipped all the way under the clear water and then sat up to face her. She followed his example. As she rose to the surface, the water streamed over her dewy face and smooth shoulders in sparkling rivulets. The soaked locks of her long hair were deepest mahogany. The small mole above her full lips and the dark tresses that lay against her translucent skin were an opulent display of exotic beauty. She wiped the drops from her eyes and blinked at him in open curiosity, clearly mystified as to what they were doing in a bathtub together.

He caught her by her slender waist and pulled her to him, the water sloshing about them in gentle waves. "This time, angel, you're goin' to be on top," said Ross. "And we're goin' to take it as slow and easy as can be."

He guided her slim legs around him, showing her how to get up on her knees and straddle his hips. He played with her gently, letting the lapping water swirl around her delicate folds as his fingers built up the need within her to a fevered pitch once again. He leaned back against the wall of oaken staves and watched as an expression of unalloyed pleasure swept over her lovely features, softened now with passion. Her lids drooped, displaying the long lashes that clumped together in dark, wet spikes. Her full lips parted slightly as she tried to accommodate the deeper breathing brought on by her accelerated heartbeat.

"Bring yourself down on top of me, sweetheart," he urged hoarsely.

With his hands bracketing the smooth curves of her hips, he guided her downward until he could feel the sensitive tip of his turgid staff press against her tight opening.

Nell shook her head and spoke in a hushed, worried tone. "I don't think it'll work this way."

"Yes, it will," he reassured her. "You just ease down on top of me, nice and slow. Spread your legs wider, darlin' and I'll enter you a little at a time. I won't hurt you the way I did before. This time there won't be any surprises for either of us."

Nell looked down into the clear water to watch their bodies join together in the mating ritual as old as mankind itself. She felt herself stretch to accommodate him as, bit by bit, she sank down on his hardened sex. The slow movement sent shafts of sweet delight radiating through her abdomen and thighs. A force so powerful she couldn't have resisted if she'd tried swept through her as she settled over him. The sensitive layers of her female tissues spread around him and rubbed against his firm flesh. In her heightened responsiveness, she was conscious of the warm water lapping about her, of the pressure of his rock-hard body rubbing against the soft inner sides of her thighs, of the movement of his callused fingers across her bare skin, which, in turn, sent the water swirling about her in little rills of pleasure.

She lifted her head and met his eyes, wondering what he'd want to do next.

"Okay, sugarplum," he said with a tender smile. "That's the difficult part. Now you just go where your feelin's lead you. We've got all night."

Nell searched his chiseled features, wondering what he was trying to tell her. "I'm supposed to set the pace?" she asked doubtfully. "I'm not sure I can do it correctly."

"There isn't any right or wrong way, punkin. You just follow your body's lead and try not to think too much with that overactive lawyer's brain of yours."

Her fingers were splayed across his hairy chest, and she could feel the vibrations of his satisfied chuckle. She grinned at his impudence. Then she bent forward and traced her tongue across his sassy mouth. With her slight movement, a bolt of pleasure rocketed through her. "Mm," she said in delight. She moved again and sighed with pure enjoyment.

"Now you're gettin' the idea," he encouraged. "I'm goin' to take you all the way there tonight. In fact, I'm goin' to take you there a couple of times before the evenin's over, just to make sure we get the hang of it this time."

He covered her lips with his. She felt him thrust up inside her at the same time he probed her mouth with his tongue. He caressed her breasts, flicking the rough pads of his thumbs across her swollen nipples. He allowed her to set the pace, as he showed her in every way possible that there'd be no inhibitions between them, no coyness, no shame, no guilt. The water surged around them, enhancing every move they made, every touch, every slightest brush of skin against skin, rocking them both in a liquid cocoon of pleasure.

This time, when he brought her to the brink, he led her over with loving expertise. "That's it, angel," he crooned in her ear. "Don't fight it. Ride it like a flood. Let it take you with it."

Nell felt the undulating ripples of her orgasm spread through her in a rising tide of rapture. The sustained sigh of her release mingled with his muffled groan of male victory as he too found satisfaction.

Ross was as good as his word. He took her three times that night, and each time she climaxed. They eventually ended up in her brass bed upstairs, where she lay cradled in his strong arms, satiated and totally depleted of energy.

Stroking his chest, she buried her fingers in the thick covering of wiry hair and traced the outline of his flat nipple with the pad of one fingertip. She couldn't touch him enough. She brought his hand to her lips and nibbled greedily on his fingers. Then she ran her tongue across the back of his knuckles.

"I thought you said a few minutes ago that you were too tired to move," he teased with a soft chuckle. His eyes glowed with tenderness.

"I can't help it," she confessed. "I dreamed so many times that you were here in this bed with me that I have to keep checking to see if you're real."

"With your tongue?"

"I go by taste."

"I know."

She tucked her head beneath his stubbled chin and felt the warmth of a blush spread over her. She could hear the beat of his strong heart thumping like a judge's gavel at the images their words provoked.

They had, indeed, tasted each other that night. Ross had introduced her to an eroticism she'd never dreamed of—wild, pagan, and unashamedly carnal.

"If you wanted me here beside you, why did you keep pushin' me away?" he asked. When she refused to look up, he shifted her slightly so he could nibble on her earlobe until she gave up and answered.

"I was afraid of you," she confessed.

His arms tightened around her. "Of me? Why?" She could hear the astonishment in his voice.

"Because . . . because you're a man." Haltingly, Nell told him of her father's abandonment of his family in order to search for gold.

Ross listened in comforting silence as she told of how her father had died in a fight over a trollop, leaving her mother to raise two children on her meager earnings. He learned in horrified amazement of Charleton Blevins, the middle-aged roué who'd seduced her in order to steal the small savings she'd inherited from her mother. Ross had assumed wrongly that the man who'd taken her virginity at seventeen had been as young and inexperienced as Nell. Given the differences in age and worldly experience, along with the conniving bastard's ulterior motives, her deflowerment had bordered on rape. With new insight, he recognized the many things she left unsaid. Probably nothing frightened her more about men than their lust for the rich metals that lay hidden beneath the earth.

Guilt at his own culpability spread through him. He wanted to admit to her that he was mining the Glamorgan illegally. But after what she'd just confessed, he was convinced she'd see the same greed in him.

Ross was determined to fight for his mining claim. He knew Hegel would gladly pirate the ore from the Glamorgan's rich veins if Ross didn't get to it first. Sean Ryan had been killed trying to discover if Hegel was doing just that. The young Irishman's loyalty to his boss had cost him his life. But Ross couldn't tell the woman he loved of her brother's bravery. Not yet.

Instead, he kissed her temple and whispered, "Marry me, darlin'."

She turned in his arms to search his face. "Ross, I . . ."

"I love you, Nell. I've loved you since the moment you walked into my office." When she only looked at him in startled wonderment, he continued in a tone of playful self-derision. "Hell, I tripped over my own feet at the sight of you. You should have known when I kicked over that damn wastebasket that I was a besotted fool."

"But . . . but I have to go back to Boston when the trial's over," she stammered in confusion. "I . . . I have to return to my uncle's law firm."

"No, you don't. You could have a legal practice right here in Butte. Look how marvelous you were at Lottie Howard's trial. You're a born natural at criminal law, and we've got more criminals in this minin' camp than a dog's got fleas." Although she hadn't said that she loved him, Ross was determined that she would, once he'd earned her trust, once he'd shown her that he wasn't like the men who'd hurt her so badly.

Nell absently smoothed her fingers across the thick comforter that covered them. "I don't know . . ." she hedged.

"You don't have to give me an answer tonight. Just say you'll think about it."

"Yes, I will." At his sideways grin of triumph, she quickly amended, "Yes, I'll think about it."

"We could get married at St. Patrick's right here in Butte," he said as he cuddled her closer.

"Oh, no. I'd want to get married in my own parish church back in Boston, with Uncle Cormac giving me away."

"That's fine with me, angel eyes," he immediately agreed. From the unmitigated satisfaction in his voice, she realized he'd have agreed to marry her in any church she cared to name, no questions asked. She also realized how adroitly he'd maneuvered her into talking about wedding plans, as though all that was left to settle was the exact date of the ceremony.

Nell pushed away from him and peered into his deep green eyes. Their gold-flecked depths sparkled with happiness. He didn't even try to hide his elation. She shook her head at him in feigned disbelief. "You are something else, Rossiter Morgan," she chided. "Haven't you ever learned the meaning of the word *no*?"

He slid down under the covers, taking her with him. Pinning her beneath his large frame, he braced up on his elbows and captured her head in his hands, his long fingers buried in her damp, tangled locks. His voice was filled with male pride. "I told you when we first met that a man never got what he wanted by cowerin' silently in the background."

"Ah, faint heart never won fair maid?" she murmured as she traced the outline of his firm lips with one fingertip.

"Somethin' like that," he agreed. "Now let's have another try at learnin' the taste of each other. I told you before that I was goin' to devour you like a pomegranate." He tracked a trail of fiery kisses across her breasts and over the bumps of her ribs, then dipped the tip of his tongue into the cavity of her belly button before continuing downward.

She clutched the tousled waves of his golden hair in her fingers. "Why, Mr. Morgan," she said in a husky whisper, "I do believe you're the boldest man I've ever known."

"And the luckiest."

Ross bent over the geological map spread across his battered desktop and thoughtfully traced the vein of ore. It was the first week in December. He'd just completed another meeting behind closed doors with his superintendent and the foreman in charge of timbering. With the help of Eben Pearce and Kalle Kuusinen, he'd continued to sink shafts and extend the exploration work farther and farther into the Glamorgan Mine. To his gratification, Ross had learned that the rich vein of ore they'd been following was even more valuable than he'd hoped. The deeper they went, the higher the grade of copper they found. In the secrecy of the long winter nights, his crew of Finns and Cousin Jacks proceeded to stope, hoist, and rush the copper to the smelter as fast as possible.

On the other side of the wall, the Irish miners of the Forrester could be heard dynamiting as well. Sometimes it seemed to Ross that the lawyers for both sides and the rum-soaked magistrate presiding over the case were the only ones still unaware of what was going on. The miners of Butte knew that it was only a matter of time until the two crews would meet head-on at the twelve-hundred-foot level. Then the battle underground would take on a whole new direction.

Ross stared down at the map with the stunned realization that he stood on top of a veritable hill of copper. The ore he'd found was in such quantity and of such a high grade, he conservatively estimated its value at twenty million dollars. Everything hinged on a favorable settlement in court, giving him undisputed claim. On his wedding day, he would be either a very wealthy man or a busted-flat mining engineer.

In her small office on Montana Street, Nell gazed in abstraction at the law book opened in front of her on the map table. She sighed, knowing she had every reason to feel happy and yet unable to quiet the butterflies inside her. Ross insisted on speaking of their engagement as a settled issue, though she'd never actually agreed to marry him. She'd told him she couldn't even think of becoming officially engaged until the trial was over. Afraid to make that final commitment, she'd insisted that they keep their personal relationship a secret. She hadn't told Ross she'd fallen in love with him. She knew that once she confessed her true feelings, there'd be no turning back. He'd never let her go.

In the past six weeks since they'd shared the sauna, they'd spent as much time together as possible, despite her many reservations. Christmas was only five days away. Ross's mansion, which had been built to resemble a French chateau, was decorated with garlands of fresh pine boughs and bright red ribbons. An enormous candlelit tree stood in the front parlor. She frequently had supper with Ross and Luke in the elegant dining room.

Nell had come to care very deeply for the ten-year-old boy. Hidden inside her was the longing for the three of them to live together as a family. Beneath her brass bed at Kuusinen's, she'd secreted the many presents she'd chosen with loving care for the two men in her life.

Whenever possible, she and Ross would spend part of the night together. It wasn't difficult, for although the boardinghouse was always busy with miners coming from or going to their shifts, the constant activity made it easy for Ross to slip inside her bedroom and leave again without notice. Well, almost without notice. She suspected Hertta knew and chose to look the other way.

There was another problem in Nell's life, and it was a big one. When she'd first told Gavin of Felix Hegel's attempted bribe, it had occurred to her that a similar offer might have been made to her legal partner. She'd quickly pushed the thought aside, unwilling even to consider the possibility that her good friend of almost fifteen years would sink to accepting Hegel's tainted money. Nell assumed that, if the unprincipled owner of the Forrester had tried to influence him, Gavin would have told her.

Little by little, however, she'd come to the unhappy conclusion that Gavin O'Connell was purposely mismanaging their representation of the Glamorgan Mine. That afternoon, she was waiting for her colleague to show up at their office. She intended to lay her suspicions on the table and give him a chance to defend himself.

She rose to greet him when he came in. Brushing the snow off the shoulders of his heavy topcoat he smiled at her in reply. Although he hadn't liked the fact that Nell had fallen for Ross Morgan, Gavin had remained constant in his friendship for her.

"Hi," he said as he removed his fur hat and tugged off his leather gloves. He shrugged out of his overcoat and moved to the steam radiator that kept their little office cozy and warm. "Brr, I don't think I'll ever get used to this Montana climate," he complained spreading his fingers over the rising heat. "I can hardly wait to get back to Boston." He looked around at her with a satisfied smile. "And that won't be long now. This blasted trial should be over in a few more weeks."

"I want to talk to you about the trial," Nell began hesitantly. She hated to accuse Gavin of doing something unethical and illegal. Acceptance of a bribe was a horrible charge to lay against anyone, let alone your own law partner. She swallowed nervously before continuing. "This morning in court, I couldn't believe you weren't going to object to the judge's denial of my model as evidence. I waited as long as possible to give you a chance to move to your feet. When you just sat there saying nothing, I had to speak out."

Gavin sank down in his chair and propped his boots up on the desk in front of him. Nell was forcibly reminded of Judge Curry, whom she'd learned to detest with good reason. "You seemed to be doing all right by yourself," Gavin said. His attractive features twisted in a sneer. "You sure as heck don't need any help from me."

"Of course I need your help!" she exclaimed. "What I want to know, Gavin, is why I never get any. You've overlooked every opportunity we've had to build a record for an appeal in this farce. How can you face Ross every day in the courtroom and not be ashamed of your lackluster performance?"

Gavin jumped to his feet. "Come on, Nell, you're not being fair. You know the outcome of this trial is a foregone conclusion. Why get yourself all in a dither over something you can't change?"

Nell's shoulders slumped as she stared down at the pointed toes of her oxford shoes. Heaven save them, Gavin was right on that score. Judge Otis Curry, who hadn't the least understanding of geological terms or mining laws, had blocked every attempt they'd made to use elaborate maps and diagrams to illustrate for the jury's benefit the testimony of their two expert witnesses. She suspected the only reason Curry had changed his mind and allowed her to submit as evidence the model she'd crafted so carefully was to afford him the opportunity to poke fun at it. He'd repeatedly referred to the exact, three-dimensional replica of the Glamorgan as "the lady's little toy mine."

During the cross-examination of Dr. Gunter, the tobacco-chewing magistrate had seen fit to allow

Shelton Broply to confuse her star witness by shooting rapid-fire questions at him and then reacting
with acid sarcasm when the bespectacled professor from Columbia had to take time to think them
through. Playing on the fact that Adolph Gunter
spoke with a heavy German accent, Broply had
twisted the elderly man's words around, until it
seemed as though Gunter's credibility was damaged beyond repair. The Glamorgan's other expert
witness, Morris Yandel, hadn't fared much better.
The burly, middle-aged man from Idaho explained
the results of his survey of the Glamorgan in clear,
precise terms—for a mining engineer. But without
the admission of the actual geological charts he'd
drawn up, the jurymen appeared unable to follow
the technical explanations.

During Nell's cross-examination of the Forrester's
experts, Judge Curry had repeatedly interrupted
her, purposely breaking her train of thought or
undermining the point she was about to make
to the jury. At other times, he'd swivel around
in his chair and stare down at her in patent disgust, as though she were asking foolish or improper
questions. He'd roll his eyes in the direction of the
jury box with obvious disdain, implying that Nell
was either incompetent or bent on misleading the
honorable gentlemen of the court.

"If we lose this case, I don't think I'll be able to
face Ross," she told Gavin with a dejected shake
of her head. "Everything he owns is wrapped up
in this trial. He stands to lose it all."

"Don't be so naive." Gavin walked over and
propped his backside on the map table. He folded his arms and met her questioning gaze. "Morgan
has no faith in your ability to win this case—or
mine either, for that matter. He never did. Felix
Hegel told me as much the night we attended
his birthday ball. I didn't want to believe it at
the time, but since then, he's convinced me of
Morgan's duplicity. Right now, Ross is secretly

removing as much copper ore as he can take from the Glamorgan."

"That's not true!" She moved away from the desk and faced Gavin with her fists clenched.

"The hell it isn't. That smooth-talking Casanova has blinded you, Nell. You can't see his driving ambition because you're head over heels in love with him. But your pair of rose-colored glasses doesn't change reality. To Ross Morgan, his copper ore comes first and foremost." Gavin straightened from his perch on the map table and took a step toward her. "Is that the kind of man you want to marry? One who lies and engages in illegal operations? The only thing that cold hearted bastard really cares about is his damn copper mine, and I can prove it to you."

Her voice shook with anger. "I don't believe you."

"Give me a chance, and I'll show you the truth about him."

"How?" Nell asked scornfully. She tossed her head, rigid with fury at Gavin's accusations.

"I'll take you down into the Forrester Mine, and you can hear the evidence of Morgan's treachery for yourself."

Chapter 18

"**N**ow there's nothing for you to be worrying about, Miss Ryan," said the shift foreman. He made a slow, downward motion with his big hand. "We're going to be dropping you nice and easy. Why, you'll be as safe as a baby in pram."

Beneath the heavy, fleece-lined jacket she wore, Nell resolutely squared her shoulders and met the stocky Irishman's blue-eyed gaze with calm determination. "I'll be fine, Mr. Coughlin. I'm not given to hysterics."

"That's my girl," Gavin exhorted with a jaunty smile. "We'll be down there and back up in no time."

They were standing beneath the tall gallows frame of the Forrester Mine. Its bare steel girders soared upward into the night sky, reaching over a hundred feet into the velvety darkness above them. Standing alongside Felix Hegel was his superintendent, Michael O'Neary, and his foreman, Paddy Coughlin. Both of the Forrester employees must have been forewarned by their boss that Nell and Gavin would be dressed as miners, complete with tie boots and two candles in their front shirt pockets. Neither O'Neary nor Coughlin had so much as lifted an eyebrow in surprise at the costume Nell wore.

"I would go with you, Nell," Hegel said in an unctuous tone of apology, "but I have some papers I need to look at this evening. And I don't want you to feel I'm pressuring you. I want you to make up your own mind about what you hear tonight. Just remember that the Glamorgan lies along the west side of the Forrester."

Nell lifted her chin and met his silvery gaze, daring him to so much as hint that Ross was engaged in criminal activities. "I'm only going on this excursion to satisfy Gavin," she insisted.

"Of course," Hegel replied with a tiny smile, unable to conceal his pleasure that she'd agreed to go into his mine at all. Dressed in a gray tweed top coat and tailored trousers, he seemed out of place in their roughly clad group. He glanced at O'Neary, his white haired superintendent, and then pointedly at the night shift foreman.

"If you're ready, ma'am?" Coughlin asked politely. He was a burly man with massive shoulders and huge upper arms that came from years of swinging a heavy sledgehammer. A shock of thick black hair stood out like porcupine quills from under the brim of his slouch miner's hat, and an enormous walrus mustache nearly covered the lower half of his craggy face. In spite of his hardened appearance, there was a fatherly gentleness in his voice.

Nell swallowed convulsively at the thought of what she was about to do. She'd never suffered from irrational fears. Heights and close quarters were no more frightening to her than to the average person. But dropping twelve hundred feet straight down into the earth at breakneck speed while enclosed in an open metal cage wasn't something the average person usually did. Just the thought of it made her feel a little woozy.

"I'm as ready as I'm ever going to be," she answered with a tight smile. "Let's get this over with."

Hegel came around behind her and lifted his hands to her shoulders. "Here, let me help you with that jacket."

Nell slipped out of the garment and gave it to him to hold. In the depths of the Forrester, there'd be no need for heavy winter clothing, even on this frigid December night. And the bulkiness of the coat would only impede her movements, exhausting her needlessly.

"Nell, I'd like you to stop by my office before you leave tonight," he continued. "If you have any questions about what you've learned, I'll be only too happy to answer them."

"Any questions I might have, Mr. Hegel, will be answered by the owner of the Glamorgan." She nodded to the foreman, signaling her wish to get started. Together, she and Gavin followed Paddy Coughlin across the steel turnsheets to the mine elevators.

Beneath the tall framework that rose above the Forrester, there were three sets of cages, two for lowering and raising miners and one for moving supplies and ore cars. These were connected to a hoisting apparatus by a wide belt stretched over a winding drum below and a great wheel perched high atop the gallows frame. Each cage had four decks stacked piggyback, one on top of the other. The station tenders and the engineer were responsible for the safe operation of the elevators, which they accomplished by a system of bells and white lines painted on the outer side of the belt.

With Gavin at her side, Nell stepped timidly into the skeleton of a box that would take them below.

"Don't worry," he told her in a creaky voice. "This thing's got safety locks in case the cable breaks." He tipped his head and fidgeted with the miner's cap that covered his thick brown hair, betraying his own nervousness.

She peeked at him from the corner of her eye, suddenly too frozen with fear to move. "Thanks."

For a fleeting moment, she wished Ross were going down with her. The tragic irony of that impossible notion almost made her sob out loud. After she'd agreed the previous afternoon to go into Hegel's mine with Gavin, she'd barely been able to face Ross. When he'd stopped at the law office to take her to supper, she'd pleaded exhaustion. His sincere concern had nearly been her undoing. In addition, she'd had to concoct an excuse for not seeing him the next evening. She could hardly tell her fiancé that she was going to be too busy trapping him in unlawful activities to spend any time with him. So she'd told him, instead, that she planned to wrap Christmas presents in the privacy of her bedroom.

The lies had filled her with self-loathing, but she hadn't backed out or confessed the truth. How he'd not heard the duplicity in her voice or read the evasiveness in her averted eyes, she'd never understand. It was probably only because her treachery had been the furthest thing from his mind. But she had to know if Ross had deceived her the same way Charleton had—from the very first day they'd met. She had to learn if, once again, she'd placed her trust in an avaricious, self-serving scoundrel.

Coughlin joined them in the elevator, squeezing his hefty bulk into the small space with an encouraging smile. "Keep your hands inside the cage," he advised them. "And your elbows too."

The station tender, a young man with a skimpy fringe of orange mustache over his pink upper lip, stepped on last and showed Nell and Gavin how to grasp a metal pipe overhead to maintain their balance. She'd already slipped off her gloves and stuffed them into her overall pockets. She was afraid she'd never be able to hang on to the smooth metal with her clammy palm. With her other hand, she clung to Gavin's arm for dear life.

"Stand steady," the station tender called.

Two sharp, loud bells rang out in the cold night air like the peal of doom. The next instant, the world dropped out from under her. Down, down, down they flew, into the bowels of the earth at the dizzying speed of an express train hurtling into oblivion. At times, the cage jerked and bumped against the side timbers of the shaft, making the platform they stood on shake and tremble. Holding her breath, Nell squeezed her eyes tight and prayed silently.

In less than a minute, they came to a grinding halt.

"We're here," Coughlin announced cheerfully.

Nell opened her eyes. They were, indeed, there. Twelve hundred feet below the surface. Her stalled heart resumed its beating as she drew in a deep draft of air and exhaled a ragged sigh of relief. She could breathe normally, she told herself sternly. She could do it, if she just remained calm and concentrated on making her lungs work for her. In and out. In and out. She was determined to ignore the horrible premonition that she was about to be crushed like an insignificant, unwary insect beneath a thousand tons of rock.

From the central station in which they stood, tunnels led outward in all directions. Lanterns cast their flickering light. There was a huge steam engine humming nearby, which Nell knew circulated fresh air by the use of large ventilating fans. Lines of pipes and wires had been dropped down a separate compartment of the shaft. Some were used to pump out water, while others provided compressed air for the drills the Butte miners had cynically labeled "widow-makers" because of the clouds of deadly dust they stirred up. Barrels of clear water with large blocks of ice stood along the wall, drinking ladles hooked to their sides.

"I'm going to be taking you two into a drift that goes right past the Glamorgan's back door," Paddy Coughlin told them. "Don't be surprised when you see track laid down on the floor and cars filled with ore. They've been sitting there since last June when our mining was halted by the court injunction. Course, Mr. Hegel has been waiting until it's legal to resume operations."

Nell ignored the implication that Rossiter Morgan hadn't been so law-abiding. Without replying, she nodded her willingness to follow Coughlin.

He led them into a tunnel that had been cut through solid rock, supported on both sides and overhead by a scaffolding of strong beams. The light from their carbide lanterns created deep shadows that seemed to leap about them with a life of their own. An oppressive atmosphere of dampness and warmth prevailed, despite the currents of fresh air being pumped into the drift.

"How can we get so near the Glamorgan Mine?" asked Nell, not making any attempt to keep the skepticism from her voice.

Coughlin stopped and rubbed the stubble of black whiskers on his chin. When he turned to face her, the light of his lamp bathed her in its phantasmal glow. "Now that's the wondrous thing about our mining camp, Miss Ryan. The entire Butte hill has been honeycombed with drifts and crosscuts which have been established in all the mines at regular hundred-foot intervals. Faith, a man can descend a shaft in Walkerville and ascend to the surface in Meaderville over two miles away."

Gavin pursed his lips and gave a low whistle. "Now that's impressive."

Nell studied him through narrowed eyes, wondering exactly when he'd taken such an interest in mining. It hadn't been during their preparations for the present ongoing trial.

They resumed their exploration, walking alongside the track that had been laid down for the ore cars. The jagged walls and ceiling had been carved out of granite by the repeated firing of dynamite. They occasionally saw crystallizations of rock that sparkled brilliantly in the lantern light. The floor along the narrow gauge tracks was rough and uneven. Frequently, they had to make their way around—and sometimes over—piles of broken rock. Nell was thankful she'd been able to find a pair of work boots small enough to fit—with the help of three pairs of heavy wool socks.

"The Glamorgan's just behind the wall to our left," Coughlin informed them. "The mine over on the far side of the Forrester has been abandoned for the last two years, so the sounds you'll hear can't be coming from the Rosie O." He led them to a heavy iron door and tapped on it silently with the tip of his finger. He spoke in a low voice. "This bulkhead seals off a crosscut connecting the Forrester and the Glamorgan. It's been padlocked shut ever since Mr. Hegel bought the Forrester from its former owner. Sure, and you can hear the work going on behind it right now."

Nell listened, her heart in her throat. From the other side of the iron bulkhead came the unmistakable sound of a mine car clanking noisily down its track, followed by the crash of a load of ore being dumped. Heartsick at what she heard and all that it meant, she turned to go.

"If you'll be coming with me a little farther into the stope, Miss Ryan," Coughlin called, "we can hear those Cousin Jacks blasting."

"I've heard enough."

"Let's do as Paddy says," Gavin urged. He caught Nell by the elbow and pulled her to a stop. They were nearly the same height, and his attractive features, only inches from hers, were drawn tight and tense. "As long as we've come this far, we might as well hear what we came to hear."

Unable to argue, Nell shook her head dispiritedly, then waved her hand in defeat. "All right. Let's go."

Together, they trekked farther into the drift. When they finally reached the end, Nell gazed around at the ragged walls, the light from her carbide lantern casting eerie shadows on the saw-toothed outcroppings of rock supported by massive timbers.

"They've been blasting in the Glamorgan every night just about this time," Coughlin explained. "We'll wait for their next firing and then be heading on back."

Nell sank down on a huge chunk of rock, too disheartened to say a word. Covering her brow with her hand to hide her face, she stared down at the granite floor. Thankfully, the two men who stood beside her seemed to sense her despair and compassionately held their tongues.

Heaven save her, she understood now why Ross had never let her inspect the site of her brother's accident. If she'd been allowed to descend to the twelve-hundred-foot level of the Glamorgan, she'd have seen and heard the evidence of Ross's unlawful mining operations. That was why he'd refused to allow Eben or anyone else to escort her down there. Sean hadn't been merely conducting a routine check on the timbering, as Ross had told her. Her young brother had been working illegally in the Glamorgan when he died. If it hadn't been for Morgan's inordinate greed, Sean Ryan would still be alive. Ross had lied to her since the day she'd arrived in Butte. And he hadn't stopped lying since.

The silent trio didn't have long to wait. The explosion in the Glamorgan shook the walls around them. Over their heads, the wooden scaffolding creaked and groaned ominously. Terrified, Nell jumped to her feet and peered at Coughlin in the dim light, unable to see his features clearly but certain he was startled.

"Jaysus, Mary, and Joseph," he muttered. "They're getting a whole lot closer than we thought."

"Let's go back," she pleaded.

"Yes, let's go," Gavin agreed, his voice thin and strained. He took her hand, ready to lead her back down the drift.

A second blast echoed, nearer and louder, sending waves of vibrations reverberating around them. It was as though they were standing inside the center of a kettle drum that had just been struck a mighty blow. The crack and shriek of splitting lumber ricocheted off the walls like an army of banshees howling down the corridors of hell. A low rumble sounded from far away. It moved steadily closer, coming down the tunnel they'd just traversed and increasing in volume, till it was a horrifying roar.

Nell clutched Gavin's hand. "What's happening?" she cried.

"God a'mighty," Coughlin said from directly behind them. "It's a cave-in."

"Oh, Jesus, no!" Gavin exclaimed.

Simultaneously, the three looked up at the drift's timbered roof. The sound of the giant beams straining and groaning to hold back the rock above them filled Nell with a paralyzing terror. Certain she was about to be crushed to death, she began a silent Act of Contrition. *Oh my God, I am heartily sorry for having offended Thee . . .*

Miraculously, the framework of lumber directly over them held. The chamber was filled with dust, blown in from the collapsed tunnel by the force of the cave-in, making the site of their entrapment seem otherworldly.

"You both wait here," Coughlin instructed. "I'll be going to see what happened."

Too frightened to argue, Nell and Gavin did as he told them. With their arms wrapped around each other's waists, they huddled together for moral support.

The sensation of being entombed alive brought scalding tears to Nell's eyes. It took every ounce of strength she possessed to keep from screaming out loud, over and over, in sheer, mindless horror.

In only minutes, Coughlin reappeared from out of the murky darkness. "Jaysus, it ain't looking good back there." His somber dust-streaked features were filled with misgiving. "The dry timbers must have cracked under the stress of the blast. We can't be reaching the bulkhead door as I'd hoped."

"How . . . how much of the tunnel collapsed?" Nell questioned hoarsely. A film of cold perspiration covered her body. She was rigid with fear.

Lifting his hat and wiping his forehead with a red checkered handkerchief, Coughlin answered with unruffled fatalism. "There's no way of knowing, ma'am."

"What do we do?" Gavin asked, his words jerky and sharp with dread.

The foreman plopped down on a clear spot on the hard floor and calmly removed a chaw of tobacco from the bib pocket of his overalls. "There being nothing else we can do, boyo, we wait. And pray."

The mine whistles wailed, piercing the night and shattering the peace of the sleeping mining camp like the clear, cold ring of a sledgehammer driving a steel bit into solid granite. As the news of the disaster at the Forrester traveled across the Butte hill, one mine after another added the shriek of its loud whistle to the rending alarm.

Residents leaped from their beds, tossed on clothing, and raced to the scene of the tragedy. Miners below ground, working on the night shifts, left their drilling and stoping and mucking to find out the extent of the calamity and what they could do to help.

Since Nell had said she was going to be busy with her holiday preparations that evening, Ross was working late with Eben in the mine office. He had done a little gift wrapping of his own that afternoon. Under the huge, tinseled fir tree in his front parlor sat a small box containing a diamond engagement ring. The secrecy, which his reluctant little darling had insisted upon, was fast approaching its end. Come Christmas morning, he was going to put his brand on Nell Ryan for all the world to see.

When they heard the whistles first start to blow, Ross and Eben yanked on their winter overcoats and hurried across the snowy yard of the Glamorgan to the scene of confusion around the shaft of the nearby Forrester. As they raced by, someone called to a friend that a woman was trapped in the mine. Ross ignored the shouted words, certain he'd heard them wrong.

A group of Hegel's Irish miners were standing on the surface turnsheets near the cages, talking quietly as he and Eben drew near. A larger crowd of men from all the mines on the Hill milled around the gallows frame, hoping to be told what they could do to be of assistance. The women who'd come at the sound of the whistles, some with children and babies in their arms, gathered in front of the Forrester's mine office as they waited to learn if it was their loved one injured or dead below. A fire wagon pulled into the mine yard, its alarm bells clanging wildly, followed by two ambulance wagons.

"What is it?" Ross asked a burly miner. "Fire?"

The man turned, his eyes filled with dread. "A cave-in."

It was one of the worst of the many accidents that could happen in mining, bringing with it an awful death, either of being crushed alive or of slowly suffocating. Every miner feared being buried alive more than anything else.

Eben shook his head in sympathy for the trapped men. "How many are down there?"

"Only three, thank God," another miner told them.

Surprised by the low number, Ross could only assume that for some reason the entire night shift at the Forrester had been detained up on top for a long while that evening. Perhaps the delay had something to do with the accident. Perhaps it was merely amazing good luck.

"One of them's a woman," said a brick-haired station tender, speaking directly to Ross. The wiry young man was thoroughly shaken. He stared at the owner of the Glamorgan with frightened eyes, clearly the only one of the group who knew the actual identities of the people trapped below.

An icy foreboding snaked through Ross. His abdomen cramped painfully, as though he'd just been kneed in the groin. "Who's down there?" he demanded. But he knew the answer before the man uttered a word.

"Miss Ryan. She went down with Coughlin, our shift foreman, and that dude lawyer O'Connell."

"Where's Hegel?" Ross snapped, ready to sprint to the cages. "Down there now?" He warded off the shock of panic that threatened to destroy his usual ability to think clearly in any crisis.

The station tender shook his head, his ruddy complexion turning scarlet. "He and O'Neary are over at the office looking at some charts. Two dozen men have already gone below to start digging them out, but it looks pretty impossible from the station."

Ross turned and raced through the group of bewildered women clustered in front of the Forrester's main office building. He flung the door open to find Hegel and his superintendent bent over an engineering map spread across a desktop. They straightened warily as he charged into the room.

"You goddamn sonofabitch," Ross said through clenched teeth. Slamming the door shut behind him, he stalked into the room.

Hegel flushed uncomfortably and then stared back down at the parchment. "That's not going to get her out, Morgan."

"Why?" Ross bellowed, taut with rage and fear. "Why'd she go down there in the first place?"

Only the width of the desk separated them, and he fought back the urge to reach over and choke the life out of the slimy bastard. But without Hegel's knowledge of his own mine, they might never get Nell out. Ross knew he'd have to wait until after she was safe to learn the answers to his questions.

He looked down at the map of the Forrester spread out across the desk. Snatching his eyeglasses from his shirt pocket, he jammed them on. "Where the hell are they?"

"Our best guess is right here," O'Neary said in the strained voice of a man suffering bitter self-recrimination. The safety of every person below ground was his responsibility, and he knew it. He pointed to a spot on the surveyor's chart. "At a set time, Coughlin was going to take them to the very end of this drift."

By then, Eben had also joined them. "They're on the twelve-hundred-foot level?" he asked with surprise. His coppery freckles stood out on his pale face. "Right alongside the Glamorgan? We blasted near there earlier this evening."

"Hell, it was your illegal blasting that caused this catastrophe!" Hegel accused.

O'Neary glanced at Hegel and shook his head in disgust, making it all too obvious that the seasoned mine super had no respect for his boss, who was even now trying to cover up his own illegal mining.

"How much of the drift caved in?" Ross demanded.

"We think the timbering along the whole blessed stope gave way," O'Neary answered, his face beet-red with guilt and shame.

Ross clenched his jaw, determined to control his rage. "How long has it been since the timbers in that drift were inspected and the rotten ones replaced?"

"Too damn long," O'Neary admitted in a low growl. "I was afraid something like this would happen." He jerked his white head toward Hegel beside him. "But the boss never wanted to do anything except pull out as much ore as he could get his hands on, as quickly as possible."

Ross gave a curt nod, acknowledging O'Neary's blunt honesty, which would more than likely cost the man his job when this was over. "Where's the nearest crosscut?"

O'Neary jabbed his thick index finger at a spot on the chart. "There's an iron bulkhead right here."

Ross looked over at Eben. "Go get the maps of the Glamorgan and bring them back here. Fast!"

Clenching his fists, he turned to Hegel as Eben raced out the door. "I swear to God," he snarled, "if we don't get Nell out of there alive, you're a dead man."

Nell sat on the granite floor with her folded arms resting across her bent knees. With one cheek laid on her forearm, she closed her eyes and waited for death. Beside her on the ground, Gavin and Paddy Coughlin sat with their backs braced against the solitary ore car that had been trapped inside the small area with them. The two men talked in low tones, probably in the hope that she would doze off and find a few minutes' reprieve from the terror that blanketed them. The flame of a single candle sent its feeble rays through the chamber. They'd put out their carbide lanterns in order to save oxygen, but not one of them was willing to sit in total darkness. The heat in the enclosed space had risen steadily, adding its oppressive humidity to their discomfort. Nell thought longingly of the barrels of ice water she'd seen near the shaft end of the tunnel.

Numb with despair, she'd reached the conclusion that she really didn't care if she was rescued or not. Dear Lord in heaven, her life wasn't worth the effort it would take to save her. If it weren't for the lives of the two men entombed with her, she'd have prayed for death. Aside from Uncle Cormac, every man she'd ever cared about had betrayed her. Her father had abandoned her as a child. Charleton Blevins had swindled her, not just out of her mother's money, but also out of her girlish, romantic dreams. Even Gavin, her good friend for so many years, had betrayed her by selling out to Felix Hegel and purposely sabotaging their court case. In every instance, the sole driving force behind their treachery had been greed. Yet nothing the others had done could compare to the perfidy of the golden-haired seducer who'd courted her and won her love.

She realized now the scope of Morgan's duplicity. She'd thought it strange, at first, that Eben had never come to the trial. Nor had Kalle Kuusinen. When she'd questioned Ross about their absence from the courtroom, he'd told her that Eben needed to stay at the Glamorgan office for security reasons. He'd implied that the burly Finn was working for some other mine owner. She knew now that Kalle and all the other Finnish miners at the boardinghouse were secretly going down into the Glamorgan at night to do the dangerous work of timbering. They slept during the day when she was busy at her law office or in the courtroom. Not one person had slipped and given away Ross's secret. Even Hertta, whom she'd begun to care for like a sister, must have deliberately kept the truth from her.

With new insight, Nell understood why Ross had taken the legal setbacks during the trial so calmly. She'd been abject at her lack of success, and he'd told her with unperturbed sangfroid that he knew she was doing her best. *Her best!* While all the time, the mercenary, conniving wretch was secretly removing his copper ore and pocketing the money. His lies, his ugly deceptions were more than she could bear. She hated Ross Morgan with all the passion he'd ignited and brought to a raging fire within her.

She'd hate him until the day she died.

The galling thought that she might not live long enough to tell him so rankled even more than the knowledge of his despicable hypocrisy.

The minutes flew past, turning into hours. Working feverishly from the Glamorgan side, Ross's crew of Cornish miners cut around the side posts of the iron bulkhead with pickaxes, only to find a solid wall of rubble. With agonized frustration, they realized it would take days to remove the broken rock and splintered timbers that filled the collapsed drift. Ross knew that if, by some miracle, Nell remained alive at the farthest end of the stope, she had to be rescued quickly, before the air supply was gone. He didn't give a good goddamn about the two bastards who had taken her there in the first place.

"We can try to smash our way through with picks and sledges from this side," Eben said, "but that'll take time. Or we can risk the chance of another cave-in and blast." His shoulders slumped in discouragement. "Either way, we stand to lose them if anything goes wrong—given they're still alive."

Ross ran his hand over his eyes, not wanting to make the dreadful choice, but knowing he had to. They'd moved to the twelve-hundred-foot level of the Glamorgan, bringing with them the survey maps and mine drawings from the Forrester. Hegel hadn't dared to protest as O'Neary casually rolled them up and tucked them under his brawny arm. The geological charts of the two mines now lay side by side on the rough granite floor, lit at each corner by a kerosene lantern.

Four desperate men, Eben, Kalle, O'Neary, and Ross, hunkered around the outspread maps, deliberating their next move. They were flanked by a crew of Cornishmen, experts in drilling and blasting, who were eagerly waiting for orders. Hegel had already returned to the surface. He had proven useless, unwilling to take responsibility for the tough decisions that had to be made any more than he accepted the blame for the unnecessary disaster in his own mine. The man was a low-bellied snake.

"A small, controlled explosion could do it," O'Neary added thoughtfully as he studied the maps from his perch on an unopened case of dynamite. "Just enough to cut into the face of the Glamorgan's east wall without endangering the people behind it."

"You're sure about the location we're aimin' for?" asked Ross for the third time. He scowled down at the charts in worried concentration. His heart lurched at the thought that they might be going in the wrong direction.

O'Neary nodded. He tapped a forefinger on the wrinkled paper with glum confidence. "The plan was for them to be at the end of the drift when you blasted on schedule this evening. The new timbering at the face of the stope should have held. But whether they're alive or no, we'll be finding them here."

"Blasting would be the fastest way to reach them," Eben pointed out. Crouched down on one knee beside the mine drawings, he brushed his fingertips nervously back and forth across his heavy red mustache. "It's your call, boss. What are we going to do?"

Ross straightened and looked steadily around the group, meeting each man's eyes, taking full responsibility for whatever might happen. "We blast."

Chapter 19

Time was running out. Every man on the rescue crew knew they dared to blast only once or risk the escalating danger of setting off another cave-in. They had to do it right the first time. After firing the dynamite, it would then be a matter of hacking their way through the wall of the stope to the other side as quickly and expeditiously as possible.

With painstaking precision, Ross measured and marked each spot for his team of veteran miners, telling them exactly how deep he wanted them to drill each hole. He intended to bring down as much rock as possible in one precisely planned explosion, without destroying any timbers that still remained upright in the Forrester. If any remained standing.

Ross estimated the wall between the Glamorgan and the Forrester to be about eight feet thick at its narrowest width. He oversaw the placing of each stick of dynamite by his Cornish crew, not willing to chance another man's error in their frantic haste. Too much explosive or too little could be equally deadly for the three people trapped on the other side.

When everyone else had withdrawn from the blasting site, he and Eben lit the fuses. Moving calmly but quickly to safety, they gave the familiar cry.

"Fire in the hole!"

The detonation shook the walls and echoed down the long granite corridors of the Glamorgan. His heart pumping madly, Ross prayed to heaven he hadn't just collapsed the roof on top of the three people he was trying to free. The dread of losing Nell sent cold bands of fear wrapping around his lungs like the arms of an insidious phantom, threatening to destroy all rational thought.

Over four hours had elapsed since the cave-in had occurred. More precious minutes ticked away as the rescuers hung back until it was safe to reenter the area after the blast. It took all of Ross's willpower to remain composed and cool-headed, knowing that Nell could be running out of oxygen or lying injured beneath a fallen timber while they waited for the noxious gases to dissipate.

Once they were able to return to the face of the stope, everyone scrambled to move the broken rock out of the way, some with shovels, some with their bare hands. Using sheer, brute strength, they tore into the wall with their picks and sledges. In the heat and humidity, the miners stripped off their shirts as they worked. Their half-naked bodies glistened with sweat in the lantern light. Eight men, including Ross and Kalle Kuusinen, crowded into the small space, every one of them strong and athletic, with muscles that knotted and bulged beneath the rigors of their labor. While several men took turns chopping into the rock with picks, others quickly hauled the debris out of the way, methodically clearing a path to the trapped victims. At last, they heard the faint tap-tap of someone banging frantically against the other side. It had to be Paddy Coughlin—using the small pick hammer he carried to dislodge ore samples— in a desperate attempt to signal them. The renewed sound of their furious digging echoed up and down the drift.

Ross was the first one to climb through the small hole they bored through solid granite. He found Nell, Gavin, and Coughlin standing side by side in front of a loaded ore car, watching him in dazed stupefaction as he crawled into the dimly lit chamber.

They were alive!

Their faces streaked with soot, their miner's clothes covered with dust, the three stared at him with round, owllike eyes, too much in shock for the first few seconds even to speak.

Ross wrapped his tired arms around Nell's slender form and cradled her tight against him, unable to say anything at all. Perspiration streamed down his bare chest and back. The matted hair on his head clung to his soaked scalp. His hands and forearms were begrimed with dirt. He was so damn filthy he shouldn't be touching her, but nothing on earth could have held him back.

His eyes burned with unshed tears. With her gorgeous frame smashed up against his body, he swallowed back the lump in his throat, unable to risk speech for fear he'd break down and cry like a prissy schoolboy. And all the while, his heart thumped wildly in delirious, glorious, jubilant thanksgiving.

God above, she was alive!

She was alive!

Eben, Kalle, and O'Neary crawled through the narrow aperture to join them. The two burly Irish miners from the Forrester clasped each other like grizzly bears in a joyous hug of deliverance, while Gavin pumped Eben's hand and the husky Finn stood by, grinning in mute happiness.

Ross's heart ached for the silent woman he held so close to his heart. There wasn't a sign of a tear track on her soot-covered cheeks. Somehow, she'd managed to remain calm during the whole horrible time she'd been imprisoned in that godawful chamber. Christ, he'd seen grown men panic over far less. Suffering from shock and delayed fright, she was as stiff and lifeless in his arms as a wooden marionette.

"Come on, angel eyes," he said tenderly. "Let's get you out of here."

Ross and Nell rode up in the lift with Eben, Gavin, Coughlin, O'Neary, and Kalle. When the rescued and rescuers reached the surface, they were greeted ecstatically by a throng of cheering miners. Dozens

of kerosene lanterns held by the waiting crowd lit
the wintry darkness around the shaft house.

People from as far away as Meaderville and
Walkerville had come to keep vigil. The men were
bundled up in heavy jackets and fur caps; the women
had thick wool shawls wrapped around their shoulders and plaid head scarves tied snugly under their
chins. Children in snowsuits jumped up and down
in the moon-drenched snow, dancing around their
parents in excitement. For anyone to return to the
surface alive after a cave-in was a cause for wild
celebration.

At the edge of the exuberant crowd of women and
children that had gathered near the Glamorgan Mine
office stood Luke with Hertta and Mrs. Rooney, the
Morgans' housekeeper, on either side of him. Like
so many others, Ross's son had been wakened from
his sleep by the alarm whistles and had raced to the
site of the accident to learn the identity and fate
of the men caught below. Mrs. Kuusinen had her
arm around Luke's shoulder, keeping him beside
her until his father was freed of his responsibilities
and could talk with him at length about the night's
events. The proud grin on the boy's face shone like
a banner of praise in the moonlight.

Nell staggered as she stepped out of the cage.
With his arm firmly about her waist, Ross caught
her before she fell. She skidded awkwardly on
the frosty steel turnsheets as though completely
unaware of her surroundings. He could sense her
blank befuddlement and wished uneasily that she'd
break down and sob out loud rather than keep up
this unnatural, dry-eyed control.

"It's all right, sweetheart," he told her softly, trying to break through the haze of bewilderment that
surrounded her. "I'm right here beside you. You're
perfectly safe now."

Morgan's hypocritical words pierced Nell's muddled confusion. In violent reaction to his two-faced
guile, she shoved him away. How could he believe

she didn't know the truth after all that had happened?

"No!" she cried. "No! I'm not safe with you!" She began shaking uncontrollably. Her voice rose in hysteria. "You're a cheat and a fraud! You've been mining illegally in spite of the injunction."

Her frenzied accusations rang out in the cold night air. Beneath the stark gallows frame of the Glamorgan Mine, the joyful conversations of the men and women who surrounded them grew hushed. Gradually, the children's voices died down to a soft murmur as they looked up in wonder at the stricken adults.

Over her shoulder, Nell could sense Eben and Kalle move closer to Ross, while Gavin hurried to stand directly behind her. The electrified tension that surrounded the dusty, dirt-streaked group was filled with an ominous silence.

Felix Hegel, still dressed in his tailored overcoat, emerged from the cluster of Irish miners who'd waited near the shaft house during the crisis. He sauntered up to stand directly in front of Ross. "Well, I guess you know why she went down there in the first place," he taunted in a voice that carried to every listener.

Ignoring Hegel's jeer, Ross scowled at Nell, comprehension slowly dawning on his rugged features. He understood now why she'd gone with Gavin into the Forrester. His words came clipped and terse. "Nell, I never cheated you."

"Liar!" she screamed, as all the tight control she'd managed to maintain while she was entombed underground unraveled like a housewife's ball of yarn. Every precious breath she took seemed to sear her suffocated lungs. "You lied about Sean's death! Didn't you? Didn't you?"

"Sean was killed accidentally when a timber fell on him, just as I said," Ross answered coldly. He started to take her arm, but she jerked away as though his very touch revolted her.

Nell ignored the people around them, not caring who heard her accusations. "Sean wouldn't have been down there at all, Morgan, if you hadn't been so greedy. If you had obeyed the law and shut down your mine, my brother would be alive today."

A muscle twitched in Ross's taut cheek. His strong jaw clenched in fury. "If you'd had any faith in me, you would have come to me with your suspicions, not betrayed me by sneaking down into the Forrester with Hegel's connivance in order to catch me doing something illegal. Your actions tonight have proven only one thing, Miss Ryan—that you've sold your integrity for thirty pieces of silver."

Aghast at his unwarranted assumption, Nell stared at him, too shocked to say another word.

Hegel moved to stand next to her. Lifting the fleece-lined jacket he held, he placed it solicitously over her shoulders, as if he were the one responsible for her well-being and not the grimy, sweaty brute who stood next to her. "What more is there to discuss?" he interjected with a sneer. "Miss Ryan certainly knows by now that you've been illegally mining in the Glamorgan since last June. I doubt any attorney, even a love-struck one, appreciates being hoodwinked by an unscrupulous client."

With blurred speed, Ross doubled up his fist and struck Hegel squarely in the stomach, then followed up with a second blow to the jaw. Hegel grunted with pain and fell to the ground.

Ignoring the motionless form crumpled at his feet, Ross met Nell's gaze. His eyes were icy emerald shards. Heaven save her, he wasn't even breathing hard. "Are you coming with me?"

Gavin stepped forward to stand beside Nell. He placed his arm protectively around her shoulders, daring Morgan to take a step closer.

She lifted her chin and glared at Ross as she gave him back measure for measure. "You despicable wretch," she said through stiff lips. "Your greed killed my brother. I'll hate you till the day I die."

Without a word, Ross turned his muscled back on them. He was still naked from the waist up. Since returning to the surface, he hadn't taken the time even to pull on his shirt. He strode away from them now, his spine rigid with disdain, his tawny head high. As he started to make his way with aloof detachment across the snowy yard to his office, the crowd silently opened a path for him.

"Dad!" Luke shouted. "Look out!"

His son's warning was all Ross needed. From the corner of his eye, he saw two brawny miners charging toward him. He crouched and braced himself as the first man jumped on his back. In one fluid movement, Ross went down on his knee, reached back, and clasped the man's neck. Using his assailant's own momentum, he flipped him over his shoulder. The beefy man crashed onto his back, striking the frozen ground so hard that his whole body bounced.

Still crouched, Ross met the second miner's assault with equal force as he rammed his elbow sharply into the man's ribs. Continuing to pivot, Ross knocked his attacker off balance and pitched him to the ground. Then Ross straightened and lashed out with the sole of his heavy boot, striking his barrel-chested foe neatly in the solar plexus. It had taken only seconds. By the time Kalle and Eben could reach his side, Ross stood between two fallen men, one groaning in agony, the other lying spread-eagle and unconscious in the trampled snow.

Ross's crew of Finns and Cornishmen immediately gathered about him, their fists clenched, their legs braced apart in a pugnacious stance of readiness. They waited eagerly for the big Micks from the Forrester to make a threatening move. The air bristled with the spine-tingling thrill that accompanies any brutal confrontation.

"Hold on just a damn minute," Michael O'Neary bellowed to his fellow Irishmen from his spot near the cages. "This fight's between the two mine owners. Let's be giving them some room so they can have it out, fair and square."

The circle of fascinated onlookers who'd gathered beneath the gallows frame quickly widened, drawing Felix Hegel into its center. Standing erect once again, he hastily removed his snow-dusted coat and rolled up his white shirtsleeves. Kalle and Eben stepped back into the cordon of men, happy to allow Ross the pleasure of beating his enemy to a bloody pulp.

With horrified dread, Nell clung to Gavin, watching the two men meet face to face on the steel turnplates that surrounded the mine shaft. There'd be no gentlemen's rules to protect the participants in this fight. A knee to the groin or a thumb in the eyes was as acceptable to the men who watched as a swift, well-placed uppercut.

Ross grinned to himself, delighted that Hegel had been foolish enough to get back up on his feet. When he'd knocked the sonofabitch down, he hadn't dreamed he'd be so lucky as to get the chance to hit him again without Hegel's crew of Irish miners swarming in to protect him. For all the bastard's affected Eastern airs, Ross knew that Hegel had been raised in the slums of Chicago. The fastidious man with the cultivated accent had the merciless cunning of a born street fighter. But Ross had learned a few tricks himself, growing up in the Colorado goldfields.

Hegel swung the first punch. Ross anticipated the move and ducked the blow with ease. The enthusiastic audience gave a shout of appreciation for the agile footwork. Twisting, Ross rammed one fist and then the other into Hegel's gut. Gratified at the sound of air being forced from his opponent's lungs, Ross shifted his weight and moved to trap his wily adversary in a headlock. Just as he started to close in, Ross's boot slipped on a patch of ice. He crashed against the nearby metal cage, striking his temple and the side of his face on its sharp edge and tearing a gash across the corner of his eye over the cheekbone. Dazed, Ross fought the blackness that swept in on him. He sank heavily to his knees, one arm braced against the side of the mine elevator.

Hegel seized his opportunity. He kicked Ross viciously in the ribs, again and again, then chiseled at the mangled cheek with his fist in a series of quick, half-arm punches. The impact of the savage blows tore a short, strangled grunt from Ross's throat. The cut on his face was bleeding freely. He tasted his own blood.

Visibly excited, Hegel panted in short, wheezing gasps. Pursuing his advantage with wild-eyed eagerness, he drew back his foot to stomp again. Ross rolled to the side. From his spot on the ground, he kicked out at Hegel, who was balanced precariously on one leg. Ross nailed him square on the kneecap and had the satisfaction of seeing his antagonist topple backward like a felled tree.

Groggy and disoriented, his face throbbing with pain, Ross crawled to his hands and knees. He sprang up from a crouch as Hegel staggered to his feet. Throwing all his weight behind his charge, Ross drove his shoulder into the other man's chest. Together they crashed to the frozen turnsheets, spattered and slickened now with Ross's blood. They skidded across the icy steel plates and smacked up against the wooden shaft house wall with a sickening thud.

Ross recovered first, clambering to his knees and sitting back on his haunches. He dragged Hegel up by the front of his bloodied white shirt and smashed his fist into the bruised face. The satisfying sound of bone and cartilage splitting asunder told Ross he'd broken the bastard's nose. Holding Hegel up by his ruffled shirtfront, he pounded his right fist into his enemy's face over and over, till Hegel's mouth was a puffy, lacerated mass, and his eyes were starting to turn purple and swell shut.

"T'at's enough, Ross." A man's deep voice cut through Morgan's white-hot rage. "He's unconscious. He can't feel a t'ing."

Ross recognized the familiar sound of Kalle's Finnish accent and realized the foreman was bending over him. Kuusinen's big hand squeezed Ross's shoulder to signal the fight was over. Ross released Hegel's shirt. The dark head dropped back down on the cold steel plate with a hollow thud, and Ross rose slowly to his feet.

The top layer of skin over one shoulder and arm had been burned away from the slide across the frozen metal. The deep gash on his cheek had congealed in the frigid air. Hell, it felt like the whole side of his face had been torn away. The front of Ross's bare chest was splattered with blood, and not all of it was Hegel's. Fiery pains shot through his bruised rib cage, making breathing a conscious act of willpower. Wincing, Ross put his hand to his side and wondered absently if he'd sustained a couple of broken ribs.

Eben hurried to offer assistance. Ross gestured him away with an impatient jerk of his head. Breathing in shallow pants, he looked around the circle of people, searching for a pair of enormous brown eyes till he found them. Nell was standing with Gavin's arm around her waist, a look of horror on her lovely, soot-stained face. Both of them, dressed in their ridiculous miners' garb, stared at him in stunned apprehension when he started to approach.

He didn't even pause as he passed them. He jabbed his forefinger at the disloyal pair contemptuously, his labored words rasping out in the hushed arena. "You're fired."

Nell looked at her reflection in the ornately framed mirror over the dressing table, and her shoulders drooped in misery. She shouldn't have come tonight. But at the time she'd accepted Shelton Broply's invitation to the New Year's Eve ball given by one of

Butte's wealthiest copper magnates, she'd been consumed with righteous anger. She realized now that she should have stayed in the seclusion of her own bedroom, where she could have secretly wept her eyes out as the clock struck midnight.

When Shelton had asked her a week ago to accompany him to the holiday celebration, she'd been determined to go to the beautiful mansion on Granite Street and act as if she didn't give a damn about Ross Morgan. But faced with the prospect of mingling with a houseful of vivacious partygoers, she found she didn't have the heart even to pretend to be happy.

It had been nine terrible days since her rescue from the Forrester Mine. Nine days filled with an aching despondency that couldn't be assuaged. Nine nights tormented with sleeplessness and an acrid sorrow that seemed to be eating away at her heart.

Somehow, she'd managed to make it through Christmas without falling to pieces in front of everyone at the boardinghouse. According to Finnish custom, she'd exchanged presents on Christmas Eve with Kalle and Hertta, Fetsi and Maija, and the taciturn but kindhearted men whom she'd come to know and respect during the last six months. She'd received a letter that morning from Lottie Howard and shared it with them. They'd listened eagerly to the news that the lovely young woman had opened a hat shop in Des Moines, which she'd named Nellie Belle Bonnets in honor of her attorney.

Then all the boarders had gathered around the candlelit tree in the Kuusinens' big parlor and sung carols. Later, Hertta had served a special supper that included *lipeä kala*, which Nell learned to her dismay was a horrible-smelling codfish to which the Finns were addicted. For dessert came a traditional rice pudding with an almond hidden in the center. When Nell discovered the almond in her dish, the broad-shouldered miners up and down the long table cheered. They said it meant she'd be married within a year and would enjoy an entire year of good luck. She'd fought back the tears at the irony of their words.

Good luck? Married? In a pig's eye!

She'd attended early morning mass at St. Patrick's alone, her heart a lump of ice inside her chest. Without success, she had tried to forget that she'd planned to attend midnight mass on Christmas Eve with Ross and Luke.

Deep in thought, Nell rearranged the silver comb and brush set on the dressing table in the mansion's guest bedroom. She touched the vials of expensive perfume which were reflected in the gleaming polished surface. Beside an imported scarlet poinsettia plant sat a round box of loose face powder. She picked up the fluffy rabbit's fur puff and rubbed it thoughtfully back and forth against her chin.

Luke had come to see her two days after Christmas. He'd brought a present for her, a lovely felt hat trimmed with white rabbit fur. She knew he'd paid for it with the money he'd saved from selling newspapers that summer. She'd lied to him and said she'd caught a dreadful cold and that was the reason her eyes were tearing and she had to keep blowing her nose. She didn't have to inquire about Ross's injuries. She'd been kept informed by the Kuusinens and Eben Pearce. The boy's father was recovering from the vicious fight without complications. Felix Hegel was also mending, though few of her friends seemed to care if he lived or died.

She gave Luke the presents she'd hidden under her bed: a fishing rod for next summer, a leather jacket with sheepskin lining along with a matching pair of fur-lined deerskin gloves, and a pair of Western boots. When she told him she'd soon be leaving Butte, he hadn't been surprised. Showing a wisdom and maturity far beyond his years, he hadn't mentioned the terrible names she'd called his father either.

The energetic ten-year-old patiently allowed her to hug him and kiss him good-by. She stood on the boardinghouse's wide front porch and watched Luke hurry up the snow-covered street to catch the trolley. Then she'd gone upstairs and cried her foolish heart out.

But all the tears in the world hadn't changed reality. Nell propped her elbows on the cherry dressing table and rested her forehead against her folded hands. She tried valiantly to regain control of her shattered emotions. After all, Ross's double dealings shouldn't have surprised her. Even Uncle Cormac, who'd provided so generously for her and Sean, and who'd treated them with such fatherly affection, had a sham marriage. Cormac Ryan's mistress had come to his law office once, and Nell had accidentally overheard them talking. The tall brunett was a handsome woman in handsome clothes, soft-spoken, intelligent, and well-bred. Nell could understand Cormac's disillusionment with his foolish, empty-headed wife. Marriage to Aunt Lydia would be tedious for any man, let alone someone as brilliant as her uncle. Oh, Nell understood, all right. But that didn't change the fact that the one man she'd admired since childhood had proved to be an unfaithful husband. She hadn't missed the lesson intrinsic in that unhappy discovery. No man could be trusted. *No man.*

Nell carefully replaced the powder puff in its pink container as she recalled the events of the past nine days. Gavin had tried to talk her into leaving Butte with him the morning after their rescue from the cave-in. She'd refused to cut and run, believing it would be unethical to depart without at least filing for a postponement of the trial. But O'Connell was frightened witless that his client would come after him, once the injuries were healed. Her dapper law partner had stuffed his expensive suits in his bags and taken the first Northern Pacific train out of the copper camp.

Judge Curry had refused her petition for a continuance so that Morgan could find another law firm to represent him. The Glamorgan trial had gone to the jury four days after Christmas. The jurymen were out a scant twenty minutes before returning with a decision for the plaintiff, as dictated by the corrupt magistrate. Nell was devastated. Not because of what it meant to Ross Morgan, she told herself repeatedly, but because the verdict was a blot on her otherwise unblemished record of legal victories.

Ross had wasted no time replacing his attorneys. Early yesterday morning, a lawyer from Philadelphia, who specialized in apex litigation, had arrived in Butte. By mid-afternoon, she'd met with Silas Armstrong in her office at her previous employer's written request and had turned over her records and notes for the trial. Meticulous and businesslike, Mr. Armstrong seemed quite capable. But all his talent and prestige wouldn't have made an iota of difference in Judge Otis Curry's courtroom. She'd learned that Armstrong had left for Helena that same evening to file an appeal in the appellate court.

That, however, was Ross Morgan's problem, not hers. Not any longer. Now that her responsibility for the lawsuit was over, she was free to leave this godforsaken mining camp. Her train ticket sat on the bureau in her bedroom. Heaven save her, in just four more days, she'd be on her way home to Boston. That thought should have filled her with elation. Instead, she had to bite her lower lip to keep from bawling.

Morosely, Nell gazed into the mirror and fluffed the deep, pointed black lace on the puffed sleeves of her new evening gown. When she'd picked out the ruby satin dress, she'd done so with Ross's approval in mind. They'd planned on going to the Thornton Hotel for dinner and dancing on New Year's Eve, then coming back to his home and spending the night together beneath the down-filled comforter that covered his high four-poster bed. She blinked back the tears that glistened on her lashes, wondering whom he was escorting to the gala at the Thornton tonight in her stead. And if the woman would take Nell's place in his warm, soft bed as well.

She rose slowly from the bench in front of the dressing table. Shelton Broply was probably wondering why she was dallying so long. She pasted a false smile on her trembling lips, glanced once more in the mirror to be sure no trace of tears remained, and left the sanctuary of the guest bedroom that had been designated as a powder room for the ladies that evening.

Shelton was waiting for her on the second floor landing when she came out the door. The tall stained-glass windows that decorated the central staircase rose up behind him like a jeweled tapestry. Attired in formal evening dress of white tie and tails, he was a pleasing sight. He smiled in open appreciation of her festive appearance. "You look very lovely tonight, Nell," he said simply. "I'm a lucky man."

"Thank you," she replied, trying her best to act pleased with his compliment. "You look pretty spiffy yourself."

More than that, she couldn't bring herself to say. She didn't want to repay him in false coin. She'd come to respect Broply as an astute adversary in the courtroom. He was a polished attorney with enormous talent. Belatedly, she had also come to realize that, overall, he'd treated her with kid gloves during their legal skirmishes. The taint of Felix Hegel's incredible wealth hadn't rubbed off on his lead counselor.

Had she never met Ross Morgan, she would have been flattered by Shelton's attentions. It wasn't Broply's fault that she'd accepted his invitation out of some perverse idea of getting revenge on the unprincipled owner of the Glamorgan Mine—an idea she now thoroughly regretted. For her escort's sake, however, she was determined not to show how much she wished she hadn't come that night.

The lilting strains of a waltz floated down the hallway. "Let's hurry," Shelton said, taking her elbow. "I think they've started the first dance without us."

The red brick Victorian mansion was decorated in magnificent style for the holidays. Everywhere Nell looked, bright red candles burned in hurricane lanterns, which had been set amid fresh evergreen boughs tied with giant red velvet bows. The main staircase's carved oak banister was also wound with pine branches and red ribbons. Over every door, huge holly wreaths hung on the etched glass transoms. The polished, inlaid oak woodwork on door jambs, windowsills, and wainscoting glowed golden in the light of the flickering gas lamps. The smell of bayberry candles and fresh pine filled every room.

Despite the lavish display of joyous Yuletide decorations, she'd found that she didn't particularly like their host, William Andrews Clark, or his daughter, Mary, who was acting as her widower father's hostess. They'd greeted Nell and Shelton, along with all the other visitors, in the spacious entry hall upon their arrival. Unlike most of the people she'd met in the democratic mining camp, both of the Clarks seemed cold and calculating, far more interested in showing off their own wealth and social status than in their guests' enjoyment.

Nell much preferred Clark's archrival, Marcus Daly, whom Ross had introduced to her during one of their many happy evenings at the Tie Lang Noodle Palace. Daly was the owner of the great Anaconda claim, the site of the biggest and richest single body of copper ore ever discovered. Although he was every bit as wealthy as their snobbish host, Daly was far more approachable and infinitely more likable. That same night, Ross had also explained that Felix Hegel was a personal friend of Clark's and, consequently, Marcus Daly's bitter enemy.

The brightly lit ballroom took up almost the entire third floor. Nell and Shelton entered to find it already filled with guests, glorious in their party attire. The four musicians, seated in a small alcove, were playing a waltz. With a pleasant smile beneath his dark brown mustache, Shelton immediately swept her into his arms, and they joined the whirling stream of dancers. As they twirled lightly around the polished oak floor, Nell returned his smile, for the first time in sincere enjoyment. Her attractive escort was a graceful dancer. She allowed herself the luxury of a cautious sigh. Maybe, just maybe, the evening wouldn't be so bad, after all.

Her smile faded at the sight that caught her eye as she and Broply waltzed around the room. She turned her head to look again, wanting to believe it wasn't true.

It couldn't be!

But it was.

He was here!

Stepping out onto the dance floor with a peaches-and-cream blond on his muscular arm was Rossiter Morgan. Nell recognized the young woman at once. Heavens, she'd seen her picture often enough in the society pages of both the Butte *Miner* and the Anaconda *Standard*. Elise Bousman was the daughter of one of the camp's millionaire copper kings. Apparently if Ross couldn't wrest a fortune from his mine illegally, he was more than willing to aspire to marry one. Gad, his greed knew no bounds.

In spite of the bandage that covered his high cheekbone, Morgan was stunningly handsome in a black tuxedo and white tie. His golden-brown hair was ruthlessly combed back from his high forehead. His chiseled features and athletic frame were shown off to perfection by the severity of his

tailored evening clothes. The spoiled, willowy socialite, resplendently gowned in mauve silk trimmed
with plum-colored velvet, was every bit as dazzling.
Hands down, they were the most beautiful couple
on the floor. As they floated across the planked oak
boards, Ross appeared to be hanging on to every
clever word Elise uttered. His hooded, gold-flecked
green eyes gazed down at his companion as though
she were the only female in the room. A smile of
enamored delight played about the corners of his
lying lips.

But Nell couldn't lie to herself, though she'd certainly have liked to try. She didn't have to wonder
any longer who Ross would find to take her place.
Or if the lovely woman would end up in his big bed
in the French-chateau mansion on Park Street. All the
heartrending images that Nell had kept at bay for the
last nine days came crashing down on her. Knowing Ross's smooth, heaven-blessed charm with the
ladies, she could easily envision him making love
to the beautiful girl in his arms. Nell was all too
familiar with the way he'd lift the wisps of Elise's
pale hair to place a sensuous kiss on the nape of her
neck, or run his thumb lingeringly across the cleft of
her chin as he whispered her name, or boldly stroke
his tongue across her open lips.

Nell barely managed to finish the dance.

"Let's go downstairs and see what kind of
refreshments have been set out," she suggested
the moment the music stopped. She ignored the
fact that her stomach had just tied itself into a
knot.

"Great idea," Shelton answered. "There's supposed to be a buffet set out in the dining room."
If he'd noticed the presence of her former employer, he was too much of a gentleman to mention
it. He was also kind enough not to ask why her
eyes were suddenly pooling with tears. Taking
her elbow, he politely guided her through the
throng that milled around the dance floor, just

as the quartet of musicians struck up another
waltz.

Throughout all the first-floor rooms, chatting
guests mingled convivially, sipping champagne.
A sumptuous feast had been laid out on the long
table that ran the length of the dining room. Fragile crystal goblets stood beside stacks of delicate
bone china plates and rows of heavy silverware
on the sparkling white damask tablecloth. An enormous ice carving in the shape of a Christmas angel
made a magnificent centerpiece. Nell and Shelton
filled their plates with delicacies and wandered
into the nearby front parlor. Several boisterous
acquaintances from the Silver Bow Courthouse
invited them to join their group in the corner.
Heartsick, Nell sank down on an upholstered
chair and found herself unable to eat. The tempting holiday food tasted like ashes in her dry
mouth.

Everyone else was in rollicking good spirits, interrupting one another, talking over the next person's
voice, beating a friend to the punch line of a familiar
joke. She forced herself to concentrate on the nearest
conversation, knowing the last thing she wanted to
do was go back upstairs to the ballroom. Merciful-
ly, Shelton seemed to understand. He withdrew just
enough to give her the time and the space to recover
her scattered wits.

The evening dragged on without another glimpse
of Morgan or his lady friend. Either they'd remained
upstairs on the dance floor, or Ross had become
involved in the billiards tournament that someone
said was being held in a game room in the back
of the house. Eventually, Nell became separated
from her escort. She wandered into the library, seeking the comfort of its book-filled peace. But even
there, she found a group of white-haired matrons
ensconced on a sofa and love seat in front of the
roaring fire, gossiping cozily. She picked up a thick
shawl from a chair, tossed it over her shoulders, and

stepped out onto the verandah that stretched along the side of the house.

The winter evening was crisp and cold. A sliver of moon was hidden behind a patch of dark clouds, and the black Montana sky was filled with a million twinkling stars. Hoping the quiet beauty of the night would bring a measure of ease to her aching heart, Nell wandered slowly along the verandah's painted white railing. She didn't see the tall, solitary figure standing by the carved balustrade and looking out on the lights of the valley below until she rounded the corner of the house. She was almost upon him before she noticed the bright red glow of his burning cigar. She stopped short. Hoping she could beat a hasty retreat before he turned and saw who'd joined him on the otherwise empty porch, she took a cautious step backward. And then another, ready to turn and flee.

Ross didn't need to look around to know who'd come up behind him. He closed his eyes for a brief moment and breathed in the wonderful scent of gardenias that wafted toward him on the chill evening breeze. "You don't have to leave because of me, Miss Ryan," he called over his shoulder. "I was just about to return to the party."

"Oh, I . . . ah . . ." she stammered. "That's . . . that's quite all right. I just wanted a little fresh air. I'm not going to stay but a moment myself."

Ross turned to find her bathed in the golden lamplight that streamed from the tall parlor windows. With an expression of wary suspicion, she guardedly studied the gauze bandage that covered his cheek. Remembering how she'd looked at him with such trusting tenderness after their lovemaking, he felt a fresh jolt of anguish. The vision of those enormous angel eyes had tortured him for the past nine days.

She was exquisite that evening in a jewel-red satin gown that just skimmed her creamy shoulders and dipped down to show a tantalizing glimpse of her voluptuous cleavage. With a quick, nervous movement, she rearranged the fringed shawl to hide the velvety shadow between her lush breasts, conscious of where his hungry gaze had lingered. What she didn't know was that a ruby necklace to match that very dress lay in an oblong box in his dresser drawer, along with another small package containing a diamond engagement ring.

Instead of the severe chignon she usually wore, she'd pulled her thick chestnut hair up on top of her head in a soft pompadour and fastened it with jet combs. Silken tendrils floated about her ears and the nape of her graceful neck. The tiny mole above her full lips beckoned enticingly. Christ, if she didn't look like a love goddess, no creature in heaven or on earth ever did.

How could anyone who looked so utterly perfect be such a heartless schemer? His pain-racked soul cried out to her in torment.

Damn it, Nell, why did you succumb to Hegel's bribery? Was it only for the money? Or was it for the phony charms of the bastard himself?

Ross had asked those tortured questions over and over, as he'd tried to bury the pain of her betrayal in one bottle after another of fine Kentucky bourbon. He was convinced beyond a doubt that she'd sold her loyalty. What he desperately wanted to know was if her luscious body had been part of the bargain as well. If it hadn't been for his responsibility to Luke, he'd have gone on a drunk to end all drunks. Jesus, he'd even thought of trying to find solace in another woman. He'd accepted Elise's invitation for tonight's highbrow shindig with that very scheme in mind—until he saw Nell and knew it wasn't going to work. Not for him. He couldn't rip Miss Elinor Margaret Ryan out of his heart anymore than he could get her out of his mind. What the hell was the matter with him? She'd sold out to the highest bidder, and he still wanted her.

God almighty, how he wanted her.

"Thank you for Luke's presents," he told her quietly, hoping to ease the tension between them. "That was very thoughtful of you."

She moved to stand beside him at the railing, where she could look down at the empty cobbled street below. Her words came barely above a whisper. "I wanted him to have his Christmas gifts. Luke's a very special young man."

"He is that," Ross agreed. He leaned his shoulder against the porch post and puffed on his thin cigar. "Thanks for bein' so cooperative with Mr. Armstrong," he added, searching for some topic that would keep her beside him. "Silas couldn't praise your expertise enough. He claims that your three-dimensional model of the Glamorgan was a brilliant inspiration. And he seems to feel certain the professional groundwork you laid in Judge Curry's courtroom will help us win our case in the appellate court."

Nell lowered her head and shrugged. "That's what I'm paid for."

Ross yearned to explain that she was wrong about her brother. Sean hadn't been killed because of his employer's greed. The young man had died when he'd tried to discover if Felix Hegel was blasting in the Forrester. The work in the Glamorgan hadn't even started until after the accident, after Ross had learned of Hegel's illegal activities. But Nell had arrived in Butte spitting and snarling about the lack of law and order, insisting on seeing everything in black and white, condemning Ross and all the other residents of the mining camp as uncivilized ruffians. So he'd kept his mining operations a secret from the stiff-necked spinster. It was a secret he'd later come to deeply regret, when there was no way to reveal it without jeopardizing her tentative feelings of attraction to him. He'd sensed from the beginning that the unspoken reasons for her hesitation had been all about trust. The more he came to love her, the more he feared losing that trust.

Ross watched her now, knowing she'd leave if he attempted to explain any of it. Hertta had told him she'd tried this past week to talk some sense into Nell. Like an obstinate, hardheaded mine mule, she had refused even to discuss it with her friend. She sure as hell wasn't going to listen to the man she hated.

The strained hush between them was broken by the sound of laughter coming from the mansion. Nell moved slightly, as though anxious to go back inside, but not quite sure how to exit gracefully.

Longing to take her in his arms and hold her against his aching heart, he strove to keep his voice cool and detached. "Luke said you were leavin' soon."

She gripped the railing and blinked up at the starry sky. "Yes, next Monday. Uncle Cormac wired that he has a complicated inheritance case waiting for me as soon as I feel ready to tackle it."

"I thought maybe you'd try to strike out on your own in criminal law. You were splendid at Lottie Howard's trial."

"To the surprise of everyone in Butte, no doubt," she answered with uncharacteristic bitterness. He'd apparently touched a raw nerve, for the acid words seemed to spill out of their own accord. "I'm sure people wondered why I was willing to publicly defend a prostitute. But I don't stand in judgment on women whose sole means of support is catering to the whims of the men who control the gold. It's a simple business arrangement, no different than what a married woman agrees to deliver in return for her husband's monetary support. Only the unlucky housewife has to scrub, and bake, and look aside when the man proves to be a philanderer." She paused and drew a ragged breath. When he failed to respond to her spiteful castigation, she continued. "As far as I can see, marriage is the best bargain a man can strike: hot meals, clean sheets, and a partner obligated to perform her duty in bed."

Stung by her caustic cynicism, Ross straightened from his spot against the wooden post and threw his Havana into the bushes. He didn't try to hide the disgust in his voice. "Do you really believe marriage is nothin' more than a business arrangement?"

"Considering the male's unending quest for power and wealth, how could I believe otherwise?" She tossed her stubborn head in defiance. "I, however, am fortunate enough to be financially independent. The services I offer for trade are in the courts of law."

They were interrupted before Ross could retort that, like the strumpet she'd represented in the courtroom, her services could also be bought and paid for by the wealthiest patron.

"Nell?" called Shelton Broply from the darkness. He came around the corner of the brick home and paused when he saw whom she was with. "Is everything all right? You'll catch pneumonia in this weather."

Ross had to give the fellow credit. Broply didn't turn tail and run when he saw the ferocious scowl on his competitor's battered face.

Without warning, Elise Bousman brushed past Broply and hurried to her own escort's side. "Ross, honey," she complained petulantly, not even bothering to glance at Nell beside him. "I've been looking all over for you." Slipping her arm through his, she pursed her carmine lips and leaned her hip against him provocatively. "It's almost midnight."

"You're right, Shelton," Nell agreed in a voice ringing with holiday spirit. "It's absolutely freezing out here." She stepped away from the porch railing and hurried to Broply's side. "Good-by, Mr. Morgan," she called cheerfully, as she walked away on the other man's arm. "I'll send you my bill when I get back to Boston."

Chapter 20

In the distance, fire bells clanged a frantic alarm. A blaze had erupted somewhere in the city on that freezing January night. The strident peal of warning seemed a fitting background for Nell's disheartenment.

She stood in the Northern Pacific Railroad Station, waiting impatiently for the call to climb aboard. Compounding her anxiety, the train from Seattle had pulled into the railway yard hours behind schedule. It was now late in the evening.

She'd insisted on coming to the depot alone. Prepared for the possibility of a long delay due to the bad weather, she'd refused to allow Hertta to accompany her.

Earlier that afternoon, the two women had said a tearful good-by on the Kuusinens' big front porch. Kalle and Eben had been there too, along with all the men who weren't at work on the day shift. Till that moment, Nell had been convinced that her benumbed heart couldn't feel any more pain. She'd been wrong. All she wanted to do was get aboard and leave the copper camp and her gnawing misery behind.

Nell hadn't been able to depart four days after the holiday ball she'd attended with Shelton Broply. Beginning on New Year's, a series of fierce winter storms had swept down from the Canadian prairies, hammering the states of the northern plains. All trains caught anywhere between Bismarck and St. Paul were stranded for days at a time. Strong winds swept the snow into drifts high enough to bury entire railroad cars. The newspapers carried stirring accounts of passengers being rescued by horse-drawn sledges and taken to local farmhouses and even barns for shelter. Several people were found frozen to death in North Dakota. It would have made no sense to leave until the tracks were cleared and trains were running smoothly again. So she'd bided her time.

God knew, it hadn't been easy.

On New Year's Day she'd received a package from Ross. It contained a magnificent ruby necklace with a card inside saying the gift was in appreciation of all her efforts in the courtroom on his behalf. Implicit in the message, though left unsaid, was his apology for deceiving her. What he didn't say was that he'd been wrong in ignoring the court injunction and continuing to mine his damnable copper in the first place. Or that he'd finally come to realize that she hadn't purposely sabotaged the Glamorgan case by being willfully inept. She'd wrapped the box back up in its silvery paper, retied it with the bright red ribbon, and returned it with a curt note, telling him to wait until he saw her itemized bill before being so generous—since she knew how important money was to him. She added with scathing sarcasm that if he lost the decision in the appellate court, he could pawn the jewelry to buy a train ticket out of town.

It was now January 15. She was free to leave Montana at last. Restlessly, she paced up and down the long waiting room, holding her full-length storm coat over her arm. She was dressed for the bitterly cold weather. A hat of dark sable covered her ears. The gored skirt of her brown wool traveling suit swirled about the ankles of her warm half boots as she moved back and forth past her stack of luggage.

The station was busy despite the late hour. Travelers like Nell, who'd been unable to embark as they'd planned for the last two weeks, milled around the waiting room, anxious to resume their interrupted or postponed journeys. Families gathered in tight little groups, saying their tearful farewells or greeting a loved one who'd arrived on the passenger train that had just pulled in from the state capital. To a morose, melancholy Nell, it seemed that the country's limitless railroad tracks, which now extended to every far-flung corner, had turned its restless inhabitants into a nation of gypsies.

She stopped mid-stride as Ross, dressed in a business suit and topcoat, entered the depot. He stood head and shoulders above those around him, and his golden hair was easily recognizable in the crowd. For a split second, she thought he had come to tell her good-by.

But she knew the truth. He was bound for Helena. She'd read in the Anaconda *Standard* that the case between the owners of the Glamorgan and Forrester mines was presently being reviewed in the Supreme Court of Montana. Silas Armstrong must have found the ear of a sympathetic appellate judge. Like her, Ross had been forced to wait until the worst of the weather had blown over before leaving to join his new legal representative.

Nell clasped her sable-trimmed coat tightly against her waist, unable to take her eyes off the devastatingly handsome man she was seeing for the very last time.

The man who'd tricked and deceived her.

The entrancing, smooth-talking, double-dealing man who'd destroyed every last vestige of trust within her.

The man she still loved.

What frightened her more than anything was the sure knowledge that she'd always love him, despite his treachery, despite his lies.

Why had he worked so hard to ensnare her with his legendary charms? The Colorado Cougar could have had any unmarried woman in Butte—and half the married ones as well, if he'd wanted them. Had he seduced her only to ensure that she'd strive her utmost to win the lawsuit for him? Had captivating her been his insurance against the chance that she might discover he was mining illegally and try to put a stop to it? Or was her initial reluctance simply too much of a challenge for a man over whom women had always swooned?

As recently as two days ago, Morgan had tried to see her. He'd come to Kuusinen's and planted himself in the front parlor, sending word up with Fetsi that he wasn't leaving until he spoke with his former fiancée. Nell had barricaded herself in her bedroom the entire day. For a while, she thought he might try kicking the door down. From what he'd shouted through the locked portal, it had certainly occurred to him. When he'd finally given up and left, Hertta had berated Nell for behaving like an idiot. She'd retaliated by telling the landlady to mind her own business. The two women ended up having sharp words for the first time since they'd met six months ago. Only upon wishing Nell a final, tearful good-by that afternoon had Hertta truly forgiven her.

Nell met Morgan's gaze across the packed station lobby, and the haunted look in his magnificent green eyes pinned her to the spot. Her heart thumped a strangely painful, syncopated rhythm against her ribs at the sight of his disfigured face. The terrible scar across his cheekbone was a visible reminder of her descent into the Forrester. Every time he looked in a mirror he would blame her for setting in motion the events that had ended in his savage fistfight with Hegel. One day, Ross might forgive her, but he'd never, ever forget.

Her mind seemed to go blank. God above, she'd never been so heartsick. Seeing him now, knowing it was for the last time, her soul cried out in heartbroken premonition, warning her that she was about to be cut off forever from everything warm and wonderful in life.

It was all his doing. No matter that she was the one who was leaving for good. He was the one who'd lied. He was the one who'd built an intimate relationship under false pretenses. He was the betrayer who'd ultimately destroyed her foolish, girlhood dreams.

Abruptly, Nell turned away, afraid he'd see the tears brimming in her eyes from across the waiting room. She placed one hand to her breast, trying to ease the feeling of suffocation that closed in on her. She knew there was nothing physically wrong with her. It was only her shattered emotions playing tricks on her tortured mind.

Suddenly, without any warning, a horrific explosion rocked the building to its very foundation. The sturdy brick walls shook with the force of the enormous concussion. All the windows rattled and cracked beneath the strain of the booming vibrations. For a second after the roar of the blast, it became deathly still inside the terminal. Then everyone shouted and called to one another as they rushed toward the main doors to see what had happened.

Nell whirled around to join the exodus. She ran straight into Ross, who'd made a beeline for her.

"Are you all right?" he asked. He grasped her shoulders and drew her toward him with a worried scowl.

She nodded in confusion, vaguely aware that he'd immediately pulled her within the shelter of his large, powerful body in a touchingly masculine gesture of protection. His concerned eyes searched hers. "I'm . . . I'm fine," she stuttered.

He took the heavy winter coat she carried and helped her slip it on. "Then let's go see what's happened."

In the night-shrouded city, hundreds of people were streaming toward the sound of the eruption. The sky to the southwest glowed red from the

light of a great fire. Ross and Nell raced hand
in hand through the streets, along with countless
others who'd been drawn from their homes and
workplaces by the horrible roar. Flames could be
seen pouring from buildings several streets away.
A cluster of burning warehouses were apparently
the site of the massive detonation.

All over the wintry landscape, remnants of lumber, iron, and steel were scattered for blocks around.
Huge timbers, used for shoring up the mines, had
been hurled through the air like javelins. Pieces
of hardware covered the frozen ground as though
some maniacal giant had upended great barrels of
bolts, nuts, screws, awls, saw blades—all the para-
phernalia that would be sold in a great hardware
store in the sky—and let the contents rain down on
the unsuspecting populace.

As they drew within a block of the inferno, Nell
could see torn and mangled bodies lying in the
snow. Pieces of the Butte fire department's bright
red horse-drawn wagons, as well as fragments of
the beautiful animals, were scattered over the entire
area. But the firemen themselves were nowhere to
be seen. Nell shuddered at the realization that the
firefighters must have been caught by surprise in
the very center of the blast.

Ross came to a sudden halt. He drew her closer
and placed his arm protectively around her shoulders, turning her toward him and away from the
blazing structures. She could sense the uneasy tension in his muscled frame.

His brusque words had the unquestionable ring
of authority. "I'm sendin' you to safety. One of those
warehouses holds a large store of dynamite."

"I can't leave these people to die!" she cried,
shocked at his callous proposal. "I've got to stay
here and help them."

He didn't bother to argue. He just grabbed her arm
and hurried her toward a hack that was driving pell-
mell up the street. As they moved rapidly away from

the conflagration, another mighty explosion roared from inside the flaming warehouses two blocks behind them. Steel, timber, and ragged chunks of the corrugated iron that covered one building flew straight up into the air like an enormous geyser.

Ross reacted instantaneously. He shoved Nell around the corner of a brick building and down into its open cellar stairwell. Steering her into the safest corner, he shielded her with his own body. The force of the blast sent shards of metal, wood, stone, and glass flying through the air above their heads. Heavy pipes and solid bars of iron were tossed about as though blown by a hurricane.

The moment the tumult subsided, Nell attempted to rise to her feet. Ross held her pinned in a crouch against the rough wall at the bottom of the stone steps. All about them on ground level, they could hear people shouting to one another to withdraw, warning any newcomers of the possibility of still another detonation.

"Wait," he ordered her. "Don't move yet."

His words were followed by a third tremendous explosion that must have rocked the entire city, sending the awesome boom of its reverberations for miles around. This time, she sobbed out loud in sheer terror.

Time seemed to stand still. The screams from the injured and dying echoed through the streets. They could hear the whoosh and howl of the blaze as it raged unimpeded, spreading to more warehouses. Ross kept Nell within the confines of his arms and the protection of his large body for what seemed like ages, as they waited to be certain there wasn't going to be another explosion.

When, at last, they cautiously climbed up the stairs to view the scene around them, they discovered a grisly holocaust. It was a sight of unbelievable horror. Bodies had been decapitated by flying steel, iron railroad plates, and lethal hardware. Arms and legs had been severed and flung through

the air like so many pieces of debris. Great timbers
lay across the fallen, pinning them to the snowy
ground. The first rescuers on the scene had become
casualties alongside the victims they'd been trying
to help.

Unable to look at the gruesome suffering that surrounded her, Nell covered her eyes with her hand.
Without Ross's supporting arm about her waist, she
would have dropped to her knees on the frozen
cobblestones. Clenching her teeth in stubborn determination, she fought the tug of inky blackness that
drew her toward its seductive oblivion.

Ross cradled her head against his chest. The steady
beat of his heart reassured her that the two of them
had miraculously survived. Somehow, they were
still alive amid a setting of incredible destruction.

"Take a deep breath," he told her. "I'll ease you
to the ground if you think you're goin' to faint."

"No, I'm all right," she lied. But she followed his
advice and drew in a deep draft of air. "Let's see
what we can do to help these poor people."

They were joined by others, who crept out cautiously from the damaged stores and homes nearby,
drawn by the shrieks of hysterical women and the
pitiful appeals for help of the trapped and partly
buried. Mingled with the screams and groans of the
wounded came the frenzied calls of their deliver-
ers. People were driving every kind of vehicle they
could find into the area to help remove the injured
to the hospitals and the dead to the morgues. The
streets, littered like an urban battleground with the
human wreckage, became further congested with
rearing horses and careening buggies.

Frantically, Nell flagged down a hired hack while
Ross bent over a blood-soaked youth in his late teens.
Using his own wool neck scarf, Ross deftly applied a
tourniquet to the victim's severely gashed leg and
slowed the pumping artery. Together, they helped
the young man hobble to the waiting carriage. They
turned to another sufferer, an elderly woman whose

hand had been partly severed by flying glass. Nell removed her own long storm coat, slipped off the jacket of her traveling suit, and handed it to Ross. Shaking with cold and shock in the frigid night air, she hurriedly put her heavy garment back on while he wrapped the brown wool around the woman's lacerated fingers and tied the material into a tight bundle with the sleeves. They lifted the sagging form into the bloodstained interior of the cab. They loaded a third victim, and then a fourth. Ross pounded an all-clear signal on the side of the coach, and the hackman took off at breakneck speed to deliver the injured to the St. James Hospital and hurry back for another load.

The ghastly landscape was lit by the brilliant glare of the reddened sky. Along the streets, the shattered storefront windows were gaping, jagged caverns, and the sidewalks sparkled and glistened with broken glass. Nell and Ross made their way through an entire city block of indescribable carnage, stopping to help as many people as they could. Ross used his topcoat to blanket a woman whose teeth were chattering uncontrollably in cold and shock. With his suit jacket, he covered an injured child being removed to safety and continued on, despite the freezing weather, dressed in his shirtsleeves. They worked their way slowly toward the site of the fire, joined by every person who had a relative or friend in the area and feared the worst. The sickening odor of burning flesh filled the frosty air. Bodies of the dead, so twisted, charred, or mutilated that they were virtually unrecognizable, were being gathered up and placed side by side in rows of a dozen or more on an open plateau just north of the still-burning warehouses. Women who suspected their loved ones had been caught in the tragic accident gathered in terrified clusters, crying and wringing their hands inconsolably.

Nell and Ross turned a corner and saw Eben Pearce nearly a block away. He was waving both his arms high over his head in an urgent signal for someone to help him. They tore up the street.

"Ross!" hollered Eben through his cupped hands the moment he recognized them. "Your boy's over here! Hurry! He's hurt!"

They raced across the cobbled intersection strewn with the dead and dying to where he stood beside Luke's still form.

The boy's crumpled body lay against the side of a wooden building where he'd been hurled by the force of the blast. Blood trickled from his mouth and one ear, staining the dirty snow beneath his cheek a bright red. His lips were blue with the cold.

Ross dropped to one knee beside the inert figure. "Luke!" he called. There was no response. Tenderly, Ross straightened his son's head and checked the pulse at the base of his neck. Both sides of Luke's face and his temples were swollen hideously. From the deep purple of the wounds, Nell suspected he must have been lying there for close to an hour.

"He's alive," Ross croaked in hoarse thanksgiving. He glanced up at Eben. "Get a coach. Fast! Steal one if you have to."

Pearce took off at a trot.

Terrified at the boy's battered appearance, Nell pulled off her silk neck scarf and used the soft material gently to wipe away the blood from his bruised face, while Ross checked carefully for broken bones. He shook his head at the unspoken question in her glance. She bowed her head in relief. Thank God, at least, for that.

In less than five minutes, Eben was back. He'd commandeered a bright blue and orange California Bakery wagon. With utmost care, Ross lifted Luke in his arms and carried him to the borrowed vehicle. Nell scrambled up into its enclosed back end. She shoved aside the big wicker baskets that, in only a few more hours, would have been filled with loaves of sourdough bread and sesame seed rolls for the morning's delivery. In an ironic twist of fate, the wonderful smell of freshly baked pumpernickel and dill rye permeated the small enclosure of their makeshift ambulance. She sank down on the floor and quickly unbuttoned her storm coat.

"Here," she urged. "Give him to me."

Ross nodded in agreement. He placed the motionless boy in her arms and clambered inside. Nell wrapped the edges of her fur-lined garment around Luke's chilled form, sharing her warmth in a desperate attempt to prevent further loss of his body heat. With a noisy bang, Eben closed the double doors on the back of the delivery wagon and hurried to sit on the high front seat with the driver. A shrill whistle pierced the air. The team of horses took off at a mad gallop.

The ride to the hospital was a nightmare. Ross crouched on the floor beside Nell, his hand on Luke's chest to be certain he was still breathing. The tortured anguish on Ross's sharp features at the thought of losing his son filled Nell with overwhelming compassion. Unable to say a word, she wiped away the blood that continued to trickle from Luke's ear with her soaked scarf. Tears poured unheeded down her face and splashed on the back of her trembling hands.

Don't let him die, God. Please, let him be all right.

God must not have heard the frantic plea uttered in the midst of such unspeakable chaos. A week later, Luke was still unconscious. In the quiet hospital room, Nell sat on a white-painted metal chair in front of the tall window and watched the immobile form beneath the bedcovers. She put her hand to her mouth to smother the sobs of fear that clogged her throat. Rising to her feet, she turned to stare helplessly out at the leaden January sky.

The past seven days had been a time of horror unlike anything she'd ever imagined. The entire city

had mourned its dead, some of whom were never
identified. Kalle Kuusinen had been killed trying
to help pull the wounded away from the burning structures. He'd gone to the site—just as Luke
and countless others who'd been wakened by the
first explosion had gone—drawn by the fascination
of a roaring blaze, the scurrying, shouting firemen
and their colorful, horse-drawn, bell-ringing wagons. There had been so many injured that dozens of
homes, boardinghouses, and even hotels had been
used as temporary infirmaries. Medical personnel
had worked day and night, gladly accepting the
services of all volunteers. In the great mining camp,
hundreds of mourners had filed past improvised
morgues seeking the remains of loved ones.

Along with Kalle, Lee Yipp and Juniper Jess had
been killed trying to help those hurt in the initial blast. Every member of the Butte fire department, save three, was gone. A public funeral for
the deceased whose bodies could not be identified
was attended by almost every resident of the city.
A solemn cortege of six hearses and three undertak-
ing wagons, accompanied by the dirge of muffled
drums, left the city hall and wended its way to the
cemetery. One large wagon alone held nine caskets.
Every store in the city closed its doors that day.
Throngs of mourners jammed the streets, making
them all but impassable. Another public funeral was
held for the heroic firefighters, while private services for the victims who'd been identified took
place all during that week.

Except for attending Kalle's burial with a distraught, nearly inconsolable Hertta, Nell had spent
every moment at the Sisters' Hospital. When she
hadn't been with Luke, she'd been helping the over-
taxed nuns tend the many maimed and disfigured
that filled the wards and lined the corridors.

Together, she and Ross had cared for his son.
They'd set aside their differences and stood shoulder to shoulder at the hospital bed, praying for

Luke's recovery. In an undeclared truce, they avoided any topic that touched on the trial, his violation of the court injunction, or her descent into the Forrester with Gavin O'Connell. Hertta had come frequently to visit the youngster in spite of her own grief. Her courage was an inspiration to Nell. Each of them had tried gently shaking Luke and calling to him. Nothing had wakened the boy from his coma.

Nell could feel Ross's presence now as he reentered the tiny room. He paused briefly just inside the open doorway, checking on Luke in silence. Then he moved across the immaculate tiled floor and came to stand directly behind her.

She swallowed back the tears, her gaze on the snowy yard beneath the window. Her lips trembled when she tried to speak. "Did you talk to the doctor?"

"Yes. He's goin' to stop by again as soon as he finishes his mornin' rounds." Nell could hear the awful, weary sadness in his deep voice.

She pressed her fingertips against the frosted glass. The teardrops she could no longer restrain rolled unheeded down her cheeks. "It breaks my heart to see him lying there so quiet. Luke was never still for a moment."

Ross laid his hand gently on Nell's shoulder. In her bright blue dress and long bibbed apron, she looked like the angel of mercy she'd been for these frightful past seven days. Unable to find the words of reassurance she sought, he bowed his head in stark, silent terror. Everything that mattered most in his life was enclosed within those four Spartan walls. Everything. He couldn't bear to contemplate what might happen if his worst fears were realized. He faced the horrendous possibility of losing the two people he loved more than his own life.

Seeing Nell at the train station a week ago, prepared to walk out of his world forever, had nearly torn him apart. Since that terrible day, though she'd stayed right by his side and helped him nurse his injured son, she hadn't indicated by so much as a word that she'd changed her mind about leaving.

Even worse was the thought that Luke might die. It filled Ross with paralyzing dread. If he lost his son . . . oh, Jesus, Jesus . . . if he lost his son . . . The bleakness of such a harrowing future sent an ache of anguish into the deepest reaches of his soul. Ross had never considered himself a particularly religious man, but he'd gone down on his knees in prayer every single morning of the last seven days.

"Boss," called Eben softly from the doorway. Ross turned his head to see his mine superintendent, dressed in work pants and a heavy corduroy jacket, tiptoeing past the quiet bed on the thick soles of his snow-crusted miner's boots.

"I'm sorry," his red-haired friend apologized, "but I have to talk with you. We just got another telegram from Silas Armstrong. This is the third one in as many days." He handed his employer the folded yellow paper.

Ross opened the wire and scanned its urgent contents with indifference. The message held nothing new. Armstrong had sent the same desperate request twice before.

IMPERATIVE YOU COME TO HELENA AT ONCE STOP YOUR EXPERT ADVICE IS REQUIRED IMMEDIATELY STOP OUTCOME OF APPEAL HINGES ON YOUR PRESENCE STOP ARMSTRONG

Ross knew that Nell, standing at his elbow, had read the text along with him. He folded the telegram and placed it inside his coat pocket. "Wire Armstrong that you're comin' to Helena instead of me," he ordered Eben. "Then get packed and get on the next train leavin' for the capital."

Pearce scowled and shook his head. His blue eyes were narrowed with self-doubt. "I can't compete with Hegel's clever corporation lawyers," he protested. "They'll twist my words around the way they did Professor Gunter's. Only I don't have Adolph's scholarly reputation to fall back on. I'll end up looking like a prize fool."

"You'll do fine," contradicted Ross. "Tell the appellate judge in your own words what we learned from the maps of the Forrester. Have the charts of the two mines placed side by side, just like we laid them the night of the cave-in. It won't take a degree in engineerin' to see that the disputed vein of copper apexes on the surface claim of the Glamorgan."

Eben pulled on one end of his huge coppery mustache in nervous apprehension. "Golly, I don't know, hoss."

Ross was unmoved by his superintendent's hesitation. The outcome of the trial was the least of his worries. There'd be other mines, other chances to make his fortune. There would never be another Luke. Come hell or high water, he was going to remain with his son. Felix Hegel, his Forrester mine, his cadre of lawyers, and the whole damn rest of the world didn't count for Jack squat.

Nell touched his sleeve. Her quiet voice carried a somber warning. "If you lose this appeal, Ross, you'll lose all chance of ever regaining your right to mine the Glamorgan."

"To hell with the mine."

He saw the astonishment in her startled brown eyes, as though she couldn't believe he meant what he said. She seemed to think he didn't fully understand the consequences of what he proposed. "I'll stay here with Luke," she promised, "if that's what you're worried about. I won't leave his side until you return. But if you don't go, and he never wakes up, you'll have lost the Glamorgan and every cent you own to no avail."

Ross's words were low and fierce with passion. "My son's going to recover. And I'm going to be right here by his bedside when he opens his eyes."

He glanced over at Eben. "Now get the hell out of here, Pearce, and get on that train."

As Eben hurried out the door, the portly hospital physician entered the sickroom, accompanied by a Sister of Charity. Ross and Nell immediately went to stand across the bed from them.

Dr. McCullar bent over Luke. He lifted one closed lid, then the other. "Patient continues to have roving eye movements," he told Sister Mary Thomasina with professional dispassion. "One pupil still dilated." He checked Luke's pulse, then raised the boy's hospital gown and listened to his chest through the stethoscope. "Heartbeat's strong. Lungs are clear."

Silently, methodically, the nun made the brief notations on the clipboard she'd taken from the foot of the bed, but Ross knew the depths of the old sister's compassion. She'd spent many sessions at Luke's side, trying to bring him to consciousness.

"Luke!" McCullar called loudly. "Luke!" He lifted the boy's hand and pinched the fleshy part of his forearm.

Just as before, there was no response. None at all. Ross heard Nell's muffled sob catch in her throat. Bravely, she covered her mouth with one hand to keep from interrupting the examination.

A deep frown creased the doctor's brow. He met Ross's gaze and gave a slight shake of his head.

"What's the prognosis, Doctor?"

The physician folded the tubing of his stethoscope and replaced it in the pocket of his white coat. He had a gravelly voice that rumbled deep in his chest when he spoke. "There's no sign of pneumonia, and that, alone, is a miracle. He also shows no loss of respiratory reflexes. But the longer the boy remains comatose, the less likely he'll ever regain consciousness. He's suffered a bad concussion. If he doesn't awaken soon, he may endure permanent impairment of the higher mental functions."

"What exactly does that mean?" Ross's sharp tone warned the doctor not to pull any punches. He wanted the unvarnished truth.

McCullar grimaced, clearly hesitant to state the worse. "Amnesia, for one thing. Blurred vision, impaired concentration, slurred speech. There's also a strong likelihood he may suffer at least partial deafness from the blow or the explosion."

Nell gripped Ross's elbow, clearly stunned by the staggering list of conditions stated so clinically, including the frightening possibility that Luke might never hear again.

Ross took her shaky hand in his, drawing strength from her loving concern. "Thanks for your honesty, Dr. McCullar."

As the physician and nurse left, Ross gazed in fearful contemplation at his son, lying motionless on the bed. The swelling on Luke's discolored face had gone down, leaving the bruises and scrapes to heal more slowly. The unruly golden-brown waves framed his peaceful features, which appeared even more childlike in repose. He looked so serene, he might have been sleeping, except for one terrible thing. He couldn't be roused. Was it because he couldn't hear them calling him? When Luke did waken at last, would it be to a silent world?

Early the next morning, Ross disappeared from the hospital room without any explanation. Nell had been dozing on a narrow cot they'd set up in the corner and hadn't heard him leave. They'd taken turns, around the clock, resting on the bunk fully dressed, so that one of them could always be at Luke's side should he waken.

A feeling of unease gnawed at her when she realized that Ross had left his son's sickroom so abruptly. Had he given up all hope for the child's recovery? Ross had been a pillar of quiet strength for the last seven days. His tenderness, his loving care had sustained and supported her. Had he cracked at last, beneath the awful strain?

Nell sat down in the chair beside the white-painted brass bed and studied the boy. She smoothed a tangled lock of tawny hair back from the high forehead, then lifted his pale, cool hand and placed it across her open palm. The fingers were long and graceful, almost delicate, just as his dad's must have been at the same age, before the years of hard work in mining had thickened and callused them. Luke had inherited his sire's strong constitution as well. Even with his heavy winter clothing and the fur-lined leather gloves she'd given him for Christmas, nothing short of divine intervention could explain the fact that he hadn't suffered acute hypothermia as he lay unconscious on the frozen ground.

Her thoughts turned to Luke's father, whom he so closely resembled. She'd been certain that the Glamorgan Mine, with its rich veins of copper and the vast fortune it was sure to produce, was the most important thing in Ross Morgan's life. She couldn't have been more wrong. He'd thrown it all away without a moment's hesitation. For the proud, ambitious mine owner, nothing had come before his beloved son.

Humbled by his enormous sacrifice, she realized that Ross would never abandon his family the way her father had. Jack Ryan had deserted his wife and children to follow the lure of gold. Ross had willingly sacrificed not only the promised millions in his mine, but everything he owned outright as well, in order to stay and care for his boy. Flushing with shame, she recalled the snide note she'd written when she'd refused the ruby necklace. The bitterness of her words had been a judgment, not on him but on her. Nell admitted to herself that she'd been blinded by her angry self-deception. Only now, schooled by the example of Ross's total commitment to his child, was she beginning to understand the meaning of unconditional love and unquestioning trust.

Her heart ached at the thought that the robust, outgoing youngster she'd come to care for so dearly could slip away from them at any moment. She loved Luke as she would have loved the son she never had. *Would never have.* If Luke died, the void he left would never be filled. And whether he recovered or not, she knew she'd never be the same egocentric, self-contained person she'd been before. Ross had taught her that a man's loved ones are the most valuable treasures on earth.

In the silence of the hospital room, the emptiness of her life seemed to sit like a great weight on her shoulders, threatening to crush her lonely spirit.

Chapter 21

Ross returned thirty minutes later, carrying a familiar brown leather case in one hand. Not bothering to remove his heavy jacket, he stepped quickly to the end of the bed. He reached across the footboard's painted brass railing, laid the case on top of the white covers, and snapped it open. Without a word, he drew out his trumpet and lifted it up before him.

Nell watched in fascination as he noiselessly fingered the valves. When he started to adjust the tuning slide, she couldn't contain her curiosity. "What are you doing?"

"I'm goin' to play somethin' by Rimsky-Korsakov," he told her solemnly, his gaze riveted on his son. His hawklike features were harsh with anxiety.

"Something Luke especially likes?"

"Nope. Luke detests classical music."

With that oblique explanation, Ross raised the shiny horn to his lips. The clear, brilliant notes soared out over the sickbed and bounced off the pristine white walls. The rich, melodic splendor of a symphonic masterpiece filled the little room.

Nell, still holding Luke's hand, felt the sudden tremor in the tapered fingers. Her heart stalled in breathless excitement. She looked down at the quiescent boy and then over to his father.

At that moment, a Sister of Charity flung open the door and hurried into the room. "I'm sorry, but you can't do that," she cautioned. "There are patients in the wards still sleeping."

"Wait!" cried Nell. She flung up one hand, her fingers spread wide in an impassioned plea. Sister Mary Thomasina nodded, her dark eyes lighting with immediate understanding. The elderly nun moved to the side of the bed across from Nell.

Ross continued to play with even greater gusto. The bright, lively, colorful strains of *Scheherezade* swirled and echoed around them.

Slowly, slowly, Luke lifted his lids, as though having been awakened too soon from a deep, exhausted sleep. A scowl of immense displeasure puckered his bruised face.

"Aw, c'mon, Dad," he complained in weary disgust. "You know I hate that stuff."

Ross immediately lowered the brass instrument. Tears welled up in his green eyes and glistened on the tips of his thick lashes. His husky baritone was filled with overwhelming joy as he grinned through his tears. "I promise, son, I'll never play any of that highfalutin' stuff in your hearin' again."

"Good," Luke answered with a tired smile, "because it's given me a terrible headache." Turning his head back and forth on the pillow, he looked from the Sister of Charity to Nell in confusion. "How come everyone's cryin'?" he asked in a whisper. "Is somethin' wrong?"

"Oh, my dear heart," Nell said, her thick voice choked with delirious thanksgiving. She squeezed his fingers, then lifted them to her lips. "Nothing was ever more right."

Ross was beside her in an instant. With one strong hand on Nell's shoulder, he bent over his son and gently, tenderly kissed his forehead. His smile was positively beatific. "The beautiful lady is absolutely correct," he told Luke. "Nothin' was ever so right."

Nell sat on the slatted wooden trolley bench and stared down at her interlocked fingers encased in black leather gloves. Sighing with unhappiness, she took the train ticket from her handbag and frowned at it. Once again, her luggage had been picked up at Kuusinen's Boardinghouse and delivered to the depot. She'd hugged Hertta good-by, holding her dear friend close, promising to write her frequently, telling her she'd never forget her and Kalle's kindness as long as she lived.

In another hour, Nell would be on her way home to Boston. She shoved the railway pass back in her bag and looked out at the snow-blanketed sights of the sprawling camp with bemused melancholy. The stark gallows frames rising up into the gray winter sky, the barren mine dumps, the smelters belching smoke, the crowded, noisy saloons and gambling halls on every block of the uptown district had become so familiar in the past weeks, she hardly noticed them. Just as the populace took it all for granted, not even aware of the ugliness and sinful corruption of the city built on the richest hill on earth, little by little, she'd come to focus less on its aesthetic drawbacks and more on its unique inhabitants. Millionaire, merchant, miner, housewife, and harlot. They were like no other people she'd ever encountered.

In a nation known for its independent citizenry, the residents of Butte were the quintessential rugged, free-thinking individualists of pioneer story and song. Not a person—man, woman, or child—seemed to question his right to be on this earth. Or the right to stake his claim to what could turn out to be another glory hole of fabulous riches. They had a shrewd, incisive ability to see right through puffed-up pretensions. They boldly scoffed at any attempt to make class distinctions. Their skeptical fatalism, brought on by the unavoidable disasters inherent in hardrock mining, was only a hard outer shell. On the night of the explosion and the week of horror that followed, she'd seen, firsthand, the openhearted generosity and unqualified self-sacrifice of their souls.

Nell pulled a lacy handkerchief from her bag and wiped her wet cheeks. Today she was seeing the wide-open, rip-roaring copper camp for the last time. Who would have ever believed, when she'd first arrived spewing self-righteous castigations about this godforsaken hellhole, that she'd cry at the thought of leaving? The crazy truth was she'd come to love and respect the hardy people of Butte as none other. Most especially, she loved and respected one rugged, strong-willed, dangerously attractive mine owner.

As she stepped down from the trolley car, she gave herself a stern mental shake. Heavens to Betsy, she shouldn't be weeping. There was far too much to be thankful for. Luke had made a complete recovery. He'd not even suffered a loss of hearing as they'd all feared. Three days ago, the exuberant boy had returned to the beautiful chateau-style mansion on Park Street, riding in a hack beside his proud, happy father. Nell had accompanied them home from the hospital. She'd helped Mrs. Rooney, the Morgans' cheerful housekeeper, get the boy settled on the parlor sofa before she left.

Nell had prayed that Ross would give some sign that he wanted her to stay with them, at least for the afternoon if not for supper or the rest of her life. But he'd been strangely abstracted. He'd barely said good-by when she'd taken leave. So she'd returned to her bedroom at the boardinghouse and forlornly packed the few things she'd pulled out of her trunks in the past two weeks.

Since the day Luke was released from the Sisters' Hospital, Ross had made no attempt to contact her. Yet she couldn't leave without telling him how wrong she'd been about him. She admitted now what she hadn't been willing even to discuss before. Ross had continued to mine his own vein, in spite of the court injunction, because if he hadn't, Hegel would have cut through the adjoining wall and pirated the Glamorgan copper right out from under him. Ross hadn't tried to get a court order to inspect the Forrester and prove what his enemy was doing, for he'd known Judge Curry would side with the crafty schemer who'd lined his pockets.

She walked up the front path and tugged on the bellpull of the rosy brick mansion, knowing she had to see Ross one last time before she left. She had to apologize for her failure to trust him and beg his forgiveness. Somehow, she had to find the words to tell him she was sorry. That she'd been wrong in her rash judgment. And that she loved him.

It was just like Ross to answer the door himself. She should have been prepared for that devastating, sideways grin, but she wasn't. Her heart leaped in admiration at the sight of him. Attired in a starched linen shirt and tailored black slacks, he had the supple, predatory grace of a cougar. All the physical longing he'd ignited within her now flamed into a roaring blaze.

Visions of bathing with him, stark naked in the sauna, or lying beside his magnificent bare body in his big, warm bed, rose up to torment her. In her mind, she saw him again in all his glorious male splendor. Memories of touching that broad chest and burying her fingertips in the crisp, golden-brown hair that covered the flat nipples, of feeling the powerful biceps and forearms beneath the palms of her hands, of smoothing her fingers across the flat abdomen, ridged with muscles, and stroking the massive, corded thighs and lean flanks left her mesmerized and embarrassingly short of breath. She stared at him, speechless, and prayed madly that he had no idea of the carnal thoughts that raced through her mind.

"Well, well, Miss Ryan," he drawled, "come in, come in." A corner of his mouth quirked in the hint of a smile. She wasn't sure if he was pleasantly surprised to see her or just amused at her temerity. Either way, he moved back to allow her to enter.

Her heart squeezed painfully. What wouldn't she give to hear him call her angel eyes or little darlin' once more? How could she have thought those loving endearments sounded trite and meaningless?

She stepped into the vaulted entry hall to find it piled high with boxes, cartons, and barrels. "I wanted to stop and see how Luke was doing before I left," she explained lamely, her glance taking in the unexpected disorder.

"Luke's as fine as frog's hair," he stated with satisfaction. "Guess it takes more than a thump on the head to slow down a Morgan for long. He just walked down to the corner to say good-by to some friends. Come on in and sit down for a moment."

Ross took her short traveling cape and hung it on the coat stand, then waited politely while she laid her handbag and gloves on the hall table before he ushered her into the front parlor.

Everything was in wild disarray. More crates, filled with household possessions, were scattered throughout the drawing room and down the hallway in mute testimony to Morgan's desperate financial straits. She hadn't expected him to be forced out of his brand-new house so quickly. Evidently, he was further in debt than she'd suspected. The pale blue settee and love seat, which had once sat at right angles to each other in front of the blazing fireplace, were shoved haphazardly toward the far wall. Their silk cushions, protected by dust covers, were piled high with boxes. Nell perched on top of an upended wooden crate in the center of the room and tried to ignore the empty spot on the rug where the huge Christmas tree had stood, not so very long ago.

Ross leaned his buttocks against the back of the sofa, crossed his arms, and gazed at her with twinkling eyes. If he found his new status as a pauper humiliating, he certainly didn't show it.

"You have to move out of your home?" she asked sadly.

"I'm goin' to take Luke to visit his grandpa and grandma. He hasn't seen them since a year ago last September. My mother's written several times in the last few months sayin' how much she misses him. Now that he's well, she wants to see him with her own eyes and make sure he hasn't suffered any lastin' effects from the concussion."

Nell gave a quick nod of understanding. Her heart went out to Ross for the brave front he was putting up for his son's sake. She knew how painful it would be for someone with Ross's pride to have to go to his parents and admit he was a broken man. He'd be forced to live off their charity until he found a job as a mining engineer for some other mine owner, perhaps in the ore-rich mountains of Nevada or Idaho. Her words were filled with quiet sympathy. "I'm sure Luke will have a wonderful time seeing his grandparents."

"Let me get you a cup of tea," Ross offered brightly. "Mrs. Rooney's taken the mornin' off, but I can put a kettle of water on. It'll be hot in no time."

"Please don't," Nell said quickly, before he could move. If she didn't tell him she loved him now, she'd never have another chance. She lowered her eyes and smoothed the skirt of her green plaid street gown with nervous fingers. "I . . . I can't stay long. I already said my good-bys to Luke when I called yesterday."

"I was sorry to learn I missed you," he said without a trace of sorrow. "I had to clear up some last-minute business."

She kept her head lowered, not daring to look up for fear he'd read the anguish in her eyes. She'd understood the meaning of his casual remark. He'd known she was going away today and had made no attempt to see her and wish her farewell.

"My train is leaving in less than an hour," she blurted out.

When he gave no response to her graceless attempt to provoke some sign of caring on his part, she raised

her lids and met his calm gaze. Lord, he wasn't
making it any easier with his cool detachment. If he
were angry, she'd at least have known he still cared.
But this complete indifference was the most painful
lesson of all. No wonder she could hardly talk.

"Be-before I do leave, I want to tell you how very
sorry I am for the awful things I said . . . and did.
How . . . how deeply I regret my lack of faith in
you. I know now that the blame for Sean's death lies
squarely on Felix Hegel's shoulders." She gulped
back her tears and went on. "Going down into the
Forrester with the idea of entrapping you in illegal
activities was a shameful thing for me to do, and I
humbly apologize."

"Thank you for that, Nell," he said quietly.

"Just for the record," she continued, "I never sold
out to Hegel. He tried to bribe me, but I refused
the money." She sadly shook her head. "I tried my
darnedest to win your court case for you, whether
you believe it or not."

"I believe you."

Nell lifted her hand and gestured toward his
injured face. "And most of all, I'm so terribly, terribly sorry for what happened to you."

He shrugged, as though the scar was of no great
importance. "The fight between me and Hegel was
inevitable. If we hadn't fought the night of the cave-
in, we'd have slugged it out eventually. It was only
a matter of time." He smiled in blithe unconcern.
"Besides, the doctor assures me that by this time
next year, I'll only have a fine line to show for my
idiotic male belligerence. Don't blame yourself."

She fought the overpowering urge to cross the
room, fling herself into his arms, and sob her heart
out. She wanted to beg him to forgive her, but the
words stuck in her throat.

"And, knowin' you as I do," he added conversa-
tionally, "I'm sure your visit here this mornin' has
nothin' to do with today's news in the Anaconda
Standard."

She stared at him in blank bewilderment. What in heaven's name was he talking about? Here she was, pouring her heart out in mortifying self-recrimination, trying to build up enough courage to tell him she loved him, and he wanted to discuss the morning's newspaper!

He cocked his head lazily to one side, indicating the folded paper lying on top of a nearby barrel.

Irritated at his exasperating complacency, Nell reached over, snatched up the newspaper, and jerked it open. The headlines blared the news.

GLAMORGAN MINING RIGHTS UPHELD IN MONTANA SUPREME COURT!
Owner Sells to Anaconda Mining for Twenty Million!!

"Ross!" she cried ecstatically as she rose to her feet. "You did it!" She gazed at him in surprised delight. He'd not only been vindicated in court, he'd also sold his mining claim for a fantastic sum to Felix Hegel's worst enemy.

"No, *you* did it, Miss Ryan," he corrected. "Silas Armstrong has been back in Butte since yesterday evenin'. The verdict delivered in Judge Curry's district courtroom was reversed in strong language by the Montana Supreme Court. Silas admitted he'd been far too pessimistic in his urgent telegrams. And Eben did a grand job, despite his reluctance. But accordin' to Armstrong, it was your careful objections that laid the grounds for our successful appeal." Ross straightened from his place against the back of the sofa and stepped closer. His deep green eyes glowed with a teasing humor. "Of course, the fact that Hegel's lead counselor was infatuated with his gorgeous legal adversary also helped to get our maps and charts entered into the record without bein' blocked by that dishonest judge. Through your tireless efforts, Nell, we managed to get enough crucial evidence admitted, includin' your exact model of the Glamorgan, to build a brilliant case for our inevitable appeal."

Nell bit her lower lip in embarrassment at the mention of Shelton Broply. The handsome attorney had tried to court her after the New Year's ball. She'd rejected his overtures with honest finality, too heartbroken over Ross to offer any hope to Shelton whatsoever. She wondered if Ross believed that her affections had been claimed by another. If he did, he certainly wasn't upset about it.

"Unfortunately," said Ross, "your legal skill also protected your co-counsel. Armstrong claims that it would be impossible to prosecute Gavin O'Connell for the unethical behavior of accepting a bribe since you covered up his deliberate ineptness in the courtroom so capably. Your colleague gets to keep his ill-gotten gain. The only consolation is that Hegel put out a whole lot of bribery money for nothin'. But if I ever meet up with Gavin O'Connell again, I'm goin' to break the little bastard's neck."

She smiled with trembling lips. "I'll hold your coat when you do."

He shook his head as he stepped even nearer. "You won't have to. That fight'll be over so fast, I won't even take my jacket off."

"Well, congratulations on your victory," Nell said sincerely. "I'm very happy for you." She drew a deep breath and forced herself to continue. "Now, I really need to be going. I hope you and Luke have a safe trip to Denver and a pleasant visit with your parents. I just want you to know that . . . I'll always remember you."

For a second, she considered reaching out and shaking his hand. But her brittle emotions wouldn't let her touch him without falling to pieces like shattered glass. Afraid he'd see the tears that had started to pool in her eyes, she turned to go, adding in a whisper, "And I'll always love you."

She must have stunned him. She'd nearly reached the door before he caught up with her. He put his hand on her arm and pulled her firmly to a halt.

"What did you say?"

Swallowing back the sobs, Nell cleared her throat. She averted her face from his searching eyes. Her words came out in a broken, undignified croak. "I love you."

"I still couldn't understand what you said."

Nell scowled in frustration at his blockheaded obtuseness. For heaven's sake, what the heck did he *think* she said? This time she lifted her chin and stared straight into his laughing eyes.

"I love you, you big idiot!"

"You don't have to shout," he told her with a slow, satisfied grin. "I heard you the first time. I just wanted to be sure you could never deny sayin' it." He clasped her shoulders, bent his head, and bussed her lightly on the brow. "We'd better get goin', or we'll miss that train for Boston."

Nell's heart plummeted to her toes. He wanted to escort her to the depot! Good Lord, she wasn't sure she could bear it. She clenched her hands and strove to hide her wretched disappointment. "Yes, I . . . I wouldn't want to be late for my train."

"Neither would I," he said cheerfully. Taking her elbow, he led her into the entryway. He took her black velvet cape down from the coat stand and placed it on her shoulders. Then he grabbed his sheepskin jacket and pulled it on. "You're sure you've got your ticket?" he asked with a wide smile.

He was certainly anxious to get rid of her. She nodded glumly as she pulled on her gloves. She had to give him credit. When the Colorado Cougar broke a poor woman's heart, he did a real thorough job of it.

"Let's have a look, just to be sure," he insisted.

Trying to hide her misery, she pulled the ticket out of her bag and started to hand it to him.

"No, you hang on to it," he said. "And while you're at it, you can keep mine and Luke's in your bag too. Just for safety." Before she could protest, he took her outstretched hand and laid two more tickets on top of her own.

She looked down through blurred eyes at the railway passes she held in her gloved palm.

Three tickets to Boston.

Three tickets to Boston on the Northern Pacific!

She looked up in openmouthed astonishment. Happiness burst inside her, glowing like the candlelights on Hertta's Christmas supper table. Maybe the Finns had been right when she found that lucky almond! Maybe she *was* going to be a bride this year!

He chuckled at her stupefied silence. "You said you always dreamed of gettin' married in your own parish church, with your Uncle Cormac walkin' you down the aisle. Well, I'm goin' to be standin' right beside that priest at the altar and watchin' you come to me in the most beautiful weddin' gown money can buy."

She nearly babbled in her confusion. "But . . . I thought . . . You said Luke was going to visit his grandparents."

"He is. I telegraphed Denver yesterday afternoon. My folks are probably on their way to Massachusetts this very moment. After the ceremony, Luke will stay with them till we get back from our honeymoon and decide where we're goin' to live." He reached up to the top rack of the coat stand and picked up his hat. "Now where would you like to go on your weddin' trip?" he asked. He placed the felt slouch at a rakish angle. "I've always thought the Caribbean islands would be fun to visit in the wintertime, but if you'd rather go to Europe, just say the word."

He didn't give her time to utter a peep. He opened the door and swept her out onto the wide stone porch. In front of the mansion, a hired coach stood waiting at the curb. The team's breath puffed like clouds of steam in the frosty morning air.

Luke thrust his head and shoulders out the window of the hack. "C'mon, Dad! C'mon, Nell!" he cried in excitement. He waved his arm for them to hurry. "We'll all miss the train!"

"C'mon, angel eyes," Ross said with a wicked grin. "There's a private Pullman car waitin' for the three of us at the Northern Pacific Railroad Station."

"Come on, sweetheart," she said, starting to skip down the stairs. "We don't want to miss that train!"

He caught her before she reached the second step and drew her back up and into his arms. The look of love in his eyes sent her heart spinning with happiness.

"First come here, little darlin', and kiss me hello."

Epilogue

July 4, 1898
Colorado Springs, Colorado

"**N**o, no, I want you over there on the left, Uncle Cormac," called Nell. "Sit down next to Aunt Lydia. That's right. Now, Dad, I want you on the other side of Mom."

The gentlemen did as instructed, moving to sit at either end of the four chairs. Though Cormac Ryan's black hair was graying at the temples now, he was still as slim and agile as ever. Lloyd Morgan walked with a cane, but beneath his shock of white hair, his deep green eyes were bright and alert. Despite the summer warmth and the fact that it was a holiday, the two patriarchs were dressed in three-piece black suits with high starched collars and striped silk neck scarves, in honor of the family portrait that was about to be taken. They sat straight and tall, each man holding his bowler hat perched carefully on one knee. Between the two men sat Lydia Ryan and Clarissa Morgan in their best Sunday gowns, their colorful satin skirts of rose and plum spread out around them.

Luke came across the lawn to stand beside Nell. "What about me, Mom?" he asked with his carefree grin. "Where do you want me to sit?" Unused to wearing a tie, he ran one finger beneath his stiff wing collar and tugged it away from his neck. He lived in Levi's, plaid flannel shirts, and Western boots and had changed into his brand-new suit just ten minutes ago, and then only at Nell's request. At fourteen, Luke was as tall as most grown men, but so lanky that, at times, he seemed all arms and legs.

Nell reached out and straightened his necktie, then brushed back a lock of his wavy hair. "Sit on the grass in front of your grandma, dear. And thank you for wearing your new suit," she added with a tender smile. "You look terrific."

"Thanks, Mom. So do you."

As Luke joined his grandparents, uncle, and aunt, Nell fluffed the lace at the elbows of her bright yellow dress. She wanted everyone looking gay and festive, including herself.

She turned to locate her husband, who'd wandered over to the nearby creek. She was just about to call him back to the group when she was forestalled by the photographer. The young man had been busy setting up his cumbersome equipment for the last twenty minutes.

"I'm almost ready, Mrs. Morgan," Fred Chilton told her. Wisps of his pale hair stood up on end. He'd ducked under the black focusing cloth on his camera several times to adjust the lenses. Chilton had the reputation of being the best portrait photographer in Denver, a true artist of the lens.

Nell hurried over to his tripod and stood beside it, trying to visualize exactly how the finished picture would look. There on the sloping lawn sat the four eldest members of the family in a curved, off-center row, with Luke sitting cross-legged on the grass directly in front of his grandmother. Behind them to the right was the brick mansion, rising up three stories into the blue Colorado sky. Everyone had assumed she'd want them seated in the formal drawing room or standing on the wide, colonnaded portico. Instead, Nell had insisted that four white wicker chairs be carried from the porch down to the small knoll on the lawn.

She held up her hands, thumbs angled to form a frame, and carefully scanned the scene. At the left of the setting, drifts of wild columbine followed the winding banks of the stream that bubbled and sparkled in the dappled sunshine. Behind them, tall aspens, willows, and birches swayed gently in the soft summer breeze.

She wanted all of it in the photograph. Her beautiful home, the gorgeous scenery that surrounded them, her precious family. Most of all, her precious family. She'd come to love Ross's parents as dearly as she loved Uncle Cormac and Aunt Lydia. She smiled at all of them now in unmitigated joy.

"Ross, bring Julia and get on over here," his mother called cheerfully. "We're just about ready to have this picture taken." She stood up in front of her chair and waved animatedly to her son. Clarissa Corneille Morgan was as outgoing, as vivacious, as full of vinegar at sixty-one as she must have been when she was the celebrated singer and dancer of the Central City saloon in which she'd met the rugged, good-looking prospector who later became her husband.

"Take the picture without him," Lloyd Morgan growled. "That way we won't risk breakin' the camera." He raised his voice so his son could hear and added, "But bring my granddaughter over here first."

"If anyone's going to break the camera," Uncle Cormac said with a chuckle, "it's going to be the two old codgers sitting in front of it right now." He met Nell's gaze and winked broadly.

Aunt Lydia giggled. She covered her mouth with one plump hand and turned to look at her husband with a flutter of her long eyelashes. Cormac smiled indulgently. The years had been kind to Lydia Ryan. Her clear skin was still smooth and fine-grained, marked by only a few laugh lines around her eyes. Her blond hair remained thick and lovely, the strands of gray barely noticeable.

Both the Ryans had become reacquainted with the eldest Morgan's acerbic sense of humor since they'd arrived for their visit six days ago. Everyone knew his bark was far worse than his bite.

Gruff and hard-nosed on the outside, Lloyd had a soft spot a mile wide where his family was concerned. Nell had learned, mostly to her delight, but sometimes to her dismay, that her irascible father-in-law doted on her and his two grandchildren. There wasn't a request he'd refuse them. And although Ross and his father argued and huffed at each other over business matters, she also knew how very deeply Lloyd Morgan loved his son. They were both so much alike—autocratic, strong-willed, ambitious, and totally devoted to their families.

Ross had taken over the Morgan Mining Corporation when he and Nell had returned from their honeymoon. Lloyd had suffered a heart seizure while the bride and groom were in the Bahamas. He'd asked his son to run his mines for him, assuring Ross that he'd have free rein to make his own decisions.

Ross assumed control of his father's company just in time to avoid a potentially violent labor dispute. He promised the miners a wage of three dollars a day for an eight-hour day, ensuring their loyalty for years to come. Then he promptly expanded the Morgan holdings, acquiring two claims near Cripple Creek with the money from the sale of the Glamorgan. The new mines were now producing gold ore of the highest grade. Once again, Ross's uncanny genius for mineral geology had paid off. Both Morgans, father and son, were now millionaires several times over.

She'd been right about her husband, though. Nothing came before his love for his family. She turned to watch him now on the bank of the stream as he crouched on his haunches behind his little girl. Julia stood within the protection of her father's muscular thighs and reached out for the purple wildflowers that grew in profusion at the water's edge. Ross bent his head, kissed the top of her chestnut curls, and spoke quietly in her ear. From that distance, Nell couldn't hear the words, but she could easily guess them. Her tall, powerful, broad-shouldered husband was telling his tiny baby girl how much he adored her.

"C'mon, Dad," Luke hollered good-naturedly. "We can't get out of these fancy duds till we get this picture taken. And I can't set off any firecrackers until I've changed my clothes. What kind of a Fourth of July is this, anyway?"

Ross scooped his two-year-old daughter up in his arms and rose to his feet. Turning to face his family, he gave them all a lazy, sideways grin. Nell knew exactly what he was thinking. He wasn't going to be hurried on this glorious summer morning. He was going to enjoy each and every minute of the Grand Old Fourth—from the group portrait that was about to be taken, to the sumptuous picnic lunch that was even now being laid out on the tables, to the fireworks they'd shoot off when the sun went down.

"Hold your horses," he called to Luke. "I'm comin'."

Carrying the child in his arms, Ross joined the others. Like the rest of the men, he was dressed in a smartly tailored business suit. His daughter's lacy white cotton dress stood out in sharp contrast against the dark wool.

Julia reached up and patted her father's jaw with her fat little hands. "Daddy, horsie," she said.

"Not now, sweetie," he replied, kissing her fingers. He looked over at his wife. "Okay, sugarplum," he called, his eyes sparkling with happiness. "Where do you want us?"

Nell pointed to the spot. "You sit down just a little to the right of your father."

Ross promptly folded his long legs and dropped down on the grass. She studied the grouping thoughtfully. The older generation sat bolt upright in their chairs, suddenly solemn. Beneath their great handlebar mustaches, Lloyd and Cormac pursed their mouths in fierce concentration. They looked so serious they could have been a pair of Supreme Court justices about to hand down a landmark decision of epic proportions. Lydia and Clarissa, their hands clasped tightly in their laps, were scarcely less tense. Even Luke had a scowl creasing his forehead at the momentous occasion of having a family portrait taken.

"Let Luke hold his sister," Nell suggested to Ross.

Her husband handed Julia to his son with nonchalant compliance. The two-year-old struggled unhappily in Luke's lap, till she managed to squirm to her feet and stand beside him. Then she wrapped one arm tightly around her big brother's neck and spoke directly into his ear. "Lukie, horsie," she cajoled.

"Not now, Ju-Ju," her brother said with a tolerant grin. "Look at the camera, Ju-Ju. Look at the camera."

Julia twisted around to face her grandfather. "Papa, horsie," she demanded.

"Come on, little dolly," Lloyd said. "Get up here." He handed his hat to his wife and set the girl on his knee, turning her so that she faced the camera.

Impulsively, Clarissa placed the derby on Luke's head, bent over, and kissed him lovingly on the cheek. "You look just like your daddy," she told him. "And next to your grandpa, he's the handsomest man in the world."

Luke moved the hat to a natty angle and grinned proudly.

"Put your hat on the baby's head," Aunt Lydia suggested to her husband.

Uncle Cormac reached over and dropped his hat on Julia's dark curls. The round black felt with its rolling brim completely covered her eyes. Just as Lloyd bounced his granddaughter on his knee, the little girl snatched off the bowler and sailed it toward her daddy. Ross caught it with easy grace and jammed it on his head at a comical angle. Julia, entranced by her father's clever feat, clapped her hands and trilled ecstatically. Everyone joined in the infectious laughter.

"That's it," Nell told the photographer, who was already beneath the focusing cloth at the back of the bulky camera. "That's the picture. Wait for me to get in it and shoot."

"But . . . but . . ." Fred Chilton sputtered from under the black covering. The glass image before him was obviously not the formal family portrait he'd envisioned.

Nell didn't waste time arguing. She raced to join the others. Kneeling directly behind her husband, she put her hands on his wide shoulders and nodded toward the camera.

The photographer obeyed, and the entire family was caught laughing with joy.

After several more exposures, the group broke up and headed toward tables that had been set in the shade and were now laden with food. Nell started to move to her feet. Ross reached up and covered her hands with his much larger ones, keeping her with him. His long fingers absently stroked hers, as though he were reluctant to let the moment end.

Together, they watched his father give Julia to Uncle Cormac, who kissed her dimpled cheek and cooed to her, while Aunt Lydia patted the little girl lovingly. Clarissa had her arm around Luke's shoulders, telling her grandson a joke from her show business days that he'd already heard at least a dozen times before. It never failed to bring a chuckle.

Nell sighed with pleasure. She knew she couldn't get any happier. Her husband tipped his head back to look at her upside down. The bowler hat tumbled to the grass beside them.

"Did you get the picture you wanted, angel eyes?"

"Mm, exactly," she said, capturing his face between her hands. She bent over him and kissed his brow, the bridge of his nose, then tenderly pressed her lips to the faint scar on his cheek.

"Well, you managed to get everyone in it," he teased.

She grinned in secret delight. "More than you know."

Still looking at her from upside down, Ross searched her eyes in puzzlement. When she continued to beam at him enigmatically, he sat up straight, pulled her around in front of him, and lifted her onto his lap. His strong arms imprisoned her in silent warning. He was going to have the truth before he set her free.

An inquisitive smile played at the corners of his mobile lips. "What don't I know?"

"Remember when I was carrying Julia, and you wanted me to have my photograph taken just a month before she was born?" She slid her arms around his neck and kissed him lightly on the lips.

Ross pulled back to look into her eyes. His smile faded. "I'd never seen anyone so beautiful," he said with a scowl, clearly still disappointed that she'd refused to go along with the idea.

"And I'd never heard of anything so shockingly scandalous. Who else but you would want a portrait of his enormously pregnant wife?"

Ross gazed into her eyes, comprehension slowly dawning. "You mean . . ." He glanced over at the empty, disarranged chairs. "Today, when . . ."

"You finally got your wish, Mr. Morgan. You have me captured on photographic plate, forever *enceinte*."

Ross grinned. "Well, hot damn, angel eyes."

"Does that mean you're happy?"

"*Happy* can't do it justice," he said in a husky voice. The gold flecks in his sea-green eyes glinted with a smoldering, sensual desire. "I knew the minute I laid eyes on you, Mrs. Morgan, that you were a love goddess come down from paradise. But I thought you were here to torture and torment me. I never dreamed I'd get to spend the rest of my life in the garden of earthly delights."

Avon Romantic Treasures

*Unforgettable, enthralling love stories,
sparkling with passion and adventure
from Romance's bestselling authors*

COMANCHE WIND *by Genell Dellin*
76717-1/$4.50 US/$5.50 Can

THEN CAME YOU *by Lisa Kleypas*
77013-X/$4.50 US/$5.50 Can

VIRGIN STAR *by Jennifer Horsman*
76702-3/$4.50 US/$5.50 Can

MASTER OF MOONSPELL *by Deborah Camp*
76736-8/$4.50 US/$5.50 Can

SHADOW DANCE *by Anne Stuart*
76741-4/$4.50 US/$5.50 Can

FORTUNE'S FLAME *by Judith E. French*
76865-8/$4.50 US/$5.50 Can

FASCINATION *by Stella Cameron*
77074-1/$4.50 US/$5.50 Can

ANGEL EYES *by Suzannah Davis*
76822-4/$4.50 US/$5.50 Can